CONDRA'S FIRE

ALSO BY S.K. RANDOLPH

VARTERELS' UNIVERSE™

(as paperbacks)

Part I - UnFolding

1. DiMensioner's Revenge

5. ConDra's Fire

8. MasTer's Reach

10. Jaradee's Legacy

Agothany 1 (Companion Shorts 2, 3, 4, 6, 7, and 9)

Part II - CoaleScence

11. Incirrata Secret

13. Corps Stones

16. Mocendi's Gambit

19. Queen's Quest

Agothany 2 (Companion Shorts 12, 14, 15, 17, 18, and 20)

Part III - Quickening

(a work in process)

Told with words and art,

contained in novels and companion shorts,

available in print and eBooks.

CONDRA'S FIRE

ILLUSTRATED BY THE AUTHOR

VARTERELS' UNIVERSE™
BOOK FIVE

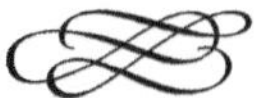

S.K. RANDOLPH

Cover and Illustrations by
S.K. RANDOLPH

ConDra's Fire: Illustrated by the Author (VarTerels' Universe™ Book 5)

Previous published as The ConDra's Fire

ISBN
Paperback 978-1-962777-15-5
eBook 978-1-962777-28-5

Self Published by S.K. Randolph
CheeTrann Creations LLC
Suite 316-160
1410 Valley View Drive
Delta, CO 81416

Web Site: www.skrandolph.com
Substack: skrandolph.substack.com
Facebook: http://facebook.com/S.K.Randolph11

Revised 2026

VU-126-J VU05-CF 260704-1512 PIBPb .vellum | 231129 PIbtA VUPt-1

VarTerels' Universe ™
SCIENCE FANTASY

CONDRA'S FIRE

Prologue

The children of many continue their course
To defy and destroy a sinister force;
The Unfolding pulls them along in its wake
Toward worlds to protect and the wicked to break.

The Unfolding—the Time of Transformation on the last remaining piece of Old Earth—picked up momentum. Currents of change, like flash floods, surged from Myrrh to the planets of Thera, DerTah, KcernFensia, and the far-off world of RewFaar.

In the Guardian's sanctuary, the oracle fountain, Elcaro's Eye, waited alone and all-knowing. Rhythmic drops of water fell into the bowl, faltered, then ceased. Restless wavelets churned the surface into a tempest. The alabaster woman kneeling on the rim gazed unblinking into its turbulent depths. An image emerged and steadied.

Massive wings cast their shadows across the vastness of a blood-red desert. Creatures of fire swooped above the sand, drank its shimmering heat, and soared out of sight. A darkened cave rose from Elcaro's blue depths and wavered into focus. The cherry-colored embers of a dying fire captured a woman's shadowed form. Writhing, fiery tendrils of hair framed her face. She uncurled the fingers of her fisted hand. On her palm, a glowing crystal shifted in hue from saffron to glacier blue.

The woman dissolved in flares of orange. On the water's surface, a convergence of light and color revealed a boy strapped to a long, narrow table, tears streaming down his cheeks.

Beneath closed lids, the boy's eyes burned. The probes inserted into his temples scorched the tender flesh. Panic surged. A horrified howl roared up from his belly as searing pain electrified his mind, flinging its slivered fragments into oblivion. A tortured shudder catapulted him into unconsciousness.

The rhythm of horses' hooves and the creak of wagon wheels called him back to himself. He squinted through swollen eyelids, but saw nothing. The rough fabric chafing his cheek reeked of dried blood and vomit. His hands and feet, still bound, ached. He lay motionless—trying to remember.

A single, shimmering tear formed in the alabaster woman's eye, slid down her cheek, and fell, scattering the image like pieces of a broken heart. The gentle sound of falling water again filled the room.

The Unfolding continued...

1
DerTah

Esán Efre stood alone at the center of an unfamiliar room. "My uncle kidnapped me." The bitter taste of bile lathered his tongue. Padding across his quarters, he poured cool water into a pottery mug and gulped every drop.

Memories of his arrival on the planet of DerTah blazed unforgettable. He sank onto the edge of the bed and covered his face with trembling hands.

As Esán fought to stop his uncle, DiMensioner Seyes Nomed, from reaching the Prima Crystal Evolsefil, a clap of thunder shook Nemttachenn Tower. Zigzagged light preceded a rolling tremor that pitched twins, Ari and Brie, to the ground, their horror-filled faces buried in a tumble of long, red curls.

With granite chunks exploding in all directions, Esán broke free of his uncle, shoved him, and ran. A swirling vortex opened beneath his feet and froze him mid-stride. Nomed's arms closed around him. The death shadow, Wodash od DerTah, howled his horror and plummeted into the gaping hole.

The twins scrambled to their feet. "No!"

The last thing Esán saw before plunging into the magnetic pull of the vortex was an aftershock tossing the twins into each other's arms. Their frantic shouts faded into nothingness darker than night, enclosing him in a silence so profound his ears ached. Suspended in time, he fought to calm his racing emotions. *Where are we going?*

Streaks of exploding color tore him free of Nomed's imprisoning arms. He shot from the dimensional portal into scalding desert heat, slid down the side of a blood-red dune, and came to a sprawled stop next to the death shadow.

A chorus of bloodcurdling shrieks sent grains of sand dancing over the dunes. Flaming carnivores, part dragon and part condor, materialized in searing waves and soared above them. Red-hot eyes drilled into their prey. Immense and ravenous, the ConDra swooped in a wide, fire-filled arc.

Nomed skidded to a halt beside him. "Don't move!" He untied his cape and hurled into the air, where it remained silver-side up. "Get under here and hold on to me! Now!"

Without hesitating, Esán obeyed his uncle's command. He knew beneath the hovering cape was the only place they would survive the Fire ConDra of Fera Finnero.

Terror tensing every muscle in his slender body, Esán's gaze darted from the descending creatures to his uncle's stern features. The next instant, the walls of a barn enclosing them in sudden dimness left them blinking.

Esán lowered shaking hands from his face and gripped his knees. *I'm on another planet.* He squeezed the bridge of his nose and sighed. *Will I ever see my friends and family again?*

A wave of fatigue washing over his too-thin body ended in a protracted yawn. He ran a hand over his bald head. "At least I'm somewhere safe." The need to rest overpowering him, he stretched out on the bed, closed his eyes, and gave himself permission to sleep.

. . .

Sometime later, he woke to a knock, followed by the immediate arrival of his uncle. Nomed peered down at him. "I'm glad you could nap."

Esán pushed himself to sitting while his uncle placed a chair by the bed and took a seat. Wistful eyes searched his face.

Esán lowered his gaze.

Nomed sighed. "I wish we had met under different circumstances, but we didn't. Now, I suggest we put the past behind us and get to know each other." He smoothed his hair back from his face. "I did not intend to kidnap you, Esán. I am, however, not sorry to have you at my side. Tomorrow you will meet Wolloh Espyro, the High DiMensioner who trained me. Please allow me the privilege of telling him what happened on Myrrh. He did not know of my intended visit."

As much as he wanted to demand that Nomed take him home, Esán pressed his lips together and kept his gaze steady.

His uncle tensed. "I know you must be angry. We will talk about this later. Now, eat and get some more sleep. The next few turnings will be busy ones. DerTah's Dreelum, the leaders of this planet, have gathered to meet you and to appraise your talents. Tonight, a servant will bring you supper, and, if you are up to it, give you a brief tour of Shu Chenaro, Wolloh's ranch house. I will see you in the morning."

He stood, returned the chair to its place at the desk, and turned with a slight twinkle in his eye. "By the way, I have released the death shadow from my service." His expression changed to serious. "You are a very talented young man, nephew. With luck, Wolloh will select you as his apprentice." A military-like about face propelled him from the room.

Esán clutched a pillow to his chest. "And what if I don't wish to be anyone's apprentice? What if I just want to go home?" He scowled. "What I desire is of no concern to anyone but me."

A soft knock ended his tirade. He tossed the pillow against the headboard, marched to the door, and yanked it open. A young servant, about his age, met his glare with wide-eyed trepidation before entering to place a large, food-laden tray on the desk. With a furtive glance in his direction, the boy laid out the meal on a table beside the window and scurried away.

Esán had just finished eating when the servant returned to clear away the dirty dishes.

Eyes downcast, the boy swallowed. "Stebben asked me to take you on a tour of Shu Chenaro?"

His instincts nudging him to pay attention, Esán smiled. "I'd appreciate seeing the ranch house." "What's your name?"

The servant's face paled, then flushed pink. "I am called Seval." His gazed lifted to Esán's face, then lowered.

"Are you from DerTah, Seval?"

"No, my home was on the planet of..." Confusion skittered across his face. Smoothing his dark auburn hair with trembling hands, he turned away. "Let me show you around."

As they walked down one hallway after the other, Esán studied his guide from beneath his lashes. *What has hurt you so deeply? Your shyness is one thing; your sad confusion is another.*

Ahead of him, Seval entered the conference room where he was to meet Nomed the following turning and stepped to one side.

From the doorway, Esán took in the subtle beauty of adobe walls, exotic paintings, and the antler chandeliers hanging above the long conference table.

He blew out a tense breath. *Tomorrow I meet Wolloh Espyro and the Dreelum of this planet.* Nervous excitement mixed with the last vestige of anger made him turn and walk away.

Seval hurried to catch up, led him to his room, and without a word, scurried down the hall.

L ate the next morning, Esán sat on the side of the bed, his bleary gaze wandering over the foreign-feeling room. He shot his pillow a longing look, rose, and walked to the window.

For a moment he stared unseeing, remembering his fifteenth Sun Cycle Celebration. *I left the hospital and visited Myrrh. Ari and Brie were there with Torgin. Our adventures together began that turning.* He sighed. *Will I ever see them again?*

Shaking himself, he gazed out the window at the desert stretching as far as the eye could see. Red-orange dunes rolled, one after the other, in wavelike repetition to the black line of the horizon. The sun rode high and close, much closer than the Theran sun. Heat from the scorched sand radiated upward in sheets of shimmering mirages. Seval had told him no one ventured out-of-doors until late afternoon.

He sighed. "I'm on DerTah whether I like it or not."

An enormous bird swooping into view prompted him to open the window and lean out. A shock of mid-morning heat slapped his cheeks as the bird flew out of sight. He ducked inside and pulled the window shut.

After nibbling on the meal left in his room, he prepared for the turning. His reflection in the mirror held him motionless. *Today I meet the High DiMensioner od DerTah for the first time.* He shivered.

Somewhere in the ranch house, a bell chimed. His curiosity quickened. He stepped into the hallway and walked toward the conference room, his eagerness waning with each step. *They won't allow me to go home. So... What now?*

From the arched doorway, he surveyed the busy room. His attention, drawn first to the silhouetted figure of a man in front of double glass doors at one end, moved on to several dark-haired men in red robes gathered around the long table. His uncle sat on the far side next to an empty chair.

Nomed glanced up and caught his eye. A smiled tugged the scar on his right cheek. "Esán, come in and join us.

The buzz of conversation stilled to silent interest as he walked around the table to stand beside his uncle.

"This is my nephew and apprentice, Esán Efre." Nomed nodded toward his associates. "These, Esán, are the esteemed Dreelum od DerTah."

Esán acknowledged the planet's leaders with a smile and waited for introductions.

A short, rotund man with one wandering eye stood. "Dreela Thaer from the Plains of DoOlb." He cleared his throat. "Welcome to DerTah." Before Esán could reply, he swept his greasy, black hair away from his face, attempted to straighten his crumpled robe, and slumped into his seat.

Craggy of face, lean, and graying, the man next to him pushed back his chair and rose. A stern voice filled the room. "Dreela Omudi." His steady gaze seemed to dissect Esán. "I am from the Towne of TiCeed on the Island of Geran."

"It is an honor, Dreela Omudi." Esán acknowledged him with a slight bow of his head.

Across from Nomed, a thin-faced man made a slow ascent to standing.

Esán's gaze climbed with him to his full height, where his shock of white hair brushed the ceiling. His smile warmed Esán. "Dreela Baroh from the TheDa Mountains." His voice, dry and kind, rumbled around the room. "I welcome you to DerTah, Esán, nephew of Seyes Nomed."

"Thank you, Dreela Baroh." Dark eyes met his and descended as the reed-like body folded back onto the chair.

The next Dreela, his short, muscular body sparking with energy, surged to standing. "I am Gidtuss. Fire ConDra are my pets and the sands of Fera Finnero are my domain." He narrowed his close-set eyes. His words licked the air like flames. "You know it, young Esán, as the Desert of DerTah." His eyes widened to a hard-edged stare. "You have felt the heat of its breath."

Before Esán could respond. The man's smirked smile, a cool compliment to his fire, formed and faded. "I am Gidtuss, the great—"

"My dearest Gidtuss—" A fluid, feminine voice filled with irony stopped him. "You are a man of heat fueled by ego."

Gidtuss scowled, stuck his nose in the air, and plopped down on his chair.

Esán turned to stare as an elegant, shapely figure draped in burnished gold flowed with languid grace from the doorway to a stop opposite him and his uncle.

"As you assured me, Seyes, he has a look of you." Her deep, velvety voice rose and fell like water in the wind. "Too bad he did not come to DerTah of his own accord."

Esán held back a gasp of surprise and gazed at the only woman he had seen since his arrival. Waves of short, dark hair framed her delicate features. Sparkles of gold flecked her slate-gray eyes; her skin glowed warm and brown.

"I am Dreelas TheLise. The Sea of Trinuge is my home. You are welcome, Esán, to visit us." Her smile held a touch of humor. "Have you ever sailed across an ocean?"

"I've never seen an ocean, Dreelas."

With an understanding smile, she took her seat. Esán couldn't stop staring.

A sharp noise at the double doors, where the silhouetted male figure extended a hand and positioned a black cane to the side, demanded their attention. Apprehension crept from one Dreelum to the next. Esán felt Nomed tense. The scar on his uncle's cheek pulsed.

Like an eclipsed moon reappearing, the man turned, allowing his facial features to emerge into the light. Spiky hair the rich brown of freshly furrowed earth; a well-formed ear; a tanned cheek; a hazel eye that glistened with mystery; and a straight nose came into view. The man stood statue-like, both hands resting on the crystal knob of the black cane, his chin high, his aristocratic profile chiseled and stoic.

A tap, step, drag, tap, step, drag carried him the length of the table. Elegance and charm accompanied him as he greeted the Dreelum, his handsome profile expressing his pleasure at their presence. When he reached Nomed, he angled his crippled body to maintain the side view of his face.

"It is good to see you, Seyes." His vibrant voice carried a slight accent. Each syllable rolled from his tongue with fluid clarity and purpose.

He tilted his head. His eye slid from Nomed to rest on Esán. His smiling mouth relaxed into a smooth line. With deliberate slowness, he rotated until the left side of his face caught the light.

Gulping down his shock, Esán schooled his expression and kept his attention fixed on the man whom he knew barely survived his first attempt to shift shape.

Accentuated by the overhead lighting, the almost translucent skin on the left side of his face exposed a web of pale, blue veins crawling over a withered cheek. A mouth trapped in a spasm of dreadful pain pulled downward. His brow, an arch of feather-like barbs, intensified the opaque murkiness of a milky eye.

Esán's gaze traveled from the upraised shoulder to the deformed arm to the clawed hand resting on the knob of the ironwood cane before returning to the High DiMensioner's disfigured face, where the osprey's vibrant presence took center stage.

Everything around him muted into a background of silent, hazy shapes. Only one man remained in focus—the man whose eyes, one dark hazel and alive and one sightless and opaque, locked him in a stranglehold. Darkness enshrouded his mind. He gripped the back of his chair, masked his mind, and shifted his gaze to a mole on the man's ravaged cheek. A low laugh pulled his focus to a frontal view of the strange face.

"You are good, young Esán. Most would not have had the presence of mind to hide their thoughts. Do you know who I am?"

"You are Wolloh Espyro, sir. Nomed's mentor."

Wolloh laid the cane on the table. "Why we are here today?"

"I don't know, sir."

"We are..." His single-eyed gaze scanned the room. "...here to meet you and assess your potential. You are a specimen, boy. Something to be examined—a bug under a microscope. How does that make you feel?"

Esán met his commanding gaze. A mind touch forced him back a step. "Please do not probe my mind, sir, and I will afford you the same courtesy."

Someone in the room gasped.

Wolloh slammed the clawed hand on the table. "Answer my question, boy. How does it make you feel?"

"Curious, sir. It makes me curious."

"Explain." The word snapped like a trap.

"If I am your specimen, then you are mine." He tilted his head. "And I am curious to know more."

A laugh began and choked into silence.

The smooth corner of Wolloh's deformed mouth twitched. "Come here. I wish to see you better."

Esán walked around the table. Twisted fingers cupped his chin. The mismatched eyes held his for what seemed an eternity.

"You will do, boy." He lowered his disfigured hand to pick up the cane and turned to the Dreelum od DerTah. Ironwood thumped the floor three times. "His assessment begins tomorrow. Now, let us adjourn to the dining room to enjoy a meal."

Nomed appeared at his elbow. "Go back to your quarters, nephew. Your mid-turning meal will be served to you there. I'll come by later."

Outside the arched doorway, Esán stopped, his mind emptied of thoughts.

"You realize you must break him, Seyes, or he will never bend to your will."

The unknown speaker made his jaw tighten. A single thought shot through his mind. *You will not break me, Seyes Nomed.*

2

Myrrh

On Myrrh, Almiralyn stood in the doorway to her sanctuary, her gaze fixed on her carved likeness kneeling on the rim of the alabaster fountain at the room's center. Water from the statue's cupped palms spilled into the large bowl with a rhythmic cadence that eased the tension of the past few moon cycles. *So much has happened.* She sighed. *And there's much more to come. It's time to go to work.*

Crossing to the fountain, she gazed into its rippling depths. Elcaro's Eye, a powerful oracle, assisted her in the performance of her duties as Myrrh's Guardian. She nodded to herself. *I am so glad the Galactic Council trusts me enough to leave it in my care.*

The water's silence called her attention back to its surface. A flash of golden light faded, leaving behind the image of the Prima Crystal Evolsefil obscured within CheeTrann's blue light in Nemttachenn Tower. Its magnificence and power combined with the arrival in Myrrh of four talented young people had triggered the long-anticipated Unfolding. This momentous event would impact her land and those she loved for a long time.

Her role—to help those who fight to bring about The Unfolding's positive conclusion—focused her attention on discovering her next move. She took a breath and waved a hand above the water. "Elcaro, the All-Seeing Eye, show me Esán Efre.

The Prima Crystal's glowing image faded, leaving behind a blur of reds and oranges that coalesced into Esán, staring out the second-story window of a rounded room.

Almiralyn leaned closer. "Where are you? Where did CheeTrann send you?"

Eddies stirred the water then grew quiet. The walls of the room melted into windswept red dunes undulating in all directions around him. High overhead, an osprey and a great horned owl flew side-by-side. Esán's expression, filled with stubborn determination, was the last thing she saw as water cascaded into the bowl, scattering the image like so much wind-blown sand.

"Wolloh Espyro and Seyes Nomed..." She ran a finger over the alabaster braid circling the fountain's rim. "So, you are in DerTah at the home of your uncle's mentor. Until you return to Myrrh, Evolsefil is not safe. Only you, Esán Efre, can move the Prima Crystal from Nemttachenn Tower back to the Cave of Canedari in the Dojanack Caverns. Our priority is to rescue you.

With a last glance at the rippling water, she strode from the sanctuary.

Arienh Lynae AsTar sat alone at the Guardian's kitchen table. Sunlight from an open window glinted off her coppery curls and warmed her fair skin and its sprinkling of freckles. With a long, frustrated sigh, she repeatedly traced a horizontal figure eight on the tabletop. "Where are you, Esán?" The memory of the DiMensioner pinning her friend against his chest made her shudder. "You disappeared down the swirling vortex in the tower." Her fist hit the table. "I wanted to help, but I couldn't get to you."

Brown eyes glinting beneath bridged auburn brows, she traced another symbol on the tabletop. *So much has happened since we met you on Torgin's fourteenth Sun Cycle Celebration.* Another infinity symbol... *We lost you to your uncle and the death shadow, found you again, and then...* She dropped her face in her hands, trying to erase the image of the tower vortex closing over him. Raising her head, she made a promise to her friend and to herself. "We will find out where Nomed took you, Esán. Then we *will* rescue you."

She stared at the tip of her finger. *I am fourteen and just met my father for the first time. Almiralyn is my aunt.* A frown curved her mouth. *I thought we were from Idronatti. Now, I've learned my father is from the planet of KcernFensia and my mother is from Myrrh.*

She traced the lines etching her life story across her palm. *What am I, anyway? Human or something else? Does it matter?* Her gaze darted to the doorway.

Brielle, her identical twin, approached the table. "Are you alright?"

"I'm fine, just confused." Ari eyed her palms and then her sister. "Are we Human?"

Brie pursed her lips and slid into a chair across from her. "What makes you ask?"

"Father said he has a longer lifespan than people in Idronatti. So?"

Brie tipped her head. "Myrrhinians are Human. Therans are Human. Does a species that lives over a century fall into that category?" She shrugged. "We are who we are, Arienh." A grin sparked. "We're pretty special, if you ask me."

Almiralyn entered the kitchen. "Good morning, girls. It seems you are in a quandary. Give me a moment, and we'll see if I can help."

With her favorite Dojanberry tea steaming in her cup, she sat down and looked from one twin to the other. "What's bothering you?"

Ari blushed. "I'm confused. Am I Human—will I live for centuries? I'm all mixed up."

Almiralyn cradled her cup in her hands and stared at the steaming liquid. "My birth planet is in a different dimension and vibrates at a different frequency, so my life cycle is different, but I am as Human as you are, Arienh."

Relief wiped the concern from Ari's face. "So I won't live for more than a century?"

"I didn't say that. You are more KcernFensian than you realize, so you may have inherited my bloodline's longevity."

Ari groaned and dropped her face into her hands.

Brie's curiosity bristled. "What do you mean we are more KcernFensian than we know, Aunt Mira?"

Almiralyn finished her tea, peered at the pattern of leaves lining the bottom of the cup, and looked up at her niece. "Please ask you parents to join us, Brie. I'd like them to be part of our discussion."

Ari peeked between her fingers at her disappearing twin, then lowered her hands and gave Almiralyn an awkward smile. "I feel like Torgin must feel when he's faced with something new. Why does it matter so much?"

Almiralyn rose to clear her cup away. "Have you thought about why it matters to you, Ari?"

Her niece's eyebrows bridged, then smoothed. "I've always known Brie and I were different. Not just because we're identical twins, something unheard of in Idronatti, but..." She tugged a curl. "No one else in the city has red hair." Her head tilted. "Brie knows stuff before it happens; I never worry about the rules. This is bigger."

Brie burst into the kitchen with her parents in tow. "Here we are!" She plopped down on the chair next to Ari.

While SparrowLyn poured a cup of tea, Allynae sat down across from his daughters. "Brie says you need us, Mira?

Almiralyn welcomed him with a slight smile. "Let's wait for Sparrow to join us." She gazed at her brother's wife, whose shiny chestnut hair, tied back with a green ribbon, framed her face. Her dark eyes, so like her daughters, sent her an inquiring look as she sat down beside Allynae.

Mentally organizing the information she wished to share, Almiralyn gazed around the table. "Ari has expressed some concerns. I didn't want to address them without you present."

Everyone's attention switch to Ari, who squirmed under their scrutiny. "I just want to know if I'm Human. If I'm not, then what am I? Almira— I mean, Aunt Mira said we're more KcernFensian than we know. We want to know what that means."

Allynae shifted his gaze to his sister. "Well, Mira?"

Almiralyn shifted hers to Sparrow. "What do you know about your parents and their families, SparrowLyn?"

"My parents were born in Myrrh. I met my father's mother once, but don't remember ever meeting my mother's family." Her gaze darted to Allynae and back. "Why?"

Almiralyn folded her hands on the tabletop. "You don't remember your mother's family because they are not from Myrrh."

Sparrow's emotions flashed by like the shifting colors in a kaleidoscope. Words as soft as summer rain filled the kitchen. "Where are they from, Almiralyn?

"Your mother is full-blooded KcernFensian and—"

"Wait!" Sparrow turned to Allynae. "That means—"

He laughed and hugged her. "It means we have the same life expectancy." He released her but clasped her hand. "So, Mira, tell us more."

The twins questioned in unison, "What about us?"

Almiralyn regarded the twins and then their parents.

An expectant silence settled over the family gathered at her table.

In Almiralyn's red barn, a tall adolescent boy with warm brown skin finished grooming the pony, Tam. He led her into the paddock, swung the big gate closed behind her, and rested his arms on top. "I'm so glad Mira trusts me to take care of you, Tamboreen."

He narrowed his summer green eyes. *What an adventure we just had! I wonder where Esán is and if he's alright? Sure wish we could help him.* Running a hand through his dark, wavy hair, he frowned. *Torgin Wilith Whalen, how are you ever going to be happy back in the City of Idronatti?* He stared up at the clear blue sky. *I've changed so much since I came to Myrrh.* He gazed at the pony. "As soon as I arrived here, I wanted to go home. Now, I can't imagine living anywhere but Myrrh. What is happening to me, Tam?"

Tam whinnied and stuck her nose through the bars of the gate. He scratched her forelock and grinned. "You are so beautiful. How many times have you rescued me since I arrived for my Sun Cycle Celebration?"

Memories of the battle to save Myrrh and Almiralyn from the DiMensioner od DerTah made him shudder.

He reached between the bars and combed his fingers through the pony's creamy mane. "Who would have guessed Nomed was Esán's uncle?" He shook his head. "My predictable life in Idronatti did not prepare me for such a bizarre adventure."

Tam nickered and nibbled his fingers.

Torgin squeezed his eyes shut and hugged himself before looking back at the attentive animal. "I wish Yaro, my Pentharian heart-brother, and his comrades hadn't left yesterday."

"Hello, young Torgin."

Solemn thoughts vanished as he turned to smile at the tall, black man who grinned at him and offered his upturned hand. Torgin touched his palm to the man's much larger one. "Where have you been, Paisley?"

"I waited for Yookotay to return to the Dojanack Caverns. The DeoNytes were sure glad to have their leader back in their midst."

"How's Skipt?" Torgin smiled at the memory of the small boy made of gray stones.

"The Enots went straight home to his mama."

Paisley glanced around as they strolled from the barn into the garden. "Where's everybody?"

"They all left yesterday, except of course for us Humans. You know Nomed kidnapped Esán, right?"

The big man nodded. "Yookotay told me. He also said Almiralyn is back and safe. Is she here?"

"She is in the kitchen with everyone else."

Paisley walked toward the cottage. "So when do ya return to Idronatti?"

Torgin kicked a pebble. "I don't want to return to the city. The PPP will erase my memories of Myrrh and all that happened here. I cannot lose who I've become, Paisley. I cannot."

"Now, now, let's see what Almiralyn has planned before ya panic. We gotta rescue Esán, ya know."

Torgin climbed the back steps, yanked open the screen door, marched into the kitchen, and went straight to Almiralyn. "I cannot go back to Idronatti. Please don't make me, Almiralyn. I want to keep my memories, and I want to help find Esán. Tam is here. The twins are..." The realization everyone was staring at him brought the stream of words to a halt.

"Slow down, Torgin." The Guardian's sapphire blue eyes sparkled up at him. "Have a seat and catch your breath. I'm not sending you anywhere yet."

Relief made him giddy. "Oh, ah, I... Thanks, Almiralyn." He squeezed in next to the twins.

The Guardian smiled at her brother's long-time friend. "Paisley, it's good to see you. What's happening in the Dojanacks?"

Paisley pulled up a chair next to Allynae and lowered his sizable frame onto it. "Everyone's home and safe. Elae is better. The Cave of Canedari is ready for Evolsefil. Other than that, it's darn quiet." He curled the end of his black mustache around his finger and lowered his eyes.

"When are we going to rescue Esán?" Torgin fidgeted in his chair. "It's already been three turnings."

"Yes, Almiralyn, what are your plans to rescue my nephew?" Esán's aunt entered the kitchen with Jordett, the PPP major who had helped to save Myrrh. He pulled out a chair, and they each perched on an edge, their focus on the Guardian.

"Good morning, Merrilea, Jordett. I'm glad you're here. We were just discussing Esán."

Ari frowned. "Wait. What about..."

Sparrow gave a tiny shake of her head.

"Where's Karrew?" The major's question shifted everyone's focus to him. "I haven't seen him around."

Allynae grinned. "You still can't believe Almiralyn's raven talks, can you?"

"I believe it. I just never tire of hearing him."

"Karrew is running an errand for me, Jordy." Almiralyn gave him a conspiratorial grin. "He'll be back soon." She looked around the table. "Since we're all here, I have a brief update. Esán is on the planet of DerTah in the Desert of Fera Finnero. That is all Elcaro's Eye has shared so far."

"Can we go there?" Brie and Ari chorused.

"I haven't decided if it's safe for you and Torgin to go anywhere." When they started to protest, she held up a hand. "You've already been exposed to enough danger. DerTah is not a friendly planet. It's the home of Nomed's mentor. Three Der'Tahan leaders hired Nomed to steal the Prima Crystal Evolsefil. If they caught you, they would use you to gain control of it. I cannot send you there."

Allynae glanced around the table. "One Man, Jordett, Paisley, and I can go. I have some experience with the planet." He rubbed his chin. "Some of my contacts may remember me."

Jordett glanced around. "Where is One Man? I haven't seen him all morning."

Torgin cleared his throat. "He left to go for a walk. Said he needed time to think."

"Time to be alone is more like it." Allynae sighed. "Being around people can be difficult. After living in solitude for so long, I imagine it's even harder for One Man."

"Plus, he just met and lost his son." Merrilea's voice quivered.

Ari's elbow in his ribs made Torgin jump up from his chair. He glared and moved aside as she slipped by.

Brie pushed her chair back. "Since you don't need us, we'll go out and enjoy the sunset."

"Please don't wander too far." Almiralyn's voice had a strange edge to it.

"We'll stay in the back garden." Brie nudged Torgin.

He frowned, torn between going with the twins, or learning more about Esán's rescue. Brie decided for him.

"Come on, Torg." She grabbed his hand and pulled him out the door after Ari.

"What is wrong with you two?" He jerked his hand away. "I want to hear what Almiralyn and Allynae are planning."

Ari did an about-face. "You interrupted a very important—"

"Ari, leave it." Brie shook her head.

He looked from one to the other. "What is going on?"

"Nothing, Torg." Brie linked her arm through his. "Almiralyn was talking about KcernFensia."

"I wanted to hear more about it, that's all." Ari marched into the barn and headed for the ladder to the loft. "Up we go. No one will hear us up here."

"No one will hear us down here. They're all in the kitchen." Torgin continued to mutter as he climbed the ladder and sprawled in the hay. He studied the twins. "What are you two up to?"

Ari nibbled on a piece of straw. "I'm not waiting for the adults to get organized. We need to rescue Esán ourselves."

Torgin scowled at her. "To do that, we have to go to DerTah. How do you propose to navigate a planet we know nothing about?"

Ignoring his testy tone, Brie continued what her sister had begun. "Wouldn't it be great, Torg, if the Compass of Ostradio worked there? I wonder..."

The straw moved from one side of Ari's mouth to the other as she studied her twin. "What's going on in that brain of yours, Brielle AsTar? Come on, tell us."

Brie pulled them into a huddle. "Tonight, when everyone's asleep, we need to pay Elcaro's Eye a visit. Maybe it will answer some questions for us. We'll meet in the kitchen at midnight."

"Good plan." Torgin stood and brushed the straw from his pants. "Let's find out what the adults are planning. We might learn something, you know." Without waiting for the twins, he descended the ladder and strode across the garden.

"What type of planet is DerTah?" He heard Jordett ask as he pulled the screen door open and waited for the girls to precede him into the kitchen. "I know different dimensions have different time frames as well."

Sparrow moved over so her daughters could join the group still gathered around the table. Torgin plunked down on a chair next to Brie.

"DerTah is quite primitive compared to Thera and resembles Old Earth in the nineteenth century." Allynae acknowledged their arrival with a nod and continued. "Some provinces have train lines. Trinuge and Geran provinces have sailing ships. Horses are the primary mode of transportation on land."

Torgin memorized every detail. He caught Ari's eye. Dropping his gaze, he watched her trace a horizontal figure eight on the tabletop. *Tonight at midnight, I will meet the twins, and we'll make plans of our own.* His ever-present anxiety fluttered in the pit of his stomach.

3
Der Tah

Nomed lay on his bed, fatigue attempting to compete with his racing thoughts. With a frustrated sigh, he stared up at the ceiling and let his mind wander.

Sunrise brought with it a summons to meet his mentor in the arena. Mumbled profanities accompanied him as he stepped into the early morning coolness. A deep, cleansing breath erased his lingering sleepiness and left him alert as he strode to the arena's center.

Wolloh, his good eye gleaming, nodded a welcome. "Seyes, join me for a flight around the ranch." Not waiting for a reply, his mentor shifted to an osprey and soared into dawn's peach and lavender sky.

Nomed shaped the great horned owl and followed. Flying with Wolloh, an unexpected treat, left him exhilarated.

Afterward, they sipped hot tea in front of a dying fire in Wolloh's study and enjoyed some time by themselves.

Not ready to share his misadventures on Myrrh, Nomed kept his gaze fixed on the glowing embers and flickering flames.

Across from him, Wolloh savored a long drink and set his mug on the side table. Angling his smooth, unblemished cheek toward him, he cleared his throat. "So, did you achieve your goal?"

"I did not." Anger clipped the words short. "I had Almiralyn encased in ice and Evolsefil within reach." He scowled and stared into his mug.

"Are you going to leave me in suspense or tell me what happened?"

Nomed hesitated. *Do I want Wolloh to know how badly I bungled things?* He set his mug down and squared his shoulders. "I underestimated my opponents, my henchmen, the Pentharian—" He shot his mentor a defensive look. "Esán and his friends exhibited talents I did not expect." With his eyes narrowed to slits of hazel, he stared at the fire. "And the sentinel of the tower in the Terces Wood flummoxed me and sent me back to Der Tah without the Evolsefil Crystal."

Wolloh's disfigured profile turned in his direction. "And how are Gidtuss, Thaer, and Omudi feeling about that?"

Nomed's heart thumped. He swallowed a lie and told the truth. "They're none too happy. How did you know? I mean... Never mind. You miss very little." He frowned. "You could have told me you knew."

"Why? You're a grown man. If you choose to become involved with likes of those three..." The grimaced mouth became more pronounced and tugged the tortured cheek taut. The head turned and Wolloh's good eye scanned his face. "Something happened on Myrrh you did not expect."

Nomed rubbed the scar on his cheek and ran a hand over his mouth and chin. "Somay, my brother, was there. He's Esán's father. The boy is my nephew, Wolloh." He swallowed. "His presence in my life has opened me up and left me raw. I don't know why."

Wolloh massaged the calf of his mangled leg and leaned back in his chair. "My dearest Seyes, for such a smart man, you are always obtuse when it concerns your emotions."

"I don't want to talk about it. Isn't it enough that I failed? Almiralyn and Myrrh have both survived. The Prima Crystal is out of reach. What a magnificent crystal!" For a brief instant, it materialized in his memory—

almost half again as tall as he was, with six smaller crystals circling its base. He sighed. "You should have seen it."

His mentor smiled. "I believe I just did."

Nomed's eyebrow shot up. A laugh burst from his throat. "You are a devil, my friend."

Nomed stretched and sat up. The rest of their conversation had centered on Esán and his upcoming assessment. He felt a rush of excitement. *When Wolloh sees how talented he is, he will never allow the DerTahan leaders to interfere.*

He splashed water on his face, smoothed his shoulder-length chestnut hair back into a low queue, and changed to a shirt of russet silk. The mirror assured him he was handsome, regardless of the scar on his right cheek. His hazel eyes gleamed with pleasure. Whistling to himself, he left his quarters in search of TheLise, the Dreelas of the Sea of Trinuge.

Esán sprawled on his bed, fuming at the conversation he had overheard after leaving the conference chamber. *No one is going to control me.*

A soft knock brought him upright; his eyes narrowed as he came to his feet. Acute senses informed him a stranger waited in the hallway. *Friend or foe? Only one way to find out.* He pulled the door open.

The man held a tray laden with food. "May I come in?" The voice, somewhat throaty and warm, held only respect. The dark, almond-shaped eyes held a smile.

Esán stepped aside. The man placed the tray on a small table. "My name is Corvus Difner." He glanced at the open door.

Closing it, Esán turned back to study the man, who watched him with a steady, quiet gaze. Tall, lean, and well-muscled beneath his servant's uniform, he appeared to be about Nomed's age. Blue-black hair lay in loose layers around a face that seemed to shift in and out of focus. A moment later, the features stabilized...a narrow nose, a mouth curved into a smile, a dimple on his right cheek that deepened when he spoke.

"I know your uncle brought you here against your will." The words were barely audible.

"What do you want?" Esán kept his voice quiet.

"May I sit down?"

"If you like." He indicated a chair next to a rosewood dresser as he perched on the edge of his bed.

Corvus leaned forward. The intensity in the black eyes demanded his full attention. "You mustn't try to escape, at least not yet. Learn all you can learn. When the right moment presents itself, you'll know. I'll be near if you need help."

"Who are you?" Esán sent a gentle probe into his mind.

"I'm your friend. You'll find nothing in my mind to the contrary."

A nod acknowledged the truth in the man's words. "They wish to break my spirit, Corvus. I will not let them."

"Play their game, Esán. Learn *everything* you can." He crossed to the door. "I'll be near." It closed behind him.

As he reviewed the conversation, the burden of being alone in the enemy's camp lifted, leaving him light-headed with relief. Hunger growling, he pulled up a chair and examined the tray. Thick, spicy soup and warm bread assuaged his hunger and strengthened his resolve.

Night air from the open window restored his good humor and swept the stale heat from his stuffy room. With a full-bodied yawn, he prepared for bed, slipped between cool sheets, and drifted into dreams of the dark-haired man.

A sharp knock left him awake and staring out the window at the lightless sky. Another knock demanded an answer. He stumbled to the door and pulled it open a crack.

The young servant, Seval, met his bleary gaze with a slight smile. "The master is waiting to receive you."

"Who?" Esán tried to shake his lingering lethargy.

"Master Wolloh awaits you in the outer yard. Please dress. Layers would be best. When the sun rises, the heat returns with a vengeance."

Esán closed the door and, leaning against it, gathered his scattered senses before he crossed to the washstand and splashed cool water on his face. He caught sight of his groggy reflection and frowned. *Meeting Wolloh with sleep still clogging my mind would be a disaster.*

A quick jog around the room woke up his heart and sent fresh blood to his brain. When he felt wide awake, he dressed and stepped into the hall where Seval waited.

The young servant shook his dark auburn hair back from his face. "We'd better hurry. Master Wolloh has only a small reserve of patience, especially in the early morning."

Esán followed him down the hall to a flight of stairs. All too soon, they stepped into the chilled darkness of the outer courtyard. A shiver made him wrap his cloak more tightly around his slender body.

Seval pulled open a wooden gate leading into a large, round arena. At the far side, the warm glow of a lantern cast a shadow over Wolloh Espyro's deformed face, creating the illusion of unblemished handsomeness. The High DiMensioner turned. The illusion shattered.

With his one-eyed gaze fastened on Esán, Wolloh dismissed the young servant with a wave of his hand and took a step forward. "Well, boy. It is time to evaluate your talents. Stand where you are and do not move."

Nomed's excitement, diminished by Wolloh's refusal to allow his participation, returned as he ducked into a darkened doorway to watch. *The boy is my nephew and my apprentice.* He shoved unruly thoughts away and moved further into the shadows. Wolloh was not someone whose anger he wished to incur.

A subtle probe of his nephew's mind almost brought a smile. The boy had masked it. Impressed, he noted his nephew's calm demeanor and vigilance. His brow arched. *Your intelligence and potential may outstrip my own.*

He turned his attention to his mentor. *What will you discover that I missed, Wolloh Espyro? Will you take Esán as your student, or farm him out to the Dreelum od DerTah?*

Esán realized he was under the microscope. He met Wolloh's demanding gaze with a steady one of his own. *By turning's end, I will have a much better understanding of you, Wolloh Espyro.* For the briefest of moments, he wondered if Corvus was near. Then, with practiced skill, he closed his mind further and arranged his expression to open acceptance.

"You need not mask your mind. I respect your request that I not probe it."

Esán remained quiet.

"We are here to learn how powerful you are, boy." His voice changed—grew sterner. "Do as I say, and you will leave here unscathed. Disobey and..."

The unfinished sentence spoke volumes. Esán shoved away a slight tremor of fear.

Wolloh limped closer and leaned on his cane. His disfigured face remained hidden by darkness but for a gleam in his sightless eye. "Let us begin." He tapped the ground with his stick. "You can teleport. Move to the gate and return here."

Esán flashed to the gate and back. *Will I ever get used to this?*

"Now to your quarters and back."

He teleported to his room, refreshed himself with a deep drink of water, and returned to the arena.

Wolloh's powerful hand gripped his neck. "Do no more or less than I ask." He dropped his hand. "Am I clear?"

"You are most clear." He ignored the throbbing in his throat.

"Now, teleport to the desert where you landed on your first visit to DerTah."

"Would that be when I came through NaiDisbo Gateway or when Nomed kidnapped me?" He kept his voice level and cool.

Wolloh's good eye sparked with an amused thought. "The spot where you first met the Fire ConDra. And, Esán, return here immediately."

His heart hammering, he hesitated. *A Fire ConDra almost killed me.*

"Now, boy! Or are you afraid?"

Fist clenched, he arrived in the desert of DerTah where he encountered his first Fire ConDra. Nothing but sand. He flashed back to the arena.

Wolloh pointed across the space. "Teleport that lantern here."

Esán focused his intent. The lantern floated to Wolloh and hovered beside him.

"Return it."

The lantern floated back and settled on the table.

A metal pole flew from the shadows. Wolloh snatched it and held it up. "Form this into a figure eight." He released to hover in the air between them.

After assessing the metal of the pole, Esán pictured it bending. Much to his surprise, it formed into the required figure and fell with a thud to the sandy ground.

Wolloh continued his commands. "Tell me who is in this arena."

"You, Nomed, and the Dreelum od DerTah—except for Gidtuss—three small birds, a myriad of crawling creatures, and a shadowy thing."

"What do you sense outside the walls?"

He stretched his consciousness outward. "The gradual awakening of life. Servants are beginning their various jobs. Animals sense the sun's return. Seval guards the gate. At a greater distance, the desert prepares for the return of the sun. A lizard scurries across the sand, a rabbit burrows deeper, a small red fox catches one last bite to fend off hunger."

"Enough. Tell me what's happening on Myrrh.

"I don't know, sir."

"You didn't try, boy. Do it now."

Focusing on Myrrh, he inhaled. Images flashed: Brie and Ari watching him disappear with Nomed into the vortex in Nemttachenn; the tower reassembling; a conversation around Mira's table; Torgin and the twins huddling in the red barn. His mind blanked. Astonishment shot through him. Relief he had seen no more made him giddy.

"Come on, boy, before I lose patience."

Esán described what he had seen.

Wolloh's deformed face showed neither emotion nor interest. "One last thing...without moving, I want you to ward off anything that is thrown in your direction, thoughts, objects, entities. Are you ready?"

"May I have a moment, sir?"

"A brief one."

Centering his thoughts, he inhaled. *Trust. I must trust my instincts. Trust.* An exhale stiffened his spine. "I'm ready, sir."

A ball of indeterminate weight shot toward him.

Motionless and relaxed, Esán never took his eye off the ball, rocketing straight for his face. An arm's length away, it smashed into an invisible barrier and bounced off. A second ball whizzed toward him. A whispered word sent it ricocheting high overhead. More objects flew from every direction, first one at a time, then en masse. A shower of small silver balls hit the barrier and bounced like raindrops over the ground.

The projectiles ceased. Tension filled the silent arena. Esán's instincts shouted a warning. His vigilance increased. Around him, his energy field crackled. A roiling cloud of gray shot straight for him. Eyes like smoldering coals stopped just short of his shields and hovered.

Wolloh held up his clawed hand. The burning eyes wafted his direction. "You may go." His voice was gentle. The smoky entity sputtered a hiss and puffed from sight.

Esán felt the protective field around him collapse. On the verge of exhaustion, he knew he would fail another test.

Nomed flashed to his side and slid an arm around his waist. "Enough, Wolloh, I told you he's ill." Nomed guided him across the arena away from Wolloh's hammering commands.

Only vaguely aware of his uncle's powerful presence and support, he entered his room and sank onto his bed. The moment his head touched the pillow, fatigue dropped him into a deep sleep. A sharp pain behind his eyes heralded his slow return. He ached all over. Thirst clawing at his throat left his tongue cracked and swollen. Someone lifted his head. Cool water slipped between his dry lips. His eyes fluttered open. Relief engulfed him.

"How are you?" Corvus' gentle tone contrasted with his serious expression.

"Exhausted—more exhausted than I've ever been, even in my sickest moments." He pushed himself to sitting and slid his legs over the side of the bed.

"You did well today. Your gifts have caused quite a stir."

Esán took another deep drink from the glass Corvus had placed in his hands. "Now they are planning how I can be of use to them." His tired, thin voice reflected his disgruntled vulnerability.

"For the time being, you must continue to show some resistance, Esán. Learn everything they can teach you. In the end, it will serve you and those you love." Corvus handed him a round object that resembled a peach with purple skin. "This is steerro fruit. It will restore you and rebuild your natural energy levels. I put more in your bottom drawer. Eat one whenever you feel drained." He moved to the door. "I must go. Take care and don't give up hope." The door closed with a whispered thud.

Esán studied the fruit with interest. A tentative nibble tantalized his taste buds. Deep salmon flesh oozed droplets of juice that threatened to escape down his arm. Taking a big bite, he savored the succulent sweetness. Energy, like a shock wave, rolled through his system. *Whatever steerro fruit is, I am sure glad to have it.* He popped the last morsel in his mouth, licked his fingers clean, and crossed to the window. The sun hung well past its zenith, scorching hot in the orange sky. *I must have slept a long time.*

"You did."

He swung around to find Nomed in the doorway. "How long have *you* been standing there?" Annoyance sharpened the timber of his voice. "And please stay out of my mind."

"You seem glad to see me." His mentor sat down on the edge of the bed. "I rescued you from more tests, you know."

"I know. Thank you."

"You continue to surprise me, Esán. And I am not often surprised by anything. Did you know you could do what you did today?"

"Only some of it."

"Well, dear boy, you are the talk of the Dreelum. They would like you to join us for dinner."

"And if I prefer to eat here alone…"

"Wolloh will be most disappointed."

Esán turned back to the window. Heat rose like a curtain from the red sand. He sighed and faced Nomed. "We wouldn't want to disappoint Wolloh, now would we? When is dinner?"

"Seval is bringing you new clothes and will help you dress. I'll be back when you're ready." He opened the door. The young servant entered and placed the clothing on the bed.

The door shut. Esán stared at the scarlet robe and frowned.

4

Myrrh

The pitter-patter of rain on the roof accompanied Brie's random thoughts as she lay beside Ari and watched the slow, steady progression of time on the face of the chronometer on the bedside table. *We have parents. How strange.* She and Ari had doubted they'd ever know who their father was, let alone meet him. SparrowLyn had refused to discuss anything connected to their birth and parentage. They'd finally quit asking.

Ari rolled onto her side, her curls a riot of copper around her face. "What are you thinking?"

"I'm thinking how odd it is to have parents, plural—a mother *and* father." Brie sat up and plumped her pillows behind her.

"Pretty amazing, huh?" Ari grinned. "If we hadn't become involved in saving Myrrh and Almiralyn, we might have never found him."

"Fourteen sun cycles apart," said Brie, "and he and Mother still love each other so much."

Ari laughed. "Now they can't stand to be separated. They're kinda cute, aren't they?"

"Yes, they are. Making up for lost time, I think. It must be nice to be loved." Brie's musings made her smile. "I mean...we love Mother, but it's different. She's happier than I've ever seen her."

"Don't you wish Torgin had waited just a few chron-clicks longer to come bursting into the kitchen? Then we would have learned more about her parents—our grandparents."

"Mother is part KcernFensian." Brie's eyes glistened with excitement. "I can't wait to hear more. Do you think Grana Gerolyn's husband is really mother's father?"

"There's some mystery about that. Almiralyn had more to say. Hey, do you think Elcaro's Eye can tell us anything about this?"

Brie shrugged. "Aunt Mira's teaching me how to use it, but it has a mind of its own. It only tells you what you *need* to know." She yawned." It's almost time to meet Torgin, isn't it?"

Ari rolled over and picked up the chronometer from the nightstand. "Five clicks and he'll be in the kitchen." She replaced it and scooted to the side of the bed. Dragging a brush through her curls, she pulled her hair back into a ponytail and secured it with a blue band, the last remnant of her Idronatti uniform.

Brie followed suit, and soon they were waiting in the kitchen, where the rain pattered on the windowpanes and splashed a constant rhythm on the sills.

"I hate rain." Ari grumbled under her breath, then shivered.

Torgin, who was bunking in the barn with Major Jordett and One Man, huddled under a large, black umbrella. Closing it and leaning it next to the porch door, he tiptoed into the room. "It's wet out there." He brushed water droplets off his pants. "Hope it stops before I head back."

"Let's go." Brie tiptoed into the hall. "Be careful of the fourth step. It squeaks."

The rain's gentle song accompanied them up the stairs to the Guardian of Myrrh's sanctuary. In the middle of the room, a peaceful Elcaro's Eye rested on its carved pedestal. From its rounded rim, the kneeling alabaster woman tipped a slow stream of water from her upraised palms into the waiting bowl.

"It's so beautiful." Torgin crept closer. "I can only see water. How's it work?"

The twins joined him beside the fountain.

Brie felt a subtle pulsing as she rested her hands on the rim. Almiralyn had told her some of its history, an intricate and mystical story cloaked in the obscurity of passing aeons. Created on the tiny planet of Tao Spirian, it had found its way to KcernFensia, where the Guardians placed it in Almiralyn's care when she completed her training and arrived in Myrrh. Vesen, the tall, slender crystal encased within the alabaster pedestal, came from the cavern where Evolsefil and her father's crystal, Novissi, were discovered. All three were as cognizant as the Human's they served.

She leaned forward and whispered the words her aunt had taught her. Brown eyes gazed up at her. Her reflection only stimulated more questions. Red hair, brown eyes, and a dusting of freckles did not remind her of either of her parents. She pushed the thought away and concentrated. "Elcaro, the All-Seeing Eye, show me Esán Efre."

Torgin and Ari gasped as the figure of their friend came into focus. Clothed in a scarlet robe and looking anything but happy, he fidgeted while a boy about his age tied a gold sash around his waist. The image dissolved.

Ari tugged at a curl. "Well, at least we know he's okay."

Torgin looked at Brie. "Who was the other boy?"

"He looked like a servant." She organized her thoughts and planned her next question. "Where is Esán?"

The surface smoothed. A turquoise full moon came into focus at the center of the Eye. Its light illuminated a sea of red sand. The image zoomed out, showing a butter yellow orb and a milky crescent moon edging their way across the night sky.

"Wow! Three moons." Ari studied the scene. "I bet that's DerTah."

Brie took a breath and exhaled. "What is the best way for us to rescue Esán?" The desert and moons vanished. The still water shimmered in the dim light of the sanctuary. "Will Torgin's compass help us navigate in DerTah?"

Torgin, with the Compass of Ostradio in his hand, floated to the surface. On its face was the picture of a sandstone arch in a red desert.

Ari pursed her lips. "Elcaro shows you in DerTah, Torg, so we must get there somehow."

"What if I don't want to go to DerTah?"

Ari punched him in the arm. "You want to rescue Esán, don't ya?"

"Yes, but—"

Brie gathered her courage and gripped the rim of the bowl. "Who is our grandfather?"

Ari and Torgin stopped their bickering and stared.

The Star of Truth sent a warning throb of pain up the back of Brie's neck. Elcaro's Eye shuddered and splashed dark, frothing water over its alabaster rim.

"I don't suppose you considered asking permission to use my fountain?"

From the corner of her eye, Brie saw Ari and Torgin whip around. She could not move. The face rising from black, stormy clouds on the water's surface sent a wave of paralysis shooting through her. Her mind filled with the piercing, intelligent eyes of a man with flaming hair. She could not tear her gaze away. A foaming whirlpool eradicated the image. But the sinister eyes remained like flares of light in her mind. The alabaster statue spilled droplets into Elcaro's bowl—the only sound in the room.

She gasped for air. Her knees buckling left her sitting on the floor in a puddle of spilled water. A voice, muffled and unrecognizable, pounded against her eardrums.

"Brie!" Almiralyn's face, nose to nose with hers, snapped into focus. "Shield your mind *now*!"

Struggling against the vacuum that threatened to engulf her, Brie tried to respond. "I...I...can't..."

"Brie." Almiralyn's hands, pressing firmly on either side of her head, pushed the penetrating eyes away. "Shield your mind!"

Like a guillotine dropping, Brie felt her mind snap shut. "I did it." A whimper of relief left her trembling.

"Good girl. I must erase the connection he is trying to forge. Be still. If he fights me, it may hurt, but not for long. Are you ready?"

Brie steadied herself. "Yes, Aunt Mira, I'm ready."

Inside her skull, a pain twisted tighter and tighter. A scream clawed at her throat. She gulped it down and gasped as the connection convulsed. Like a snake slithering into hiding, it was gone.

Almiralyn's arms supported her. "Breathe, dear one. Just breathe. You'll be fine. I'm right here."

Ari knelt beside her. "I'm here, too, Brie."

Torgin stood looking down at her, his wide green eyes brimming with alarm.

Remorse choked her. "I'm s-so sorry, Aunt Mira. I asked about our grandfather. When his eyes found me..." A tear ran down the side of her nose. She brushed it away. "He wouldn't leave me alone. I felt like he was dissecting my brain to discover everything about me."

"I think we thwarted his attempt, Brie, but now he knows he has a granddaughter." Almiralyn studied her face and then turned to her twin. "Ari, please wake up your parents and Merrilea. Have them join us in the kitchen. Torgin, fetch the Major, One Man, and Paisley. We have much to discuss."

After they had darted away, Almiralyn helped her to stand. "I'm sorry I used Elcaro's Eye without your permission, Aunt Mira. Is our grandfather a good man?

"Your grandfather is someone I had hoped you would never meet." She sighed. "It's only a matter of time."

Ari sat next to Torgin at the kitchen table. Allynae, Jordett, and One Man were deep in conversation across from her; and Paisley sat near the door, leaning against the pale yellow wall. Her mother moved over to make room for Merrilea to sit beside her. Ari saw the question in her eyes.

"What were you doing in Mira's sanctuary in the middle of the night?" Sparrow's tone held a note of disapproval.

Ari kept her eyes focused on the tabletop. "We wanted to make certain Esán was safe." Somehow, the justification sounded hollow.

Almiralyn entered the kitchen with Brie. "You were planning to go after Esán. Now we have a serious situation on our hands."

Ari felt herself blush. Before she could stop them, angry, defiant words gushed out. "We did nothing wrong." She glared at Brie.

"Ari..." Sparrow admonished.

"It's okay, Mother." Brie slid into a chair next to her sister. "I had to tell her, Ari."

"It's not your plan to rescue Esán that worries me at the moment." Almiralyn put both hands on the tabletop. "It's what the image in the fountain learned that has me concerned."

The sense of foreboding in her voice sent chills racing up Ari's spine.

"She saw your birth father, Sparrow." The Guardian sat down. "And now he knows he has a granddaughter."

"And who is my birth father, Almiralyn?"

The Guardian hesitated.

"Well?" Allynae leaned across the table. "Are you going to tell us who he is, Mira?"

"He is the Largeen Joram of the planet of RewFaar."

"RewFaar!" Allynae jumped up and gripped the table. "Are you sure? RewFaar! The Largeen Joram..." He sank onto his seat and put a protective arm around his life-mate.

Sparrow pressed closer. "I think you should explain, Almiralyn."

"I suppose I should."

Ari watched her aunt search for the right way to begin.

5
DerTah

Esán slipped the scarlet robe over his head. *What are they planning for me?*

Seval finished tying the gold sash and stepped back to check his handy work. "You look good, Master Efre."

"Esán." His snapped response widened Seval's eyes. He softened his tone. "Please, call me Esán."

"It would not be appropriate for me to address a Tyro in that manner." Seval lowered his eyes.

"I'm not a Tyro, whatever that is. I'm only in DerTah because my uncle kidnapped me." The anger in his voice surprised him. "Can you at least call me Esán when we're alone?"

"If you wish." Seval opened the door. "Come, Master, the Dreelum await you."

Master. Esán swept from the room, his long scarlet robe swishing as he walked. *I am no one's master. And I will allow no one to be mine.*

Outside the dining room, he prepared himself for a tiresome evening. It irked him that everyone inside would attempt to read his mind the moment he entered, and that they were discussing him now. Masking his thoughts and transforming his frown into a gracious smile, he entered the room. All eyes swept his direction. Speculation, greedy interest, fear, laughter—all flashed through the gap between them.

Wolloh welcomed him with a distorted smile. "Ah, our guest of honor. Come in and join us, Esán. We were just talking about you." A wicked light gleamed in his hazel eye. He reached out his good hand and drew him into the circle of Dreelum.

TheLise flashed him a disarming smile. "You look quite dashing in your robe, Esán. Has anyone explained to you what it means?"

"No. I was just told to wear it."

Baroh peered down from his immense height. "It is the symbol of power in DerTah, Esán. The gold sash denotes a Tyro." The words tumbled like pebbles down a steep hill, one dry syllable after the other.

"Am I correct in assuming no one told you what a Tyro is?" TheLise's teasing smile made the blood rush to his cheeks.

Wolloh cleared his throat and turned the handsome side of his face to TheLise. "I believe dinner is served, Dreelas." He offered his good arm. "May I escort you to the table?"

Her gray eyes sparkled as she placed a hand on his arm. "I'm always delighted to walk by your side, Wolloh."

"But not to follow where I lead." His teasing tone held a touch of displeasure.

TheLise gave a deep, sensual laugh. "I am who I am, Wolloh. Would you want it any other way?"

"Never, my dear." He patted her hand with his twisted claw and guided her to the table.

Captivated by the exchange, Esán's eyes followed them as they continued their banter, his thoughts speculative. Wolloh, with his distorted features, seemed to be two distinct personalities.

Nomed placed a hand on his shoulder. "Interesting, isn't he?"

Esán moved apart from his uncle. "He is clearly a man of power."

"Esán." Wolloh sounded amused. "Please sit across from me so I may... observe you more closely." He laughed and turned his handsome face back to TheLise.

Esán moved around the table. *I continue to be under the microscope. So be it. I will also learn about you, Wolloh Espyro. And I intend to learn a lot from you, as well.*

After dinner, Nomed relaxed in his room. All evening, he had waited for Wolloh to announce his plans for the boy. At one point, he wondered whether his mentor was tormenting him on purpose with his silence. The dinner, a pleasant affair, took shape in his mind.

Rarely had he seen his mentor so charming or so witty. Wolloh's taste for society ran to the occasional meeting with the leaders of DerTah. Teaching his initiates was more to his liking.

Nomed's eyes gleamed. Memories of his training flickered. The Arts of DiMensionery focused on the innate gifts of man, not on magic, spells, or fortune-telling." He smiled. Esán showed an abundance of these gifts and more were certain surface. He returned his errant thoughts to recent events.

When dinner was complete and the dessert plates cleared, a dignified servant poured an after-dinner cordial smelling of fire and roses into small, shimmering crystal glasses. Wolloh stood, his fragile glass in his uninjured hand, and turned his handsome face to the gathered company. The room grew quiet. All eyes rested on the High DiMensioner od DerTah.

Lifting his glass higher, Wolloh gazed from one guest to the next. "To a most enjoyable evening." He took a sip, savored its robustness, and held up his glass again. He turned his head—his sightless eye staring at Esán. The glass and the eye gleamed. "And...to my new apprentice."

"Here! Here!" The room vibrated with the chorused response. Everyone drained their glass and threw it with relish against the wall behind the new Tyro. Esán stared at the disfigured face, set his glass down, and walked, straight-backed and proud, from the room.

Wolloh laughed and continued his charming discourse with the Dreelum as they disbanded for the night. As the dining room door closed behind them, Wolloh turned and smiled. "You have done well, Seyes." His hazel eye glinted. "I am delighted you brought the boy to me. What spunk he has! You were older when you first arrived in DerTah, but filled with the same self-righteous rebellion." He chuckled. "What a fiery temper you had! Esán has a different temperament, but he is definitely his own person. My challenge will be to make him mine. What is his bloodline? Is he, like you, of mix-blood?"

Nomed's stomach clutch. Memories of Esán's mother always brought with them a flood of emotion. "His mother, Tianna, was from Myrrh."

Wolloh, his face hidden in the shadows, turned to pour a last drink. "That explains much. It will be interesting to see what other gifts the boy carries." He handed Nomed Esán's untouched cordial. "To you and your nephew."

They downed the fiery liquid and hurled the glasses against the wall.

Nomed struggled with the mixed emotions that surged through him. *I've gotten what I wanted, haven't I? The master High DiMensioner of the Inner Universe will train my nephew, and when his training is complete... what then? Will he be more powerful than me?*

Esán stripped off the scarlet robe. "Did it ever occur to anyone it might be nice to ask *me* whether I wanted to be a Tyro?" He wadded it and the gold sash into a crumpled ball. "I realize I don't have a choice but..." He scowled and pitched them into the corner. "I would prefer they had asked." Scrambling into his own clothes, he continued to mumble under his breath about the stupidity of adults...well, not all adults, but for sure Wolloh and Nomed.

From his window, he watched the moons of DerTah parade across the desert sky. Buttercup yellow and full to bursting, the largest and most distant moon had begun its disappearing act below the horizon. A turquoise moon arcing overhead, its fullness cradled within a glowing double corona, cast cool light over silhouetted taccus trees and buildings. The tip of the third moon, white and crisp as the snow in the Central Mountains, pushed its crescent phase above the ranch as though straining to catch up with its companions. The immenseness of the scene awed him.

He grabbed his cloak and threw it around his shoulders. "Perhaps a brisk walk will cool my temper."

Esán loved nighttime aromas, the chill of the air against his skin, and the stark beauty of the sky. The myriad of stars was so different from those on either Thera or Myrrh. *I wonder if any are the same. What are my friends doing? How is my father? Aunt Merrilea must be so worried. Will I ever see them again?*

The crunch of a footfall made him pause in the shadow of a tall taccus tree. Careful not to touch the sharp quills covering its surface, he ducked behind it and waited. A low voice whispered—another answered. Esán caught his name and strained to hear more. The footsteps and the voices came closer.

"Do you think we can coax the boy away from Nomed?"

Esán frowned at the unfamiliar voice.

"Maybe we just kidnap him. He'd be a great bargaining chip."

That's Gidtuss. I'm positive. Esán crouched lower, wishing he dared to use telepathy.

"Do you think Wolloh would care about the boy's life?" The unknown voice dripped with sarcasm.

"We don't bargain with his life. We bargain with his talent. He's loaded with it, and when he's trained... Look out 'cause we'll all be in trouble." Gidtuss and his companion stopped to gaze up at the night sky. Esán could just make out their silhouetted figures.

"Will anyone else be interested in helping?" Heads bent close together, they continued their conspiratorial stroll through the desert night.

Esán's thoughts raced. *Who owns the second voice? Why do they need a "bargaining chip"?* He bit his lip. *"By the Fathers, I need help, or I might be—"*

The rustle of fabric behind him kicked his heart into his throat. He turned, ready to fight.

"Corvus." His relief was instantaneous. "How did you know I—"

Corvus put a finger to his lips and stepped closer. "Teleport back to your quarters. I'll join you there when it's safe."

Esán nodded and arrived in the middle of his small room.

"Don't move." The soft voice hissed through the darkness. The door's lock clicked into place.

6
Myrrh

Almiralyn cleared her throat and addressed Sparrow.

"Your mother, Gerolyn, was born and raised in the Temple of Mahyinaeh on the planet of KcernFensia. The summer of her eighteenth sun cycle, she received an invitation to become a priestess in the temple and swore an oath to serve. That same summer, a delegation from RewFaar arrived and with it the Largeen Joram and his son, Lorsedi.

"It is important to understand several things. KcernFensia is a matriarchy. Although men do lead, most often the rulers are high priestesses of Mahyinaeh. RewFaar, KcernFensia's antithesis, is a patriarchy ruled by its military leaders. RewFaaran women are cloistered from birth and raised in an area known as LaTenge Famele. They remain separate from the male population, unless required for official functions or to mate with a man. RewFaarans would never accept or tolerate a woman as their leader. The delegation that summer came to KcernFensia in search of new breeding stock."

"You mean they were there to get women?" Brie's eyes widened.

"They were, and not just any women. They wanted young priestesses raised in the temple and trained in the healing arts. The delegation was not popular. Glenet Evol, the high priestess, welcomed them only because she had no choice. They had threatened war."

Allynae's brow knitted. "RewFaar is a military dictatorship whose entire society and government are based on waging war. Warfare is their aim, and raw fear is their game."

Torgin's eyes widened. "No wonder she had to let them visit."

Almiralyn nodded. "Glenet knew the Largeen Joram's threat was real. He had set his sights on a high priestess to join with his son. Prior to their arrival, she sent all but three priestesses into the hills to hide. Gerolyn's twin sister, Tissent, and two other young priestesses had volunteered to give up their lives in the Temple to save the planet they loved."

Excitement lit up Brie's face. "My grandmother is a twin? Maybe that explains why we're twins. Perhaps it runs in the family."

"Maybe." Ari tugged a red curl. "That was really courageous. What happened next?"

"Unwilling to leave her twin unsupported, Gerolyn, disguised as a visitor, reentered the temple grounds. An accidental meeting between her and Lorsedi spawned love at first sight and doomed them to live their lives apart. Gerolyn had taken her vows to serve in the temple and refused to leave with Lorsedi and betray her planet. Contrary to the traditions of his culture, Lorsedi did not wish to share her with his fellow soldiers.

"For the duration of the RewFaaran visit, they kept their love, and Gerolyn's presence, hidden. As negotiations neared completion and the three young priestesses prepared to depart with the delegation, Lorsedi and Gerolyn, secretly sealed in the ways of KcernFensia, consummated their love."

"How did Glenet plan to keep KcernFensia safe?" Torgin chewed his lip. "I mean, couldn't RewFaarans come back and demand more women?"

Almiralyn's gaze narrowed. "As the gateway swallowed the delegation, Glenet sealed the path from RewFaar to KcernFensia for time and eternity. The men of RewFaar could not return, at least via dimensional travel."

"Gerolyn soon discovered she was with child and requested a meeting with Glenet Evol. They realized Lorsedi would guess and find a way back to KcernFensia, so the high priestess sent Gerolyn to me. Their Joining by sacred ceremony meant she could not remarry nor could she bear another man's children. Standin agreed to be her protector and to raise you, Sparrow, as his daughter."

"He has always been so good to us." Sparrow shook her head. "What a sacrifice."

Brie's gaze shifted from her mother to Almiralyn. "Did Lorsedi ever return to the temple?"

"He did. Many sun cycles later, business took him to DerTah, and he used a gateway there to return to KcernFensia. When he discovered Gerolyn was gone, and Glenet refused to tell him where, he was furious."

Sparrow looked puzzled. "Why are you worried about him now?"

"I received word he is searching for you and your mother." She looked over at Brie. "Today, he learned he has a granddaughter."

Ari squirmed in her chair. "Why is that so bad?"

"For a generation, RewFaaran men have bred within the same bloodlines. They are desperate for a new strain. With your KcernFensian blood and the fact that you are two generations removed from Lorsedi, you are the perfect potential mates. Also, you have the red hair of the ruling class."

Ari sat back and folded her arms across her chest. "I'm not the least bit interested in living in RewFaar with a bunch of other women. I don't intend to be a breeder. Her expression dared anyone to contradict her.

Almiralyn smiled. "You don't need to worry about that yet, Ari." She stood up. "If you will excuse me, I need some time to reflect." *And I need some answers.*

As she hurried up the stairs, her mind grappled with the issues facing her and those gathered in the kitchen. Evolsefil topped the list. The longer the Prima Crystal remained in Nemttachenn, the greater the risk to it, to Myrrh, and to the Clenaba Rolas System. Ancient law stated that the person who removed it from the cave must return it. Esán's rescue, therefore, headed the list of what had to be accomplished. The squeaky fourth step made her pause. Esán's gifts also made him a target for the Dreelum od DerTah. Their lust for power could turn him into a battleground. She continued up the stairs. *Now, we also have to deal with RewFaar.*

She entered the sanctuary and hastened to the fountain. *Curiosity has just put Myrrh and Thera and even KcernFensia in jeopardy.* Resting her hands on Elcaro's rounded rim, she gazed at the rippling water. *It is possible all is not lost. I must contact Standin.* She slowed her ricocheting thoughts and passed a hand over the Eye.

Lorsedi's face flashed to the stilled surface. The fountain quaked as Almiralyn dodged from his line of vision. She focused power and her intent on success and fought him for control. With all the formidable strength he possessed, the Largeen Joram tried to wrench it from her.

The water roiled, foamed, and shot up into the air where it froze, suspended in a splashed arc above the round basin. In the shallow puddle remaining on the bottom, fiery red hair caught the light and eyes as deep and dark as the pits of Sedah blazed with desire and frustration.

Almiralyn made her last stand. Swirling her hand above the fountain, she clapped three times. The image disintegrated into the bubbling return of the water to the bowl. With exhaustion threatening to overwhelm her, she recited an ancient text.

> *"Evil comes—cease to flow.*
> *Empty now, Elcaro's bowl.*
> *Water turn to air and light*
> *Until recalled when all is right."*

The carved woman on the edge stopped spilling water from her open palms as steam rose to fill the sanctuary. Almiralyn clapped three more times. The steam vanished, leaving the fountain's alabaster basin empty on its carved pedestal and the tip of the Vesen Crystal exposed at the bottom of the bowl.

She hugged herself. "Lorsedi, how did you gain control of Elcaro's Eye?"

While the discussion around the kitchen table continued after Almiralyn left, Allynae pondered all she had shared. Sparrow, his chosen life companion, was not only KcernFensian but also carried the royal bloodline of RewFaar. His daughters, the granddaughters of the Largeen Joram, were royalty on both planets. Life grew more complex by the turning.

He glanced up as his sister reentered the kitchen. Her expression spoke volumes. So did her pallor. A tense silence settled over the kitchen. No one spoke as she sat down at the table.

Brie leaned close to Ari. "She's seen our grandfather."

Ari nudged her and flicked her gaze toward their father.

Allynae sat next to Sparrow, his impatience to know radiating around him. His cool blue eyes flashed to his daughters and snapped back to his sister's drawn face.

"Tell us, Almiralyn." Sparrow's voice was soft, but urgent. "We can help only if we know what we're up against."

Brie felt Torgin press next to her and slipped her arm through his. Ari stiffened. Jordett looked on with interest. Next to him, Merrilea remained wrapped in her personal sadness. One Man, a silent spectator, rested a hand lightly on her shoulder. Paisley faded into the background.

Almiralyn lifted fatigue-infused eyes. "I've shut down..."

Brie strained to hear the murmured words.

With a shake, Myrrh's Guardian spoke with more energy. "Lorsedi fought me for control of Evolsefil. I've shut it down."

Jordett broke the stunned silence following her announcement. "Does he know who you are?"

"Could he tell where you are?" Allynae's concern flared and sputtered.

Merrilea broke her sad silence. "How did he get control of your fountain, Mira?"

Ari jumped to her feet. "We won't know what's happening if Elcaro isn't working."

Sparrow remained silent. One Man's intent gaze rested on the Guardian of Myrrh.

"Are you alright?" Brie's question brought all eyes to Almiralyn's face.

"I'm frustrated but fine, Brie." Her serious gaze traveled the concerned faces around the table. Lorsedi did not see my face, but he won't take long to trace the path he forged to Elcaro's Eye. We have limited time to make decisions. "

Torgin leaned forward. "He cannot find you if you shut it down, right?"

"I did my best to erase the connection. However, he has spent time and energy tracing it, or he wouldn't have had such a powerful hold. Had I not used Elcaro's Eye when I did, he would have taken complete control." Her eyes narrowed. "Lorsedi may prove to be a fearsome enemy."

Jordett tapped the table with a fingertip. "Lorsedi is a military leader. He had strategies in place before he saw you. My guess—he's already on the move."

"The major's right." Almiralyn's voice regained its authority. "We have two primary goals. One is to rescue Esán. He is the only one who can return Evolsefil to the Cave of Canedari."

One Man cleared his throat. "I also believe the Dreelum od DerTah will attempt to turn Esán into a pawn in their power games. We can't allow that to happen any more than we can allow Lorsedi to find Sparrow's family."

Almiralyn acknowledged her agreement with a nod.

"Moving quickly on both fronts is vital." Jordett leaned forward. "I suggest we contact Sparrow's parents as soon as possible. Lorsedi may have already sent soldiers to Thera."

Brie felt Ari's hand tighten on her arm as their mother's face paled.

"Aren't they safe in Singtil?" Sparrow's voice shook.

Jordett and Almiralyn exchanged glances. The Major's eyes narrowed. "Not if Lorsedi discovers Myrrh."

Allynae hugged Sparrow and then turned to his sister. "What about Novissi, my crystal? Can we use it to contact them?"

Almiralyn shook her head. "Its connection to Elcaro's Eye will make it Lorsedi's next target.

Paisley tugged at his mustache. "Do Sparrow's parents need to come here so we can protect 'em?"

Hope flooded Sparrow's face. "Then we could all hide together."

Allynae frowned. "None of you should hide in the same place. Not even the twins."

Ari's brown eyes snapped beneath half-closed lids. "You want to separate Brie and me?"

"If you are together and Lorsedi finds you, he has you both. If we send you to different places, he will have to search that much harder." Allynae shook his head. "It's not what I *want*, Ari. It's what has to be."

Ari bit her bottom lip. Her chin jutted out. "I'm going where Brie goes. You can't make me do anything else."

"Please, Ari." Sparrow shook her head.

"Leave it, Sparrow." Allynae hugged her again. "Let's see where our plans take us."

"What about Esán?" Brie's soft voice cut through the discussion.

"Yes, what about Esán?" Sarcasm leaked into Ari's voice. "Are you going to leave him on DerTah by himself while you worry about us?"

Almiralyn ignored her tone. "Although it's important to bring him back to Myrrh, Esán is safer than you are at the moment. Nomed will not harm him."

"But One Man said he might become a political pawn." Torgin squirmed on his seat. "That doesn't sound safe to me."

"You're right, Torgin. We don't want to leave him too long. One solution is to send you and a twin with Jordett to rescue Esán." Almiralyn caught Ari's eye.

"And the other twin?" Ari surged to standing and glared at her aunt. "What do you intend for her?"

"Ari." Allynae's face was stern. "Give Almiralyn time."

Ari's cheeks blazed. "You may be my father, but that doesn't give you the right to order me around."

"Arienh!" Sparrow reached out to lay a hand on her arm.

Jerking away from her mother's touch, she stormed across the porch and into the back yard, slamming the door behind her.

Brie looked around the suddenly quiet kitchen.

7

DerTah

Esán searched his quarters with his fast-developing senses and stiffened. One person stood near the door. A mind touch revealed nothing. The strike of a match made him jump. A flame flared. A face appeared and then vanished.

"What are you doing here?" Esán realized his voice expressed his contempt.

Nomed lit a candle and placed it on the table. "You're in danger. I'm here to teach you how to place a ward around your room."

Esán folded his arms. "Am I in less danger from you than from the Dreelum or Wolloh?"

"You are my nephew and my apprentice. I don't need to fight for your allegiance. Do you know why you're in danger?"

"I heard Gidtuss talking to someone about kidnapping me. It appears my gifts are a coveted prize. I would be expendable if not for my talent." His eyes sparked with resentment.

Bizarre shadows flickered across Nomed's face. Esán wondered if he looked similar in the strange light.

"Trust Gidtuss to let himself be overheard." Nomed's disdain for the Dreela dripped from his statement. He crossed to the window and closed it. "To create a ward, envision a shield of light in front of all doors and windows. Begin as far below the building's foundation as you can and draw the light upward. Define what it wards against. Secure it, saying, 'Ward of Light, protect against the entry of…' in this case I would suggest you secure against all who approach meaning you harm."

Esán shut his eyes and visualized the entire round room. A shield of violet light shot up, surrounding them. His eyes flew open. "How did I do that?"

"Seal them, Esán, and then we'll talk."

"Ward of Light, protect against all who would do me harm." He held up his hand and drew a symbol in the air. "Seal and secure."

Nomed's scar yanked the corner of his mouth into an almost fierce expression. "Your gifts continue to astound me, Esán." He unlocked the door. "I'll meet you for morning meal. Afterwards, Wolloh will begin your training." Narrowed hazel eyes glistened in the candlelight. "I wouldn't wander abroad again tonight if I were you." He slipped into the hall.

Esán sank onto his bed, his thoughts in a tangle. *Now what? I need a map of DerTah. Nomed said 'don't wander,' so I won't. I'll teleport.*

He pictured a darkened corner in the library and teleported. He remembered seeing a lock on the hall side of the door. After making sure the room was empty, he crossed the carpeted floor, edged the door open a crack, slid his hand through, and grasped the key. With a sense of satisfaction, he inserted it in the keyhole on his side. Its soft click made him smile. *I'd rather be safe than sorry.*

Books covered the walls of the room. Beneath a shuttered window sat a multi-drawered map cabinet. Inside, Esán discovered several maps of DerTah. He selected two, one of the desert of Fera Finnero and another of the entire planet. Rolling them together, he walked over to a tall bookshelf, shut his eyes, and pictured the room. *Show me books about DerTah.* He smiled. On the shelf in front of him, he found what he needed. *Have to admit my talents are useful.*

He pulled a thin, leather-bound book from the shelf, skimmed its table of contents, and slipped it in his pocket. With the maps tucked under his arm, he unlocked the door, replaced the key on the opposite side, and arrived in his quarters.

The candle still burned. Corvus sat on the bed, his countenance serious.

N omed made his way with ghost-like quiet to his quarters. His mind knotted itself around Gidtuss and the others who plotted against Wolloh via Esán. *What are they after? How will my nephew help them acquire it? And who owns the second voice?* Alerted by a whispered probing in his mind, he calmed his thoughts to the mundane activities of preparing for bed. Another nudge. A quick *"meet me"* and the probe was gone. The signal was clear.

Preferring not to alert the Dreelum, who monitored his every move, he cracked open the door and surveyed the dim hallway. They would all be gone by mid-turning tomorrow. Until then, he preferred to appear ignorant of their game. He stepped into the hall and, with predatory stealth, walked past Baroh and Omudi's quarters. Gidtuss came hurrying around the corner.

"Good evening." Nomed watched him squirm.

"What are you doing out this late?" The man's voice held a note of alarm.

Nomed smiled his crooked smile. "I might ask you the same, Dreela, but I'm not that interested." Sidestepping around his adversary, he continued down the hall.

Behind him, the man's thoughts flapped like frightened birds. *I hate you, Nomed. Just wait... Does he know? What if he finds out? I have to...* His mind clamped shut.

Nomed relished his power and Gidtuss' obvious fear before stepping into an elegant sitting room. He shut the door and turned. Cool eyes met his, their warning clear. A wall slid away, and his companion beckoned him to follow. An oil lamp sprang to light as the gap in the wall closed.

Nomed assessed his fellow conspirator. "You look lovely, my dear TheLise." He inspected the small space. "When did you discover this little hideaway?"

"I found it when I was a girl training with Wolloh." She smiled her intriguing smile and then grew serious. "We have a major complication about to descend on our doorstep, Seyes." Her eyes darted to the wall.

Nomed placed a finger on his lips. Together, they strained to hear the conversation on the other side.

Esán sighed with relief to find Corvus in his quarters.

A curious smile deepened the man's dimple. "You've created quite a stir. The Dreelum are all in a twitter about Wolloh's new apprentice and how they can use your gifts to further their personal causes." He raised a brow. "Who put wards around your room?"

"I did. Nomed came by and showed me how." Esán unrolled the maps on the bed beside his guest and placed the book on top of them. "Are any of the Dreelum honest?"

"Baroh is the least likely to become involved in the games of his fellow leaders, and perhaps TheLise. She's definitely independent—a wild card. The others...they're a selfish, self-serving lot, and so are their followers."

"And Wolloh?"

Corvus shrugged. "That's a closed door. I would doubt anyone knows his mind."

Esán kept his voice low. "He's still interested in Evolsefil, the Prima Crystal."

Curiosity lit Corvus' almond-shaped eyes. "How do you know that?"

"I saw it in his mind when we first met. He either didn't realize I could read his thoughts, or he wanted me to know. I think the latter is correct."

"I agree." Corvus picked up the book on DerTah and flipped through its parchment pages. "Are you planning to go somewhere?"

Esán shrugged. "I decided I'd better prepare for a speedy departure, just in case." He studied the man opposite him. "I need to return to Myrrh, Corvus. The longer I'm here, the more difficult it will be for my friends and family."

"Don't leave without me." The man smoothed out the maps and studied them. We need to find gateways to either Myrrh or KcernFensia."

"I know about the one in the desert, but I hate the idea of Fire ConDra." Esán gave him a rueful smile. "One almost barbecued me for lunch—something I don't wish to experience again."

Corvus examined the small book. "The author certainly packed this with information. Can you read this?" He held it closer to the candle. A strange symbol marked a spot on the shoreline of the Sea of Trinuge. Below it, written in tiny script, were three words...'Oreo Tey Omoc.'

Esán analyzed the symbol and the words, then searching through the book, he found two identical symbols with the identical written phrase. "I'd be willing to bet these are gateways and the sacred Key to open them." He angled the book nearer to the candle. "Corvus, check this out."

In the margin nearest the flame, faint letters began to form. B...e...war...e t...he p...or...tal of G...

A soft knock prompted him to slip the book into his pocket. Corvus hid the maps under the bed and moved to the door.

"It's Seval." Esán mouthed the words. He could feel fear prickling around the servant.

Corvus nodded.

Esán opened the door, pulled the boy inside, and shut it all in one movement.

"The Dreelum aren't..." The servant began, saw Corvus, and clamped his mouth shut. He looked at Esán for direction.

"It's okay, Seval. This is Corvus Difner. He's a friend."

Seval took a hard look. "I haven't seen you before. What do you do here?"

"I work with the birds of prey Wolloh uses for hunting. I'm rarely in the big house." His tone was reassuring. "You're the one everyone is calling the mystery boy."

Seval looked vague. "How did you know?" He sounded less worried.

"Word gets around. You know how people talk."

"Yeah, especially in front of inconsequential folks like us." He looked at Esán. "The Dreelum aren't leaving for a few more turnings. While they're here, you're in danger."

"Any idea why they're staying?"

Corvus, his expression alert, crossed to the door. "I have to go. Take care, Esán, and remember what I said."

Before Esán could reply, he was gone.

8
Myrrh

The back door slamming smashed against the silence set in motion by Ari's furious departure from Almiralyn's kitchen. Brie's first inclination was to follow, but she realized nothing she could say would ease the anger and frustration her twin was feeling. She addressed the group instead. "She's worried you'll separate us. We just spent several crazy weeks apart, helping to save Myrrh. Isn't there any way we can stay together? Our grandfather doesn't know there are two of us."

"But if he were to see you together, he would know you are twins. You're as alike as two Dojanberries on a bush." Almiralyn watched her with understanding, but no willingness to give in.

"What if we make ourselves appear different?"

"Like what?" Sparrow looked at her with interest.

The back door opened. Ari walked to Allynae's side. "I'm sorry, Father. I didn't mean to be so rude."

He put an arm around her and gave her a quick hug. "We're all worried and edgy. I know you want to stay with Brie. How to keep you safe and together is the problem."

"What if I cut my hair and dress like a boy?" Ari used a low voice.

Torgin laughed. "You'd still look like twins."

"Not if I changed my hair color?" She released her ponytail and let her red curls fall around her face.

Almiralyn walked around the table to stand beside her. "Ari, try something for me. Close your eyes and visualize how you would look if you changed your appearance."

Ari squeezed her eyes shut and furrowed her brow in concentration. Every muscle in her body seemed to quiver with effort. Imperceptibly at first, her feminine facial features began to blur. Her brow smoothed as they came back into focus, more sculpted and masculine. Long, red curls shrunk to an unruly crop of chestnut brown waves. When she opened her eyes and fixed her gaze on Almiralyn, her once brown eyes gleamed as blue as her aunt's.

Sparrow gasped.

"By the Fathers, Ari!" Torgin's eyes bulged in amazement..

Ari glared. "What are *you* staring at?"

Brie jumped up and pulled her into the hall, where a mirror hung above a small table.

Astonishment, surprise, and suspicion flitted across Ari's transformed face. She whipped around, marched back into the kitchen, and, hands on hips, confronted her aunt. "Did you do this, or did I?"

Almiralyn smiled. "You are part KcernFensian, Ari. We can all shape shift once we figure out how. You never tried before.

Ari threw back her head and laughed, a deep laugh filled with wonder and delight. "I do have talent! Thanks, Aunt Mira." She blushed and gave her aunt an awkward hug. "How long can I keep up my alternate appearance?"

"I would suggest we cut your hair and dye it so you don't have to work so hard to hold the illusion in place. Then I think you can maintain it indefinitely. It's not like changing form. You are still Ari. You just look different."

Ari gave Almiralyn a cocky smile. "Kinda like when you're Mira, right?"

"Exactly."

Ari let the façade go and shook her curls back from her face. "Now, can we stay together?"

Almiralyn hugged them both. "You can."

Ari pulled away and looked at her aunt. "So when do we leave to rescue Esán?"

"Sit down. Let's plan." She returned to her seat at the head of the table.

Ari and Brie slid into their seats next to Torgin. "I sure wish I could do that."

"You never know, Torg. Stranger things have happened." Ari shot him a knowing smile.

"Right. I'm just plain old Theran. Bo-o-ring!"

Brie laughed. "Have you ever really listened to your music, Torg? You could *never* be boring."

Jordett listened to the exchange with half an ear and half a smile, his military mind planning a way to spur the group into action. He cleared his throat. "We can't hope to track and protect all of Sparrow's family if they're scattered over three planets. I believe Sparrow and her mother would be safest in the Dojanacks with Yookotay and the DeoNytes."

"What do you think, Sparrow?" Myrrh's Guardian gazed at her sister-by-Joining.

Sparrow frowned. "How will we get word to Gerolyn and Standin?"

Merrilea surveyed the group. "I could go to the Central Mountains and find them."

The worry faded from Sparrow's face as she leaned toward Almiralyn. "Let me go with Merrilea. It will be quicker, and she shouldn't go alone. When we get back, I will hide with Mother."

Almiralyn shook her head. "I don't—"

"I'll go with them, Mira." One Man cut in. "I spent several sun cycles in the Central Mountains. The journey will be quick, especially with Sparrow along. She can navigate us around Singtil, an area I don't know well."

"Let's hope the PPP isn't watching Demrach Gateway." Merrilea looked thoughtful. "I know a route to Singtil that will allow us to avoid public transport."

Allynae slid an arm around Sparrow. "I'm not sure Sparrow should go anywhere. Let Merrilea and One Man go."

Sparrow looked up at him. "I *need* to do this, Alli. We'll be back before you know it."

Allynae looked at Almiralyn for support. "She's right, Alli." His sister continued. "The journey will be much faster with her along. Her presence will convince Gerolyn and Standin of the danger."

"Da'am blast, Mira." Allynae bristled at his sister's betrayal, and then sagged. "I just want you safe, Sparrow. I don't want to lose you again."

"We'll be fine. I'm more worried about you and the twins."

Almiralyn looked relieved. "What's next, Jordy?"

Much to Ari's delight, Karrew chose that moment to fly through the kitchen window and settle on his perch.

Jordett grinned. "Good to see you, Karrew."

The big raven tipped its head and blinked a shiny ebony eye.

"I think we need a break." Almiralyn walked to his perch and offered an arm.

Sparrow filled the kettle. "We've been up half the night. I'll make a snack and some tea."

Allynae pushed his chair back. "I'll check the pantry and see what I can find.

Ari stretched and regarded Torgin and Brie with a half-smile. "Let's walk in the garden." She strolled out the back door.

Torgin joined her. "How long have we been talking?" He scanned the sky where pale golden light announced the sunrise.

"Too long." Ari leaned against an ancient maple tree. "You realize they will not allow us to help with Esán's rescue?"

Brie skimmed a small stone across the pond's shimmering surface and watched it skip three times. "I almost think we would be safer on DerTah. Our grandfather is not someone I wish to run into, and I bet he is on his way here."

"DerTah sounds like a horrid place." Torgin shuddered. "I wish we didn't have to go."

Ari scowled. "You never like anything new, Torg." She picked at a piece of bark that refused to pull loose from the trunk. "I'm going to rescue Esán. If you want to stay here, stay." The bark moved. "I bet if we go to Nemttachenn, CheeTrann'll send us through the vortex."

"Only if he's sure it's our destiny." Brie pursed her lips, then smiled. "Of course, Elcaro showed Torgin on DerTah, so maybe—"

"That was a quick visit." Torgin pointed skyward, where Karrew, silhouetted against the soft gray of morning, flew out an upstairs window and over the Terces Wood.

"Wonder what he's up to." Brie stared after him. "He's never far from Aunt Mira for long."

Ari shrugged. "He's probably off on another errand." The piece of bark broke free. Eyeing it, she flicked it across the garden. "How do we gather what we need for the trip?"

Torgin listened to the twins' whispered plans with some misgiving. The knot in the pit of his stomach lurched as he sidled closer to the twins. "I'm coming, too, but I wish we knew more about that planet."

Ari clapped him on the back. "Glad you've come around."

"We can check Aunt Mira's library." Brie cocked her head. "She might have something on DerTah."

"We'd better get organized." Ari ran a hand through her tangled curls. "Wish I could hide my thoughts like you, Brie. Almiralyn can forage around in my mind, and I can't stop her."

"Aunt Mira won't do that unless she's worried, so just act natural."

"You mean be belligerent and pout a lot?"

Torgin chuckled. "That sounds normal to me."

Ari scowled before joining in his laughter. "You got me, Torg."

"Come on." Brie started across the garden. "Since Karrew's off again, I imagine they're reconvening in the kitchen to snack and talk."

"Do we really need to be there?" Ari stomped after them.

It was Brie's turn to laugh. "Normal it is, Ari. Normal it is."

9
Der Tah

In the hidden room, Nomed and TheLise strained to hear the muffled conversation on the opposite side of the wall.

"He...serious trouble..."

"Evolse..."

"Hide...DoOlb...Lots..."

"...caught..."

"We can't..."

The room went silent. The hall door closed with a muted click.

Questions swam around Nomed's mind. He opened his mouth to speak. A quick shake of TheLise's head snapped it shut.

She moved away from the wall to pick up the lamp from the table. "Stand beside me."

The whispered words sounded sultry in the darkened space. Nomed slipped an arm around her waist.

"You assume much, Seyes." Reaching above her head, she pressed her thumb into a well-hidden indentation. The wall rotated, carrying them to the other side. A soft clunk and it stopped. A long passage stretched away in front of them.

"You were very busy when you were a girl." His lopsided smile tugged. "Where does this lead?"

"To the garden near the arena. It will look less suspicious if we return to the house from there." Her low voice held a hint of laughter. "Who was in the room?"

"Gidtuss, I would bet, and perhaps Thaer. Plotting with Gidtuss is about his speed. I didn't dare use telepathy."

"Nor I. They're definitely after Esán, though." TheLise led him down the passageway. "Someone keeps this clean. I wonder who." She stopped.

Nomed found himself eye to eye with her. An unsettling current ran through his body. "Yes?"

TheLise gave him a coy smile. "It is rather nice to be alone, don't you think?"

"What do you want, TheLise?"

"Two things." Her face grew serious. "An important visitor has demanded to see Wolloh. Since I couldn't read his mind, I'm uncertain who, but all of DerTah's leaders are staying for the visit. How are we going to protect Esán?"

"Esán's well-equipped to take care of himself—just inexperienced. All we can do is stay alert and keep our eye on him. If things become too dangerous, I'll simply disappear with him. Second?"

"Tell me about the Evolsefil Crystal. Did you find it?"

Anger tasted bitter on his tongue. "I almost had it...almost." He swallowed his frustration. "Someday I'll share the story."

"Someday?"

"It's not finished yet." A momentary memory of the Prima Crystal's beauty and power left him feeling deprived and unfulfilled.

TheLise's body, pressed against his, demanded he return his thoughts to her. In the dim light, her gray eyes teased, taunted him, dared him to...what? "Don't be such a temptress, TheLise. I may surprise you, and you'll get more than you bargained for."

Her laugh was husky and deep. "You are a man of ice, Seyes. I find I am not too worried." She brushed her lips against his. "Don't disappear without me."

Nomed watched her move with seductive grace ahead of him down the passage, grateful for the darkness that hid his flushed face. He placed his hand over his chest to muffle the agitated beat of his heart.

Corvus' sudden departure left Seval and Esán staring at the door. Esán transferred his gaze to the young servant. Fear still clung to him like a cloak of gray smoke. His round face was puffy, and Esán suspected his eyes were red from crying. On a planet where hatred and anger most often defined choices and expectations, Seval's gentleness intrigued him. "Are you alright?"

He sniffed and wiped his nose on his sleeve. "I miss..." He hiccuped and looked bewildered. "I am so sorry."

"You're fine, Seval." Esán put a reassuring hand on his shoulder.

The boy shrugged it off and muttered to himself. "This is my home now." He straightened his rumpled tunic and edged closer to the door. "You must be careful. The Dreelum are a danger to you, to anyone they can use. You have much power, Master...Esán." His eyes darted toward his escape route. "I go now."

"Wait." Esán touched his arm. "Please stay. You're safe here."

The boy's mouth puckered. "I'm not safe anywhere, but I don't remember why." With a stiff bow, he exited the room.

Esán stared after him. A gentle telepathic touch left him shocked. Seval's memories hung like tattered cobwebs in his mind. Only his present excruciating sadness remained intact. *Will I ever learn what happened to him?*

He shook himself free of the young servant's puzzle and pulled the maps from under the bed. *My best bet is to learn more about DerTah.*

With the map of the Desert of Fera Finnero spread out on the bed, he studied the perplexing sameness. *If I have to cross it, how will I navigate it?* He pulled the small book from his pocket, opened it to the chapter describing the desert, and submerged himself in learning.

A disturbance in the hall plucked him mid-sentence from the book.

Nervous voices and hurrying footsteps prompted him to ease the door ajar. Seval, his face clean and his tunic fresh, hurried by without a glance. Esán pressed his back against the closed door and let his senses explore the house. A radical change raised the hair on his neck. He hid the maps under the mattress and tucked the book away in his bottom drawer.

A soft knock alerted him to his uncle's presence. Esán frowned.

Wolloh hid in the shadows by his sitting room window, watching his servants bustling back and forth, preparing the guesthouse for important company. A contingent of soldiers had already arrived and set up camp near the border of the ranch and the desert. Their commander sent word he expected to be received within the chron-circle.

Wolloh limped to his chair and lowered his weary bones into its soft contours. His agile mind reviewed the events that had brought him to this planet's blood-red desert.

The recklessness of youth and the misguided belief he was indestructible had led to several ill-judged choices. He had played right into the hands of the Mocendi League, a galaxy-wide organization devoted to finding and training potential DiMensioners. He found himself banned from his home planet and headed for a penal colony at the outer rim.

Self-righteous anger propelled him toward a path of self-destruction. The discovery of his mentor, Relevart, and the Art of DiMensionery had saved him. With single-minded purpose, he buried himself in his studies.

He plucked at the feather-like streak on the deformed side of his head. The temptation to shape the osprey and fly away made him close his eyes in anticipation. Flight always reduced his stress and restored his sense of well-being. And it removed him from sad memories, as well as the scheming politics of the Dreelum and their ilk.

A timid knock made him scowl. *Speaking of which...* "What is it?"

The opening door offered him a view of a wide-eyed male servant. "Dreela Thaer would like to see you, sir."

"Tell him I'll see him in my office." Wolloh's good eye scanned the servant's face. Curiosity, and the fear in the boy's eyes, made him ask a gentle question. "What's your name, boy?"

"Seval, sir."

"How long have you been in my employ, Seval?"

He looked puzzled, shook his head, and responded, "I don't think very long, sir."

An unobtrusive mind touch provided a startling picture. "I see. Please give Thaer my message. Do you know Seyes Nomed?"

He nodded.

"Find him and the Dreela TheLise and ask them to join me there, too."

"Yes, sir." He backed from the study and closed the door.

Hm...that is the boy Stebben told me about. Life becomes more complex.

Again, the temptation to take flight nudged. He sighed, settled back in his chair, and let his agile mind carry him back to that sun turning so long ago, the turning he had forsaken his mentor's instructions for the simple thrill of defying him and the egotistical need to prove his skill.

"Shape shifting..." He laughed. "No matter what Relevart says, I know I'm ready to shape an osprey." With the arrogance of youth, he ignored his nagging doubt and launched into flight. The shift stalled in its beginning stages. Pain ripped through the left side of his body—an arm fought to become a wing, a leg—a taloned foot, his face—the feathered head of an osprey. Excruciating pain pitched him to the ground, unconscious. He awoke to find Relevart sitting next to him in a dim room. The distress in his mentor's eyes filled Wolloh with despair.

Time healed the torn flesh on his arm and leg, leaving them maimed but usable. His left hand remained a crippled claw. The scarring on his left cheek horrified him. When they removed the eye patch and he was blind, he railed against the stupidity of the healer and blamed his mentor. It took many sun cycles for him to confront himself and admit the arrogance of youth.

Struggling to redefine himself, he left Relevart's home planet to travel throughout the galaxy. He discovered life's infinite variety and became an expert in galactic history and diplomacy. Eventually, his love of DiMensionery sent him back to study with Relevart. Wisdom gained from adversity made him an exceptional student, one of the very few to attain the rank of High DiMensioner.

Caught in his musings, he massaged his withered cheek. Disfigurement had become a reminder to be circumspect and to exercise patience. Relevart had coached him to use the disastrous results of his hard-learned lesson to his advantage. The tragedy of his youth now informed his choices and actions in ways that left him grateful. It did not, however, make him tolerant of stupidity, sloth, or those who presumed more power than they possessed.

Though he was loath to leave his study and his reverie, the present awaited his involvement. He allowed himself one more moment of absolute quiet before peeling his fragile bones away from the chair. He picked up his cane, a gift from his master, and eyed the crystal knob. A desire to see its mother crystal, Evolsefil, filled him with longing. He released it with the blink of his sightless eye. The arrogance of youth, disguised as a RewFaaran officer, was about to pay him a visit. Perhaps he would teach the young man a lesson, one that would make the next few turnings less fatiguing.

10
Myrrh

Brie hoped, when the discussion around the Guardian of Myrrh's kitchen table ended, her Aunt Mira hadn't read her thoughts...or Ari's. She pressed her lips together. *We are to be hidden on the mainland of KcernFensia.* Her nostrils flared in distaste. And Torgin— *How can they send him back to Idronatti? The PPP will erase his memories and assign his profession.* He had looked miserable. She understood.

At the end of the conversation, it was decided that Merrilea, her mother, and One Man would rest up and use the Demrach Gateway the next morning to travel into the Central Mountains to warn her grandparents. Jordett and her father would leave for DerTah in two turnings.

As everyone dispersed to prepare for what was to come, Sparrow had suggested she cut Ari's hair. Brie declined an invitation to join them, headed upstairs to her room, and watched morning's brightness spreading over the garden. *Mother's father is hunting for us.* She felt like an animal pursued.

With a shake of her head, she shed her fear and tiptoed down the stairs. Once in the library, she eased the door closed. *I require information to help us navigate DerTah.* Stepping closer to the bookcase, she read the strange titles...*David Copperfield, Stranger in a Strange Land, Sense and Sensibility, The Earthsea Trilogy, The Time and Writings of Ga...*The door creaked open. She turned, her face flushed with guilt.

Almiralyn shut the door behind her and held out a thin leather-bound book. "I believe this is what you're looking for."

Brie took it and sank into a chair. The title read Demography and Customs of DerTah. She looked up at her aunt in bewilderment.

The Guardian sat down opposite her. "As much as I dislike it, I know you have to go to DerTah. It's your destiny and Ari's. I'm not sure about Torgin, but he doesn't deserve to have his memories cleansed by the PPP."

"Why didn't..."

"Your father's journey and yours are not the same, Brie. He would not have understood, nor would your mother. I have packs ready for you under the back porch. CheeTrann will help you go to DerTah. Unfortunately, you will arrive in the desert where the Fire ConDra live. I don't know how you'll deal with them, but I know you'll manage."

Brie examined the book in her hands. "Will Torgin's compass help us in DerTah?"

"It will, but you must learn the trigger verse to make it work. As soon as you arrive in the desert, have Torgin hold the compass face parallel to the ground. Recite this verse and watch the small white flecks on the back.

> *"DerTah's patterns, deep and rare,*
> *Desert, ocean, mountains fair,*
> *Absorb these secrets into thee,*
> *And all else that we should see."*

"The flecks are stars. You will know the patterning is complete when they form new constellations."

Brie repeated the verse. After several repetitions, the Guardian leaned back in her chair and stared into the distance. When she sat up, her expression was serious. "Ari should take Efillaeh. The Remembering Stone will aid you in learning what you need to know. I don't know what you will encounter on DerTah, Brielle. I only know you must go."

Brie leaned forward. "Can't you come with us?"

"I'm needed here to deflect your grandfather's interest elsewhere and to protect your mother and grandmother."

"Aunt Mira, one more thing." Brie's gaze searched her aunt's face. "Can I shift shape?"

"You possess the talent. When the need arises, it will manifest.

"I'm so glad Ari discovered it first." Brie smiled as they stood up. "She needed to feel like the special one for a change."

"You are both more special than you know—your gifts are just different." Almiralyn tugged a tendril of silver-blonde hair, her expression thoughtful. "We must discuss one more thing, Brielle. The Star of Truth creates a dilemma. You understand that, because of it, you cannot lie."

The small, red star on the back of her neck tingled. Brie nodded.

"If anyone asked you and Ari what your relationship is, the Star demands you tell the truth, which is dangerous for all of you."

A flood of dismay washed over her. "I hadn't thought of that, Aunt Mira. What should we do?"

"I'll meet the three of you in the barn at sunset. With a little help, I think we can manage a safeguard. Get some rest. You're going to need it."

Brie put her arms around her aunt. "Please take care of my mother and grandmother." She stepped back, her gaze fixed on her aunt. "Please help Father to understand."

"I'll do my best. You bring Esán back as soon as you can. Evolsefil waits." Almiralyn kissed her forehead and glided from the room.

Brie watched her go with a rush of uneasiness before returning to her chair. For a time, she sat absorbing the quiet of the house and the love surrounding her. *Will The Unfolding ever quit complicating my life?*

The book in her lap demanded her attention. Holding it closer to the lite-stick, she began to read. Frustrated by the slowness of the process, she shut her eyes, and, remembering *EmitEnil*, the Book of Time's way of imparting its wisdom, closed the book and held it to her chest. Information about DerTah, like yesterday's memories, saturated her mind.

Ari preened in front of the mirror, admiring her haircut and the richness of its new, dark brown color. "What do you think, Mother?"

Sparrow's apprehension about what was to come showed on her face. "I love your red hair, but the brown looks good. Show me what you will look like as a boy."

Ari shut her eyes and pictured the changes she wished to make. When she opened them, her mother's astonished expression made her check her reflection. "Oh my." She laughed to herself. The boy in the mirror was taller than she expected. His face, reminiscent of her father, gazed back at her with a touch of rebellion. The brown hair was thick and unruly, the eyes wide set and blue.

Her mother tipped her head. "I think you should get rid of the freckles."

Ari concentrated on the reflected image. The freckles blended into tanned skin. She laughed. "And I didn't think I had any talent." After she examined herself from different angles, she pointed at the curve of her breasts. "These should go." Her chest flattened and broadened as she spoke. Facing her mother, she rotated. "Well, what do you think?"

A deep voice answered from the doorway. "I'm not your mother, but I think you look great. Kinda like me when I was young...pretty darn handsome."

Ari grinned and chucked a pillow at her father. He caught it and tossed it back. "Walk for me, Arienh."

Tossing the pillow on the bed, she strode across the room. "Well, do I walk like a boy?"

"Give your walk more weight...more attitude." He watched her circuit the room again. "Much better. You'd fool me."

"And me." Brie joined them. "You look amazing!" She tipped her head and batted her eyelashes. "Kinda cute, too."

Everyone laughed.

Ari experienced a rush of surprise. "We feel like a family."

Allynae put an arm around each of his daughters. "We *are* a family."

Sparrow joined them in front of the mirror. "A pretty good-looking family, I might add, especially our son."

Brie grinned at her sister. "I can't wait for Torgin to see you, Ari. What shall we call you?"

Ari ran a hand through her brown locks. "Ira Raast. I'm Torgin's pal."

The light went out of Sparrow's smile. "Tomorrow you're off to KcernFensia, and I go to Thera. I wish we could all stay together."

Ari watched her boy's face grow sullen. "I still don't see why we can't help rescue Esán. When he's safe, we could go to KcernFensia and hide from Grandfather."

"We've been through this." Allynae addressed their reflections in the mirror and then chuckled. "We sure look alike when we get testy, Ira."

The tension for the moment broken, the family moved apart.

"Get some sleep. It's been a long night." Sparrow hugged them and nudged Allynae toward the door.

"We'll see you later." Allynae seemed to memorize their faces before following Sparrow into the hall.

A moment of uncertainty as her parents left made Ari shiver. "Now what?" She looked down at her twin.

Brie held up the small book and explained what had occurred in the library.

"You mean Almiralyn is *helping* us?" Ari's blue eyes widened in disbelief.

"I don't think she's too happy about it, but she knows in her heart we have to go. We have a little homework to do. Then we collect Torgin and meet her in the barn at sunset."

"I don't know about you, Brie, but we've been up forever. Let's get some sleep before we tackle the sands of DerTah."

Brie eyed her twin with interest. "I've never slept in the same bed with a boy."

Ari gave a deep-throated snort and shifted, serious brown eyes meeting her sister's. "I wonder if this is the last time I'll be Ari?"

"You will always be you, no matter what form you take." Brie flopped onto the bed. "Let's catch some rest."

Torgin tossed and turned, but sleep continued to dodge his attempts to claim it. He glared at the ceiling, anger and frustration roiling again. *Almiralyn is sending me back to Idronatti. How can she sentence me to erased memories and a profession I'll hate?*

Swinging his long legs over the side of the bunk, his feet came to rest next to a pair of navy sneakers. With a sad sigh, he slid them on. *The twins bought them for me on the way to Myrrh.* He finished tying the laces. *Sure hope a walk will discharge some of my anger.*

The garden, under the late afternoon sun, glimmered with a pale gold glow. Memories flitted ghost-like through his mind—being trapped in an ice cage with Almiralyn's bird form cradled in his arms; his first encounter with a Pentharian; Buster lying in a pool of blood; and Brie's map bursting into flames—haunted him. A soft breeze chased past dramas away and sent autumn smells to tickle his nose. The melodic rustle of gold-tipped leaves made him stand still to listen. A spasm of loneliness washed over him. *Do my parents miss me? Have the PPP put me on their Watch List?* He sighed. *Maybe a visit to Tam...*

He wandered back to the barn and made his way to Tam's stall. The tan pony nickered a welcome as he opened the gate and wrapped his arms around her neck. "I'm scared, Tamboreen. We are going to DerTah to rescue Esán." A chill made him toss his head in a Tam-like fashion. *Why am I always anxious about everything?*

He grabbed a currycomb. Stroke-by-stroke, the pony's coat grew silky beneath his hands. And stroke-by-stroke, his fear melted away. "How do you do that?" He combed her creamy mane. "You always make me feel better."

She nickered.

"I wish you were coming with us, but it is too dangerous." He replaced the comb.

Tam nibbled his fingers with her soft lips. Taking her head in both hands, he rested his forehead on her forelock.

"It's time to go, Torg." The voice, deep with laughter hidden between the words, seemed somehow familiar.

He turned to find a strange boy regarding him, his stance casual and easy.

"Who are..." His jaw dropped. "You're Ari!"

"You got it, Torg." The boy grinned.

Brie stepped into view. "Even better than yesterday, huh?"

Torgin walked around Ari, looking at her from all sides. "Much better than yesterday. You look—real!"

"From this moment, Torg, I am Ira Raast, your best pal, and I'm very real."

"Ira." Torgin savored the name. "Ira. I like it." A rush of dread flushed his cheeks. "Are we truly going?"

"We sure are. Almiralyn even packed these for us." Brie pointed at the backpacks she had set on the ground. "She wants us to meet her at —"

The Guardian of Myrrh appeared in the doorway. "Trouble comes our way. Quick! Stand here in front of me and listen carefully. Unless you believe without reservation Ari is Ira Raast, you won't be safe. I am going to place an illusion of forgetting over all of you. You'll remember your time together, but with Ira as Torgin's friend rather than Ari as Brie's twin. When Brie gives the sign, one I have already imbedded in her subconscious, you will remember Ari as Ari. Do you understand and agree?"

Brie nodded and reached for her sister's hand. "You are my heart, Ari."

Her twin grinned and nodded. "Another adventure. Wow!"

"And you, Torgin?" The Guardian gave him a questioning smile.

He shrugged. "Why not?"

She held up her right hand, two fingers extended, and whispered a phrase. Then she touched each of them on the forehead. Alarm shifted her expression. "Take your backpacks and hide!" She shoved them deeper into the barn.

The urgency in her voice made Torgin wish he were anywhere but Myrrh.

11

Der Tah

Esán braced himself and opened the door. Nomed stepped through. "Close it." The curt order rang through the room.

Obeying without question, Esán faced him. "What's going on? Why's everyone dashing around?"

"The forward guard of one of the most powerful leaders in this solar system marched through a portal on the Plains of DoOlb and scared Thaer's people to death. They have demanded an audience with Wolloh, who's furious at their lack of courtesy and the assumption that they can command him to do anything."

"You seem upset, too." Esán watched the scarred cheek twitch.

"The Dreelum are staying to help entertain what will be a most interesting entourage, which means you're not safe."

"They won't try anything with Wolloh on full alert, will they?"

"One cannot count on a couple of them to think beyond their own desires, so you must be vigilant. We will disappear if things become too dangerous. Don't wander anywhere at night; keep your wards up and strong, and use your gifts to keep yourself safe. I must go." His hand on the doorknob tensed. A dark eyebrow shot up. A sudden yank brought a startled Seval flying into the room. The door shut with a crack.

"Why were you eavesdropping?" Nomed rose to his full height and loomed over the young servant.

"I-I-I came to g-get you."

"Who sent you?" Nomed glared.

"M-m-master W-Wolloh, sir."

"Stop your stuttering, boy. I won't hurt you."

"You could have fooled me." Esán gave him a withering look.

Nomed shot him an irritated glance, pulled the door open, and shoved the young servant through. "Take me to Wolloh."

Esán watched him vanish down the hall after a scurrying Seval. "You could at least have told me who's coming," he muttered, allowing himself a small slam of the door. He sprawled across his bed. "Hope I can sleep through the ruckus."

Nomed and TheLise arrived outside Wolloh's private office at the same time. Servants scurried in various directions. Some appeared harried, others terrified. Thaer of the Plains of DoOlb backed his pudgy body into the hall, glared at them, and waddled away, sputtering and swearing under his breath.

"Don't just stand there. Get in here." The voice demanded immediate compliance. Nomed ushered TheLise in front of him and closed the door.

Wolloh's handsome face met them. "The gall of expecting me to march to their demands." He laughed.

TheLise regarded him with inquiring gray eyes.

Nomed remained unmoved.

"Where's Esán?" Wolloh looked from one to the other. "I want him here where I know he is safe. These da'am Dreelum are maddening." He gave TheLise an appraising look. "You excepted, of course, my dear. They think they can use him against me. We shall see."

"I believe Esán is trying to sleep." Nomed took a seat. "He put up wards...very good ones, I might add...so I suggest we let him be. Both TheLise and I are keeping tabs on him."

"If anything happens to him..." Wolloh raised his disfigured hand and watched its claw-like fingers curl into a fist. "The boy's smart. We shall see how he copes. Now..."

A sharp rap on the door cut him short. Annoyance flashed. "Enter."

"The guard has arrived and *demands* your presence." The servant bowed and closed the door.

Nomed peered out the window. "It seems they are impatient to see you."

"They can wait." Wolloh smiled at TheLise. "Are you prepared to play a game?"

"That depends on the rules." She tilted her head. "You know I only play by mine."

Wolloh laughed. "It's a good thing you are so charming." His good eye sought Nomed. "And you? Are you ready to play?"

"You know I love a good game, but like TheLise," he too smiled, "I prefer to play by *my* rules."

Wolloh grabbed his cane and turned his mutilated cheek to his former apprentices. "In this game, there is only one rule, my friends." He dragged his damaged leg to the center of the room and stood between them. "Stay alive."

Before he could raise an eyebrow, Nomed found himself standing amid nine mounted soldiers, whose horses pranced in nervous circles, raising red dust and intensifying the scorching heat almost beyond endurance. Wolloh lifted his clawed hand. The horses backed into a wide circle, the arrogance of their riders replaced with frustration and a touch of disquiet. Nomed waited with interest for the High DiMensioner's next move.

An officer urged his horse forward. It balked and backed further away from the circle's center. Jumping to the ground, he threw the reins to his lieutenant and strode toward Wolloh. The clawed hand lifted again, the crystal knob of the cane glowed. An abrupt halt left the officer's angry face flushed as red as the desert sand.

Wolloh spoke in an undertone that only the officer, TheLise, and Nomed could hear. "You are?"

"Tinpaca Granier." His reply hissed through bared teeth.

"I require time alone with you, Tinpaca. Send your men back to your camp. Tell them they will find a good well and plenty of firewood on the east side of the ranch." His voice, hypnotizing and calm, held the weight of authority.

The officer's eyes flashed. "I demand…"

Wolloh's head turned, his scarred and deformed profile made more frightening by the harsh light of the DerTahan sun. A growl issued from the grimaced lips. The officer's mouth clamped shut. Pivoting, he faced his men. "Return to camp and move it further east until you find a good well and firewood. I will join you later."

In unison, eight armed men wheeled their horses around and galloped toward the gated entrance of Shu Chenaro, leaving a cloud of red dust in their wake. Tinpaca Granier reversed his pivot and saluted Wolloh.

Nomed almost laughed out loud when Wolloh's good eye winked at TheLise before it refocused on the officer. "Leave your weapons with your horse and join me in my office." A slight hesitation from the Tinpaca brought Wolloh's clawed hand up for the third time. Looking dazed, the man removed his holster, two knives, and a hidden pistol.

A satisfied expression settled over Wolloh's face as he led the way through the house, with the docile Tinpaca following. Nomed and TheLise, acting as rear guard, exchanged amused glances. In Wolloh's office, the soldier first sagged and then came to life, his stance erect and his eyes furious. "How dare you—"

Wolloh's cane thumped against the floor. The man's mouth clamped shut. "Allow me to begin." The High DiMensioner's sightless eye gleamed. The distorted grimace became exaggerated. "You are on *my* planet and in *my* home. While you are here, you will abide by *my* rules and *our* laws. First and foremost, you and your men may never carry weapons of any kind when visiting Shu Chenaro. You will show unerring respect to everyone in my household, and you will represent your planet and your leader with behavior befitting the dignity I know he would demand if he were here. If you ignore my dictates, I will dispatch you and your men back to your planet in disgrace. Am I clear?"

"Yes, sir." The officer saluted and remained at attention.

Wolloh changed the angle of his head. Granier stared at the handsome smoothness. "It is late." The High DiMensioner's mouth curved into a gracious smile. "I am certain that you and your men need to rest. We will meet at mid-morning to discuss your needs. If you require anything for your comfort or that of your men, my Major Domo will have it delivered to your camp."

The door opened to admit a tall, dignified man. "Stebben at your service." He acknowledged Wolloh with a nod. "Please come this way." He bowed before stepping into the corridor.

Tinpaca Granier clicked his heels together, saluted, and strode after the Major Domo.

Nomed closed the door.

TheLise sank into a brown leather chair and laughed. "You were quite wonderful, Wolloh. Will Stebben be able to handle him?"

Wolloh's good eye sparked with humor. "Stebben can handle almost anything, my dear. As with both of you, I trained him myself. Now, we need to place a ward around the ranch so we can sleep.

Nomed helped TheLise to her feet. Forming a circle with Wolloh, they joined hands. Energy glowed around them, its throbbing hum permeating the quiet office. When Wolloh released their hands, the handsome side of his face relaxed into a weary smile. "What an interesting time." He turned to both of them. "Off you go now. I'll expect you and Esán to join me for morning meal. His training begins tomorrow."

"Are you sure working with Esán is a good idea?" Nomed raised an eyebrow.

"What better time, Seyes, to show the power we wield? Tomorrow."

TheLise kissed the handsome cheek and swept from the room. Nomed shared a momentary smile with his mentor and followed.

The Dreelas slowed her pace as he joined her and slipped a hand into his. "So you think he made his point with Granier?"

"I think he couldn't have been clearer." They stopped by her door. "Sleep well, TheLise. May I walk you to morning meal?"

A sultry smile played around her mouth. "And tonight?"

Nomed calmed his momentary desire and kissed her hand. "*Tonight* we sleep, my dear. Goodnight."

Her seductive laugh followed him down the hall.

12

Myrrh

Following Almiralyn's urgent command, Brie shoved Torgin ahead of her past several stalls. At the door to the tack room, she motioned the boys inside. Her aunt had assured her the hidden lever to open the Intersect was behind the rack of bridles on the opposite wall.

Torgin peeked out a small, dirty window. "By the F-f-fathers! Soldiers are sneaking around in the Terces Wood."

Ira grabbed his arm. "Get down, Torg. Hurry, Brie, someone's headed this way."

Anxiety made her fingers clumsy. *Where is it? Come on...* Relief eased her agitation as she found the lever, pulled it, and watched a door open onto a steep stairway. Ira shot past her. A muffled command somewhere outside sent Torgin sprinting down the stairs.

"I'll search the barn." The voice came from the garden.

Brie followed, pulled the lever on her side of the door, and ran down the steps. At the bottom, she allowed herself a moment to scan the Intersect skyscape, where a multitude of bright, jewel-colored stars sparkled in an endless expanse of sky. In the distance, the creamy moon hung, full and radiant. The root system of Myrrh's Terces Wood, silhouetted against this breathtaking backdrop, intertwined in intricately woven patterns. Where root crossed over root, iridescent turquoise light formed discs of color. *I'll never get used to the Intersect.* She let out a soft sigh and stepped onto the platform between the boys.

Torgin shook his head. "It's hard to believe all those swirls of color are Intersect platforms."

"It is spectacular, isn't it?" Ira looked down at Brie and grinned. A momentary flash of confusion lit his sapphire blue eyes.

She started to speak but couldn't remember what she had wanted to say. *What am I forgetting?* Her brow furrowed, she returned her attention to the beautiful panorama. "We need to keep moving. Ready?" She slipped her hands into theirs.

"ZeeAck od Thrice." The chorused Key sent them flashing through space. When they arrived on their destination platform, they huddled together, absorbing the vastness and the beauty, not knowing when or if they would see it again.

"Are you sure we should have left?" Torgin sounded doubtful. "What if Almiralyn needs help?"

"She needs us to get away, Torg." Ira's deep voice sounded tight. He headed up the steps. "I'd be willing to bet those were Lorsedi's soldiers you saw in the woods, Torgin. Could you tell how many there were?"

"You grabbed me, remember? I didn't have time to count." Torgin panted as he climbed. "These steps are sure steep."

"Shh! We don't know if anyone is outside." Brie pulled the lever. A soft swoosh and sunset's glow beckoned. She crawled into the hollow of a large tree and peered into the woods.

Birds chirped a song welcoming turning's end. A squirrel scurried through dried leaves. Somewhere above them, a crow cawed. Nothing else moved. Ira and Torgin crept up beside her. The panel slid back into place.

"Let me go first, Brie." Ira took off his backpack and handed it to her. He crawled into the open and stood up. Nemttachenn Tower's rough, granite walls loomed above him as he slipped between tall trees at the edge of the clearing.

Staring out at the tower, Brie experienced a wave of anticipation. Images of the turning Esán had disappeared flooded her mind. She would never forget Nomed's burning anger or the fierceness in Esán's expression as CheeTrann's swirling vortex swallowed them. Nemttachenn had then flown apart and later, at Almiralyn's bidding, reassembled itself to protect the Evolsefil Crystal. One Man's despair when his son vanished pierced her heart again. She pressed a hand to her chest and remembered the children of many singing to bring the crystal heart of Myrrh back to life and the joy of seeing Almiralyn and Karrew reappear at Evolsefil's center. The high cost of the battle nearly overwhelmed her; Almiralyn's return had eased her sorrow.

Ira stepped into view and waved. "Come on."

She crept from the hollowed trunk into the sunlight. Torgin followed, stretching his long body. "Sure glad to be out of there."

Hurrying through the woods, they joined Ira by the tower entrance.

Brie handed him his backpack and stepped into the dimness, where Evolsefil's luster glowed through the blue curtain-like haze enveloping it. Tiptoeing through the mist, she placed a hand on the crystal's smooth surface. Quartz, threaded with gold, thrummed against her palm. "We'll hurry, Evolsefil."

She beckoned her friends to follow and, pressing her hand to her heart, walked to the center of the tower. Her voice rang out as clear as a song. "CheeTrann, CheeTrann, come to our aid!"

The ground pitched and settled. "Daughter of KcernFensia, how may I serve?" The Sentinel of Nemttachenn's booming voice filled the tower.

"Almiralyn sent us to you for help. We must go to DerTah."

"Who stands beside you?"

"Ira Raast and Torgin Whalend. Please send us to the planet of Seyes Nomed's mentor."

The deep voice questioned. "Soldiers of another land march through the Terces Wood. Are they in search of Evolsefil?"

"They search for my mother, my grandmother, and me." Brie glanced over her shoulder.

"Stand together at Nemttachenn's center. Be Quick!" CheeTrann rumbled.

Ira grasped Brie's hand and squeezed. He shot Torgin a reassuring smile.

Brie clutched Torgin's hand. "We're ready, CheeTrann."

A roar thundered through the tower as a whirling vortex opened at its center. Torgin's hand yanked free. With a terrified shriek, he tumbled into the gaping mouth. Brie plummeted after him, hauling Ira behind her. They plunged into nothingness so empty she fought to draw a breath. Ira floated beside her. Nothing else seemed to move until Ira's hand slipped from hers. He drifted after Torgin, like a falling a feather in an endless tunnel of swirling night. Blurs of mesmerizing color shot toward her. A terrified shriek from Torgin accompanied their sudden and accelerated descent into white-hot light. Red sand spewed in all directions as they hit the ground and tumbled down the side of a steep incline.

"Don't move." Brie's eyes darting over the dunes.

Beside her, Ira and Torgin froze.

At the cottage, Almiralyn woke Allynae with a whispered warning next to his ear. "Don't make a sound. Wake up Sparrow and take her to The Borderlands. Soldiers are hiding in the Terces Wood."

Grateful that she had insisted everyone nap in the house, she hastened down the hall and knocked on Jordett's door.

He answered, already dressed, and not, she was glad to note, in his PPP uniform. "Trouble?"

"Soldiers in the woods and closing in on the house."

He stepped into the hallway. "I'll wake the others."

Bustling into the kitchen, she put on a kettle and set out bread, cheese, and fruit. "We must look ignorant, normal, and non-threatening." Shifting to Mira's more benign persona, she studied her reflection in the window. Her short, round body, flyaway gray hair, and wrinkles appeared far less dangerous than her true form. She scanned the kitchen one last time.

Jordett, the first to join her, watched her from the doorway. "Twins?"

The quiet question sounded an alarm in her head. "Gone, I hope. I'll explain later."

Before Allynae could shake the sleep from his brain, Sparrow sat up, her brown eyes full of questions. "What about the twins?"

"Almiralyn will take care of the twins." Allynae climbed off the bed. "Put your shoes on."

Grabbing clothes, he stuffed them in the backpack he'd planned to take to DerTah and flung it over his shoulder. He slipped on shoes, tying them with fingers that felt clumsy and cold. "I'm too old for this."

Sparrow came around the bed and pressed her body next to his. "I'm afraid."

"We'll be fine." He held her at arm's length. "Do exactly what I say."

She nodded, clipped her sleep-tangled hair back from her face, and prepared to follow.

When they reached the bottom of the stairs, Allynae pulled Sparrow after him down the hall to the front door. Two uniformed men prowling the perimeter of the cottage kept them hiding in the shadows like rats in a trap.

From his position near the kitchen door, Jordett watched Merrilea enter the room, followed by One Man. A yawning Paisley trailed behind.

"What's the plan?" One Man looked from Mira to Jordett.

"Everything must appear normal." Mira straightened her rainbow-striped apron. "You are all neighbors visiting for Jordy's Sun Cycle Celebration."

A pounding knock on the back porch door sent apprehension reverberating through the kitchen.

Jordett kept his eyes focused on Mira as she poured steaming water into her flowered teapot. Another pounding knock heightened the throbbing tension in the room. One Man moved closer to Merrilea. A hoarse shout and more pounding brought Paisley around the table to Mira's side, his eyes wary. The Guardian's gaze met Jordett's. She nodded.

His expression curious but neutral, he crossed the back porch and opened the door. "May I help you?"

A young, arrogant face glared at him. "We are here to see Myrrh's Guardian."

The arrogance made Jordett wish he didn't have to be so careful.

"Who is it?" Mira walked up behind him. "Oh my, who are you?"

"Are you the Guardian?" The officer's tone held a note of condescension.

"I am." Mira's voice remained unassuming.

Jordett suppressed a grin.

The officious young man placed his hand on his weapon. "I'd like to speak with you alone."

Mira smiled a sweet smile, put her hand on Jordett's arm, and looked past the officer into the garden. "How many of you are there? I didn't make enough tea for an army."

"We're not here for tea." A sneer of disdain twisted his mouth.

"Why *are* you here?" She looked puzzled. "I don't remember anyone asking permission to bring armed men to my land."

"We don't need permission." He took a menacing step toward her.

Jordett tensed, but waited for Mira to take the lead.

She lifted her hand. The man stopped. "Tell your men to join you."

The officer blinked several times, shook his head, and turned. "Front and center!"

Six men ran into the yard from various directions and formed a straight line, weapons at the ready.

"Tell them to relax, and you will join them shortly."

He gave the orders. His men secured their weapons, but remained at attention in dusk light. He faced them, his expression dazed.

"Please join us for a cup of tea." Mira opened the kitchen door.

The officer walked past her. Jordett prepared to follow, then paused.

For a moment, Mira remained standing in the open porch doorway. Another small wave of her hand, and the soldiers in the garden began talking amongst themselves. When she turned to face him, she smiled. "That should do. Let us see what we can learn. She preceded him into the kitchen, where Merrilea arranged the teapot and cups on the table. Her wary gaze darted to the ill-at-ease young officer. Mira took charge. "Please, everyone, sit down."

Chairs scraped the floor as the occupants of the kitchen settled around the table. The man remained standing, his stubborn expression making him look young and petulant. A benevolent and understanding smile lit Mira's face. She patted the place beside her. Blank-faced, he sank onto the edge of the wooden seat.

"What's your name?" Mira poured a cup of steaming, fragrant tea and put it down in front of him.

"Tranwar Nagry, at your service, ma'am."

Jordett stifled a grin and wondered what exactly Mira had done to the man opposite him. He had seen his eyes glaze over when she raised her hand. *Much more potent than an empty threat.* He looked around the table at Mira's little army.

Allynae watched the two soldiers dash around the corner of the house and pulled Sparrow closer. "The portal is just beyond the front gate. Squint, and you can see it glowing in the sunflowers. The Key is Eero Tye Como. Are you ready?"

Noise from the kitchen chased them from the cottage and down the walk. Their eyes glued to the portal, they dodged through the sunflowers, repeated the Key, and jumped. Their feet hit the ground in a dingy basement room filled with piles of dusty furnishings.

Allynae glanced over his shoulder as a large keyhole faded away on the surface of an oval mirror in an antique frame. A single diagonal crack ran from the upper left to merge with a series of spider-web breaks near the bottom. "Sure wish Almiralyn would do something about that crack." He grimaced and rubbed his arm.

Sparrow smiled at him. "At least we're not in Myrrh anymore. Did you bring clothes for me in that pack?"

He chuckled. "We'd look a little odd walking down the street in night clothes. Here, see what you can find."

They dressed and climbed the rickety staircase to the first floor of *Antiques by Q.* "We need to find Dom. After that, we'll find you someplace to hide."

"Isn't Dom the man who told Nomed you're the twins' father?"

"Yep. He owes me one." Something rubbed against his leg. "Hello, Majeska. Just the cat we were looking for. Where's Dom?"

The smoky gray cat, her tail waving them forward, led them to a paper-cluttered office, where an old man snored in an overstuffed chair.

Allynae picked up a thick book, held it at eye level, and dropped it. The loud smack brought Dom upright, his gaze darting over his glasses. "What the... By the Fathers, Alli, did ya have to scare me to death? I gotta weak heart, ya know." He pushed his spectacles up on his nose and peered at Sparrow. "You must be the twins' mother."

"I'm SparrowLyn." She didn't smile.

"What brings you here? I'm hearing there are strange soldiers in Idronatti. I hope you're not headed there."

"Sparrow needs a place to lie low for a few sun turnings. Any suggestions?"

The old man picked up a crystal paperweight and peered at it. When he looked up, his magnified eyes were serious. "It's morning here in The Borderlands, so I'd go find Fadin in the Market. He can hide her. What's going on?"

Allynae's brows arched.

"I know." The old man lowered his eyes. "Gotta earn your trust again." He replaced the paperweight on the desk. "Sure wish Elcaro's Eye wasn't down."

"It makes communicating tough, doesn't it?" Allynae urged Sparrow into the hall. "If anyone comes through the mirror or if soldiers show up in The Borderlands, send Majeska to warn us."

"Will do. You two take care."

"You stay alert, Dom. Mira may need you."

After a careful inspection of the narrow lane in front of *Antiques by Q*, Allynae guided Sparrow into the shadow of a deserted building.

"Who's Fadin?" She peered up and down the lane.

Her voice, low and tight, made him hug her. "There's a group of Borderlanders who make it their business to outwit Idronatti's patrollers. Fadin helped me escape from the PPP when I headed back to Myrrh after I found you. Come on. I want to get you to safety."

It didn't take long to make their way through the narrow, winding streets of The Borderland's outer reaches. When they walked casually into the town square, the Outdoor Market was in full swing. People milling about created excellent cover, so they plunged into the crowd. They found Fadin setting up shop in a booth near the market's center.

Allynae leaned on the counter. "Got a moment."

Fadin looked up and grinned. "Well, how ya be? Who's the pretty lady?"

"This is Sparrow, the twins' mother. We need your help."

A disturbance across the square froze Fadin's smile.

A quick backward glance showed Allynae the crowd parting to let a group of soldiers pass through. Piloting Sparrow around behind the tent, he frowned. "Lorsedi sure works fast."

Fadin joined them. "This place is hoppin'. The PPP showed up on their own. Now, they're back with soldiers from off-planet." He jerked his head toward Sparrow. "Better hide her. Then we can decide what's next." A calloused finger pointed at a red and white tent. "That be Saaul's. Remember him?"

Allynae nodded.

"Take your lady over there. I'll meet ya just as quick as I can."

With his arm around her waist, Allynae ambled with Sparrow toward the red-striped tent.

13
Der Tah

The sun had not yet risen above the red dunes of Fera Finnero when Torgin, Ira, and Brie tumbled from the vortex onto the night-cooled sand. Torgin glanced at his friends where they lay unmoving at the base of a tall, wind-rounded dune. "What do we do now, Brie?" He struggled to keep his panic in check.

With exaggerated slowness, she sat up and looked around. Nothing moved. She smiled. "The first thing we do is change the patterning in your compass, Torg."

She explained Almiralyn's instructions. Torgin removed the leather thong from around his neck and held the compass with the face parallel to the desert floor. "Do I need to say the verse?"

"No, I'll do it. Let me know when the change is complete. Ready?"

Both boys nodded and stared at the blue back with its sprinkling of stars. Brie recited the verse Myrrh's Guardian had taught her.

"DerTah's patterns, deep and rare,
Desert, ocean, mountains fair,
Absorb these secrets into thee,
And all else that we should see."

"Would you look at that?" Ira sounded surprised.

Torgin looked at her with round, astonished eyes. "The stars shifted."

"They did, didn't they?" Brie felt a rush of relief. "I wasn't sure it would work without Aunt Mira. Tuck it away, Torg. We need to go." When the compass was back beneath his shirt, she stood up and offered her hand.

He grasped it and let her pull him up beside her. His awed expression melted into doubt as his gaze darted over the red dunes. "Are we about to be eaten by Fire ConDra?"

"I think we're safe in the shade, but once the sun is higher in the sky..." She shrugged.

Ira scrambled upright and brushed the sand from his short hair. "What does the book say about Fire ConDra, Brielle? It won't be long until there's no shade to hide in."

"It doesn't say much except that water can destroy them." She pulled a lightweight, hooded cloak the color of the desert sand from her pack. "And wearing a DerTahan kcalo will make it harder for them to sense you." She slipped her arms into the long, wide sleeves. "It also protects you from the sun's heat and the cold at night."

Torgin slid his pack off, pulled out his kcalo, and draped it around his shoulders. "So, what do we do with these?" He held up the ankle length cords attached to the neck of his robe.

Ira twirled his cord over his head. "Yeah, Brie. What about these?"

"Get serious, Ira. We may not have much time. Watch. First you tie these three small ties to close the kcalo in front." Brie demonstrated as she spoke. "You cross the cords over your chest, pull them around back and cross them again, then bring them around your waist, and knot them to one side. There you have it." She patted her completed knot.

Ira finished tying his cords and adjusting his kcalo. "Okay, Torg, time to ask for directions."

Torgin glared at him. "Who made you the boss?" He turned his back and addressed Brie. "What do I ask? We don't know the name of anything."

"Wolloh's place is called Shu Chenaro od DerTah." Brie took a drink from her canteen and fastened it to the cord around her waist while Torgin pulled out the compass for the second time. "How do you know so much?"

"I like to read." Brie grinned and shrugged her pack onto her back. "Go ahead, ask for directions."

"Yeah, come on." Ira nudged him in the ribs. "We need to go."

"Cut it out, Ira." He shot him a dirty look and slipped the thong off over his head. "Repeat for me, Brie."

Brie pointed at her shoe. "Shu." She touched her chin. "Chenaro."

"Here we go." Torgin held out the compass. "Show us the safest way to Shu Chenaro od DerTah."

Ira scowled, slapped the compass from his hand, and sent it flying over the sand. "Not the safest way, Drotti. We need to know the shortest way."

Torgin's face turned bright red. His palm smacked Ira in the chest. "Stop pushing me around. Stop telling me what to do. And don't call me Drotti."

Ira's arm jerked back. A cacophonous shriek stopped his fist mid-way to Torgin's chin.

Torgin swung around, searching the dunes. "What's that?"

"Down! Quick!" Brie dove for the sand and pulled Ira with her.

The compass forgotten, Torgin watched the celestial brilliance of the DerTahan sun push its blazing crest higher in the sky. Blistering heat poured down the side of the dune, chasing the shadows before it and bathing him in blinding light. The desire to hide surged through him. Paralysis held him still. Another shriek, closer and more heinous, drove the sweat on his scalp down his face and onto his kcalo.

"Torgin, get down." Brie's urgent call fell on dread-deafened ears. He remained standing, a beacon emitting a message of mortal terror.

Fiery red eyes rose above the dune and locked onto his. Taller than the tallest man, the ConDra soared upward. Its powerful wings beat flames into a raging inferno that engulfed it from its snarling, beak-like snout to the tip of its long, lashing tail. A tongue of liquid lava licked the sand on either side of him. Sparks shot into the air and rained down around him. Higher and higher, the creature soared.

Torgin's brain screamed silently, *"It's preparing to strike!"* His body refused to respond.

Desert heat soaked through Brie's kcalo and penetrated her skin. Next to her, Ira's fear held him rigid. Hot air pounded their bodies. The sight of Torgin, frozen and staring, his skin russet from the intensifying heat, forced her to her feet. Slipping off her backpack and dropping her canteen to the ground, she raised her arms. The malevolent monster, lickerish and hungry, raged toward her, its mouth a gaping, fiery pit.

At the base of the dune some distance away, an Atrilaasu Dansgirl, her black eyes glistening in her reddish-brown face, stared at the young trio. She had felt them arrive and knew their danger. Too late to help, she watched the Fire ConDra rise and prepare to feast on human flesh. Horror and heat burned her throat.

Beneath the blazing beast, a cloak-draped figure rose. Curls the color of the ConDra's flame burst free of the kcalo's hood. A feminine face emerged, glowing golden in the fiery light. Fragile arms reached out in supplication, an entreaty…a plea. The ConDra shrieked, lashed its lava tongue, and shot higher. The Dansgirl crouched lower in the sand and hid her face behind her hands. Another high-pitched scream raised the hair on her neck. She peeked through V'ed fingers. Her mind blanked and sputtered back to life.

The red-haired girl sung one high note that cut the air into vibrating frequencies. She grew taller, broader, and less distinct. With her arms out to her sides, she arched her body and tipped her face to the heavens. Her features shimmered silver. Her arms morphed into glistening wings and launched her skyward—a Water ConDria soaring above the dunes. Iridescent, liquid, and cool, she faced her conflagrant foe. Eyes the color of cascading water captured and held the Fire ConDra's scorching stare. Fearless and frightening, they circled in the ravaging heat of the Desert of Fera Finnero.

Raging red and dazzling silver fenced—moving forward and back, parrying water against flame. A song flowed forth from the Water ConDria's throat. She folded her wings and spun around herself until glittering droplets of water formed a halo of liquid diamonds around her. The Fire

ConDra hovered, wings crackling and snapping. It whipped its tail in a blistering, hissing arc and soared upward, barely missing its aqueous adversary.

The Water ConDria swooped in a wide crescent until she seemed to stop mid-air, shimmering red reflected in her outstretched wings. Again, her throat opened. A song filled with the roar of water, free-falling through space and crashing on the shores of the world, shook the dunes and sent them rolling like waves before the wind. The Fire ConDra screeched in response and streaked upward. A shower of cascading sparks sizzled and died as she rose to meet it. A glistening gem beneath the orange sky, the Water ConDria hovered, her wings undulating and wide. Flames blazing hotter, the ConDra charged.

Unwavering, she met the assault. Her clear, liquid wings wrapped around its fiery body. The death scream of the Fire ConDra filled the air as flames quenched in a hiss of heat against water sent a geyser of vapor into the orange sky.

Scorched, blackened bones plummeted toward the red sands of DerTah. With a final trembling cry, the Water ConDria landed and collapsed as a Human girl into the waiting arms of her friends.

In the miracle's aftermath, the Dansgirl fell to her knees and wept. She had never seen a Fire ConDra fall from the sky, nor beheld anything so beautiful as the Water ConDria, nor heard anything so fearsome as its song.

The morning at Shu Chenaro arrived on the heels of scurrying servants who had spent the night preparing for Wolloh's unknown guest. Esán rolled onto his side and plopped a pillow over his head. *I start my training today and have slept less than a wink.* A sharp knock brought him to sitting, the pillow clasped to his chest. "Come in."

Seval peeked around the door.

"What?" Esán knew he sounded grumpy.

The boy flinched. "Master Wolloh asks that you join him in his private office for morning meal. Please wear your robe."

"Thanks, Seval. I didn't mean to grouch at you." He glanced at the crumpled pile of scarlet and gold and grimaced. "I guess I should have hung it up last night."

The servant slipped into the room. "I'll press this." He scooped it up and hurried away.

After the door closed, Esán padded to the window. Annoyed that he had no say in planning his life, he allowed himself a moment to savor the cool breeze of early dawn before he closed it and threw the lock. By the time he had cleaned up, Seval was back with the robe, looking as good as new.

The boy seemed reticent to engage in conversation, so Esán refrained from asking the questions buzzing around his brain. *Why can't I read your mind? What has torn your heart to shreds?*

Seval's face remained blank as he held the robe for him to step into. Tempted to disobey Wolloh, Esán hesitated. The High DiMensioner's hands around his throat during the assessment, a clear and present reminder of his power, set him in motion. "Thank you, Seval." He turned and allowed the boy to put the gold sash around his waist. Stepping back, he smiled. "Will I do?"

"You look like a Tyro." The young servant returned the smile.

Rebellion tightened Esán's jaw around the curse he wanted to shout. Swallowing both his need to rebel and the curse, he folded his arms. "What is a Tyro, exactly?"

"One who seeks hidden knowledge and learns." The boy's quiet response cooled his annoyance.

"I suppose I do seek knowledge, and I want to learn." He moved to the door. "We'd better go before I decide to play truant and get myself in trouble."

Nomed tapped on TheLise's door.

"Just a moment."

The thought whispering through his mind was tantalizing—sensual. He masked his own thoughts and turned his back to the door, annoyed at being left to kick his heels outside her quarters.

When she stepped into the hall, he had to admit she had been worth the wait. "You look lovely, as always." Her hunter green riding togs stressed her perfect figure. "There is something about you in britches..."

"Behave yourself, Seyes." Her smile lit her eyes. "Wolloh is waiting."

"And if he weren't?" His increased heart rate surprised him.

She took his arm and laughed the low sensual laugh that always made him squirm. "Today he is. Therefore, your question will have to remain unanswered."

Footsteps behind them made them turn. She smiled. "Good morning, Esán. I gather from your robe that Wolloh intends to show you off today."

"It seems so, doesn't it?" Esán scowled.

Releasing Nomed's arm, TheLise glided toward him. "Don't take things so seriously. It is just a game, Esán. Never forget that." She drew his arm through hers.

Nomed pursed his lips. "It may be deadly in its intent, but as TheLise so aptly put it, it is still a game. Good morning, nephew."

"Good morning, sir." The rancor left his voice.

"Well now, we don't want to keep Wolloh waiting any longer." Nomed beckoned to Seval, who had remained quiet during their conversation. "Run ahead, boy, and tell Master Wolloh we are on the way."

Under the desert sun, Ira's arms formed a protective circle around Brie. The features of the Water ConDria lingering in the lines of her face faded. He bent closer, scrutinized her pallor, the damp, red curls, and the sprinkling of freckles tiptoeing over her nose. Something stirred in his memory. Something... He shook his head. Tears spilled from his eyes and fell, mingling with the droplets shimmering on her cheeks.

Torgin, his eyes rounded in astonishment, shook his head. "Did you see what Brie did?" He sank down on the sand beside her. "She shifted to a ConDra made of water."

Ira held her closer. "She was so beautiful, and she saved us, Torg. She saved us from certain death."

"Is she alright?"

"She's breathing." Ira stroked her cheek. "Brie, wake up. We need you, Brielle. Please open your eyes."

As though emerging from a deep slumber, her breathing changed. From some unfathomable place, she released a sigh that shook her entire body. Her eyelids fluttered open. For a moment, she gazed up at the sky, and then, seemingly unaware of Ira and Torgin, she sat up and smiled.

"You don't have to hide." She wiped a droplet from her chin. "We won't hurt you."

Ira followed her gaze and stared.

A young girl rose from the sand a short distance away. Eyes the color of coal stared at the trio. A colorful beaded band held thick, dark hair back from a brown face that hinted at the red of the desert. Beneath her orange kcalo, her loose-fitting clothing blended into the sun and the sand. With a grubby hand, she scrubbed a tear from her cheek.

Torgin looked from the girl to Brie. "Who the—"

"My name is Brie. Do you understand?"

The girl knelt and bowed her head. "You ConDria. Please, not hurt me." The accented words were halting.

"What is a ConDria?" Brie's words sounded soft as a summer song.

The girl kept her eyes lowered but peeked at Brie from beneath long, dark lashes. "Ancient stories tell of magic times. ConDra filled the skies. They killed our people. A ConDria rose—saved the ancestors. You ConDria...a girl who becomes a Water ConDria." She touched her forehead to the sand and straightened.

Brie looked around at the scorched bones scattered down the slope of the dune. Her eyes sought Ira. "Did I shift shape?"

"Into a ConDria. You were so beautiful and so terrifying."

"And how did..." She pointed at the bones.

"You wrapped your watery wings around the Fire ConDra." Torgin threw his arms wide. "The fire went out with a gargantuan hiss, and the bones fell to the ground."

"Talk about shape-shifting!" Ira laughed and then sobered. "Do you remember *anything*, Brie?"

"Only a delicious coolness flowing through my body. Then I woke up in your arms." She looked at the desert girl. "What's your name?"

"I tell name, you hurt me."

Brie knelt in front of her. "I won't hurt you, nor will my friends. Will you hurt us?"

"I have no power." She pointed at Brie. "I serve. Never hurt."

Brie rose and offered her hand.

The girl hesitated, wiped her hand on her cloak, and placed it in hers. As she climbed to her feet, sunlight glittered on an object that slipped from beneath her kcalo.

"Look! She has Mira's compass." Torgin started forward.

Ira caught his arm.

Suspicion flashed across the girl's face as she clutched it in her hand. She tossed her head. "He fed to desert. It not belong to him now. Nichook, Atrilaasu Dansmen od DerTah, claims this desert gift."

"It is not..." Torgin stopped when Brie's eyes flashed to his face.

She looked back at the girl. "Nichook? Is that your name?" Her voice was gentle—soothing.

The girl placed her hand on her heart. "Nichi. Me called Nichi."

Brie smiled. "What a beautiful name. Come with us, Nichi, and be our guide."

"I keep the gift." Her dark, watchful eyes narrowed.

Brie touched the Star of Truth. Ira read the message in her expression and spoke for her. "It's magic, you know. You can keep it if you dare, but only the one chosen by the Guardian of Myrrh can use it without fear of death."

The Dansgirl glared at Ira. "You lie."

Ira shook his head. "I would like to be your friend, so I tell you what is true."

Nichi removed the compass from around her neck and held it out to Torgin. "You keep. I not ready to die."

Torgin accepted the compass. "Thank you. I am very grateful to have it back, Nichook."

The girl rubbed her hands against her kcalo and looked at Brie. "We comrades now?"

"We are comrades, Nichi. This is Ira." She squeezed his shoulder. "And this is Torgin, Bearer of the Compass of Myrrh."

Esán looked across the table at the smooth-cheeked side of the High DiMensioner's face as he flirted with the Dreelas TheLise...*what an interesting pair*. To his right, Nomed fingered his scar, a sure sign of his displeasure. The attraction between the men and the Dreelas had been apparent to Esán from the first time he had seen them together. Now, listening to their back-and-forth banter over their morning meal of DerTahan fowl and desert fruit, he smiled.

"What's up, boy?" Wolloh's good eye gleamed. "Are you enjoying your meal or our most interesting conversation?"

Esán wiped all expression from his face. "The meal, of course, sir. It's delicious."

"What do you think, dear TheLise?" An osprey-like cock of his head brought his murky eye in line with the bird on his plate as the twisted fingers of his lame hand tore a chunk of meat loose. "Is it the conversation or the food that makes our young Tyro smile?" The meat disappeared into his mouth.

TheLise responded with an innocent smile. "The fowl is succulent, Wolloh, and the fruit is tender and juicy. The conversation, however, is laced with innuendo and sarcastic barbs. Which would make you smile?"

Wolloh laughed, eyeing Nomed with his good eye. "And you, Seyes. What are your thoughts on the direction Esán's mind is taking this morning?"

"My nephew is perceptive. I imagine he is enjoying his morning repast and smiling at the undercurrents in our conversation."

Esán kept his eyes fixed on his plate.

Wolloh pushed his chair back from the table and stood up. "Well, my children, shall we go? Tinpaca Granier will enter our gate in less time than it will take us to teleport to the arena." He paused and turned to Stebben.

Esán heaved a silent sigh of relief as the Major Domo joined them.

"Please have the table cleared, and bring Granier to us when he arrives."

"Yes, sir." Stebben prepared to leave.

"Wait," drawled Wolloh. "You, my trusted man, what do you think Esán was smiling about...his meal or our conversation?"

"I imagine he was smiling at your wit, sir." With a slight bow, he departed.

"The cheek of my servants." Wolloh called after him, then angled his feathery brow in Esán's direction. "It is time to begin your training as a Tyro. Come."

With Wolloh's cane tapping the way, the four walked through the sheltered garden at the house's center and into the open courtyard. The heat took their breath away. Esán resented the scarlet robe even more than usual as sweat crept down the back of his neck. They entered the arena. Wolloh's tap, step, drag stopped. He turned to TheLise and Nomed. "Off you go. Meet Granier and escort him on a tour that allows him to *think* he has seen much, and then bring him here to watch our power at work."

Esán observed their departure with a touch of regret. With TheLise around, Wolloh's attention seemed less focused in his direction. *Now my training begins.*

"Indeed, it does, boy." Wolloh's laugh as Esán took a step backward held a note of sarcasm. He lowered his head in a mock bow. "I will stay out of your mind, especially during training, unless you are in danger. Now, let us begin."

14
Myrrh & Thera

Sparrow and Allynae huddled together at the back of Saaul's red-striped tent, surrounded by the bustle of The Borderlands' Outdoor Market. Even with Allynae's arm around her, Sparrow felt the fear in her stomach churning in concert with her anxious thoughts. *How safe will Ari and Brie be in KcernFensia? Are PPP already in Singtil? Are my parents alright?* Anxiety made it difficult to think. And right now, she needed her brain to work. The shuffling of boot-clad feet close by compounded her fear. She caught Allynae's eye and tried to smile. His responding hug didn't help.

A boy's frightened face peeked around the curtain. "Mom says you'd better slip away. The soldiers are coming here next."

"Tell you mother thanks." Allynae lifted the back edge of the tent and surveyed the area behind it. "All clear."

Sparrow's stomach convulsed as she nodded.

He scrambled out, took another quick look around, and helped her duck under the canvas edge. A commotion at the front of the tent sent them scurrying into the crowd. Not far ahead, Fadin leaned lazily against the counter of a food tent, talking to its owner. With a quick flick of his wrist, he signaled them deeper into the throng.

Sparrow leaned her head on Allynae's shoulder. "Where to now?"

"Keep walking." Allynae guided her away from the market onto a side street that led away from the town square.

As they reached the corner, Saaul popped his head around the door of a run-down shoppe and hurried to meet them. "Get back to Dom. Majeska brought a message that Myrrh is clear. Tell Mira the PPP and off-world soldiers are in The Borderlands and Idronatti. They're looking for a red-haired girl and her ma." He withdrew. The door shut with a soft click.

"We have to go back to Myrrh." Sparrow shivered. "They're after Brie."

"And you." Allynae led her down another littered lane. A yell from somewhere close by spurred them into a jog. At the next corner, he pushed her behind him and peered up and down the street. He whispered over his shoulder. "Chance Lane is our goal. It's about three blocks that way. There's nowhere to hide, so we need to act like we belong here." Dumping their backpack into a half-empty trashcan, he pressed the lid down on top. "Ready?"

"Ready as I'll ever be."

Submerged in conversation, they walked causally along the narrow street. A dog sniffed its way past them. A grimy boy stepped from an alley. "Me ma is pretty sick." He sidled closer to Sparrow. "Ya gotta repoc, lady? It'd sure help."

Allynae flipped a coin down the street. The boy scrambled after it. Sparrow glimpsed him on hands and knees, searching, as they crossed the street and dodged onto Chance. Once in the shadows cast by the dilapidated buildings, they threw caution to the wind and ran until *Antiques by Q* was only a street away. Ducking under a tattered awning above a deserted shoppe entrance, they paused to catch their breath. Allynae held her close. "Dom's place may be under surveillance. Both of us are on the PPP's Watch List, so there's no guarantee someone won't recognize us."

The sound of running pressed them further into the shadows. Halfway down the block, Saaul dodged a PPP officer and sprinted away from *Antiques by Q*. Several soldiers in unfamiliar uniforms gave chase.

When the pounding of boots faded into the distance, Allynae urged her from one doorway to the next until the vacant, dirty windows of Dom's shoppe gaped at them from across the way. Majeska sat on the stoop, eyes gleaming like faceted amethysts. She licked a paw and scrubbed her ear.

Allynae studied his feline guide. "Must be safe, or she wouldn't be sitting so pretty."

Ears twitching, the cat nudged the door open and vanished inside. Sparrow grabbed his hand, and they dashed into the shoppe, closing and bolting the door behind them.

Dom emerged from his office in the gray cat's wake. "Soldiers have overrun this place all morning. I'm surprised you two made it back without getting snatched. Who do they think they are, tearing through my shoppe?"

Allynae's gaze darted down the dusty hall. "Did they find the mirror?"

"Weren't looking for it, I guess. Don't know what they were after. Just tore through here—a band of brigands on a raid. You two'd best get yourselves gone, or we'll all end up in the Five Towers."

Majeska gave a clipped meow and trotted down the hall.

Dom urged them after her. "She's warning ya."

Allynae started to speak. The old man shook his head and shoved his spectacles higher on his nose. "I'll be fine. They've already ignored me twice. Go."

A shout exploding in the street, sent them racing after Majeska. A weapon fired. The hidden door to the basement clicked into place, cutting off another urgent shout.

In the dusky light at the bottom of the stairs, they found the mirror. Allynae held Sparrow's arm with one hand, pressed the other one against the surface, and whispered the Key. The handprint curled into a fist. The index finger pointed straight at them. It completed drawing a keyhole at the mirror's center as the door at the top of the stairs flew open. Majeska shot past them and leapt through the keyhole. The next thing Sparrow knew, she was standing in a field of sunflowers, watching Majeska's shadowed form dart through the open front door to Mira's cottage.

Allynae grinned at her. "There's no place like home!"

Sparrow squeezed his hand and refused to think about what lay ahead.

After a fruitful discussion with the RewFaaran soldier, Almiralyn had sent Jordett and Paisley to escort him and his men to the Demrach Gateway in the Terces Wood. Tranwar Nagry would be chagrined to know how much information she had gleaned from their seemingly innocent conversation. She hummed to herself as she set the table for an evening meal. In her Mira form, she appeared so benign and inconsequential he had dropped his guard. A mental probe had then helped her to achieve her goal.

He and his soldiers had departed to inform Lorsedi there was no red-haired child living in Myrrh, and Almiralyn had no information regarding his daughter. Her respite would be brief. She looked up from her preparations and smiled to see Merrilea entering the kitchen with Majeska at her heals.

The back screen door banged shut. Jordett strode into the kitchen with Paisley. "They're on their way." The major smiled his relief and sat down next to Merrilea.

"Didn't think much of them soldiers." Paisley scooted his chair closer to the table. "They're pretty darn rude. Are all RewFaarans that arrogant?"

Almiralyn handed him a cup of tea. "Good and bad people exist on RewFaar, just as they exist on Myrrh and Thera."

Jordett sat down and accepted his favorite steaming brew. "Uniforms make some people feel like they don't need to pay attention to how they behave."

Paisley tugged at his mustache. "Ya mean like the uniform says 'I'm powerful, so whatever I say is right'?"

"Sometimes just like that." The major sipped his brew.

"What are your plans now, Almiralyn?" Merrilea's dusky, gray eyes appeared troubled.

"It's imperative we conceal Sparrow and Gerolyn." She sat down at the table. "The twins and Torgin are in DerTah."

"They're *where*?" Allynae's voice from the doorway made everyone jump.

"Back so soon?" His sister smiled.

"Mira, you sent the twins to DerTah, and you didn't tell me?"

"I let them go because they were going with or without our permission. I preferred to send them well prepared. Besides, Allynae, it's their destiny."

"By the Fathers, I know you know what you're doing, but..." He scrubbed his upper lip with a finger and glowered.

Sparrow appeared beside him and slipped her hand into his. "Did you say the twins are in *DerTah*? How could you let them go without one of us, Mira?" Sparrow's brown eyes searched her face. She sagged against Allynae. "Never mind, Almiralyn. I don't like it, and I am terrified for them, but I understand it's their destiny."

Allynae put a protective arm around her. "Dom sent you a message, Mira. There are off-world soldiers in The Borderlands and Thera. The PPP is in an uproar."

"We'd better go to Gerolyn soon, or we'll be too late." Jordett's steadfast calm faded, replaced by what Almiralyn knew was an urgent need for action, one that mirrored her own.

"Where's One Man?" Allynae pulled out a chair for Sparrow and sat down next to her.

Almiralyn smiled. "He's about to walk through the back door."

Paisley peered across the porch. "How do ya know that?"

"Because he let me know he's on the way."

"But..." The big man's face scrunched around his confusion.

One Man pushed the screen door open and strode into the kitchen. "I knew you were back." He smiled at Allynae and Sparrow. "Now we can go for Gerolyn and Standin. When we return, I'm going to DerTah to find my son."

Merrilea put down her cup. "How soon do we leave?"

One Man looked at Almiralyn. "How soon, Mira?"

"If you leave within the chron-circle, you'll arrive in Demrach Canyon before middle-night. You can camp near the gateway and begin the hike to Singtil in the morning." She opened a cupboard and pulled out three backpacks. "These are ready for you."

"So..." Allynae loomed over her. "One Man, Merrilea, and Sparrow will head for Singtil while I sit here tracing Ari's infinity symbol on the tabletop."

"I need you, Jordett, and Paisley here, Alli. Lorsedi will send more troops, and this time they'll be playing a very different game." Chagrin weighed her brother's return to his chair. She gave him a moment to gather his thoughts. "When the Largeen Joram discovers we misled the Nagry

Tranwar, he'll wish he'd never heard of Myrrh." She sighed. "And so will we."

Allynae grasped Sparrow's hand. "You're certain you want to do this? You don't have to, you know. We can hide you in the Dojanacks now."

Serious, intelligent eyes met his. "I have to go, Alli. Gerolyn is my mother. Standin protected us at great sacrifice to himself. I owe them both. Don't worry. One Man will take good care of us." She squeezed his hand and stood up. "I need time to prepare. We left in a hurry. I'll be quick." She gave him a brief smile and headed upstairs.

Merrilea pushed her chair back from the table. "I'd better get ready, as well." She hurried after Sparrow.

Paisley hoisted his ample girth to standing. "I'll go saddle the horses. How many?"

"Four. I'll help." Allynae's tone verged on belligerent. "I'll escort them, Almiralyn, and bring the horses back." His expression dared her to disagree. He strode from the kitchen, slamming the door behind him.

She put her cup in the sink and turned to find Jordett watching her. "You did what you felt was best, Almiralyn."

"It's the twins' destiny, Jordy. I just wish Elcaro's Eye were still functional, so I could keep track of them." She fingered her long braid. "I wish I could have gone with them."

With strong misgivings, Allynae watched Sparrow, Merrilea, and One Man leap into the whirling mouth of Demrach Gateway and flash from sight. He stared at the empty portal, unable to make himself leave the deserted clearing. His lips still tingled with the pressure of Sparrow's last kiss. His arms ached to hold her one more time. *If I can't be with her, I should be with the twins.* He rubbed his top lip.

With the reins of three horses looped around his hand, he prepared to mount the stallion, Gemlucky. Hair rising on the back of his neck made him hesitate. He ran a hand down the stallion's sleek, black side, dropped to his knee, and let his eyes scan the clearing's shadowed edge.

Around him, the horses moved uneasily. Gemlucky snorted. Allynae released their reins and stared between restless legs at the vortex. A flash of color in the trees flared and darted deeper into the forest. A twig snapped. The sound of running tempted Allynae to give chase. Instead, he gave a low whistle.

Gemlucky raised his head and whinnied. Two horses trotted into the trees. The third waited, ears twitching. More running feet, an oath, and silence held Allynae tense and alert. Gemlucky nickered. With an exclamation of frustration, a soldier staggered into the moonlit clearing. Nudged by his captors, he stumbled to a stop in front of Allynae. The four horses formed a barrier around them.

"Well, what do you know..." Allynae reached into Gemlucky's saddlebags and pulled out a length of rope.

The soldier's hand moved to his sidearm.

"I wouldn't if I were you." Allynae kept his tone conversational. "Gemlucky won't take kindly to any sudden move on your part. I suggest you drop your weapon and hold your hands out in front of you."

The soldier's stern face reddened. But he did as instructed.

As Allynae moved toward him, a fist whizzed by his chin, slammed into his shoulder, and sent him staggering backward. Quick as a cat after its prey, the soldier was on him. They crashed to the ground in a heap of flying arms and flailing legs. With all the strength he could muster, Allynae sent his attacker rolling. Scrambling on hands and knees, the soldier headed for his weapon. Gemlucky's nose sent it skittering into the underbrush. Allynae lunged, caught the soldier around the knees, and flattened him to the ground. Gemlucky sunk strong teeth into his uniformed-shoulder. The man went limp.

"Don't move." Allynae gulped in air. "Or I'll let these horses do whatever is necessary to keep you from escaping. Do you understand?"

The soldier grunted and remained still.

Allynae stuffed the man's weapon in the saddlebags and grabbed the rope. "Stand up!"

Gemlucky released the soldier's shoulder but kept his muzzle close to his ear. Ignoring the blood soaking his uniform shirt, the man grimaced and climbed to standing. Hatred glinted in his eyes.

Allynae trussed his hands in front of him. "You have a choice. You can either ride or walk back to the cottage. Which will it be?"

"I'll ride." He flinched and clenched his teeth.

"Good." Allynae helped him onto a horse's back, gathered the reins in his hand, and mounted Gemlucky. His prisoner had seen Sparrow, Merrilea, and One Man depart through the gateway. He prayed he was the only spy.

I n Demrach Canyon, One Man, unable to hear anything but the water cascading over the falls, squinted in the light of the full moon and frowned. He knew two soldiers had seen Sparrow jump into the vortex when she and Merrilea escaped to Myrrh.

"We need to keep moving." He glanced around. "We can't camp here. You know this area, Merrilea. Is there somewhere close enough we can reach it before the moon starts it's descent?"

"We can slip behind the falls. There's a cave of sorts hidden quite a ways back under it."

"Is there another exit?"

"Yes—one that takes us to higher ground and then down into the valley."

Sparrow's eyes narrowed. "I suggest we move. My instincts tell me we won't be alone much longer."

Esán's aunt made her way through the tumbled rocks to the near side of the waterfall, where flat, wet stones shimmered in the cool light. "It's slippery, so pay attention." She tested a foot-sized stone before scrambling from there onto a large, wet rock.

One Man helped Sparrow and prepared to follow. A night bird called, another answered. A chill shimmied down his spine. *We aren't alone.* He hurried after the two women. *Thankfully, they won't panic.* Catching up with them, he whispered a warning. "We've got company on the way."

"We heard." Sparrow stepped to the next rock.

Merrilea jumped across a small chasm and landed beside the plummeting falls. Spray splattered her clothing as she shrugged off her pack and rummaged inside. Withdrawing a lite-stick, she tucked it in her belt, hugged the pack to her chest, and maneuvered around an overhanging branch onto a narrow, moss-covered ledge. Her spine against the rocky cliff face, she sidestepped behind the curtain of water and vanished.

Sparrow clutched her backpack in front of her. Imitating Merrilea, she ducked around the branch, stepped onto the ledge, and made the crab-like journey.

A bird called. The answer was closer.

Too close. One Man scowled. A couple more steps and he would be behind the water. Ahead of him, Sparrow stopped. The word *'company'* flashed through his mind. A quick backward glance showed him nothing. His next step took him under the falls. Crashing water roared around him. "*Hurry.*" The urgent telepathic message plunged through his thoughts like a stone.

Sparrow felt, rather than saw, Merrilea disappear. She stopped. A hand on her arm guided her forward in the dark. Her foot found firm ground, and she knew she was no longer on the ledge.

Merrilea pitched her voice above the boom of the water. "The surface is smooth...but wet. Go on ahead. I'll help One Man."

Moving with care, Sparrow traversed a short distance over the slippery ground and stopped. *I wish Alli were here.* Her hand moved to the gold locket she wore hidden under her shirt. She had only been eighteen sun cycles when Allynae appeared at her mother's back door. It had been love at first sight. The locket, warm and smooth between her fingers, reminded her of that fateful summer. Inside it was the V-Chip that contained the record of their secret Joining. Fourteen sun cycles ago, unbeknownst to Allynae, their daughters had been born. Their time together as a family had been short-lived. Now they were scattered from Myrrh to Thera to DerTah.

Diffused light brushing the falls with momentary warmth snapped her out of her reverie. *The soldiers are at the falls.* Her pounding heart rivaled the roar of water.

One man slid his foot along the ledge. A hand gripped his arm and guided him onto a flat, solid surface and further back into the gloom.

More lights glittering beyond the falls sent Merrilea scrambling behind a large rock. Sparrow followed. One Man squinted, trying to see through the water.

"One Man, hurry!" He took one last look and slipped around the rock.

The women huddled together a short distance ahead with their backpacks in place. As he shouldered his pack, they began a steep climb up a narrow, pebble-strewn path. The sound of falling water covered their retreat.

"They haven't discovered anything yet, but they haven't given up either."

He shook his head, puzzled.

"It's me, Sparrow."

"Sparrow?"

"Yes...I hear you."

"Telepathy!"

"Of course."

"How did you—?"

"Later."

The women came to a halt.

He edged closer. "What's wrong?"

"I lost my lite-stick. Should I go back?" Merrilea's frightened whisper matched the intensity of the pounding water.

"You two keep moving. I'll see if I can find it." He started to backtrack.

"One Man, they found it. Come on!"

15
DerTah

Torgin trudged through the sand, sweat dripping down his face. For the hundredth time, he wiped a wide kcalo sleeve across his brow. Nichi led the way. Although she knew all about Shu Chenaro, her response to taking them there had been mixed. Wolloh, High DiMensioner od DerTah, was well respected and much feared by her people. Brie's promise to protect her convinced her to stay with them.

In response to their concern about Fire ConDra, she fell to her knees in front of Brie. 'Not attack ConDria.' They now trekked at a slow but steady pace over the sand, somewhat less encumbered by the fear of being a feast for a bird of fire...at least Brie, Ira, and Nichi were. He looked over his shoulder several times, certain they were being followed.

Another swipe of the already dry sleeve soaked up a drop of sweat from the end of his nose. *This journey is altogether uncomfortable.* Grit crunching between his teeth made him want to spit, an absolute 'no' in Idronatti.

Idronatti. He savored the word. *Would I want to be home right now? Probably not, but I can't help wondering what my parents are doing.*

Cramped muscles returned his thoughts to the heat-soaked desert. After stretching his calves, he sipped water from his canteen and stared at the dunes, rolling one after the other all the way to the horizon. *Does it ever end?* He gave the sand a savage kick. *I'm dirty and grumpy and too blistering hot.*

Ira glanced back, his eyes as blue as the Myrrhinian sky. A momentary tug at his memory made him frown. *Wish I had some kind of talent.* Sweat trickled down his back. *I am just too normal for words.*

Ira pushed his hood back and ran a hand through his short, unruly hair. Unhooking a canteen from his belt, he drank a ration of water and let it slide, tepid and wet, down his parched throat. Fera Finnero stretched endlessly ahead. After another small sip, he recapped the canteen and trudged after Brie and Nichi. Torgin trailed behind. Ira waved him forward. His friend's face, grim and sweaty, provided a hint of his mood.

Torgin trudged to his side. "I have developed a distinct dislike for deserts."

Ira grimaced. "Nichi says it's almost time to rest." He pulled his hood forward to shade his eyes and gazed up at the orange sky, where the sun hung white-hot and blazing just short of its zenith. "Mid-turning is the hottest time and the most dangerous for travelers. I won't mind a break." He twitched his hood and squinted at Torgin. "You look unhappy."

"What makes you say that? There's sand in my hair, in my shoes, in my mouth, and everywhere else; and I'm hot, thirsty, and tired. I'm definitely not happy. How much longer?"

"Can't say." He shrugged. "We'll get there when we get there."

"How do we even know Nichi knows the way?"

Torgin's petulant tone caught Brie's attention. She said something to Nichi, and they stopped. "What's up, Torgin?"

He scowled and pointed at Nichi. "How do we know she isn't lost?"

The Dansgirl smiled. "I not lost. Sand guides me. I know songs for dreaming tracks."

"What are dreaming tracks?" Ira's curiosity sparked in his blue eyes.

"Paths across the sand and sky created by desert spirits to guide all tribes."

"So you sing or what?"

"Songs tell signs to look for. I sing or say words to make me know where I am going." She touched her heart. "Desert knows Nichi."

Torgin's face blanked. "You are kidding, right?"

Nichi looked at Brie. "What kidding?"

"It means teasing or not telling the truth."

"I not lie. Desert lives. Watch." Nichi turned and began to walk. A faint trail appeared in the sand.

Torgin gaped. "That wasn't there before. How did you do that?"

"Yeah." Ira stared. "How'd you make the trail appear?"

"I whispered song. Desert show way." She looked at Brie. "You believe?"

"Of course, I believe you. I can sense your connection to the desert."

Nichi smiled. "You smart ConDria. We rest now. Sun is high. Too hot to travel."

"So we just sit here and roast?" Torgin rubbed a hand through his damp curls.

Nichi pulled a stick-like thing, not much longer than her palm, from a pouch at her waist. "Teska." She held it up and, with deft movements, unfolded it into a rod just over half her height. She chose a spot at the western base of a dune where the sun had not yet heated the desert floor and drove it into the sand. Then, she draped her kcalo over the rod and spread the flowing folds of fabric out to form a tent. She tipped her brown face up to the sun and then smiled at them. "Not much room, but we can be in shade."

"I wonder..." Ira shrugged off his pack and dug through its contents. "The Guardian packed these, and she knew we would be in the desert. Ah ha!" He held up a compact teska identical to Nichi's. "Thanks, Almiralyn."

Brie and Torgin followed his example. Soon, four makeshift tents lined the base of the dune.

"No lie on sand. Too hot. Many bugs." The Dansgirl arranged a section of the kcalo to serve as a sleeping mat. She then scooped sand onto the back edge of her tent, crawled under, curled up, and slept.

"Wow." Ira looked down at her. "She's out like a lite-stick."

Copying Nichi, Brie crawled into her tent. "It's only going to get hotter." Within a short time, she lay curled, kitten-like, in the small square of shade cast by her kcalo.

Ira gave her a quizzical smile. "You'd think you'd been here all your life, Brielle."

Brie yawned. "Get some sleep, Ira." Her eyes closed.

Wide-awake and sure he would remain so, he crawled under his kcalo, yawned, and glanced up at Torgin. "Are you just going to stand there, Torg?"

The tall boy shrugged and settled into his tent. His sand-speckled face grimaced with disgust. "I hate sand and heat and—" He flicked a small brown spider off his sleeping mat. "—bugs."

Ira laughed. "Get used to it, my friend. There seems to be no end to any of it...sand or bugs."

Torgin scowled. "I'll lie here, but I won't sleep."

Ira closed his eyes. A shadow creeping down the side of the dune woke him to Torgin's soft snores. A peek under the edge of his kcalo showed only the unending sand. A short distance away, Nichi sat beside Brie, speaking as much with her hands as her voice, her previous shyness gone. The urgency in Brie's body language chased away his last traces of sleepiness.

She glanced over. The message in her eyes made Ira scan the dunes with a sense of nervous expectation.

"Wake up, Torgin, and join us." Brie returned her attention to Nichi.

Her soft call added to his apprehension. He crawled from beneath his shelter, stood up, stretched, and, kneeling beside Torgin's tented-kcalo, gave him a gentle shake. An eye cracked open.

"So...you won't sleep, huh?" The expression he'd seen on Brie's face made him keep his voice low.

"I wasn't sleeping, Ira." He groaned and stretched his long body.

"Right." Ira smothered a laugh. "You always snore when you're awake."

Torgin ignored his teasing and scooted feet-first from his tent. "Brie looks upset."

"She does." Certain that Brie didn't have good news, Ira donned his kcalo, jammed the teska in his backpack, and joined her. "What's up?"

"Nichi says four desert rohes—a type of horse—head this way. They carry men. She's afraid." The worry soaking her reply made him even more uneasy.

Torgin joined them, yawning. "Men? What men?"

Ira sat down beside the Dansgirl. "Why are you afraid?"

Nichi sniffed the air and lifted fear-filled eyes to his. "Many dangers in desert. Fire ConDra not all. Tribes of Sebborr roam dunes. They very bad men. Take us away to be slaves."

"I cannot hear anything." Torgin shaded his eyes with his hand and scanned the dunes. "And I don't see anything either."

"Neither can I." Ira focused on Brie.

"Put hands on sand and shut eyes." Nichi instructed them with growing urgency.

Ira gasped. The hot sand trembled beneath his fingers. His gaze darted from Nichi to Brie.

Torgin knelt next to the Dansgirl. "I don't feel any... Ohhh." A startled expression flashed. "How far away are they?"

Nichi pressed her palms into the sand, forefingers and thumbs touching, then placed her ear in the created diamond and shut her eyes. "They not far." She sat up and blinked. "Maybe this many." She opened and closed the fingers of her right-hand one time. "No place to hide."

"Well, they can't know we're here." Ira glanced at his hands and then at Brie. "I guess they can. Now what?"

"ConDria knows what to do." Nichi's adoration for Brie filled her voice.

Ira raised his eyebrows. "Well, Brielle. *Does* the ConDria know what to do?"

Apprehension made Esán's palms sweat as he waited opposite Wolloh in the arena at Shu Chenaro. He squinted at the twisted side of the DiMensioner's face. The sightless eye held a gleam that made his heart race. *I don't know what to expect.* He calmed his anxiety. It would not do to show fear.

"So, young Esán, your time has come. Henceforth, you will never be the same. Today, you begin to challenge the very core of who you are. Your uncle tells me your mother was from Myrrh and your father from Thera. He is incorrect. That you carry the Seed of Carsilem belies that erroneous fact. So...we begin."

"What is the Seed of Car-si-lem?" Esán measured the word out in soft syllables.

Wolloh leaned his scarred cheek so close its rough surface touched his. "When I want you to speak, I will let you know. Until then—"

A fury-filled shriek interrupted him. "How did you do it? How in the name of SeDah did you destroy my Fire ConDra?" Sparks crackling around him, Gidtuss hurled his stocky body across the arena toward Esán. His abrupt halt short of his target reddened his face with confused rage. He slammed the air in front of him with a flattened palm. It hit an invisible wall. A dog-like snarl echoed around the arena. He stared at his hand and then at Esán. "You little—"

"Gidtuss." Wolloh's voice held an edge of danger not even the Dreela could ignore. "You are not welcome in this space. Leave immediately."

Esán admired the dramatic effect Wolloh achieved by the slow angling of his disfigured side to the Dreela.

Gidtuss glowered at the High DiMensioner. His nostrils flared as he stabbed the air with a chubby finger. "That boy destroyed a Fire ConDra and—" His words sputtered out like a gutted candle. Time held him motionless.

Stebben entered the arena and took the stunned Dreela by the arm. "Come along, Gidtuss." A nod to his master, and he escorted their intruder out the gate.

Wolloh turned his smooth cheek to Esán. The intelligent eye smoldered with unknown secrets. "So, Esán, who do you suppose killed the Fire ConDra? I know it wasn't you."

Esán remained quiet and curious. The intensity of his desire to search the red dunes for the culprit shook his carefully preserved calm. Dare he hope?

"You may speak."

"Sir, what will destroy a Fire ConDra?"

"Water."

"But..."

"There is water in the desert, but not where Fire ConDra roam. It is an interesting mystery, don't you think? Can you shed any light on it?"

"No, sir."

"Then let us get busy."

Esán did his best to listen to Wolloh's explanation of the theory of teleportation in its varying stages and levels. He performed each task the High DiMensioner proposed and surprised even himself when he arrived in a small, dark room he had never seen before. Reappearing in front of Wolloh, he did his best to contain his overflowing excitement.

"Where did you find yourself?" More secrets danced in Wolloh's good eye.

"In a small room I've never been in before."

"Remember it, Esán. It is well-hidden and only four trusted people, now five, know it exists." He turned his sightless eye to the gate where Nomed, TheLise, and a military officer waited. "We have more company, boy." He picked up his cane. A flick of his clawed hand brought the group forward. "So, Granier, did you enjoy your tour?"

"It was most instructive." The officer's eyes avoided Wolloh's face and looked a question at Esán.

Wolloh ignored his interest. "Mid-turning repast is about to be served. Shall we?" He gestured with deformed fingers toward the gate. Grasping Esán's arm with his good hand, he leaned heavily on his cane. The drag of his bad leg seemed exaggerated. Esán glimpsed a wicked smile on the High DiMensioner's face. At the gate, he postured his uninjured side to his guests. "Please go on ahead. I will be there soon."

Esán, detained by the grip on his arm, remained by his side.

"Your job, prior to meeting me later this afternoon, is to find out who destroyed Gidtuss' fire creature. And, boy, stay out of the Dreela's way. He is not overly bright and may forget he is in my home. Understood?"

"Yes, sir. But, sir, how..."

"Don't be obtuse, boy. You know how to discover the truth of it. Seval will come for you later. Be off with you."

Esán pressed his lips tight, stifled the emotions churning inside of him, and strode down the hall. Behind him, Wolloh's tap, step, drag died away. Teleporting to his empty room, he locked the door, checked that his wards were secure, and sank down on the bed. With eyes closed, he held out his hand and visualized the book on DerTah. His palm tingled. His eyes flew open. He held up the book and laughed. "I still can't believe I can do that." With his elbows on his thighs, he thumbed through the pages. "Now...who on DerTah killed that Fire ConDra?"

Much to Nomed's disgust, he and TheLise had spent the morning giving Granier a superficial tour of Shu Chenaro. The man's arrogance continued to annoy him. Only TheLise's hand on his arm made him keep his temper in check. His dislike of the man grew in proportion to the officer's inability to grasp the precariousness of his situation and in whose home he was a visitor.

Now, sitting at the luncheon table waiting for Wolloh, he observed TheLise from under half-closed eyelids. She tilted her head and smiled at the overbearing RewFaaran...that sultry smile that made men worship her. Granier's full lips remained uncommitted to a return smile, his expression stoic. A charming question...another smile. Nomed's anger grew stronger. *What's wrong with me?*

TheLise caught his eye. "*Control yourself, Seyes.*" Pursing pretty lips in a very feminine pout, she arched a well-shaped eyebrow and shifted sparkling, gray eyes back to their unwanted guest.

Nomed felt his scar pull the corner of his mouth into a sneer of astonishment. *Am I jealous?* Emotion propelled him to standing. "I'll discover what's keeping Wolloh." TheLise's taunting laughter made his scarred cheek pulse.

In the hallway, he stood undecided. Where would Wolloh and Esán be? Walking briskly to help dissipate his unwelcome emotions, he headed for his mentor's office. As he approached, an angry voice erupted from behind the closed door. A low and indiscernible reply brought it to a halt. The door flew open with a bang. Gidtuss stormed into the hall, his face as red as the sands of his desert home. Nomed's appearance seemed to exacerbate his anger.

"Your nephew destroyed one of my Fire ConDra." He glared back at his host. "Wolloh refuses to tell me how." Swinging his gaze back to Nomed, he clenched his teeth and growled. "I hold *you* responsible."

"And Esán did this when?" Nomed's disdainful sneer irritated the fuming Dreela even further.

"This morning. And don't sneer at me, Seyes. I take this seriously."

"You mean Esán, who was training with the High DiMensioner, quenched a Fire ConDra's fire in the middle of Fera Finnero? Or...are you accusing our host of using the boy to do this dastardly deed?" His sarcasm appeared lost on the furious man.

Unaware of the dangerous path he trod, Gidtuss cut his eyes at their host, who observed him from the doorway. "*He* made him do it."

"Calm yourself." The High DiMensioner's tone held a touch of sarcasm. "We will discover the culprit, and you may punish as you see fit." Appearing taller than usual and assuming the air of the magnanimous host, Wolloh stepped into the hallway. "I have a guest to entertain." He turned his back on the red-faced Dreela. "Come, Seyes, we have a game to play."

Gidtuss called after them. "You will pay, Seyes Nomed. Mark my words. And you too, Wolloh." He turned on his heels and marched away down the hall.

"What a very foolish man." Wolloh limped forward.

"Esán destroyed a ConDra?"

"No, he did not, but he will find out who did."

"And how will…"

"Seyes, luncheon is waiting."

Nomed pressed his lips together, but could not quell the questions chasing around and around in his mind.

16
Myrrh & Thera

Mira paced a restless path around her back garden. Without the insight provided by Elcaro's Eye, she didn't know what was happening with the children—or anyone else. She fingered a pebble she'd picked up in her wanderings and tossed it from hand to hand. *Where is Allynae? He should be here by now.*

Near the barn door, Paisley and Jordett spoke in solemn undertones. They were as impatient as she was for her brother's return. Her head cocked in a bird-like fashion, she strained to pick up a hint of his whereabouts. With a flip of her wrist, the pebble flew over the pond. Brushing the dirt from her hands, she stretched her height to its fullest and focused on the trail leading from the Terces Wood.

The percussive sound of galloping horses announced Allynae's appearance at the edge of the trees. Next to him rode a subdued but angry soldier.

Jordett strode to her side. "A spy?"

"Beyond a doubt." The apprehension haunting her now had a name.

The chaos of four horses arriving at the barn cut off any further discussion. A grim Allynae dismounted and handed Paisley the reins while Jordett helped the secured soldier off his mount.

"I'll take care of the horses." Paisley cast a look of concerned curiosity in the direction of the uniformed man.

"Thanks, Pais." Allynae joined Jordett and the soldier. "Where do you want our guest, Mira?"

"Take him to the kitchen. I'll join you shortly."

While she considered her next move, Allynae and Jordett escorted the man across the garden and into the cottage. Lorsedi's soldier and the taut anticipation exuded by the Terces Wood heightened her sense of impending doom. "The trouble's just beginning, Paisley. Keep your ears and eyes open. More soldiers are on the way."

"Can we stand against 'em, Mira?" A dark cloud of worry swirled around his towering height.

She smoothed gray hair back from her face. "We must find a way, my friend. Deal with the horses and then join us in the kitchen."

Midway across the garden, Mira shifted to Myrrh's Guardian, and hurried to the back door.

"I can leave you hog-tied, or you can behave and I'll release your hands. It's your choice." Allynae's voice as she entered the kitchen held a note of distrust.

All eyes focused in her direction.

The change from Mira's dumpy roundness and flyaway gray hair to Almiralyn's tall, slender body and white-blonde braid coiled into an elegant bun inspired a nod from her brother and an appreciative smile from Jordett. Summoning her full power, she traversed the short distance to the soldier and peered down at the awed surprise registering on his face. "You will behave, will you not? I think you know it would be foolhardy to try anything unwise."

Gathering his dropped jaw back into a stern-lined grimace, he offered a single nod.

"Please, Allynae." She indicated the ropes at the soldier's wrist with a gracious lift of her hand.

Allynae worked the knots loose, coiled the rope, and placed it near at hand on the tabletop. He remained on guard beside the chair.

With a warrior's inscrutable expression, Almiralyn motioned Jordett forward. "This is Major Jordett of the Peoples Progress Planners in Idronatti on the planet of Thera. He has some questions for you. I suggest you answer them without guile."

A stern military Jordett dissected the younger man's face with cold, impersonal eyes. "What is your name and rank?" Cordiality, like a kid glove, encased the command in his question.

The soldier folded his arms and glared. As Paisley's massive frame appeared on the back porch, his gaze flicked to the doorway.

Almiralyn gazed down at him. "There is no escape for you. Please answer the question."

"I have nothing to say." He dropped a hand to rest on the seat of his chair.

Jordett's next question cut through the strained atmosphere in the kitchen. "Why are you still in Myrrh?"

The soldier stiffened and slumped forward. In one fluid movement, his chair flew sideways into Allynae's knees, and he slammed into Jordett's chest. With cat-like instincts, he recovered his balance, dashed down the hall, and out the front door. Paisley launched himself into the back garden, while Jordett and Allynae hastened after the soldier.

Almiralyn surveyed her empty kitchen with a bemused smile. *It's been a long time since I've been engaged in battle. I should have seen that coming.* She shifted to her white and gold bird and soared out the open kitchen window in pursuit of Lorsedi's runaway soldier.

Behind the water fall at Demrach Gateway, Sparrow followed Merrilea up a narrow, rocky incline. Her heightened senses alerted her to the fast approach of seven RewFaaran and PPP soldiers. Merrilea's lost lite-stick, found by their leader, warned them someone hiked up the trail ahead of them. With increased urgency, she pressed forward, grateful for One Man's protective presence behind her.

Something snagged her pant leg. She swore under her breath and twisted to look over her shoulder. *"My foot's stuck."*

One Man knelt and slid his hands around her ankle. *"Your pant's hem is caught."* A muffled expletive behind him ricocheted up the tunnel. Whipping out his pocketknife, he cut the coarse fabric. *"Go!"*

Filled with a burning desire to put distance between herself and a fast approaching enemy, Sparrow scrambled forward. A bubble of panic burst in her throat. *If I'm captured, the ramifications for all concerned will be disastrous.* She swallowed her fear. *Panic will only get us caught.*

Not far ahead, she found Merrilea at a fork in the trail.

"They're almost here." Sparrow glanced back. "Hurry."

A panting One Man joined them. "I rolled a big rock across the path, but it won't keep them long." He peered into the darkness. "Which way?"

Merrilea jogged down the right-hand fork. At first, level and smooth, it became steeper and more irregular as it wound upward. She came to a standstill at a wall of tumbled rocks.

"I may have gotten us trapped." Misgiving filled her whispered words.

One Man stepped ahead of her. After testing the stability of a large stone, he began to climb. Lithe and confident, he hoisted himself up onto a boulder and reached down. Merrilea grasped his hand and clambered up beside him.

Sparrow whipped around. *"The soldiers have found the fork."*

"Sparrow." One Man's hand reached for hers.

She grasped it and leveraged her way onto the boulder. The hair on the back of her neck twitched. *"They're here."*

"Go! I'll catch up. Don't stop and don't look back."

Quiet as a cat, he jumped to the trail below.

"Go, Sparrow."

Forcing herself to move, she followed Merrilea up the rocky incline.

She had no choice but to leave him behind. If caught, she would be a weapon for the PPP and for the Largeen Joram.

Merrilea's hand grasped her arm. "Where's One Man?"

"Stop in the name of the PPP." The barked command provided the answer.

Merrilea shoved her up the precarious embankment. "We must get you out of here. One Man can take care of himself."

Above them, light filtered down through a jagged crack. Sparrow climbed silently toward it—grateful for Merrilea—scared for One Man on the trail below.

The RewFaaran soldier careened across Almiralyn's front yard and dashed for the trees, heading with unerring accuracy for the portal in the Terces Wood. Almiralyn flew above him, her eyes glued to his running form. Below her, Allynae and Paisley plunged through the underbrush in pursuit of their escaping prisoner. Gemlucky erupted from the barn with Jordett on his back and galloped down the trail that led to Demrach Gateway.

The soldier dodged onto a track leading through a thick stand of trees and picked up speed. If he maintained his pace and stayed out of Jordett's path, he would beat the men to the portal. Almiralyn streaked skyward. She would be waiting when he arrived.

Landing in the clearing, she shifted to Human and prepared to protect the gateway. The men raced in her direction, each pounding step sounding an alarm throughout the woods. The soldier burst into the open, and, sprinting for cover, plunged into the underbrush. Twigs and small branches snapped beneath his boots as he ran. Allynae and Paisley stopped, half-hidden in the trees, their footsteps no longer adding to the cacophony of running sounds. Gemlucky's hooves beating the ground like a drum thundered closer. As the stallion reached the clearing, Jordett reined him in and cast a questioning look in her direction. A thick silence settled over the forest.

An expletive in a foreign tongue exploded the quiet. Boots pounded back toward the clearing. Another bellowed howl elicited a snort from Gemlucky. Jordett dismounted and took up a protective stance by her side.

Paisley and Allynae started forward. Almiralyn shook her head and focused her attention in the direction of the soldier's last cry.

"What now?" Jordett questioned in a soft undertone.

"Wait."

The soldier's next cursed expletive was cut short as he stumbled through the underbrush.

A black panther broke free of the trees, its long, supple tail whipping the air. Golden eyes gleamed in the diffused light. Behind it, three more predatory cats herded the soldier, white-faced with alarm, into the clearing.

The lead panther shaped shifted. Almiralyn smiled. Voer the Pentharian, deep blue, half Human and half Reptilian, his thick braids cascading over his shoulder, bowed and extended a tattooed hand. Gold rings in his right eyebrow and ears glistened. His strange tattoos glowed.

In the way of his kind, she placed her right hand on his and her left hand on her heart. "Welcome, my dear friend."

He rested a long-fingered hand on his heart. "We come to serve the Guardian of Myrrh." The warmth of his smile faded into a warrior's seriousness. "This man is a spy?"

"He is indeed." Allynae strode from the woods with Paisley.

Color filled the clearing as Yuin, Stee, and Jeet shifted to greet their friends.

The soldier's face went blank. The odds had changed, and not in his favor.

Held firmly in Stee's grip, the soldier observed blue, green, red, and orange Pentharian shake hands with Human men and pay respectful homage to Myrrh's Guardian. He knew Pentharian by their reputation and shuddered. *I must get word to the Largeen Joram.*

Terror ripped through him as the creature holding his arm turned piercing gold eyes to stare into his.

At the foot of the rockslide, One Man faced a stern young officer. In the dim light of the lite-stick he held in his hand, a PPP insignia blazed on his uniform hat. Behind him in the gloom, more enemies loomed. With luck, they would think he was the only explorer.

"Who are you?" The officer looked him up and down.

"Name's Eno Namman." He kept his voice steady and his face blank. "Have I done something wrong?"

"What are you doing here?" The question contained the hint of a threat.

He allowed his mind to appear unprotected and answered. "I live in the valley and enjoy exploring the area. Today, I'm reliving younger times." From behind his reminiscent façade, he gazed around the space. "When I was a boy, I used to hide here with friends to avoid doing chores."

Another officer pushed his way forward. "Who is with you?"

One Man noted the RewFaaran uniform. He let his gaze travel to the PPP officer. "Are you no longer in charge?"

"Answer the question." The RewFaaran shoved his nose in his face.

"I'm alone." A mind probe tingled in his head. He smiled a benign and witless smile.

The RewFaaran officer glowered. "You and you take him back to camp. Secure him so he can't try anything stupid." A dangerous gleam lit his eye. He barked an order at the remaining four soldiers. "Explore this cave from end to end and make sure he's not lying."

One Man allowed himself to be led away from the rockslide—away from Sparrow and Merrilea.

The captured soldier, trussed to a hard wooden chair in a stall in Almiralyn's barn, could not take his eyes off the blue Pentharian. Ropes at his wrists and ankles cut into his flesh and kept him alert. Based on what he knew about the mercenaries of ReTaw Au Qa, he could not be certain that he could continue his stoic silence. *How much time before I die?*

"You know my race by reputation." Voer appeared relaxed and cordial. "Our venom is deadly. It can stun or kill in an instant. We choose not to kill in our true form, nor do we injure the innocent. "However, my friend, you are in Myrrh as a spy whose job is to bring harm to those I care about. Consider what I can do to remedy this—beginning with you. Answer my questions, and you will remain unscathed. Refuse and..."

The Pentharian shifted. The soldier held his breath as a panther circled his chair, inhaling his scent as though memorizing it for future reference. A damp black nose sniffed his face. The smell of rancid death spilled from its cavernous mouth—choking him—clogging his throat with sticky warmth. His muscles contracted to the point of trembling. A low growl pressed him against the chair. Bile rose like swill to fill his mouth. Again, the low growl rumbled deep in the muscled throat. It burst through bared teeth and exploded into a resounding roar. Huge fangs snapped the air close to his face. Golden eyes beneath heavy black lids locked onto his. A paw, claws unsheathed, came to rest on his chest. The golden eyes opened wider. Cloth ripping reverberated in his head. Razor-sharp claws grazed his exposed skin. A drop of warm blood left a trail down his chest. Silent screams collided in his brain... *"Just kill me!"*

Panther features grew hazy. Paws and claws melted into the sleek and slippery scales of a snake. Whispered hissing grew louder as its slimy length slid around his body in a tight coil. Air exploded from his lungs. The snake's triangular, blue-black head swung around in front of his face. Its forked tongue, red as fresh-let blood, flicked in and out, tasting the flesh of his cheeks. The head darted closer. His eyes cleaved it in two—two snakes hovering, hissing; two tongues flicking; four eyes boring straight through his mind.

The Pentharian's tattooed features flashed into being as close and as startling as the snake's. A shudder quaked through the soldier's body. Fighting to regain his self-discipline, he focused on Voer's black obsidian nose ring.

The Pentharian stepped back and stared down at him. "Do you understand?"

Another shudder rattled along his spine. "I can tell you nothing, or I will die a traitor. Better I die at your hand and be heralded as a hero."

Almiralyn appeared in the doorway.

Voer joined her. "He is well trained. I can break him, but torture is not my style. Nor do I believe it is yours."

Their exchange brought with it a sense of relief. He sat up straighter, aware that his death would come another time.

Myrrh's guardian crossed the stall. "What is your name and rank?"

"Grantese Tesilend." He responded without hesitating.

"Grantese Tesilend, since you refuse to give us information of your own free will, I will need to do a mind probe. If you fight or try to hide what I need, it will be painful. If you remain calm, you will only feel a slight tingling." She placed her hands on either side of his head.

Rigid and resistant, he tried to pull away.

Strong tattooed hands clamped him to the chair. Pain stabbed through his brain. Unbidden, tears spilled down his cheeks.

"Don't fight me, Grantese." The Guardian's voice, firm but gentle, penetrated his wall of fear. "You cannot resist for long. But if you try, you will suffer more pain than you ever imagined possible. And it will linger unabated for many turnings."

Her fingers pressed again into his temples. His brain writhed like a trapped cobra. He gasped. Darkness swallowed him.

17

Der Tah

B rie sat in the late afternoon shade, slipping down the side of the dune, and cast her senses outwards. Four men drew nearer with each chron-click. *How can we avoid discovery?* Her agile mind flipped through various plans, rejecting each as impractical or just plain unworkable. *I wish Esán were here so we could disappear.* Heightened awareness informed her the Sebborr were over halfway up the far side of the dune. *What will slow them down?* Her eyes widened.

A silhouetted rider appeared atop the ridge of red sand. Sharp, dark eyes bored into hers.

Ira's fingers dug into her shoulder. "What now?"

Nichook fell to her knees. "Please, ConDria. Please, not let them catch us."

A second rider materialized, dark and threatening against the orange sky. Torgin groaned and pressed closer.

The Sebborr, their mounts sidestepping in a diagonal down the red DerTahan dune, advanced toward them.

Nichi knew only fear. Stories of the Sebborr swirled through her mind. They raped. They murdered. Their prisoners were rarely seen again. Those few who escaped told heartrending stories of their tortured lives as Sebborr slaves. Behind her, she heard the bellow of a rohes. Falling to her knees at Brie's feet, she prayed to the ancient spirits of her people, asking them to support and inspire the ConDria.

In the quiet of his room at Shu Chenaro, Esán studied the map of Fera Finnero and then read the book's description. Impatience nagged at him. Something he could not quite grasp made him uneasy. *Who killed Gidtuss' Fire ConDra? I'm sure Wolloh already knows, so I don't understand why he wants me to discover it on my own.*

A commotion in the hall scattered his thoughts. A knock on his door made him grimace. *Why can't people just let me be?* With one quick movement, he shoved the book and maps under his bed, then marched to the door and yanked it open. Seval stood poised to repeat his knock.

"What now?" Esán placed fisted hands on his hips and glared.

Seval dropped his hand and cringed as though he'd hit him. "I came to warn you Wolloh's important guest arrived in the city of Inev on the Plains of DoOlb yesterday. He will soon be here with his escort."

Esán forced himself to appear relaxed. "Who is this guest, Seval? Do you know?"

The boy paled. His mouth opened as though he were about to speak, then clapped shut. Confusion and fear flitted over his face. "I can't remember. I thought I...I'm sorry, master...Esán. So sorry..." Sagging under the weight of whatever tormented his spirit, he pivoted and scurried away.

Esán leaned against the closed door. *I must remember to be gentle. I have no desire to add to his trauma.* This admonition carried him back to his bed. *What happened to Seval? Why is he fine one moment and terrified the next?*

The servant's problems faded as Esán smoothed the map out on the bed and let his eidetic memory absorb every detail of the Desert of Fera Finnero. Overflowing with its beauty and its variety, he whispered the question upmost in his mind. "Who destroyed a Fire ConDra? Who?" His breath caught in his throat. *What the—?* The beat of his heart echoed through his ear canal, threatening to destroy his ability to concentrate. He disciplined his mind and refocused.

By the Fathers of Thera!

Nomed sipped a glass of sweet wine and listened to the conversation at the luncheon table in Wolloh's private dining room. The excellent mid-repast calmed his agitation. Across from him, the officer who had interrupted their lives appeared to be mesmerized by TheLise. Her voice, hypnotic and sensual, wrapped around him, unraveling his defenses one by one.

An amused smile tugged at Wolloh's distorted mouth as he observed his guests. His eye, however, shone cold and calculating in the warm light cast by a single chandelier.

Stebben appeared at the door.

Wolloh pushed his chair back from the table. "Please excuse me. I will return in due course."

Nomed noted the drag of his crippled leg was barely a hindrance as he moved, unhurried, to join his Major Domo. TheLise caught his eye before turning back to Granier, who couldn't seem to decide whether to watch Wolloh disappear down the hall or to keep his eyes on the beautiful Dreelas.

Nomed relaxed and let his inner mind focus on his mentor while appearing to be present in the dining room. He tensed. Speculation replaced his benign thoughts. *Wolloh's important guest has arrived on DerTah. Soon I will meet one of the most powerful men in the Inner Universe.* More speculation... *Why this sudden, unplanned visit to DerTah and to Wolloh?*

"Seyes, come back from wherever you are and join us." Although TheLise smiled, her gold-flecked eyes held a question and a reprimand.

He returned her smile, his gaze shifting to Granier. "And how long do you plan to remain in DerTah?"

Suspicion replaced the enamored expression on the officer's face. "As long as it takes." An implied threat laced his tone.

Nomed kept his smile in place, ignoring TheLise's warning glance. "As long as it takes to do what?"

Granier lunged to his feet. "I think it is time I rejoin my men." Back ramrod straight, he marched from the room. His boots pounded a distinct and threatening rhythm on the tiled floor.

TheLise's slate-gray eyes caressed his face. "All my work ruined, Seyes." Her smile teased him as she glided to the double doors at the opposite end of the room. "Will you ever learn to be patient?"

He relaxed back in his chair, enjoying the supple sway of her body and his heightened response to her beauty.

She adjusted the blind and peeked out at the bright desert sun. "I miss the sound of the sea and the feel of the damp wind on my face." The blind clattered back into place. Unhurried, she retraced her steps and looked down at him.

He noted with a connoisseur's appreciation how the dark waves of her hair capped her well-shaped head and emphasized her large, luminous eyes. "How long do you think you'll stay at Shu Chenaro?"

"I'm most eager to return to Trinuge, but..." The arch of her eyebrows spoke volumes. "And you, my dearest Seyes, how long will you stay? Esán's training will take some time."

"A good question. One I don't have an answer for." His gaze roamed the length of the hall. "Do you think Wolloh will return?"

TheLise ran a finger across his shoulders as she passed behind him on her way to the door. "I think he has much to do. Come. The other Dreelum plot and plan. Shall we see what we can discover?"

He laughed and joined her. "They are rather obvious, aren't they?"

As they approached Wolloh's office, Stebben appeared and held open the door. "He would like you to join him."

"Thank you, Stebben." TheLise sailed past him.

"So much for plots and plans," Nomed murmured and followed.

Conscious of Ira and Torgin beside her and Nichi kneeling in front of her, Brie watched two more Sebborr top the dune and follow their comrades' diagonal trek down its red sandy side.

The rohes, a cross between the camels of Old Earth that she'd read about in Almiralyn's library and a Marwari horse, ambled in a controlled skid done the steep angle of the dune. Long-necked and limber-legged, they moved with an awkward grace she found mesmerizing. As they drew closer, she could discern extra-long lashes screening their slightly bulbous eyes. Wide nostrils at the end of an elongated horse-like face snorted, filling the air with a noisy, nasal chorus. Their long, narrow tails swished back and forth. She found them delightful and would have smiled had the situation been different.

Her gaze switched to the Sebborr, who wore kcalos the color of night. Secured by a woven band, the draped folds of their shoulder-length black headdresses left only their eyes visible—dark eyes that seemed to hold her and her friends prisoner already.

Each carried a sword, at least one knife in his belt, and another tucked in the top of a boot. What could she do against such savage fighters? *If only I understood how I became a Water ConDria before.*

The lead Sebborr arrived at the base of the dune. His eyes raked across her face before moving on to Ira and Torgin. Unaware of or simply uninterested in Nichi, he reined in his rohes and waited, relaxed and menacing, while his comrades formed a tight circle around them.

Ira's grip on her shoulder tightened. Torgin's fear scented the air. At her feet, Nichook pulled her kcalo over her head and curled into a small ball of trembling terror.

Brie kept her eyes fastened on the Sebborr leader. No fear showed on her face, although the careful probing of his thoughts made her heart creep into her throat. Her gaze steady and her expression bland, she created a call for help in her mind. With the force of a hurricane, she blew it out over the dunes. Sand whirling into eddies lifted into the air. Wind whipped it higher and sent it swirling up to surround them. Another silent message brought an audible answer. The shriek of a Fire ConDra shook the dunes.

Torgin groaned but stayed at her side. Ira's steady hand on her shoulder sent a wave of confidence through her. Nichi's frightened eyes peeked from beneath her kcalo, widened at the sight of the Sebborr, and disappeared.

Rohes scrambled, stomping and snorting their terror, while their riders fought for control. Only the Sebborr leader's mount remained unaffected. Atop its back, the man's menacing gaze fastened onto hers. Throwing his headdress back from his face, he drew his sword. Silver and flashing in the sunlight, it hovered above her head.

She scrutinized his features—the brown, pockmarked skin; the cruel line of his mouth; the narrow, hooked nose; and the dark, merciless eyes that snapped at her from beneath a bridge of shaggy brows. Nothing in his rugged countenance suggested generosity or kindness, only a deep and ruthless intent. Relief shot through her when a shrill shriek, announcing the imminent arrival of the Fire ConDra, allowed her to look away.

Wings stretched wide, it sailed above the horizon and cast a sudden shadow over the top of a neighboring dune. With another shriek, it swooped toward them.

The Sebborr leader tensed. The tapered point of his sword came to rest against her throat. Its sharp tip cut the top tie on her kcalo. Desert-hot blood oozed from a skin-deep zigzag that ran from the 'V' at the base of her throat to the place on her sternum, where her heart thumped against the bone.

He slammed the sword back into its scabbard, and, leaning out of his saddle, he grabbed her chin between hard, calloused fingers. "You wear my mark, ConDria. You belong to me." A malicious laugh scorched her face. Wheeling his rohes, he summoned his comrades. "Fly from the fire of death!" They galloped away over the dunes—kcalos whipping in the wind and sand flying in their wake.

Intense relief cooled her cheeks and dulled the sting from the shallow cut on her chest. Above her, the ConDra beat its fiery wings against the desert heat. Sparks igniting around it like fireworks, it followed the Sebborr until they vanished amid the rolling, red dunes. A wide arc carried it back in their direction.

The Dansgirl lifted trust-filled eyes to her face.

Brie fumbled for the blue Remembering Stone and prayed she had not brought death to them all.

18

Myrrh & Thera

Merrilea resettled her pack. Above her, the tumbled chaos of precariously balanced boulders formed a risky ladder to safety. *One misstep...* She forced negative thoughts from her mind and peered up at the narrow, jagged entrance. *At least it gives us a bit of light.* Her fingers scurried over the broken edge of a large, flat stone in search of a secure handhold. Its surface, less moist and mossy than lower down, told her they now climbed above the falls. Verifying that it would support her weight, she wedged her toe in a narrow crevice and followed Sparrow's unerring ascent, glad for her company and her courage.

With a jolt, she realized Sparrow's dim figure had come to a halt. Dark eyes flashed from her face to the entrance. She pointed at a spot beside her. Merrilea scrambled onto the large boulder. Again, Sparrow's eyes grabbed hers and darted up the rockslide.

A flash of light near the crack-like entrance made her duck lower.

Sparrow went rigid beside her. Murmuring voices, more flashing lights... Merrilea pulled her to kneeling as small stones bounced their way downward.

"We have to hide, Sparrow." She searched the dim rockiness next to them and discovered a gap between two larger boulders.

More light and more voices—a body blocked the cave entrance. Booted feet appeared. A dull thud indicated the arrival of a soldier above them.

Merrilea edged her way closer to the opening and peered into the gap. Another dull thud warned her more soldiers joined the hunt. With no other option presenting itself, she pulled Sparrow after her into the crevice.

At the soldiers' camp, One Man bided his time. The ropes at his wrists hung limp, ready to be sloughed off at the right moment. He waited. Time stretched and bent back on itself in his mind.

An image of Tianna, his life-mate and Esán's mother, formed. His heart throbbed with the love and the longing that filled him. An illness only curable on their home planet of Tao Spirian had forced her to leave soon after the birth of their son. Before she left, she had made him promise to leave Esán on Thera with Merrilea, her blood-bonded Myrrhinian sister, and to find a secluded place on Myrrh to await the quickening of his Seed of Carsilem. His memories of those first weeks in Myrrh still brought an ache of blurred emotions. Thanks to Almiralyn, he had survived.

The time he spent as a hermit in Timreh Pass in the Dojanack Mountains had allowed the power of his Tao Spirian birth gift to mature unhindered and unnoticed. Wind in the trees and whispering grasses had soothed his soul and salved his sorrow. Fifteen sun cycles passed. The Seed's Time of Quickening was complete. His restlessness began, and his destiny called. The Unfolding on Myrrh summoned him back to the world of men. Until the completion of its cycle, he would fight to protect the last vestige of Old Earth. Only then would he be free to join Tianna on the distant planet of their fathers.

Rough voices outside the tent alerted him to the return of his captors.

He dropped his chin to his chest. Soft snores, like a lullaby, floated into the night.

Almiralyn left Grantese Tesilend in Voer's care and hurried from the barn. Shafts of sunlight shot through the trees of the Terces Wood, splashing patches of light in random fashion over tree trunks and branches and diffusing, for the moment, the deep shadows of late afternoon. Love for Myrrh, its forests and plains, its spectacular Intersect, and its mountains and caverns, washed over her in an overwhelming rush. The parallel between the setting sun and The Unfolding of Myrrh was not lost on her. She could only hope, like the sun, Myrrh would rise to fullness again.

Tesilend's rigidly organized mind had provided some important information, but not as much as she had hoped. It went against her instincts of respect for individual privacy to use a telepathic search, but he had given her no choice. *What shall I do with him? I can't hold a prisoner for long.*

Yuin held the back door open for her. As always, she found herself awed by the Pentharian's alien beauty. Jordett, Paisley, and Allynae, deep in conversation with Jeet and Stee, turned to greet her, their faces filled with questions.

Allynae spoke first. "What did you discover?"

She joined them at the table. "We'll have company sooner than we expected. Once Tranwar Nagry returned to RewFaar, he realized we'd tricked him. Tesilend arrived back here in time to see Merrilea, Sparrow, and One Man enter the gateway. He knows they're headed for Singtil, but not why. He relayed a message to the Largeen Joram."

"Lorsedi may assume why." Jordett frowned. "Does Tesilend know who Sparrow is?"

"Not as far as I could tell. His training gave him powerful defenses against a telepathic probe, so it's hard to know for certain what he knows and what he doesn't."

Allynae stroked the bristled beginning of his new mustache. "There are RewFaaran soldiers in Thera and The Borderlands, and I'm betting they're also in SumnerTyme, since the PPP saw Sparrow and Merrilea in the mountains near there. They may even be in—"

Almiralyn motioned for quiet. Conversation ceased. Her mind filled with flickering pictures of One Man, Merrilea, and Sparrow. Expectant faces watched her massage the smooth, satiny grain of the tabletop with the tip of her fingers. She inhaled, preparing herself for Allynae's response. "They've captured One Man."

Allynae made a strangled sound. "Sparrow and Merrilea?"

"The soldiers have not discovered them, Alli."

Allynae stood and leaned over the table. "How do you know?"

"One Man carries the Seed of Carsilem. He let me know."

"The Seed of Carsilem!" Stee let out a soft whistle. "What a rare and wonderful gift. So our hermit is from Tao Spirian." He looked at Allynae. "You need not worry about Sparrow if she is with One Man. The Seed of Carsilem has greater power than a DiMensioner."

"Except he's a prisoner, and that leaves only Merrilea to protect her." Allynae smacked the tabletop with his palm. "I'm going to Demrach Canyon, Mira. Don't think for a moment you can keep me here."

Jordett sat back in his chair and spoke with unassuming quiet. "Both the PPP and RewFaaran soldiers are guarding the gateway. Are you ready to be captured and tortured? They won't even bother to take you to the Five Towers, Allynae. They will extract information—you know everything they need to know to find your family—and when your life serves no further purpose, they will kill you. Lorsedi will use your death to weaken those you love. The game we're playing is serious. The soldiers we fight against are the best in the Inner Universe."

Allynae's nails raked the wood grain as he sank into his chair.

Almiralyn understood his desperation and his fear. "One Man will not be a prisoner for long, Alli. Also, I have sent Karrew to make sure Sparrow and Merrilea are safe until One Man can rejoin them."

"By the Fathers, Mira, why didn't you say so?" Relief tempered his anger.

Jordett rested his forearms on the tabletop. "My biggest concern, Almiralyn, is how they'll get back here when they've found Gerolyn. The gateways in Demrach Canyon and Idronatti are well guarded."

"They won't need to use either Idronatti's or the canyon's gateway. I created a temporary one from Standin's farm to Nemttachenn. But they will need the sacred Key or CheeTrann won't let them through." Almiralyn kept her voice steady.

Stee tugged an emerald green braid. "It seems it would be best for Pentharian to scout out the situation and deliver the Key. We can go unseen. If need be, we can assist without revealing ourselves."

"I agree." Voer entered the kitchen and placed a hand on Allynae's shoulder. "You, my friend, are too important to send on this mission." He turned to Almiralyn. "Stee and I will go."

"Grantese Tesilend?" Allynae raised a brow.

Paisley hoisted his large body out of his chair. "I'll guard him well."

"Thank you, Pais." Allynae turned back to his sister, who continued to set her plan in place.

"Yuin and Jeet, please accompany Voer and Stee to the gateway and remain there on guard. If the soldiers compromise the portal in the clearing, Voer, the Key to reach the tower is Mite Skil Wren."

"How will we know if it's compromised?" The blue Pentharian leader's gold eyes did not leave her face.

"Jeet will wait at the waterfall to warn you." She addressed Jordett and Allynae." Please travel to the Dojanacks. Take the Intersect and inform Yookotay of what has occurred. He will need to prepare a hideaway for Sparrow and Gerolyn."

"That will leave you here alone." Allynae's expression verged on rebellion.

"Paisley and I will manage. Keep your trip to Meos short. If things develop here, you'd better come back via Nemttachenn. Don't return to the cottage unless one of us gives you the word. Now go. All of you. We have very little time."

The room emptied. Almiralyn crossed to the window. Four vultures flew over the woods. Allynae and Jordett headed to the barn to advise Paisley of the plans and to begin their journey through the Intersect.

A silence filled with unanswered questions and uncertainty settled over the kitchen. Out of its depths came a message so clear it sent her hurrying up the stairs to her sanctuary. Elcaro's Eye, emptied of the water that enhanced its power, held her motionless in the doorway. Light from the window made the carved statue's sapphire eyes glisten. Almiralyn strode forward and gripped the bowl. At the bottom, the tip of the Vesen Crystal caught the sunlight and sent tiny rainbows skating over the fountain's alabaster sides. "I cannot leave you here to become a weapon in the hands of Lorsedi."

Warrior instincts sent her to the window. *Soldiers are on their way. I can feel it.* Returning to the fountain, she moved her hand in a circle above it.

"Elcaro, the all-seeing Eye,
Must be hidden from those who try
To steal it for their evil plan
And use it for their brigands' band.

Smaller and smaller, let it be,
So the crystal within stays free,
Until a time when it's made clear
Elcaro's Eye may return here."

One, two, three sharp claps ricocheted around the room. Elcaro shuddered. In the blink of an eye, it shrunk to the size of her palm. Almiralyn picked it up and pressed it to her heart. Tucking it a way in a pouch at her waist, she hurried down the stairs.

On Thera, the narrow, dark space between the two rocks where Sparrow crouched next to Merrilea felt just big enough to hide them both. Above, on the cave's ledge, she imagined soldiers preparing for their descent down the steep rockslide. Her heart hammered against her breastbone. A shadowed form emerged from the dimness in front of the entrance to their hiding place. Near panic pressed her deeper into the enclosure.

Whoosh... Something touched her cheek, eliciting an almost silent cry. Merrilea squeezed her knee. Sparrow could imagine her soundless "sshhh." Another soft whoosh made her scoot further back in the crevice. Gasping, she tumbled backwards down what she discovered was a short drop. Cool, moist air rustled through her hair. Surprised and somewhat fearful, she scrambled to her feet.

Merrilea projected a tremulous whisper into the darkness. "Sparrow? Where are you? Are you alright?"

Sparrow turned toward the sound. "I'm fine. Careful, there's a small drop." She listened to Merrilea's tentative approach as she shrugged off her backpack and set it on the ground. Kneeling, she began a search for her lite-stick.

A surprised yelp on the rockslide made her look up. Rocks smashing together and a smothered cry presented the clear picture of a fall. Boulders grated against each other. The rockslide shifted. A resounding crunch left Sparrow immobilized, her mind screaming...*The gap is closed. We're trapped!* Her fingers closed around the lite-stick. She pulled it out and thought it on.

Merrilea perched at the edge of the drop off, her face pale in the soft light. "The gap closed. Now what?"

Sparrow offered a hand. Drip. Drop. Drip. The sound of water hitting a wet surface matched the beat of her heart against her ribs as Merrilea clambered down beside her. Surprised wonder replaced her friend's fear of the previous moment. Holding the lite-stick higher, Sparrow pivoted to follow her rapt gaze.

"Oh my." She stared, transfixed.

At the base of a rock-strewn slope, where level ground reached away into nothingness, stalactites and stalagmites of various sizes and colors glinted in the soft light. A pockmarked pattern of pools created over time by the drip, drop, drip of water were scattered throughout. Light vanished—absorbed rather than reflected—on their inky surfaces.

Swoosh. Whish. Whish.

Merrilea gave a startled gasp as a dark shape landed on her shoulder. Whipping her head around, she could only stare.

"Karrew? Is that you?" Sparrow offered her arm.

The big, black raven hopped down from Merrilea's shoulder and cawed, "It is."

Merrilea gave a nervous laugh. "You scared me to death. Next time, warn me you're preparing to land on my shoulder."

"We're so glad you're here." Sparrow blew out a relieved breath. "How did you find us?"

Ignoring her question, Karrew cocked his elegant head to listen. "We need to go."

A sound akin to the rustling of autumn leaves moved in a wave across the cavern. Goose bumps raised the hair on the back of Sparrow's neck. "What the..." She grabbed her backpack and slung it around her shoulders. "Where are we?"

"This isn't Vascorrie, is it?" The trepidation in Merrilea's voice did nothing to allay her fear.

"Quiet." The raven's terse tone reflected his alarm. "Extinguish the light and crouch as low as you can. Stay close together."

Sparrow dropped to her knee, her hand resting on Merrilea's backpack. The lite-stick flicked out, pitching them into abrupt and complete blackness.

Karrew's great wings wafted through the air above their heads. "No matter what happens, don't move."

Sparrow's hearing, made more acute by the lack of light, picked out Merrilea's rapid breathing, the steady drip of water, wings pressing against air...not just Karrew's. Wings, too many to count, beat against the cool moistness of the cavern and circled above her head. "What in the name—"

"Don't even breathe." Merrilea pulled her lower, her whisper hoarse with fear.

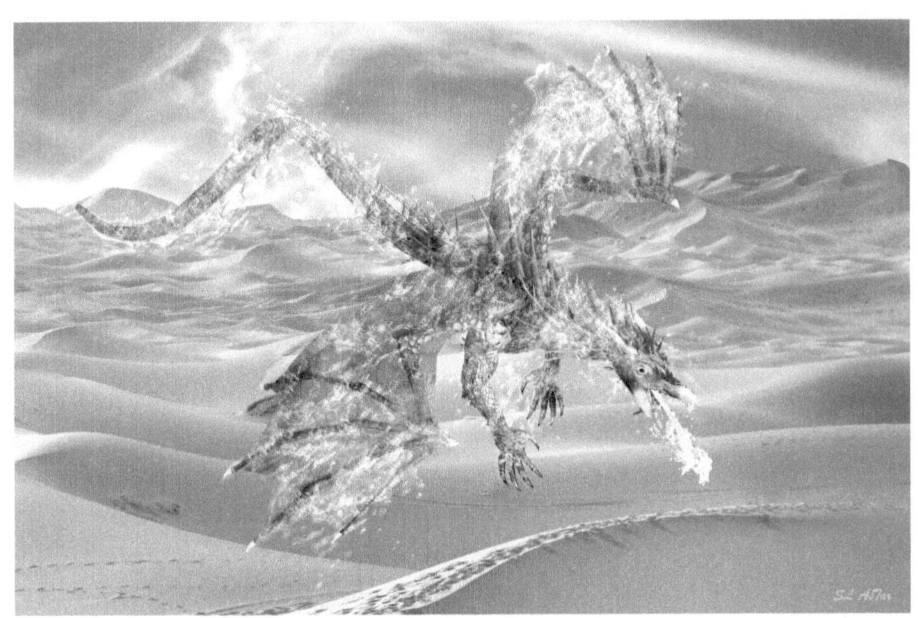

19
DerTah

Torgin, half blinded by wing-whipped sand, could barely make out the blazing form of the Fire ConDra, where it hovered above them. Through squinting eyes, he tried to bring it into focus. The massive breadth of its wings pulsed, whisking the sand into a swirling cyclone. Fire-gold eyes reeled him into its hypnotic gaze. More fascinated than scared, he watched the vicious beak smoke like a volcano ready to erupt. It shrieked and plunged toward him, its fiery tongue licking the air. Sand stung his cheeks. His eyes watered in defense against the light blazing around him. All he wanted—home—safe, comfortable, boring home.

Brie stepped away from him. A high, sustained sound flowed from her throat and burst into a cascade of quivering notes. Her body faded until it glistened translucent, then vanished altogether as the Water Condria lifted into the air. He gasped and grabbed Ira's arm.

"ConDria rises." Her hood thrown back and eyes never leaving Brie's shifted form, Nichi rose.

Soaring up to meet her foe, the Water ConDria's silver body soaked up the red of the desert. The two ConDra met and danced a wild dance...a quick step...a swooping and soaring grapevine that wove its way across the late afternoon sky.

Torgin's ear tuned to the sung chorus that passed between the two magnificent creatures. One song filled with watery changes of key melded with the other steady burn of notes. "What are they doing?"

"Why ConDria not destroy it?" Nichi cowered beneath her kcalo hood.

Ira shaded his eyes with a hand. "Just watch."

Desert light changed as the sun followed its cycled-course, withdrawing reflected color from the Water ConDria's form as it went. Phosphorescent silver and fire-orange soared side-by-side in a wide circle. Wing stroke for wing stroke, they matched each other in another intricate pattern of loops and arcs.

Torgin watched the breathtaking *pas de deux* with rapt attention. When they dropped out of sight behind a dune, he felt an acute sense of loss. "Where are they?"

Nichi pointed at the top of the dune, where two back-lit figures appeared in silhouette.

Torgin stared, rubbed his eyes, and stared again.

Ira gave a low laugh. "Well, I'll be..."

Together, the figures descended the dune, taking on substance and form as they exited the sun's lingering light. Brie's face glistened where sparkling stars of water clung to her fair skin. Beside her walked a Pentharian, tall and proud, his eyes glued to Torgin.

"Yaro! Yaro, is it you?" He ran forward to meet his heart brother. In the ways of ReTaw Au Qa, they touched palms, then foreheads, and then each other's heart. "*How* did you know we needed you?"

"I came to discover you, my brother, and to help rescue Esán. Rumors suggest a ConDria has risen in the desert of Fera Finnero." He bowed to Brie and smiled at Ira. "I have also been told the tale of Ira."

Torgin almost laughed at Dansgirl's expression. Then he remembered seeing Yaro for the first time in the Dojanack Mountains on Myrrh. "This is my heart brother, Nichi. He is a Pentharian from the planet of ReTaw Au

Qa, and he is our friend. Yaro, this is Nichook, Atrilaasu of the Desert od DerTah and our guide."

Yaro bowed his head and smiled at the wide-eyed girl. "Thank you for helping my friends, Nichook." He grew serious. "I have much to share. Our danger is greater than you know."

Torgin's excitement at seeing Yaro backslid into dread. *I want to rescue Esán and return to Myrrh. Why do I think this will be harder than it sounds?*

The results of his search of DerTah's desert made Esán's heart sing one moment and plunge into the depths of despair the next. *The twins and Torgin travel this way. My rescue is their goal. Wolloh also knows, and he wanted me to know. Why? I sure could use Corvus' advice.*

Repeated knocking interrupted his racing thoughts. Seval pushed the door ajar and peered at him. "Master Wolloh would like you to join him." His eyes, bright with excitement, noted Esán's red robes lying on the bed. "Please wear your robes. I will help." He scurried across the room.

Esán scowled and scrambled into his Tyro costume.

"*He's* here." Seval tied the gold sash with a flourish. "He's here, and *you* are to meet him."

"So, the mystery guest has arrived. Who is it?" Esán felt a rush of expectation.

Seval's face dropped. Excitement melted away in a blank, lost look.

Esán touched his arm. "It's okay, Seval. I'll know soon enough, and then I can tell you. Take me to Master Wolloh."

Seval seemed even more confused. "You must go to the inner garden."

"Aren't you supposed to come with me?"

The boy shook his head. A tear slid down his cheek. He flicked it away and stared at his wet fingers. Blood drained from his face. "I must go. Corvus says to be careful. Give nothing away." He opened the door and motioned Esán through.

"Wait, Seval, when did you see Corvus?"

"Later." He sidled past him and padded away toward the back of the large, ranch house.

Esán watched him go with his usual mixed feelings. *It's time to find out who this mysterious guest is.* He masked his mind. *I wish I had discovered my friends after this meeting. No one else must know they're here.* He squared his shoulders and strode down the hall.

Two uniformed soldiers stood guard at the double doors leading to the inner garden. He approached them with some misgiving.

His uncle, who waited beyond the door, talking with Baroh and several official-looking men, caught his eye. Nomed excused himself, spoke with a guard, and then beckoned him forward. "Hello, nephew. You look charming in your robes." The hazel eyes held a knowing gleam.

"Wolloh ordered me to wear them." Esán wrestled with his growing annoyance.

Nomed laughed. "We all dance to his tune, you know. Shall we find a spot where you can take stock of the situation? Being forearmed is always an excellent strategy." He led the way to a quiet, shaded corner of the garden. "I'll leave you here. Take time to observe the guests and then join me." Nomed waded through the crowd to the Dreelas TheLise's side.

Alone, at least for the moment, Esán surveyed the area. Body language spoke volumes. The posturing of everyone in the garden magnified the undercurrent of tension. A serious game enacted by a serious group of players held everyone in check. He let his gaze wander. Dreelum, positioned strategically around the garden, intermingled with dignitaries from DerTah and elsewhere. Esán noted several women. Soldiers guarded all entrances.

Wolloh's sightless eye found his corner. "Ah, my dear Tyro, join us." He spoke from the midst of a group gathered near the garden's center. "I have a special guest for you to meet."

Esán wove his way through the crowd, his eyes fixed on the back of a tall man who wore power like most men wear their own skin. Authority hung, chiseled and sharp, around him. Everything—the way he moved his head, the wave of his hand, the carriage of his solid frame—suggested complete control. The set of his shoulders implied a man used to getting his own way. He inclined his head as though listening. His laugh, hard-edged but full of charm, made several others in the room cast a furtive look in his direction.

Aha...Wolloh's guest. Finally, I'll find out who it is.

The man tensed, then turned. Esán fought to catch his breath as dark, penetrating eyes fastened on his face. Red hair flashed in the light. A trap ready to snap shut touched his mind. Sheer will power kept him still.

Wolloh's voice at his side broke the spell. "Let me introduce you to my apprentice, Tyro Esán Efre." The High DiMensioner's good hand drew him forward. "Esán, this is the Largeen Joram of the planet of RewFaar and..." He paused, Esán felt sure, for dramatic effect. "...the grandfather of your friends, Brielle and Arienh AsTar."

Esán's defenses slammed into place around him as the tingle of a telepathic probe began for the second time. His eyes flashed with anger, but he held his ground.

"My apprentice does not appreciate having his mind probed, Lorsedi. Am I correct, Esán?" Wolloh's complacent drawl almost made Esán smile.

He looked at the twins' grandfather. "It is rude and uncalled for. If you have a question, sir, you only have to ask."

Aware of the hush engulfing the garden, he kept his gaze fixed on the Largeen Joram's face. Wolloh's hand still rested on his arm, the fingers relaxed but firm. The tick of an old-fashioned clock marked the slowed passage of time.

A sound filled with discovery broke the tension as the Largeen Joram gave a wholehearted laugh of delight. "Well, boy, Wolloh told me you were full of surprises. It appears we will need to sit down and talk. I am most curious about my granddaughters. For now, let us call a truce and enjoy this gathering." A smile warmed his dark eyes and dispersed the cool calculation that lurked there.

"As you wish, sir." Esán turned to greet TheLise, whom Nomed had brought to his side. "Dreelas, it is a pleasure to see you." He noted the warning in her smile.

"And you, young Tyro. Please introduce me to your new acquaintance." She bathed the twins' grandfather in the fullness of her electrifying charm.

Wolloh took charge, allowing Esán to fade from the foreground of the man's attention. "Dreelas TheLise of the Sea of Trinuge, may I present the Largeen Joram of RewFaar? Lorsedi...TheLise."

The abundance of red hair flared as the leader of RewFaar clicked his heels together in a military salute and bowed over TheLise's outstretched hand. "Tinpaca Granier told me of your great charm and your beauty. He did not do you justice."

A smile, both cool and enticing, accompanied her response. "It is a pleasure to meet you, Lorsedi. Welcome to DerTah."

"And this is Seyes Nomed, Esán's uncle." Wolloh's misshapen face caught the light as he introduced his former apprentice.

Esán observed the twins' grandfather change tack as he switched his focus to Nomed. His fair face, with its sprinkling of freckles, became more intense. Ruggedly handsome features morphed from charm to conjecture. Taller than Nomed, he gazed down at him with interest. "I understand you have spent time on Myrrh."

Nomed shook his offered hand. "I have. Are you looking to travel there?"

"Perhaps." The noncommittal reply masked an interest expressed more fully in his next question. "I believe you have met my granddaughters?"

Esán made his way toward the door. Lorsedi's power, a vibrant and subtle threat to his defenses, followed him. Holding his thoughts in tight control, he conversed with Baroh and paid his respects to Omudi. Behind him, fragments of conversation held him captive. He glanced over his shoulder.

"How did you find the twins?" Nomed's question seemed casual enough, but Esán knew better.

The Largeen Joram let his eyes roam the room. They lingered on his face. Speculation curved the stern mouth into a smile before he returned his attention to Nomed. "What do you know of Elcaro's Eye?"

Esán felt Lorsedi's focus shift like a release from bondage. Relief almost made his knees weak. He nodded to the RewFaaran soldier stationed at the door and was about to slip out of the inner garden into the late afternoon heat when a languid voice brought him up short.

"Ah, there you are, Father."

Esán pivoted, letting his gaze scan the room until it came to rest on a tall man who had joined the group around Lorsedi. His hawkish face bore a slight resemblance to the Largeen Joram. Any similarity ended there. Military cut black hair and a deep tan made blue eyes, as cold as the ice on a mountain stream, appear even colder. A well-trimmed mustache curved over a tight-lipped mouth, down his cheeks where his laugh lines might have been, and connected to a square-cut, black beard, which ended below his chin. The total effect gave his face a sinister and intimidating appearance. Esán glanced around the room. No one else seemed to notice the hatred roiling around the man. He crept closer.

Lorsedi's eyes narrowed. He acknowledged the man with a nod. "This is my son, Nissasa Rattori."

With a cool bow, Nissasa acknowledged Wolloh. Holding TheLise's hand to his lips, he gave her a lascivious smile, which the Dreelas did not receive with her usual charm. Finally, he shook Nomed's hand. "Was that your nephew? The one everybody is so excited about?"

Esán did not stay to hear Nomed's reply. Instead, he masked his thoughts and made his way unobtrusively from the inner garden. *Where can I go to think? Not my room. Not the library.* He kept his conscious mind focused on the drop of the sun behind a dune and the gradual diffusion of light. *Ahhh.*

In a heartbeat, he arrived in the small, dark room he had discovered during his training that morning. An oil lamp softened the edges of a rough-hewn table, where a pitcher of water and a small glass glowed in its warmth.

He pulled out the wooden chair and sat down. His mind, unbound, ran a speculative race through recent events. *The Largeen Joram wants very much to find the twins.* Elbows on the table, chin resting in his hands, he stared at the flame in the lamp. *Do they want to be found?* His instincts shouted no. He reviewed his time at the party. *Nissasa Rattori was the man with Gidtuss, the man who wants to kidnap me.* Clarity hit like a blast of cold air. Lorsedi was a threat to the twins, but Nissasa was the greater menace. Danger bristled around him—danger for anyone who got in his way and extreme danger for himself and for Ari and Brie. That certainty left him breathless. *I wish I knew more about RewFaar. I wish I knew why the Largeen Joram is interested in Elcaro's Eye. More than anything, I wish I knew Nissasa Rattori's game.*

His hand traced the crown of his head. The prickle of short hair on his palm arrested the movement. He still looked gaunt and far too thin, but he felt healthy. Since his arrival on DerTah, the disease that had tormented his body seemed in remission—at least for now.

He sat back in the chair and tapped his lips with a finger. *What's my next step? I sure wish Corvus were here.* A long sigh lost itself in the shadowy interior of the room. He reached for the pitcher of water. Beneath his hovering hand, an envelope materialized on the aged wood of the tabletop. He traced the four hand-printed letters...**ESÁN**. Curious but cautious, he picked it up and opened the flap. Inside, he discovered a single folded sheet of parchment. Pulling it free, he opened it and read... **WARN YOUR FRIENDS. TAKE SEVAL. DISAPPEAR.** After he read it a second time, it shredded into tiny pieces and vanished.

Who do you suppose—? Breathing in the darkness behind him made him jump to his feet. A hand clapped over his mouth.

20
Myrrh & Thera

In Vascorrie, cackled ravings and murderous mutterings chased Karrew higher as he led the winged-ones away from Sparrow and Merrilea. *I have no desire to be dinner for a batch of Primavers.* These tiny, humanesque creatures with bat wings and a rat's tail and ears had razor-sharp teeth that could devour a man's flesh in no time. He didn't think about how fast they could feed on a raven.

Behind a stout stalactite, he landed on a ledge, where darkness formed a curtain of protection around him. The Primavers began a gradual resettling. When sounds in the cavern had returned to the drip of mineral-filled water, he flew in silence to where Sparrow and Merrilea crouched in the dark.

A muffled caw warned them of his return. "I'm here a short distance in front of you. If you want to escape alive, don't use the lite-stick." He hopped closer. "Follow my exact path—no deviations. These pools contain their own set of nightmares."

"Karrew, I can't see you." Panic tinged Merrilea's breathless whisper.

Sparrow murmured in her ear. "I can see him, Merri. Just hold on to my pack." She sidled in front of her friend and prepared to follow Almiralyn's raven.

Relieved Sparrow had discovered her ability to see him against the black of the cavern, Karrew hopped between pools. Keeping them on track was vital. One false step...

"Karrew, can you hear me? It's Sparrow."

He peered back at her with one shiny eye. *"So you've discovered your telepathic voice, too."*

"How long?"

"If we don't keep moving—too long." He could hear the distant murmuring of Primavers preparing to take flight.

"I hear it, too. Hurry!"

Karrew picked up his pace. Open air, their only salvation, seemed too far away.

A splash...a muffled oath...

"Sparrow, what was that?"

"Merrilea stumbled. She's fine."

"Did she disturb a pool?"

"Yes."

Karrew ruffled his feathers instead of a groan. *"What rotten luck."*

"Karrew?"

"Move away from that pool." He led them around a group of smaller stalagmites to an open space where he hoped they would remain safe. *"I don't want to leave you, but I need to scout ahead."*

"Something's following us." Merrilea's whisper shook. "It sounds like it's sniffing."

"Got any food in your pack? Smelly cheese or something with a strong odor?"

"Mira packed goat cheese. Will that do?" Sparrow fumbled around in Merrilea's pack. "Found it."

"Scatter it on the ground and follow me." He half flew, half hopped in front of them for a good distance and stopped. "Let us hope the cheese obscures your scent."

"Karrew, the primavers are on the move."

"So, my dear, are the tarwish, and I'm not sure which is worse."

At the RewFaarans' camp, One Man pretended to sleep as a soldier entered the tent. A tentative hand shook him. He yawned and opened his eyes.

Inexperience clung to the young man like a cloud. He cleared his throat, began to speak, and cleared it again. "I-I am..." He coughed. "You will answer my questions." The lack of authority in his bluster made him blush.

Sitting upright in his chair, One Man raised dulled eyes to his face. "I took a walk through my memories and look where it got me. There's nothing to tell." He made himself seem small and tired.

The soldier rubbed his chin. "How many were with you?"

A crooked, almost dreamy smile played across One Man's face. "Just me, son, me and my past."

An officer marched into the tent. "What have you learned?" He addressed his underling but glared at One Man.

The young soldier snapped to attention. "Only that he says he was alone, sir."

The officer studied One Man's placid countenance.

"The boy's right, sir." One Man babbled away. "I can only tell what is. 'Specially, I can't tell you what's..."

A hard stare shut him up. He painted a harried expression across his face and slumped against the chair.

The officer strode to the door. "Don't let him out of your sight." He glared, then exited.

The young soldier stared after him. When he turned back, relief made his features appear even younger and more inexperienced.

One Man remained non-threatening. "You must be pretty good, since he trusts ya to watch me." His voice held just the right degree of awe.

The soldier bristled with self-importance and sat down on a chair inside the tent flap. "Don't try anything." He gave him a fierce look and stifled a yawn.

"Since I'm trussed to this chair, I imagine I won't go far." One Man dropped his chin to his chest. Through half-closed eyes, he watched the soldier slip into sleep, jerk awake, and finally settle into a comfortable, rhythmic snore.

Sloughing off the ropes at his wrists, he made quick work of the knots at his ankles. Silent as a cat, he padded to the soldier's side and placed hands on his temples. The boy's breathing slowed. Deep sleep carried him into oblivion.

With a quick mind search of the camp, One Man located its headquarters. A thought propelled him through the dusk-lit trees to a large tent, where he listened to the three-way conversation taking place inside.

"All the men are back. They found nothing to prove he's lying."

A younger voice interjected. "I found this fabric caught between a couple of rocks. It doesn't appear to belong to the prisoner."

One Man's quick mind assessed his options. If his luck held, they wouldn't check, at least not immediately. He continued to listen.

"Did you find anything else to suggest a companion?"

"No, sir. Nothing. The tunnel was empty, and we found no one on or near the rockslide."

A murmured conversation ended in the dismissal of the younger man.

After he departed, the voices continued. "Although he may not be who we're looking for, let's keep him under guard. Tell your men to stay alert. It never pays to fall into disfavor with the Largeen Joram."

One Man felt a faint mind touch. "*Sparrow?*"

"*Primavers. Help!*" The urgent appeal faded in and out.

One Man dissolved into shadow and slipped through the trees. He knew of Vascorrie, the den of the Primavers. He hoped he could reach it in time.

Paisley rested his arms on top of the wooden gate. At the back of the stall, the RewFaaran Grantese sat tied to a chair. He seemed unafraid. Bloodshot eyes were the only sign he had experienced stress of any kind.

Paisley's curiosity got the better of him. "What's RewFaar like?"

"It is a planet of great beauty. Our mountains are wilder and more desolate than your Dojanacks. There are many rivers and lakes. Rainforests cover large portions of the planet's lower hemisphere, while open plains stretch across the north. It is much bigger than Thera, with less ocean and more land mass."

"I always lived in Myrrh." Paisley twisted the end of his mustache around his finger. "Traveling from dimension to dimension isn't somethin' I'd care to try."

Tesilend shrugged. "You get used to it."

A peaceful silence settled between them. Paisley broke it. "Can I get ya some water?"

"I could use a drink."

"I'll get you a bite to eat as well." Paisley tested the knots at his ankles and wrists before exiting the stall. Not wanting to leave his post for longer than necessary, he strode through the barn into the garden. Gooseflesh prickling up the back of his neck made him stop to survey the area. Unsatisfied and even more uneasy, he scanned the blue sky. A vulture reached the apex of a high arc and dropped toward Almiralyn's cottage. Its silent speed bespoke trouble.

Almiralyn crossed the garden to stand at his side. "Well, our moment of respite is over, my friend. I imagine we have company."

Yuin materialized as soon as his vulture talons touched the ground. "A platoon of infantry soldiers came through the portal. They're on foot and traveling this way. They mean business, Almiralyn. You can't stay here."

"I'm ready to leave. I have one thing to do with Grantese Tesilend before we go. And we need to release the animals."

"How much time do we have?" Paisley glanced beyond the Pentharian. His lip gave a nervous twitch.

"Moving at their current pace, they should be here in less than a quarter turn of the chronometer." Yuin sniffed the air." We must be gone when they arrive, so we need to hurry."

Almiralyn led the way toward the barn. "Yuin, check on the Grantese. We'll be with you shortly. Come on, Paisley. Let's get the animals moving."

Paisley followed. *How will I escape? Can't shift shape...can't outrun 'em...* He pushed his fear to the back of his mind. It wouldn't help him face what was to come.

At the barn door, Almiralyn stopped. With a hand shielding her eyes, she searched the thick border of trees at the edge of the Terces Wood. Unusual stillness heightened her sense of urgency. Nothing moved. No birds sang. Even the trees stood tall and silent.

Where are Lorsedi's men? How can I keep everyone safe? A glance at Paisley's worried face sent her at a brisk walk to Gemlucky's stall. Strength and intelligence gleamed in the big stallion's eyes. She patted his side. "You, my friend, must take care of the other horses."

His ears twisting in her direction, he snorted.

She ran a hand along his muscled neck. "Take them into the foothills and hide. Avoid the soldiers in the woods at all costs. I'll call you when it is safe to return."

He nuzzled her shoulder before trotting into the paddock where Paisley had assembled the other horses and the pony, Tam.

"Open the gate, Paisley."

The big man swung it wide.

Gemlucky whinnied and galloped along the edge of the Terces Wood. Passing the main trail into the forest, he led his charges down a little used track that would take them away from the Demrach Gateway.

Satisfied Gemlucky would keep them out of harm's way, she hurried back to Grantese Tesilend's stall. "Yuin, please wait outside. Keep your eyes open. We'll be right with you." She nodded to Paisley. "I'll need your help."

The Grantese watched them with wary eyes.

"You will soon rejoin your fellow soldiers." She halted in front of him. I must perform a mental block."

Rigid with resistance, he jammed his feet against the ground. A quick push propelled his chair backward. It crashed against the wall.

"Paisley, please help Grantese Tesilend hold still." She spoke with quiet authority. "This won't take long. If you fight me, it will be painful. I suggest you remain calm."

With Paisley negating the RewFaaran's ability to pull away, Almiralyn placed her hands on the man's temples and blocked only those memories pertaining to the Pentharian. Lorsedi must not know of their presence in Myrrh. They must remain her secret weapon.

Finally, she whispered a quiet word and removed her hands. The RewFaaran's eyes closed and a series of small snores mingled with barn dust and hay. She looked down at her prisoner. "You are well trained, Grantese Tesilend. May your battles be great ones and your sun cycles long."

She looked up at her loyal friend and protector. "Untie him and lay him on the ground. His comrades will wake him when they arrive."

She exited the stall and walked into the sunlight, Paisley, a shadow behind her.

Yuin emerged from the gloomy interior of the barn. "What are your plans?"

"Fly back to the gateway. Send Jeet through with a warning to return to Nemttachenn. You stay on guard. I'll send word as soon as everyone is safe in the tower."

"What about you and Paisley?"

"We'll take the Intersect. Paisley can wait at the tower for Jordy and Allynae while I warn the Wood Tiffs and the Nyti to stay hidden." She smiled at the ruby Pentharian. "Thank you, Yuin."

Yuin returned her smile. "It is an honor to fight by your side." He bowed and shifted. Vulture wings carried him over the Terces Wood, high above the advancing enemy.

21
Der Tah

After greeting Yaro, Ira stepped apart from his friends to catch his breath. Unable to shake the nagging feeling that he was forgetting something important, he looked down at his body, felt the weight and the breadth of it, and ran a hand through his short, cropped hair. He closed eyes as blue as Almiralyn's. When he opened them, Yaro studied him from across the way. As though the Pentharian understood his thoughts, he blinked. The strange pupils in the gold eyes dilated and narrowed. The corner of his red mouth turned up momentarily.

Ira studied the shape of his hands and frowned. Their sturdy squareness seemed strange to him, but he wasn't sure why. He shoved them in his pockets and forced himself to focus on Brie as she explained to Yaro what had occurred since their arrival on Der Tah.

The Pentharian's tattooed face showed no emotion as he listened. Ira marveled at his alien beauty. Intricate tattoos covering his face, torso, and arms depicted his clan and lineage. Gold and silver loops ran from the tip of his ears to his jeweled lobes, signifying initiations and successes in battle. A carved stone ring piercing the cartilage of his nose symbolized his passage from Penthary to full Pentharian, from adolescence to adulthood. His eyes traveled from Yaro's mass of long braids down his humanesque torso to his scaled legs and tail, the tip of which twitched as Brie talked. Ira pulled his hands from his pockets, gave them a speculative stare, and looked back at Yaro. *Does it feel strange to shift form? Brie did it. Maybe I should ask her what it's like to be a ConDria.*

Yaro seemed to sense his confusion. The Pentharian's slight nod and brief, thin-lipped smile made Ira feel less alone.

Brie, her expressive face displaying a mix of emotions, listened to Yaro. RewFaaran soldiers gathered in Myrrh's Terces Wood. The Pentharian's comrades had traveled to Myrrh to assist Almiralyn.

Lorsedi's soldiers march in Myrrh. The drop of the sun below the horizon compounded the cold that crept into Ira's body. He tugged his kcalo closer around his broad shoulders and glanced at Torgin, who watched his heart brother with admiration and relief. Yaro made the world seem less frightening for the boy from Domlenah Uptown Blue in the city of Idronatti. Standing apart and timid, Nichi tried not to stare. Ira understood. He would never forget his first meeting with a Pentharian.

He studied Brie's face. *She has changed so much I hardly recognize her.* And the ConDria—he found it hard to believe Brie could shape shift a water creature that sang with a voice like ringing crystals. He tugged at a short curl. *Why am I so confused? I can shift shape, can't I?* Uncertainty chased his thoughts back to the start of this strange adventure.

Introducing Torgin to Myrrh on his fourteenth Sun Cycle Celebration had seemed like a good idea. Mira had been delighted to see them. They had met Esán and headed into the Terces Wood with the pony Tam and Buster, Mira's dog. Ira's throat tightened. Buster had died trying to protect them. He couldn't shake his guilt at not being able to save him. And then—the adventure had really begun.

Now here they were in the middle of a red desert on the planet of DerTah. Life twisted and tramped him through one escapade after the other. He looked at the distant horizon. *Wonder what's next?*

In the small hidden room at Shu Chenaro, Esán's assailant whispered next to his ear, "Don't make a sound. Nod if you understand."

Esán moved his head in response. The hand pressed over his mouth relaxed. Its owner stepped into the light.

Stebben put a finger to his lips and pointed at the floor. Esán moved to stand beside him. Wolloh's Major Domo reached up and pressed his thumb into an almost invisible indentation just above his eye level. The wall rotated inwards, carrying them with it. When they arrived on the far side, it closed soundlessly behind them.

Stebben produced a lite-stick that drove the darkness away and illuminated a narrow passage. "You can speak now."

"How did you know where to find me?" Esán regarded the man with a touch of suspicion.

Stebben's lips pursed and then shaped a barely perceptible smile. "Master Wolloh sent me to await you. He realized you wouldn't return to your room.

The Major Domo produced a change of clothing and waited silently while he slipped out of his red robes and into jeans and a T-shirt. When he'd dressed, Stebben exchanged his Tyro costume for a reddish cloak and the small leather book. "It is urgent that you disappear and take Seval with you."

Esán slipped into the kcalo, tied the ties, and wrapped the long cords as though he had always worn one. The book on DerTah went into his pants pocket. "Where do I find Seval?"

"He will be in the arena." The Major Domo gave him a second kcalo. "You understand he is a troubled boy?"

"I do. Can you tell me why?"

Stebben shook his head. "Master Wolloh says you must discover the answer. He requested I share two things: the boy is in grave danger and the twins can help." Reaching behind him, he grabbed two backpacks and handed them to Esán. "You'll need these. Go. The party will break up soon."

A faint noise on the other side of the wall brought Stebben's finger again to his lips. "Go." He mouthed.

Esán shut his eyes, pictured the arena, and arrived in a deep shadow opposite the gate. Squinting through the dimness, he searched for Seval.

Curled around himself, the boy formed a forlorn heap near the entrance. In the space of an instant, Esán arrived beside him.

"Seval?" He touched the still figure.

The boy came to his feet in one startled movement. "Why am I here?" The uneasy question quivered around them.

"We have to leave, Seval. I need you to trust me. Do you understand?"

"Leave? Where? Why?"

"I'm uncertain why you need to leave, but I know why I do. Wolloh told me to take you with me. Here, put this on." He handed Seval the kcalo and helped him tie it in place. "I have friends who are in the desert near here. Take my hands. We'll go to meet them." Confusion brought color to Seval's face and a stutter to his words. "I-I-I c-can't l-l-leave here, Esán. I h-h-have t-to…" A blank look wiped all expression from his face.

Esán took the boy's hands. "Shut your eyes. I promise everything will be fine."

Footsteps pounding in their direction made Seval's hands clutch harder.

Sure, I wish I had more time to discover where the twins are. Esán squeezed Seval's icy fingers as the gate flew open.

Brie's index finger traced the zigzagged cut on her chest as she listened to Yaro describe what he'd learned of the events in Myrrh. The salt from her fingertip made it burn. The Sebborr's face flashed into memory.

"Brielle, they hurt you." Yaro's concern drew her back to the present—the desert, her companions, the burning.

Ira pulled Efillaeh from its scabbard. "Here, let me help."

Brie held the jagged edges of her shirt aside. The knife's silver tip touched the shallow cut. The redness paled, leaving a faint white scar. Ira looked perplexed. "Why didn't it disappear?"

Nichi's brow furrowed. "When Sebborr leader leaves his mark, it is for life. ConDria must bond with him or she die. No other man dares claim her. If another man touches her…" She shivered.

Ira's hands flew to his hips. His expression darkened. "Brie's not bonding with that horrid man."

"We have more important things to worry about than Sebborr." Brie shivered. "Night is almost upon us." She looked at the Dansgirl. "Do we make camp, or do we travel further?"

Nichi played with the rope at her waist. Indecision held her tongue quiet. The subject of her concern looked down at her. Understanding dawned in his alien eyes. Gathering her courage, she made herself answer the ConDria's question. "We must travel to the camp of my people. But..." Words stuck in her throat. Blood flushed her cheeks with color.

The Pentharian named Yaro knelt in front of her. "You do not know me, Nichook. I am strange to you. Perhaps you fear I may be a danger to your people?" She nodded, her eyes never leaving his face.

"What can I do to help you know I mean you no harm?"

Brie placed a hand on the strange creature's shoulder. "I swear to you, Nichook, that Yaro is our friend. I pledge my life forfeit if he should prove untrue."

Torgin stepped to his other side. "Me, too."

"We all swear." Ira moved next to Brie.

Nichi gripped the medicine bag at her throat and bowed her head. Her inner knowing spoke in her heart. "I honor your trust and your truth, ConDria." She tucked the medicine bag beneath her kcalo. "Yaro, you not come to camp as Pentharian, or my people act in fear."

"I can shift to another form. What will not frighten your people?"

"Be desert fox?"

As quick as the snap of a spark, a rust-red gold fox sat in his place—its tail wrapped around its haunches, its golden eyes bright and alert.

Astonishment erased Nichi's last vestige of fear. "You good, Yaro. Now we go to WoNadahem Mardree."

"And who is WoNadahem Mardree?" Ira snapped his mouth shut.

Nichi scowled at the brown-haired boy. "She Atrilaasu Oracle and head of tribe. Come, we hurry. Be there before the sun goes."

22

Myrrh & Thera

Karrew sped on dark wings toward the entrance to Vascorrie, searching out a safe path for Merrilea and Sparrow. Their danger escalated with each passing moment. Fresh air lifted him in easy flight and drew him up into the night. Landing on a bare branch, he tipped his head to watch the silhouette of a blue heron cross the path of the moon, Norio. An urgent need to turn his attentions elsewhere drove him to focus on the job he must complete here. He soared upward.

"Karrew! They've taken flight." Sparrow's urgent message sent him swooping back into the Primavers' lair.

Hundreds of tiny, rustling wings made his nerves shudder. Time was of the essence.

Sparrow led Merrilea between tarwish infested pools. Tarwish... She only knew of them through the folklore of the Central Mountains—water wraiths that hungered for Human brides and launched into feeding frenzies when Human men appeared on the scene. Between them and the Primavers, she and Merrilea would be lucky to make it out of the cavern alive.

A soggy sound not far behind them tempted her to grab Merrilea's hand and run. Instead, the whir of miniature wings overhead sent them both into a low crouch. She wrapped an arm around her friend's trembling shoulders.

"They're gathering. We have to move." Merrilea inhaled panicked gulps of air.

Sparrow's mind searched the cavern. *"Karrew, where are you? We need you."*

The wafting wha wha of raven wings alerted them to his arrival. "I'm here. This way." He half-flew, half-hopped ahead of them through the dreadful dark of Vascorrie.

Sparrow, her gaze fastened on his blue-black feathers, guided Merrilea around one pool after another. The sudden scent of night filled her nostrils. *We're almost there.* Heady with relief, she stumbled.

Merrilea's hand steadied her, then froze on her arm. "Don't even breathe." Her teeth chattered, crushing the words.

The sound of something breaking the water's surface, the wheeze of an exhaled breath, and the stench of decay made Sparrow's heart leap into her throat. Pupilless, iridescent yellow-green eyes gleaming in the darkness, stared directly into hers.

A chorus of cackling laughter exploded over their heads. Merrilea grabbed her hand. "We can't escape." Her horrified whisper evaporated into sheer terror.

Sparrow hugged her friend to her. The pounding of their hearts melded, vibrating like a timpani. Thick, mucousy moisture trailed down her arm. She felt Merrilea flinch away from something and held her tighter. A slimy tongue licked her cheek. Tiny hands plucked at her hair. Primaver fingers yanked it in all directions. The volume of their crazy cackling increased as they pulled it harder and tighter. Her scalp burned in protest. Tears filled her eyes. Dread overwhelmed her as something wrapped her in its waterlogged length. *Alli, I love you. Ari, Brie...*

More tiny wings, too many to count—more cold wetness that clung to her body—more sucking, licking sogginess brought her to the point of screaming. Merrilea sagged against her, unconscious. Sparrow held her, sobbing.

A sudden gust of fresh air fanned her cheeks. Bright white light burst the darkness into silver edged pieces. Primavers howled, their razor-sharp teeth gleaming, and clung to her hair and clothing and backpack. With a sucking sound, a snakelike creature detached itself from her body and, with several others, splashed into pools and vanished.

The light shimmered into the translucent form of a man. From his open mouth, golden sparks spewed forth and whirled through the air. They sought out Primavers and sent them screaming into the black depths of Vascorrie.

Sparrow felt the weight of Karrew on her shoulder. A relieved sob rocked her body. The light dimmed, and One Man strode to her side. Scooping Merrilea up in his arms, he led the way down the path. Too dazed to think, she stumbled after him. Her knees gave way. Strong arms held her upright, lifted her. She knew no more.

When she opened her eyes, moonlight softened the darkness. Stars sprinkled the night sky like tiny pinpoints of hope. Fresh forest air washed her lungs clean and cooled her feverish cheeks. Merrilea and One Man knelt at her side. "I—"

"*Shhh. Soldiers fill the woods.*" One Man's face, half hidden in shadow, looked worn. Merrilea's blonde hair hung in sodden tendrils around her face.

"*How?*" Sparrow looked around for the man who had carried her from the cavern.

"*Later. Can you stand?*" His arm slid around her shoulder and leveraged her to sitting.

Ignoring the throb in her head and the aches in every part of her body, she struggled to her feet. At first, her legs refused to support her weight and then they steadied.

One Man helped Merrilea to stand. He placed a hand on either side of her face and whispered soft words. Color rushed to her cheeks. He turned to Sparrow and repeated his actions. Her fatigue fled. She knew she could walk.

One Man dropped his hands. His eyes glazed over, then cleared. "They've discovered I'm gone." His whisper shifted a curl on her forehead.

"Karrew?" Sparrow asked.

"Gone." One Man guided them through the underbrush.

Sparrow glanced over her shoulder. No sign of their passing marred the landscape. Her curiosity about Esán's father quickened. He was more than he seemed, but she was sure he had not carried her from Vascorrie. So, if not him, who?

Merrilea stiffened beside her. "What was that?"

One Man laid a finger on his lips.

Almiralyn surveyed her cottage, her garden, and her barn. She would not allow the soldiers of RewFaar to denigrate them. The Pentharian had disappeared over the Terces Wood. It was time for her to take Paisley and do the same.

"Paisley, wait by the barn." When he reached his post, she faced her cottage. Lifting her outstretched hands, she whispered an ancient spell.

"Time is illusion—something but not.
It holds things together. I untie the knot.
Delude those who trespass, a trick of the sight.
The spell holds unbroken 'til I make it right."

She clapped her hands. Her beautiful cottage flickered in the late summer light and crumbled into an antediluvian ruin where ivy and moss crept over a heap of stones, housing a myriad of insects. The garden disappeared into forest trees and underbrush. Large spiders spun webs that glistened with sticky spittle in the waning sunlight. She walked to where a nonplused Paisley stood shaking his head.

"How d'ya do that?" Puzzlement made his expression solemn. "Can ya bring it back?"

"When the time is right, it will return to normal. This way, Paisley, we must be gone. The soldiers draw near." She led him through the barn to the tack room and, rummaging behind a stack of leather goods, she pulled out a pair of saddlebags. "Take these. They will supply you with everything you require to remain hidden at Nemttachenn for as long as need be."

Paisley draped them over his shoulder while she pulled the lever behind the rack of bridles. The door to the Intersect gaped open.

"What about the barn? You leavin' it standin'?"

She gave him a tight smile. "No. I'll join you on the platform."

The cottage and surrounding gardens had been her home for many sun cycles. It tore at her heart to leave, knowing the soldiers would soon overrun her acreage. She sighed, waved a hand, and whispered her spell. A quick glance assured her the Grantese slept soundly amidst the settling rubble. Clambering down the steep steps, she sighed. At least the RewFaaran soldiers would not ransack her cottage and barn, nor would they find Elcaro's Eye. Only the memory of what had been would greet them. And then what?

Allynae and Jordett had journeyed to the Dojanack Caverns and now waited in a small meeting chamber in Meos for the DeoNyte ReDael. Yookotay and his son, Zugo, had helped to save Myrrh from the DiMensioner. Surely, they would come to their aid in this fresh crisis.

Glad for the flames blazing in the fire pit, Allynae soaked up its warmth. More ancient than Old Earth, the DeoNytes had lived in deep caverns within the Dojanack Mountain range for time untold. Until Seyes Nomed's attempt to destroy Myrrh, they had rarely ventured into the outside world. Even then, only Yookotay and Zugo and the DeoNyte healer, Owae, and her granddaughter, Elae, had dared to leave the caverns.

A male DeoNyte of medium height and build entered the chamber. Like the majority of his people, Yookotay was lithe and lean with startling pale blue eyes and white fur that covered skin as black as night.

"Welcome to Meos, my friends. It is good to have you visit our home." The blue eyes lost their welcoming smile and hardened. "I understand trouble plagues our land once again. Please tell me how the DeoNytes may help." He sat down on a bench on the opposite side of the fire.

Leaving Jordett to explain the details with the efficiency of his military training, Allynae stewed over his sister's recent choices.

Yookotay listened to Jordett's description of events. When the Theran major had finished, he looked at Allynae. "Life, like clouds in Myrrh's sky, changes shape and forms new patterns with each new decision. It is the Time of Unfolding. Choice equals change equals transformation." He studied the weary face of Almiralyn's brother. "It is good you came to me. We will prepare a safe place for Merrilea, Sparrow, and her mother." The look on Jordett's face at the mention of Esán's aunt told him much. *Life is indeed complex.*

"Soldiers from RewFaar already fill the Terces Wood." Jordett held his hands over the fire. "How do you intend to keep them from invading the caverns?"

"We allow them to enter at select spots and let the labyrinth and the Giests that still roam take care of them. They will not find Meos. Almiralyn has already secured the boundaries of the city and the surrounding area, including the Cavern of Tennisca and the Cave of Canedari. And you say the twins and Torgin are in DerTah? And Esán? How does the Guardian track them without the help of Elcaro's Eye?"

Allynae barely heard the conversation. Anger at Almiralyn for putting his daughters in danger still rankled. His heart told him Sparrow needed him, and here he was, a world away from her. *Has One Man escaped and rejoined her?*

"Allynae..."

I've only just found her again. What if she's hurt or imprisoned or... Pain rose from his heart into his throat.

A hand squeezed his arm. "What?" He looked from Jordett's understanding expression to Yookotay's dark face.

The ReDael's white fur glowed in the firelight as he stood up. "You worry about your Sparrow. I have something to show you."

He opened a wooden door and led them into a room where a carved map of Dojanack Caverns covered one wall. At its center, a sapphire matching the one he wore around his neck gleamed. Yookotay touched it. Blue light flooded the map. The topography faded, leaving a silvery mirror in its place. A mist roiled up, obscuring the surface, and flowed onto the chamber floor.

Jordett gasped beside him.

Almiralyn's face shimmered into focus.

"Hello, Alli." She nodded to Yookotay and the major. The serenity in her face belied the sorrow in her voice.

"Sparrow? My daughters?" His voice shook.

"One Man has escaped and rejoined Sparrow and Merrilea. They continue their journey. The twins are still in the desert. Yaro has joined them. They live out their destiny, Alli. You must believe they have the resources to succeed."

"But they are children, Almiralyn. And you sent them alone to a foreign planet." The understanding in her eyes brought him to the realization she, too, ached with concern. The anger dropped from his voice. "What do you suggest we do?"

"We wait. So far, the soldiers' focus is the cottage. Paisley is at Nemttachenn. Meet him there, and I will join you when I can."

Jordett interjected one soft word. "Esán?"

"I have heard nothing." The image began to dissolve. "Take care of yourselves."

The map reappeared.

Yookotay laid a hand on his arm. "Sparrow is safe, my friend."

Allynae rubbed the fatigue from his eyes. "But for how long, Yookotay?"

The three men stared at the map.

In the Terces Wood, the soldiers of RewFaar surrounded Almiralyn's land. Predatory and silent, they began to close their ranks, constricting the perimeter like a hangman's noose. The Largeen Joram would not tolerate another mistake. Their very existence depended upon their success.

23
Der Tah

Wolloh's sitting room welcomed him with warm colors, the fragrance of a fresh-lit fire, and his favorite chair. He paused in the doorway, enjoying the comfortable silence but aware it would not last. Leaning heavily on his cane, he limped to the chair and sank into its leather-smooth softness. The cane's crystal knob glistened as he propped it against a small table. Staring at the fire, he smoothed dark hair away from the uninjured side of his face, shut his eyes, and allowed the stillness to absorb the fatigue from his body.

Stebben's arrival, carrying a tray laden with the brandy, desert fruit, and the four glasses he had requested, ended his time of quiet. "Your guests will be here shortly. Is there anything else, sir?" He set the tray on the low table in front of him and waited.

Wolloh's eye wandered from the fire to the tall, elegant man in the burgundy and black uniform, who would remain standing with patient respect until he answered. Stebben's heavy-lidded eyes gleamed with a touch of humor. His full-lipped mouth twitched.

Wolloh indicated a chair. "I require just one more thing."

"Sir?"

"You, Stebben. Please sit. Tell me what you learned of the boy? Did you feel his power?"

"I agree with your assessment, sir. Esán is indeed extraordinary. He carries dual seeds of Carsilem. With time and training, he will be a force to be reckoned with. Were any of the Dreelum, the Largeen Joram, or Nissasa Rattori to gain control of him, havoc would ensue."

Wolloh shifted his body to ease the agony in his deformed hip. "And what of Nissasa? Were you able to read him?"

Stebben rubbed his chin, and for a moment, turned his gaze to the fire. Intelligent eyes blinked and refocused. "Anger, fear, guilt—hate—all boiled around him like the bubbling mud in the fire pits of DerTah. His power reeks of the Mocendi League."

"Good work, Stebben. Few would have picked up on the subtleties of his training. The Mocendi League..." Wolloh rubbed his hip and frowned. "Hatred taints the League's members—hatred and ambition."

"He is danger personified, Wolloh. You and Lorsedi are targets for his wrath."

"We are not the only ones in danger—"

A knock interrupted him. Stebben rose and crossed to the door. Wolloh nodded. With a slight bow, the Major Domo ushered three guests into the room and departed.

With Ira at her side, Brie followed Nichi up the side of a low dune. Something about him haunted her, something just beyond her mental grasp, something important. Peering up at him from under her lashes, she studied the strong profile. *Who do you remind me of?* He grinned down at her. She smiled back, enjoying the ease of their friendship. Her heart told her they shared more than either of them realized. The effort to match his long stride began to take its toll. He slowed his pace and allowed her to take the lead. She wiped the sweat from her face and trudged onward.

At the Atrilaasu's camp, there would be water and food and perhaps a tent where they could rest. It occurred to her she and her friends might not be welcome. *Time will tell.*

Torgin growled behind her. She swung around in time to see Ira's fist hit him in the gut hard enough to double him over.

"What is wrong with you two *now*?"

"He won't let me be. He always has to make fun." Torgin glared at Ira, his fists poised ready to do battle.

Nichi looked from one to the other. "WoNadahem make you fight. Then you be done with it."

Torgin didn't need any urging. His fist shot out and clipped Ira's chin. Ira lunged, caught him around the waist, and knocked him to the ground. Red sand flew around them as they kicked and rolled, fists flying, smacking, thunking against flesh—

A flash of light froze everyone in place. Astonishment turned to exclamations of wonder and excitement. Esán stood grinning at them. Next to him, a strange boy gaped in horror as Yaro changed to his natural form. Nichi fell to her knee, her face hidden in her hands. Ira grabbed Torgin and yanked him to his feet.

"Esán!" Brie's relief at the appearance of her friend made her lightheaded. "You found us. I am so, so glad."

The boy beside him cowered, his expressive face a picture gallery—fear, awe, confusion, sadness... It was the last emotion that brought Brie to his side. "I'm Brie. We won't hurt you." She glanced at Esán.

"This is Seval." The compassion in Esán's voice made her look at the boy more closely.

"Esán, it's so good to see you." Ira thumped him on the back.

For a moment, their eyes met and held. Esán's expression shifted from curiosity to understanding. He gave his friend a playful punch in the arm and gazed up at the tall Pentharian. "It's good to see you, Yaro. Hey, Torg." Esán grinned, then turned to Nichi. "You're an Atrilaasu Dansmen, aren't you? What's your name?"

Shy interest replaced her initial look of suspicion. "I Nichook. You know of my people?"

He smiled. "Your people are ancient and wise. Are you headed to your camp?"

She nodded and touched Brie's arm. "I take ConDria to WoNadahem Mardree. Others follow."

"ConDria?" Esán's eyebrow arced in a question. His fingers traced its curve. Brow and hand dropped. *Ugh. Nomed does this.*

Brie intertwined her fingers through his. *"You aren't like your uncle. You are you, Esán."*

He smiled his thanks. *"You are the ConDria?"*

"I can shape shift."

"It was you who killed one of Gidtuss' Fire ConDra. I should have known. It's good to see you're discovering your talents." His gaze sought Ira and then returned to her face. "A Water ConDria. Boy, I would have liked to have seen that!"

Yaro interrupted. "I think it would be wise to continue this conversation later. The sun will set quickly, and the night will catch us unprepared." His shift to a fox brought a gasp from Seval.

Nichi moved to the boy's side. "We take good care of you, Seval. Not worry. Just come."

Like a wilted flower drenched with cool rain, he grew taller. Nichi offered a hand. Seval's smile transformed his face as he grasped it and walked beside her.

Torgin and Ira, with the desert fox trotting between, trudged after them.

Esán's eyes followed Seval and Nichi. "That's interesting. Very interesting, indeed." He squeezed Brie's hand. "I have so much to share. And we have so much to do."

Brie shivered. Was it the sun sliding toward night or the message in Esán's words that chilled her to the bone?

Nomed allowed TheLise and Lorsedi to precede him into Wolloh's sitting room. The Dreelas shot him a questioning look as she swept past. The quizzical widening of her gold-flecked eyes elicited a cautious smile from him. Lorsedi's craggy, impassive features matched the rigid set of his shoulders.

Wolloh did not rise but postured his good side to greet his guests. "I apologize for not getting up. My hip keeps me stationary after long chron-

circles of standing." He waved at the three chairs facing him on the opposite side of the low, round table. "Please, take a seat. It has been a long turning. I thought a nightcap might be in order."

With sultry grace, TheLise sank onto the middle chair, forcing Nomed and Lorsedi to flank her on either side. Nomed took his seat and wondered at her game. The Largeen Joram gave the High DiMensioner a slight bow before joining them at the table, where brandy and fruit waited.

Wolloh angled his face to present the smoothness of its uninjured cheek. "Seyes, would you be so kind as to pour?"

"Of course." He turned to Lorsedi. "Wolloh has an exceptionally fine wine cellar. Holding up the crystal decanter, he swirled it. The light of the fire added its warmth to the deep honey color of the brandy. "This was aged in barrels made from the Tirips trees on Myrrh. Would you care for a glass? I think you will find it most delicious."

"You have piqued my curiosity, Nomed. However, I would prefer to determine for myself whether it lives up to your glowing description."

After favoring Lorsedi with a slight nod and the hint of a grin, he turned to TheLise. "And you, Dreelas?"

She picked up an etched crystal glass and held it out. "Myrrhinian brandy. A rare treat. Thank you."

He filled her glass, passed one to Lorsedi, and poured another for his mentor.

Wolloh accepted it, cleared his throat, and surveyed his guests with his good eye. "A toast..." The gleaming eye came to rest on Lorsedi's striking features. "To the achievement of our goals."

Four glasses, raised. Firelight caught the amber light and flickered it from face to face as Wolloh turned his injured side toward them. The sightless orb burned golden; the scarred landscape of his profile absorbed the warm color, deepening the anguished grimace. He shifted in his chair, the handsome side of his face eclipsing the tortured profile.

Lorsedi blinked. "To our mutual success."

The glasses lifted higher and touched with a soft clink. Murmurs of appreciation followed the first shared sip.

Lorsedi smiled. "Lovely, Wolloh. I must have a bottle to take back to RewFaar."

"Consider it done, Lorsedi, a gift from the wine cellars of Shu Chenaro.

Shall we discuss our goals? You asked about Elcaro's Eye. Tell me what you know."

The Largeen Joram settled back in his chair, took another sip, savored it, and swallowed. "It is a fountain of unimagined power. The seven-faceted Vesen Crystal encased within its pedestal, when connected to Evolsefil, makes its reach galaxy-wide. Almiralyn is its steward. It is in Myrrh. That is how I discovered my granddaughter." He smiled at Nomed. "Seyes has since informed me I have two granddaughters, identical twins whom he has met. They sound quite extraordinary. I want them. I want their mother and grandmother, and I want Elcaro's Eye."

Nomed studied the older man. "So then, what brought you to DerTah?"

The question hung in the air.

Esán plodded along beside Brie. A deep sense of relief and a touch of wonder made him smile. Her face flashing through his mind had enabled him to teleport to her side with Seval. *Will I ever get used to the power I carry?* He glanced at the girl beside him. *What is the power you wield, Brie, without realizing it?*

Ahead of him, Seval walked with Nichi. Something about her calmed his fear. Yaro's desert fox trotted between Torgin and Ira as they climbed the dune, sharing bits of information. Esán's delight at seeing Yaro was almost overshadowed by his curiosity regarding Ira. Had Almiralyn's spell not warned him, he would have exposed Ari's secret and put them all at risk, in particular Brie. The Star of Truth would blister her to her core if she attempted to lie. *Thankfully, the Guardian set the spell to warn me.*

Nichi and Seval stopped near the top of the dune. She motioned everyone to gather around her. "We at camp. I go down. Talk to WoNadahem. You hear horn blow, you come." She hiked the remaining distance to the top, waved, and descended the other side of the dune.

Esán could feel the tension mounting in his companions as they waited in the late afternoon coolness. Strain lined Seval's face. Ira and Torgin started to bicker. Only Brie and the red fox seemed unconcerned. He slipped his hand into Brie's and let his senses scan the far side of the dune. Nothing alerted him to danger.

The sound of a deep horn blowing announced the acceptance of their presence. The fox trotted up the dune and paused at the top, ears twitching and nose sniffing. Torgin and Ira followed. Seval held back. Brie took his hand. "It is safe here, Seval. I can feel it, and so can Esán. We won't let anything happen to you—I give you my word."

Ira's excited voice urged them to hurry. "Hey, you three, come see what's on the other side."

Esán placed a hand on Seval's shoulder. The muscles beneath his palm contracted. "Don't you want to see where Nichi lives?"

"I don't—"

Nichi appeared at the top of the dune and waved.

Seval's tension vanished as he waved back and climbed toward her.

"That *is* interesting." Brie smiled. "You must tell me about Seval as soon as we have some privacy. He is so sad and frightened."

Before he could respond, they reached the top and gazed down at the first touch of green they had seen in the desert.

24

Thera

One Man studied Sparrow and Merrilea from beneath lowered lids. The horror of Vascorrie had taken its toll. Fatigue draped them like a blanket. *How soon will they be able to travel? Are my pursuers closing in?* His Carsilem trained senses, tuned to the sounds of night and the gloominess of predawn, failed to detect the approach of two sleek, black panthers that melted out of the tall ferns and evergreens and shaped Pentharian, one blue and one green.

"Well, I'll be..." His arm steadied Merrilea when she gasped in surprise.

Voer's blue braids tumbled over his shoulder as he bowed to the women. Sparrow placed her hand on his palm and on tiptoes, touched her forehead to his. Surprise registered on the alien face.

"SparrowLyn, oid eo daize rao." The guttural greeting was so soft, One Man's ears strained to catch it.

"Voer, oid eo daiza raa." She stepped back. Her own surprise tugged her lips into a half smile. "I didn't know..."

The Pentharian placed a tattooed hand on his heart. "It is good, Mother of Twins." He turned to One Man. "We must leave. Many soldiers move this way."

Stee, his face still registering his astonishment at Sparrow's grasp of his native tongue, joined the group. "We can't fly in trees this close, and we can only carry one Human adult on our panther backs."

One Man's senses picked up a vibration in the ground that urged action. "Take the women. I'll follow. Hurry! Merrilea knows the way. I'll meet you at Singtil Pass."

Merrilea started to protest. He touched her face. "I'll be very close."

A subtle shift in the forest sounds made everyone fall silent. A soft, whistled note sent them into a nearly soundless flurry of activity. The Pentharian melted into panthers. The women mounted. Quiet paws carried them into the predawn shadows of the forest.

One Man set his course to lead the soldiers in the opposite direction. Like a deer startled into sudden flight, he shook the hip-high ferns and dashed through the trees. He felt the soldiers catch his sound and focus their search in his direction.

Intent on leaving a clumsy trail, he dodged over the rough terrain. Ferns slapped at his legs. He slid down a rock-strewn hill and circumvented a large boulder. His goal—to give Sparrow, Merrilea, and the Pentharian a substantial lead—took him to the edge of a swamp in a long, narrow gully.

With the goal of confusing his pursuers, he ripped strips from the bottom of his shirt and shoved them in a pocket. Eyes on his target, he teleported to a bush a short distance over the sodden ground. He draped a scrap over a bare branch. Another quick trip...a broken twig...a footprint... another scrap...all marked his journey. Finally, he reached the far side of the swamp and stood silent, listening.

An uneasy quiet settled over the woods. Birds ceased their song; a small creature stood on its hind legs, ears twitching. One Man stretched his awareness until he found the soldiers grouped at the other side of the swamp. Would they take his bait?

Teleporting above the rancid water, he made his way to a tall, leafy beech tree, and shimmying up, he swung his legs over a sturdy branch, and pulled himself up. The climb from there was easy, and although he could have teleported, he savored the touch of rough bark beneath his hands and the physical exertion that brought sweat to his brow. Close to the top but still hidden in the foliage, he stopped and pressed his body against the trunk.

Eyes narrowed against the sun's encroaching brightness, he searched the surrounding terrain. A flash of light bounced off the swamp's murky surface. Muffled expletives reached his ears. A soldier slogged his way through the hip-deep water. He stopped and held up a scrap of shirt.

"Over here." His shout was cautious, but loud enough to reach the men who skirted the sloping walls of the gully.

One Man prepared to wait, hidden by the leafy treetop. Now, patience would be his best friend. The soldiers had no dogs to follow his scent, so he could observe their activities and listen to their orders without fear of discovery. Even if they stayed until nightfall, the darkness would force them to discontinue their search until morning.

Close to the beech tree, an officer standing at the edge of the swamp ordered his men into the tepid water. "Search for anything that will lead us to him. He can't have gone far."

RewFaaran soldiers and PPP patrollers slogged through foul-smelling mud and stumbled over submerged roots. Frustrated expletives tainted the air. Two men paused beneath his hideout and looked toward the officer, issuing the orders. "Guess he doesn't want to get his shiny boots wet. We don't even know for sure it's our guy leaving a trail so easy to follow."

The second man took off his cap and mopped his brow. "How soon will he call it quits?"

"You're talkin' about Old-Never-Give-Up. He could keep us here until DerTah's desert freezes over." The first soldier waded toward the opposite side of the swamp.

"Shite." The second man slapped his arm with his hat. "I don't wanna be eaten alive." He swatted his cheek with his hand and examined his palm. "The little bugger drank half my blood." Wiping his hands on the seat of his pants, he labored through the muck after his comrade.

A subtle change in the air left One Man alert and tingling with anticipation. He peered up at the forest canopy. An almost imperceptible breeze, heading in the direction the Pentharian had taken the women, sent the faint odor of smoke rustling through the trees. His uneasiness escalating, he searched for Sparrow's mental signature.

A shout from the far side of the gully reminded him to pay attention. His present circumstance continued to put him at risk. As much as he wanted to teleport to Sparrow's side, every instinct warned against it. An answering shout told him the soldiers moved back in his direction.

The sun rode high, erasing the shadows between the fallen and tangled trees scattered throughout the swamp. Soon there would be no cover. He climbed down from his sturdy branch, landed soundlessly at the base of the birch, and shifted.

Across from him, a soldier stepped from behind a tree and drew his weapon.

One Man unfurled his heron wings and lifted into flight. A shot rang out. The bullet whizzed by him, cutting a trajectory through a radiant flash of sunlight.

Sparrow shuddered and clung to Voer's panther back, welcoming the warmth and power of the muscles rippling beneath her hands. Letting her exhausted body soak in both, she gave herself a mental shake. Memories of her close call in Vascorrie clung to her like a spider's web. Flashes of Primavers and tarwish made her cringe. *Who carried me away from sure death? One Man carried Merrilea. Powerful arms lifting me are all I can remember.*

Her hands gripping Voer's black fur held her steady as she peered ahead through the trees. Although Pentharian could not converse in panther form, they could understand their riders. Merrilea's whispered directions to Stee had helped to put distance between them and the soldiers who hunted One Man.

Up ahead, Merrilea leaned low over Stee's back. His ears twitched. He slowed, then stopped. She dismounted and stretched. Voer's easy gait decelerated to a standstill. Sparrow swung a leg over his back and slid off. Both Pentharian shifted, their lizard-gold eyes inspecting the woodlands.

Voer touched her arm. "Daughter of KcernFensia, can you sense anyone in pursuit?"

Sparrow closed her eyes and stretched her sensory skills. "Nothing follows. Birds sing. Small animals forage for food. A predator close by stalks an unaware rabbit."

Voer's expression eased. "One Man has done well. How far are we from Singtil Pass?"

"We will be there by nightfall if we can keep up this pace." Merrilea sighed and leaned against the broad trunk of an ancient tree. Her eyes drifted shut, then opened slowly.

Sparrow's hand rested on her stomach, where uneasiness churned for no apparent reason. Seeking to understand, she wandered a short distance from her companions. Something in the distance moved toward them, something not of the planet of Thera. Her eyes widened and flashed to the faces of her companions.

Voer closed the gap between them in one long stride. He held her gaze, understood the urgency he saw there, and nodded. Signaling Stee to shift, he followed suit. Without a word, Merrilea mounted. Fear flashed over her face. She shook her head, clearing it, and whispered directions to Stee.

Sparrow took one more moment to confirm her discovery. The strangeness creeping through the forest could not be mistaken. She leapt onto Voer's back and leaned close to his ear. "Odi dimenic!" A growl told her he understood. She crouched lower. The muscles in his back engaged, and they were in motion.

Trees blurred by as Voer raced through the forest. Catching up to Stee, he growled. Merrilea's frightened gaze fastened on Sparrow's for an instant before her mount picked up speed.

More quickly than Sparrow expected, the foursome reached the U-shaped bottom of Demrach Canyon and stopped in the trees flanking the flatlands. Voer and Stee stood together in natural form, speaking in low, guttural tones. Merrilea remained quiet and watchful.

Sparrow scanned the width and breadth of the canyon. Her brow furrowed. *Is it safe to continue to Singtil? Or will I be taking danger to my parents' door?* Again, she searched the flatlands for any sign of movement. Nothing stirred. *Is that good or bad?* She scrutinized the sky where the sun continued its descent to the horizon. *It's taken most of the turning to get this far. Will waiting for its disappearance to drape darkness across the valley be the safest way to traverse it?*

A blue heron soared overhead, skirted the tree line, and landed some distance away. Voer moved to her side as it strutted toward them. Stee placed himself near Merrilea.

Sparrow's mouth rounded and then curved into a smile. "I should have known." She stepped free of the trees.

The heron unfurled its beautiful wings. Merrilea gasped and grabbed her arm as the bird disappeared in a flare of light and One Man appeared in its place.

"*Sparrow, back in the trees.*" His telepathic message was a command.

As she moved to retreat into the forest, Merrilea jogged across the distance that separated her from her brother-in-law. Silent sobs shook her shoulders as One Man's arms wrapped around her. He said something. She nodded and moved from his embrace. Taking her hand, he pulled her into the shelter of tall trees and the lengthening shadows of late afternoon.

Relieved to have Sparrow back in his care, One Man directed his focus to whatever followed through the trees like an arrow to a bull's-eye. Unable to identify their stalker, he debated the wisdom of investigating it.

The group huddled around him. He explained his concern. "I don't know what it is, but I'm sure we're its target."

Voer pursed thin, red lips. "We must discover what tracks us. Sparrow tells me it is not of Thera."

One Man looked at the twins' mother. "You can feel it?"

"I began to experience a strangeness in the forest—something that made the trees cringe as it skimmed their tops—when we took a break at mid-turning."

Not for the first time, One Man found himself impressed by Sparrow's rapidly growing gifts. "Any idea where it's from?"

"None. I only know it's closing in as we speak."

He turned to Voer and Stee. "If I can get close enough, I'll be able to tell what we are dealing with, but I need to maintain Human form to do so. Would one of you be willing to carry me?"

Voer stepped forward. "I can do this."

Stee nodded his agreement. "I will remain with the women."

One Man caught Sparrow's knowing gaze. She understood the danger. "Sparrow, do you know how to set up a screen to diffuse your scent and obscure your whereabouts?"

"I've never had the occasion to try. Tell me how, and I will do my best."

"Time is too short for an explanation. May I place the knowledge in your mind?"

She nodded. "Of course, One Man. I trust you."

With two fingers on her temples, he shut his eyes. When he opened them, Sparrow smiled." I understand."

One Man put an arm around Merrilea. "Promise me you will stay hidden and quiet."

"I promise, Somay. Please be careful." She hugged him and moved closer to Sparrow.

With Voer at his side, he stepped from the trees into the open canyon land and looked up at the tall Pentharian. "You understand the danger? If it senses us, it will be harder to destroy it."

Voer's golden gaze held his. "We made the choice, my friend." He shifted form.

One man mounted and pressed his chest against the broad vulture back. One powerful movement launched them skyward. Voer's wings sliced through the air as One Man tried to imagine all plausible scenarios. But without knowledge of their stalker, he couldn't plan an attack. *What if I made the wrong decision? What if we should have pressed on to Singtil?*

25
Myrrh

Almiralyn and Paisley arrived at Nemttachenn Tower without incident. She left him to settle in and shifted to her bird form. Her goal—Allynae's cabin to cloak his crystal, Novissi. Its link to Elcaro's Eye would enable anyone finding it to locate the fountain.

I must hurry! Dropping lower, she skimmed through the trees. Soldiers prowled everywhere. Allynae's cabin, midway between Demrach Gateway and what remained of her barn, lay right on their path. She swooped through an opening in the forest canopy and landed on the branch of a Tirips Tree.

The cabin, tucked at the back edge of the clearing, felt empty. No suspicious sounds or movements alerted her to danger. Still, it never hurt to be careful. Flying a zigzag pattern between tall trees, she came to rest on the shaded rooftop of an outbuilding. Across the way, Majeska leapt onto the cabin's front stoop, her tail switching from side to side. Gray ears twitched; amethyst eyes widened. Almiralyn knew her time ticked away.

A window at the back of the cabin gaped, wide and dark. Gold-tipped wings carried her through it into the musky coolness of Allynae's home. Only Allynae's essence hung in the air. Shifting, but remaining within the shadows, she made her way to the fieldstone fireplace.

The crystal Novissi, as large as an ostrich egg, sat on the mantle. The center glowed a welcome as she approached. Its tie to Elcaro made it imperative that she not keep both the crystal and the Eye in her possession. Her only choice was to hide it. Cradling it in her hands, she recited in a soft whisper.

> *"Achieve a size to keep you hidden,*
> *So those who come to you unbidden*
> *Will look beyond your shining light*
> *And only see the dark of night."*

As Novissi reduced to the size of an acorn, its pulsing warmth cooled. Almiralyn held it between her thumb and index finger, inhaled, and blew. The light in the crystal extinguished. She tucked it in a darkened triangle created by two books on the bookshelf and stepped back to view her handy work. Novissi was invisible.

Majeska meowed from the windowsill. It was time to go. Shifting, she flew out the window and into the trees. A pair of soldiers moved with trained stealth to hide behind the outbuildings. Two more darted towards the cabin.

Although other duties called, she remained a watcher, a protector, perched in the shadows. With luck, the four men would find nothing of interest in Allynae's home.

With a sense of misgiving, Paisley stood in the east-facing entrance to Nemttachenn and studied the clearing. *What will I do if the soldiers come here? How can I fight them off alone?*

A cool breeze brushing his cheeks sent goose bumps leaping up the back of his neck. He turned and choked down a gasp of surprise. Encased in a misty, blue light stood a tall, almost transparent figure of a man. *Is it a ghost?* Paisley rubbed his eyes and stared.

White-gray hair glowed bluish in the light and fell from a center part to the man's shoulders. Deep-set eyes, so dark Paisley couldn't see the pupils, bored into him from beneath shaggy, white brows. Under the fleshy nose, an upper lip, almost hidden beneath a white mustache, stretched in a smile to show a full set of healthy teeth. Brushing the man's collarbone, a white beard trimmed to the shape of his elongated chin completed the picture. The most astonishing thing, however, was his height. Paisley rarely found himself eye-to-eye with anyone; but here he was looking up at... He cleared his throat. "Who ya be?"

The bearded chin lifted. The massive chest swelled. "I am the Sentinel of Nemttachenn and the Protector of Myrrh. I am CheeTrann."

Paisley twisted his mustache around his finger. "Ahh. I've heard ya speak, but never expected to see ya." He let his hand drop and shuffled a self-conscious step backward.

CheeTrann, fists resting on his hips and continued his intimidating stare. "You do not need to worry about the soldiers who tramp uninvited through Myrrh's woods. Almiralyn left Evolsefil in my care. I can protect it and you."

Paisley smiled at the grandness in the tone. "I appreciate your help, CheeTrann. My question is, how do we to pass time?"

Laughter rolled through the tower. "Time? You know nothing of time." Another laugh ended in a thoughtful expression. He pointed at Paisley. "You play chess?"

A broad grin spread across Paisley's face. "My favorite game."

CheeTrann swirled a hand in the air. Beneath the staircase spiraling up the tower walls, a round table materialized. In the glow of a lantern sitting on top, a chessboard appeared. Carved pieces lined up on either side awaited the pleasure of the players.

"Shall we?" CheeTrann made a grandiose sweep of his hand.

Paisley gave his mustache a tug and grinned. "I'd be honored."

CheeTrann settled his body on a chair designed for his enormous frame. "I plan to win." His claim rumbled through the tower.

Paisley took the chair opposite and looked him in the eye. "Oh, do ya now? So do I."

The ancient spirit of Nemttachenn picked up one black pawn and one white, put them behind his back, and then held out his fisted hands. Paisley tapped the right one. The big hand opened. Taking the white pawn from CheeTrann's palm, Paisley replaced it on the board. He had won the first move.

The soldiers at Allynae's cabin searched it and the outbuildings and jogged away through the woods. Satisfied they wouldn't return anytime soon, Almiralyn flew to warn the Wood Tiffs' leader. Materializing outside Tibin's treetop bungalow, she knocked. Sibine, Tibin's mate, opened the door with a wee baby Tiff on her hip.

Brown, almond-shaped eyes fluttered in surprise. With a self-conscious smile, she patted a flyaway brown curl into place, bobbed a curtsy, and smiled. "Almiralyn, how can I help you?"

"Is Tibin here?" Almiralyn forced the worry from her voice.

"He is. Please come in." The Tiffet stepped aside. When Almiralyn had ducked through the doorway and straightened, Sibine nodded at a flowery sofa. "Please have a seat while I fetch him. Would you like to hold Adin?"

Almiralyn reached for the Tiff with a smile. "How did you know I wanted to cuddle your son?"

Sibine laughed. "I saw it in your eyes, my lady." She sobered. "I also see trouble. I'll get Tibin."

Adin sucked his tiny fist and kicked his chubby legs.

"You are quite beautiful, you know." Almiralyn touched his soft brown curls and kissed the top of his head, savoring the magic of a new life and the peace and gentleness of the TreeOm.

The patter of feet signaled Tibin's arrival with Sibine, who hurried to gather Adin in her arms and scurried away down the hall.

Tibin bowed. "How can I be of service?"

"Please sit, Tibin. I have much to share."

Sitting, he interlaced his fingers over his round belly, and raised troubled brown eyes to hers.

With precise detail, she shared with her stalwart supporter all that had occurred since their last meeting. After inhaling a sustaining breath, she provided the most frightening detail of all. "A platoon of soldiers from RewFaar came through the Demrach Gateway and advances on my cottage as we speak. You must warn the Wood Tiffs to stay hidden. I also need you to find Kieel, leader of the Terces Nyti, and inform him of the danger."

Tibin's face blanched. "RewFaar, the planet of warfare." He shuddered. "I can't believe RewFaaran soldiers have invaded the Terces Wood. How many are in a platoon?"

"Anywhere from sixteen to fifty. Yuin said he counted twenty-four."

Tibin squeezed his knees with trembling hands. When he looked up, determination set his usually merry face in stern lines. "Besides telling my people and the Nyti, what can I do to help?"

"Remain hidden, my friend. These men will not hesitate to detain and torture anyone to gain the information they require. You know too much about the twins. Your capture would be fatal for you and for them. If I need you, I'll send a message." At the door, she paused. "Your son is quite special. Keep him safe, Tibin."

Ducking onto the small veranda, she shifted form. Her white bird soared up through the forest canopy. The soldiers advancing on her cottage were pulling their noose tight.

Sibine had settled Adin in his cribett and slipped down the hall in time to hear Almiralyn's description of a military platoon. *So many soldiers marching through the Terces Wood...* Fear choked her.

Tibin turned and opened his arms. She threw hers around his neck and planted a kiss on his pale cheek. "Oh, Tibin, life has become so..." Unable to find a word to describe her turmoil, she shook her head.

"We have to be brave, dearest." Gentle hands smoothed her hair away from her face. He lifted her chin. His kiss, filled with all his mixed emotions, left her shaking. He hugged her, then grabbed his hat. "Don't leave the TreeOm. I'll be back as soon as I can."

The silence left by his departure made her heart ache. *Soldiers from*

RewFaar in the Terces Wood! She shuddered and scurried down the hall to check on her son.

Almiralyn landed in the thick foliage of an oak tree at the most distant border of her land. Soldiers in camouflage circled the perimeter of what had been the gardens surrounding her cottage. Large spiders scuttled around their webs in alarm. A snake slithered into hiding. Still unconscious, Grantese Tesilend sprawled where she had left him. Somewhere, a man swore and received a whispered reprimand. A murder of crows swooped above the ruins, soared skyward, and disappeared over the forest. Silence, like an oppressive watcher, settled over the acreage.

Bushes rustling disturbed the hushed stillness. Soldiers crept forward, their weapons drawn. An officer stepped into view and raised his arm. Eight men spaced around the clearing hunkered low. The officer dropped his arm. The men, dodging from tree to ruin to tree, skulked into the open.

Two crouched beside Tesilend. One alerted the officer, who hurried toward them, a medic at his heals. A quick conference sent one soldier disappearing into the trees. The others remained vigilant—on guard—half hidden in the rubble.

The medic knelt next to the prone Grantese and made a quick exam.

"How is he?" The officer scanned the rubble and glared down at him.

"He's coming around, sir."

Tesilend's eyes opened to the sight of his commanding officer. Helped by the medic, he sat up and sipped water from the man's canteen. As he handed it back, he caught a glimpse of his surroundings. "What the..." With a frantic look around, he struggled to standing. "Where am I, sir?"

The officer flashed him a look of surprise. "We're at the coordinates for the Guardian of Myrrh's cottage, but these ruins are all we've found."

Tesilend inhaled a long breath as his gaze darted over the land. "I swear to you, I saw a cottage and a barn..." He hesitated. "The ruins have been here awhile. So have the spiders." The grimace of disgust ended in a cough. "They weren't—"

"How did you get here?" The officer interrupted. "You were supposed to return to Der Tah."

"Sir, someone captured me and brought me back to a cottage." He told what he could remember of his story.

Almiralyn smiled when he made no mention of the Pentharian. Her gentle mind probe had been more effective than she expected. Grantese Tesilend remembered her, Allynae, and Jordett. Paisley was a vague figure he only thought he recalled.

She glanced at the amassing soldiers, her mind full of unanswered questions. *Why did Lorsedi send a well-armed plat*oon? *What does he really want? Elcaro's Eye is only part of it. His granddaughters, Sparrow, and her mother...all are important but—*

"Let me go!" A frightened childish voice squawked from the trees.

"Stop kicking, you little brat." A soldier marched from the woods with a squirming Tiff under his arm and deposited him in front of the officer. "Found this little varmint spying from yonder trees."

The youngster, glared straight at the officer's kneecap, straightened his shirt, pushed a tangled brown curl away from his face, and glowered. "I belong here. You don't."

"You have a lot of spunk for one so small." The officer looked down at him with obvious curiosity. "My guess is you're a Wood Tiff. What's your name?"

"I'm Sibee, and you'd better let me go or my friend will be angry."

"I think, Sibee, I'll take a chance on your friend's anger." He turned his attention to the soldier who had discovered him. "Take him and keep him out of trouble. I'll question him later."

The soldier grasped the Tiff by the arm and marched him back toward the trees.

"Jordy will save me. You just wait and see." Sibee shouted the brave words over his shoulder.

Almiralyn ruffled her feathers in despair. *Oh, Sibee, you are in more trouble than you know. And how on Myrrh am I going to save you?*

26
DerTah

Brie and Esán joined the group at the base of the DerTahan dune, where Nichi, still holding Seval's hand, pointed at the desert palm fronds breaking up the monotony of the sandy vista. "My home there. I show you Eissua. You see gift from desert spirits to Atrilaasu."

Hurrying ahead with Seval, she led them along a faint path between thick clumps of tall, stocky trees. As they hiked, the shade of late afternoon wafted cool air through the weave of their kcalos, drying the sweat and drawing the heat from their bodies.

The trees increased in number, shaping a circular border at the top of a rise and casting long shadows across the sun-washed sand. Nichi stopped and pointed. "Eissua Oasis, home of my people, the Atrilaasu Dansmen."

Brie could only gaze in wonder at the dramatic and beautiful landscape spreading out like a mirage in the setting sun.

"Wowee!" Ira's exhaled exclamation said it all.

As though a skilled hand had scooped the sand away, a basin stretched from the bottom of the rise to a rocky outcropping on the far side of a glistening expanse of water. Trees and desert shrubs clustered not only along the water's edge, but in groupings that climbed the rolling dunes on three sides of the oasis. Sprinkled throughout were black tents in varying shapes and sizes. Bright banners on either side of the tent flaps fluttered in the slight breeze, creating a symphony of color.

The sun hovered, round and red, above the rocky outcropping, staining it deep shades of crimson and gold and painting the water with streaks of turquoise, rose, and purple. Flowing from the rocks, a small waterfall glistened in the last moments of dusk. Amongst all this beauty, men, women, and children gathered to stare at the strangers who gazed at their home in awe.

"It is so beautiful." Torgin sighed. "I did not realize someplace this spectacular could exist in all this sand."

Nichi, pride shining in her eyes, led them down the slope. Seval clung to her hand, his sadness softened by a smile of wonder. Torgin and Ira walked side-by-side. Yaro in his fox form trotted beside his heart brother.

Brie lagged behind with Esán." When I read about Eissua Oasis, I didn't guess I'd ever see it."

Esán fingered the book in his pants pocket. "Neither did I. I can't remember if it's fed by an aquifer or an underground river, but water is sure a welcome sight."

The group ahead of them stopped. Nichi motioned them to one side and then she turned, her eyes seeking Brie's. Lowering to one knee, she placed her hand on her heart and bowed her head. Those gathered behind her followed her lead. Seval knelt. Torgin and Ira exchanged glances and joined him. Esán squeezed Brie's hand, stepped to the side, and knelt.

A lone woman remained standing. WoNadahem Mardree, the Headwoman and Oracle of the Atrilaasu, waved her closer. Brie walked several steps and stopped. Her breath caught in her throat as she stared into eyes so remarkable she could not pull her gaze away.

The woman's hand brushed her cheek. A sudden rush of coolness flooded Brie's senses. Her heartbeat quickened and slowed as her arms stretched wide and the surrounding air began to shimmer. The sound of rushing water, the luscious feel of it against her skin, and the realization that she had become a fluid and liquid force lifted her with underwater slowness above the oasis into the arc of the red sky. A song of wonder burst from her throat. The notes rained down on the upturned faces of the kneeling Dansmen.

Conscious of her transformation for the first time, she pressed her watery wings against the air and soared over the sands of DerTah. Beneath her, the oasis shone like a star sapphire in an expanse of undulating sand. *"Brie, come back!"* The words rustled through her mind like a breeze. She hovered above the clear desert lake and gazed from glistening blue eyes at the magnificence of the creature she had become. One word formed in the part of her that remembered Human. *"Esán!"*

Below her, the Atrilaasu of Eissua Oasis rose, cheering. Esán, in his kestrel form, circled around her. Dwarfed by her size, he escorted her in a wide arc and then flew to land on the hand of the Oracle, WoNadahem Mardree.

"ConDria, shift." Rang out in her mind.

"How?"

The Danswoman held out her hand. Esán's kestrel form fluttered to the ground and shifted. He opened his arms. "Brielle, come back to me."

Her wings stretched wide, she pressed them against the arid atmosphere and glided downward until her water talons touched the sand. The shift to Human was instantaneous. A moment of confusion made her stumble. Esán caught her arm and steadied her. Again, the crowd cheered.

Brie's gaze came to rest on the headwoman's face. A tear-shaped crystal hanging at the center of her forehead caught the light of the setting sun, momentarily obscuring her features. The Atrilaasu leader turned her head. Her face re-emerged. Her haunting eyes, where the dark edges of fully dilated pupils encircled two light-filled pools of color, one the yellow of saffron and one glacier blue, glowed. Fire-red hair, held back by an intricately beaded band, flared around her head like living flames. High cheekbones and a long, narrow nose accentuated the planes of her extraordinary face and provided a canvas for thin-lined, blue-black tattoos. Brie found herself unable to look away or to speak.

WoNadahem Mardree smiled, held out her right arm, and tapped the back of her hand. A small, orange serpent slithered from beneath her kcalo sleeve and sniffed the air with its tiny tongue. A series of hisses elicited a nod from the Oracle.

Her strange eyes gleamed. "Welcome, ConDria. The Atrilaasu offer you and your comrades shelter in our home of Eissua. Tomorrow, after the rise of the sun, you and I shall share time."

The snake hissed again. The headwoman's strange eyes came to rest on Esán as the crystal on her forehead flared. "We, too, shall meet on the morrow." Her gaze dropped to Yaro's fox form. "Join me, red fox."

She beckoned a man forward, gave him instructions for housing their guests, and turned to her people. Those gathered parted, allowing her to pass between them. Her small serpent hissed. The desert fox walked by her side.

The man bowed. "I, Narrtep, show you a place to rest." As he led them along the people-lined path, the Dansmen whispered, "ConDria od Eissua, ConDria od Eissua..." and slipped away one by one until Brie and her friends were alone with Narrtep in the glow of dusk's last moments.

As they walked beside the lake, a cool breeze carrying the scents of water and night fingered Brie's damp curls and chased the heat from her clothing. Small campfires sprang to life. Laughter and song drifted around her.

The man stopped by a rectangular tent. "This is for young men." He gave them a toothy grin. "I come for you when the repast is ready."

Ira looked down at her. "You alright alone?"

She nodded. "See you at dinner." He hugged her and followed Torgin and Seval into the tent.

Esán put an arm around her. "Rest, ConDria. When we have time, I will share some things to help you with shape shifting." He gave her a quick hug.

"Thanks. I'd like that." She watched the flap fall into place and followed Nichi and Narrtep further along the curve of the basin.

Near the outcropping, a round tent nestled between palms trees and within hearing distance of the waterfall. Narrtep touched his heart. "This ConDria tent. You need anything, you tell to me or Nichi." He bowed and disappeared in the gathering night.

A shy smile lit Nichi's face. "Atrilaasu honor you. You need me, I there." She pointed at a tent midway between Brie's and the boys. "Tonight, big celebration. ConDria rising makes all happy." She, too, touched her heart. "Thank you for showing ConDria to my people. Many did not believe. Now do." With a wave, she scurried back toward her tent.

For a time, Brie remained still, gazing over the water, listening to the sounds of tribal life, and reviewing the events of the turning. She filled her lungs with cool desert air and exhaled with measured slowness. Grateful for time alone, she opened the tent flap and stepped inside.

Nomed's question seemed to repeat itself in the minds of the four people gathered in Wolloh's sitting room. "So then, what brought you to DerTah?"

Lorsedi's expression remained inscrutable. A look of intense interest replaced TheLise's irresistible smile. Wolloh's good eye, fastened on the Largeen Joram, did not blink.

Nomed sat back in his chair and brought the small crystal glass to his lips. He did not doubt that his question had struck a chord. He placed the glass on the table and observed the RewFaaran leader.

Wolloh broke the silence. "Lorsedi may not be ready to share his plans, am I correct?" His good eye reflected the firelight as he, too, set his glass on the table.

Lorsedi's long fingers held the brandy halfway to his mouth. Dark brown eyes glistened as he savored a sip. "I have many reasons for visiting DerTah. Not the least of which, Seyes, was to meet you. Rumor has it you discovered the Evolsefil Crystal during your visit to Myrrh. Did you, by chance, run across a compass of rare beauty and design?"

"I did not. Would you care to expound upon its importance?"

The Largeen Joram's laugh held little humor. "I imagine our host can explain it better than I, can you not, High DiMensioner?"

Wolloh rearranged his maimed body in his chair. His voice when he spoke held a note of mystery. "I believe you refer to the Compass of Ostradio. To my knowledge, no one has seen it in many aeons."

TheLise leaned forward, her luminous eyes on Lorsedi's face. "If I'm not mistaken, the Compass of Ostradio and the Evolsefil Crystal are linked. I believe it would be most interesting to find out how. It is said to absorb the patterning and geography of the planet or place in which it resides...a formidable tool for a warmonger." She gave Lorsedi her intrigant's smile.

Nomed wondered at her audacity as Lorsedi inclined his head in her direction, a slow, caustic smile showing even white teeth. "I hope, TheLise, that you do not think RewFaarans are warmongers because we enjoy the art and science of warfare."

Her lips curved into a sardonic smile. "I admire those who pursue the arts and sciences. Those who would destroy for the sake of destroying are the ones I find oppressive. In fact, I chanced to overhear just such a conversation this evening." She lifted her glass, held it to the light, and drank what remained of the amber liquid prior to setting her glass with studied care on the table.

"A conversation?" Nomed could not help himself, even when Wolloh's expression told him no.

Lorsedi's attention remained fixed on the Dreelas. "And why does this overheard bit of gossip color your impression of my world?"

TheLise glanced at Wolloh. His good eye blinked. She returned her attention to the Largeen Joram. "Your son and one of our less intelligent Dreela were engaged in a heated discussion about finding and kidnapping Nomed's nephew. Nissasa expressed a willingness to help in exchange for assistance in finding the compass...and Elcaro's Eye." She paused.

At the mention of Nissasa, Lorsedi's eyes narrowed. His hands balled into tight fists. An enigmatic expression sculpted his face into a mask. Uncurling his fingers, he rested his hands on his upper thighs and leaned closer to the Dreelas. "I assume, my dear TheLise, there is more?"

Her expression suggested an inner struggle, one Nomed was uncertain existed. When she spoke, it was with surprising candor. "He seems intent on destroying not only Myrrh and Thera but also those who rule RewFaar. Oh, yes. He will leave the Evolsefil Crystal to the Dreelum. I think that rather odd, don't you?"

Nomed could almost hear her purring as she reclined with catlike grace against her chair. Neither Wolloh nor Lorsedi moved. The fire's sputtering sounded too loud in the veiled silence.

Wolloh cleared his throat. "It appears we have a situation brewing that could create problems for all of us." His tone changed. "I am sorry about Nissasa, Lorsedi. It seems he aspires to become the Largeen Joram in your place. I fear he sees both you and me as his enemies."

The twins' grandfather rose and crossed to the fireplace. Resting a hand on the rustic wooden mantle, he stared at the flames.

Nomed glanced at TheLise. She had straightened, her eyes fixed on the man whose lifestyle she had challenged. A lift of her chin implied the game had not ended quite the way she had expected. She left her chair and walked to the Largeen Joram's side. "I apologize, Lorsedi. I should have told you in private."

He looked down at her, his eyes hooded. "You played the game well. And," he turned, "both Wolloh and Nomed deserve to know what Nissasa is planning." He looked again at the Dreelas. "I am a politician, a soldier, and the leader of my people. War is RewFaar's game, and we are good at it. But we never wage it with a flippant disregard for life or for those with whom we do battle...at least *most* of us don't." He returned to his chair and picked up his glass. "Perhaps another taste of your excellent brandy, Wolloh?"

The High DiMensioner nodded and, when Nomed finished pouring, raised his glass. "I suggest we drink to our mutual enemy and his imminent downfall."

Lorsedi, the first to follow his lead, held up his brandy and smiled at TheLise. "To a game well played." He emptied the glass, swallowed the fiery liquid, and held her gaze. "You seem to enjoy taking risks. How willing are you to play a dangerous game?"

She did not look away. "It depends on the game and the goal."

"The game and the goal are the same...to bring Nissasa to his knees."

"And what role am I to play?"

"The bait." Lorsedi poured himself another glass of brandy.

Nomed felt a rush of adrenaline. Wolloh's hand on his arm kept him silent and sitting. He glanced at the tortured profile of his mentor. *Will you truly allow TheLise to put her life on the line for the Largeen Joram of RewFaar?*

27
Myrrh & Thera

Voer, the Pentharian, carried One Man high above the Theran forest—the goal—to spot the creature that followed Sparrow and Merrilea before it spotted them. Driven by an urgency that matched his rider's, Voer pressed his wings against the air with a constant and powerful rhythm. A sudden blast of heat warned him of a change below. Banking to get a better view, he swooped downward. Like a dissipating cloud of smoke, a filmy shape skimmed the forest canopy. Voer circled. With the intent to remain undetected, he maintained a course above and slightly ahead of the almost invisible entity he pursued.

Attention focused on the hazy presence, One Man sent out a gentle telepathic probe. The thing's insubstantial consciousness diffused at his touch. A second probe following on the heels of the first discovered sadness and anger, a third—the urgent need to fulfill its directive. As quickly as these thoughts surfaced, they wavered and melted away.

Pressing his knees into the vulture's sides, he squeezed a prearranged signal. The enormous bird dropped through a break in the canopy, landed, and folded its wings. One Man slid off.

Voer appeared, his tattooed face worried. "Is that what I think it is?"

One Man frowned. "If you think it's a Tabagie od Ro-ec, you're correct. How close are we to Stee and the women?"

"As the panther runs, only a short sprint." He shifted.

One Man jumped on his back, and they bounded through the forest. As the panther rounded a clump of short-needled pines, their companions came into view. One Man slid off and hurried to the spot where Stee waited between the two women. Voer, in Pentharian form, followed.

Sparrow watched One Man advance toward them. Clearly, he was not happy. Voer's expression confirmed her fear. "Did you find it?"

Merrilea and Stee pressed closer.

"The creature that follows us is from DerTah." One Man sounded even less happy than he looked.

Merrilea tensed beside her. "What is it, Somay?"

"It is from the netherworld of DerTah, where it lives at the planet's core. I've never seen one, but I know them by reputation. What I don't understand is how it got here?"

Voer shrugged his thick braids behind his shoulder. "My understanding is that the Tabagie requires heat generated by the planet's core to maintain itself, so it never ventures far from home. Stee fingered the jewel on his earlobe. "Unless someone captured it and pressed it into service, I can't imagine it risking a trip to the planet's surface, let alone a journey through a portal to Thera."

"What do we do now?" The strain in Merrilea's voice had intensified.

One Man put an arm around his sister-by-Joining. "The Tabagie will not attempt to cross the valley in the daylight unless it sees movement it believes to be its prey. I will try to lead it away from you. Voer and Stee, what are your thoughts?"

Voer walked to the edge of the trees and peered at the sun, where it floated like a ball of pale butter above the horizon. His face, when he turned to retrace his steps, was serious. "The Tabagie dislike sunlight, and they dislike open spaces. They're most comfortable in the dark."

Sparrow couldn't contain her curiosity. "Why did it fly above the trees, then?"

Stee tipped his head back and scanned the forest canopy. "It would have started a forest fire had it flown through the woods. The treetops were no doubt preferable to the open sky."

One Man released Merrilea. "*And...*provided it with a means of maintaining its insubstantial body. In the turning's light, it struggles to hold itself together. The trees beneath it helped it to define itself. Besides, it was tracking you. We need to move. Voer, can you make it across before the sun sets?"

"It will be close, my friend. But I see no choice. Staying here is as dangerous as being out in the open. My biggest fear is night's darkness."

"I'll do my best to lead it far enough away that you'll have time to hide. I can't imagine you can make it to Gerolyn's before tonight."

"We don't want to lead it to the farm. What are we going to do?" Sparrow didn't even try to hide her concern.

One Man prepared to shift. "One step at a time. Who knows what will happen next? Take care of each other." He kissed Merrilea on the cheek and changed form.

The blue heron lifted into the air, its extended legs trailing and its long neck an arrow pointing toward the Tabagie od Ro-ec.

On Myrrh, Almiralyn flew deeper into the Terces Wood, landed, and shifted in a small clearing. "How on Myrrh am I going to rescue Sibee without creating a furor?"

Two tiny voices whispered close by. "Almiralyn, we can help."

The voices and the murmur of miniature wings made her turn. She held out her hands and waited for two tiny figures to land. "I thought you were told to stay hidden." She scolded them in a gentle tone.

The Nyti alighted, their sandals tap dancing on her palms. One with a thatch of unruly, reddish hair spoke up. "We want to help Sibee."

The second tipped his thimble-sized top hat. "Mumshu at your service. Please, my lady. He's our friend."

"How do you propose to help? The soldiers have him well guarded, and you are tiny."

The copper-haired Nyti's grin broadened. "Beg pardon, Almiralyn. I'm Ashor." He bowed from the waist and straightened. "We can warn Sibee not to do anything silly. Later tonight, when it is dark, we can create a diversion so he can sneak away."

Almiralyn studied the boys. Nyti, the smallest folk of the Terces Wood, had gossamer wings and hands and feet that seemed too big for their miniature bodies. They were fun-loving and enjoyed a good frolic, but they were also quick and smart. If their leader agreed, they might keep Sibee from getting himself killed or worse...tortured.

She held the tiny boys at eye level. "Does Kieel know you're here?"

Ashor's infectious grin shrunk to a self-conscious smile. "Of course... well we..."

Mumshu coughed. "Ah, no, my lady."

"How quick can you be?"

"Super quick, my lady."

"Then bring Kieel here. I can't allow you to become involved without his permission."

The Nyti darted away. If their leader was willing, they might help. One thing was certain, she couldn't risk her capture or theirs'. Too much was at stake.

The covert tread of footsteps among the trees alerted her to Human company. *Soldiers? Who else could it be?* Pressing against an ancient maple tree, she matched her molecular structure to its trunk and melted into bark. Only her eyes remained unchanged. She lowered her lids.

"I'm telling you, I heard a woman's voice." A soldier ducked behind a tree and crouched at the edge of the clearing.

His companion shot him a doubtful scowl and began a cautious search of the area. "There's no one here. Only animals have passed this way. We'd better keep moving. The Tinpaca can get pretty cranky."

"Yeah. Especially since the Guardian and her cottage and barn have disappeared. Tesilend swears he sat in her kitchen and later she questioned him in a stall in the barn."

"The man's confused, that's all." The second soldier traversed the clearing, his weapon drawn.

From beneath half-closed lids, Almiralyn observed the first man pause at the tree line. His body tensed; his head slightly turned to listen. He swung around. Narrowed eyes darted around the clearing, locked onto hers, and widened in disbelief. By the time he reached the maple, her eyes had snapped into invisibility. The man swore and ran a hand over the bark.

"What in SeDah are you doing?" His comrade peered from the shelter of the trees.

"I thought I saw..." He let his fingers trail over the rough bark. "Never mind—it was nothing." Still, he remained by the tree, his hand pressed against the trunk. "I could have sworn..." Muttering under his breath, he gave the tree a hard look and strode across the clearing. When he reached his comrade, he glanced back. "This is one strange forest. I can't wait to return to RewFaar."

Almiralyn didn't move until she could no longer hear the tread of their steps. When her senses assured her no more soldiers roamed close by, she returned to Human form. Three Nyti flitted from the shadows and landed on a branch at her eye level.

The tallest Nyti pointed his walking stick at her. "Much too close, Almiralyn. Much too close. I was about to fly out and bite his ear. You must be more careful." Kieel tapped the stick against the branch to stress each word.

"I know, Kieel. Thank you for coming." She smiled. His tidy appearance, from his tie tucked neatly beneath his sienna vest to his spotless, olive green pants, spoke to his love of neatness and detail. The only thing about the Nyti leader that suggested disarray was his thatch of thick, auburn-gold hair.

"It appears we have trouble in the Terces Wood." He placed a finger on the high curve of his distinctive nose. His stern expression morphed into speculation. "The boys tell me their Wood Tiff friend, Sibee, has got himself captured. How can we help?"

"They tied him to a tree behind what used to be the barn."

Kieel pursed his lips. "Ashor informed me your cottage and barn have disappeared. Is this so?"

Almiralyn sighed. "It's a long story, Kieel, one I am happy to share at another time. We must rescue Sibee before the soldiers have time to question him."

The Nyti leader nodded. "It sounds like we need a distraction. I suggest we scout the situation and then make a plan."

"Any closer than this to the soldier's camp, I am safest in bird form. You can talk to me and I will understand, but I won't be able to answer. If I agree, I will bob my head once...if I disagree, twice. If we need more discussion, I'll fly further into the forest, and you can follow. Right now, ride with me." She shifted, and the Nyti settled on her white-feathered back. Taking care to remain in the shadows, she flew to a Tirips tree near the RewFaaran camp and landed on a broad branch covered with silver leaves. The Nyti would scout and report back. She could only wait, hidden and worried about the lives of her people.

Kieel understood the responsibility for rescuing Sibee rested on his shoulders. The young Wood Tiff knew too much. The youngster was brave and determined. That wouldn't be enough if the RewFaarans tortured him. He also realized Almiralyn dared not show herself, even in bird form. The foreign soldiers would know about her ability to shape shift. They'd be on the alert for a white bird with gold-tipped wings.

Leading the boys away from Myrrh's Guardian, he flew to a tall evergreen and motioned them to land. He kept his voice low and his face serious. "This is not a game."

Ashor and Mumshu moved closer to each other. "We understand."

Kieel heard the quaver in their voices and nodded. "Our first goal is to find Sibee. Stay high above the heads of the soldiers and well within the cover of the trees. Do not fly in the open. Meet me back here as soon as you can." Pointing them in opposite directions, he watched them zip away with the speed of hummingbirds from one tree to the next. Satisfied they would do nothing unwise, he secured his walking stick between the long needles of the pine and darted closer to the camp. Perhaps a little eavesdropping would net him some much-needed information.

From a vantage point above the tents lining the perimeter of the vine-covered ruins, he studied the camp layout and selected his goal—a tent that appeared to be the camp headquarters. Landing in the trampled undergrowth, he crept from stone to stone and from clump of dirt to clump of dirt until he crouched near the back of it. Large feet striding by sent him shimmying under the canvas edge. Inside, he ducked behind a duffle bag and peered under a campstool at the enormous lower legs of a uniformed Human.

Kieel ducked out of range and forced himself to listen to the heated discussion thundering around him.

"The coordinates show the cottage and the barn right here." The first man frowned. "Grantese Tesilend is positive they didn't move him."

"Tesilend was unconscious when we found him, so his opinion is invalid." The second man removed his spectacles, wiped a lens with a pristine handkerchief, and replaced them. "The Wood Tiff creature confirms his story. Do you think the guardian woman made them disappear?"

"Doubtful, Cantruto." Broad shoulders shrugged. "But when you consider we're looking for twins, of which there is no sign, two women, a magic fountain, and giant crystal..." The words trailed into silence.

Cantruto narrowed his eyes. "Maybe Nissasa is right. Maybe the Largeen Joram is senile."

"I'd be careful if I were you. Tents have ears, and Lorsedi has a long reach." Although the response was calm, the man closest to Kieel straightened, and his chin came up.

Cantruto achieved his full height in an instant, leaned across the table, and glared a challenge. "You threatening me, Mondago?"

The Tinpaca rested the tip of a stylus on the table. "No, I'm warning you." He held it upright with an index finger. "I suggest you remember whom you are addressing. It would be unseemly for my adjutant to end up in the brig on such an important mission." The stylus clattered on the tabletop.

"Yes, sir." Eyeing the stylus, Cantruto sat down.

"After our meal, you will interrogate the Wood Tiff."

Cantruto unsheathed an evil-looking knife. *It should be easy to break the little bugger. I'm betting that all I have to do is cut off one finger—*"

"The Wood Tiff is a child, not a spy, Cantruto." Tinpaca Mondago's face was neutral; his voice was not. "We will question him together."

Kieel had heard enough. Rescuing Sibee was a priority. He and the boys needed a plan in place. Then he'd report to Almiralyn.

28

DerTah

Brie rotated slowly, taking in every detail of her tent at Eissua Oasis. Woven hangings in muted blues and golds circled the dark walls and created an alcove for sleeping. Blue and burgundy striped rugs thrown over black canvas covered the ground. A raised bed draped in blue, a soft-looking chair, a washstand, and a small table with an oil lamp glowing on its top created an atmosphere of comfort. Large cushions scattered around the space added cheerful splashes of color. Brie sighed. *So much has happened.* She stifled a yawn. *By the Fathers, am I tired!*

Nichi poked her head in the tent flap. "ConDria like be clean?"

"Would I!" Brie grinned.

Nichi held up a robe and towel. "This way."

Tucked in a group of trees behind the tent was a goatskin-draped cubicle. Three buckets of water steamed beside it.

"Hot water!" Brie shook her head. "Where on DerTah did you get hot water?"

Nichi grinned. "Hot springs close by. Narrtep and Dansboys bring." She showed her how to hang a bucket on a big hook attached to a thick rope. A pulley system positioned the bucket above her head. The Dansgirl handed her a stick with a hook on the end. "Tip with stick and water rains. When need more, change bucket. Goat soap there. You good?"

"I'm good. Thank you, Nichi." She stepped into the cubicle, stripped off her sand-laden clothing, and tossed them outside. With the stick, she tested the tip of the bucket. It tilted and dumped. Water drenched her from head to toe. Delight gurgling up from her belly turned to spontaneous laughter. With the goat soap, she worked her hair into a cap of lather and scrubbed the dried sweat from her body. Enjoying the luxury of a two-bucket rinse, she pictured her fatigue draining away with the dirty water.

After toweling off, she slipped on her robe and stepped from the cubicle. Not finding her clothes, she scurried around the tent and ducked into its cozy warmth. Fresh clothing and a kcalo the color of midnight lay on the bed.

Taken aback by the generosity of the Atrilaasu, she held up a creamy blouse. Red, blue, and orange embroidery decorated the neckline and created a wide band of color at the bottom of the long, full sleeves. She slipped it over her head, stepped into loose-fitting pants of the same color, and fastened them with embroidered ties at the waist and ankles. After sliding on her goatskin sandals, she rummaged around in her pack for a comb. Much tugging and pulling ended with her red curls tamed into a semblance of order and a beaded headband in place. The small mirror on the washstand reflected the results of her labor. *Not bad.* Donning her kcalo and tying it in place, she stepped from the tent into the chilly desert night.

Ira sprawled on a cot in the boys' tent. Torgin, Esán, and Seval had gone to shower. Time alone was worth being dirty for a little longer. He'd go when they came back.

"What a crazy turning!" He counted off on his fingers... "Fire ConDra, Brie becoming the ConDria, Yaro appearing, Esán showing up like a phantom. If Nichi hadn't come along, we'd all be stumbling around in the desert, freezing to death."

What's next? He sat up, rested his elbows on his knees, propped his chin on his hands, and tracked the intricate pattern on the woven rug. *I'm angry all the time. Why? Torgin makes me want to punch him. Seval is more afraid than Torgin. Esán is always taking up Brie's time. Why does that matter?* He straightened and ran a hand through his unruly hair. *Something is lurking on the outskirts of my memory...something important. What is it?*

Laughter heralded the return of the others. He gathered his things together, including the new clothing provided by the Dansmen, and pulled the tent flap aside. Cold night air whooshed through the opening, ushering Torgin in first, then Seval, followed by Esán.

"Just wait until you see the shower." Torgin shivered in his towel and hurried to his cot and his new clothes.

Ira ducked out the door. Laughter followed him as he strolled around the tent. *Why am I staying to myself? Maybe I'll feel more sociable after I'm clean.*

Three buckets of steaming water waited by the shower cubicle. He stepped in, stripped, and tossed his dirty clothes over the side. Sand and sweat, followed by his bad mood, washed away with warm water and goat soap. He dried off, dressed in the new loose-fitting shirt and pants, and slid a pair of sandals on his feet. Satisfied with his attire and delighted to be clean, he skirted the tent and walked to the lakeshore.

Two full moons reflected on the water's calm surface held him spellbound. A glance up at the strange sky filled him with wonder. The colors of the moons—one huge and saffron yellow, already sliding down its descending arc; and one smaller and glacier blue high overhead—intrigued him. At the far end of the basin, a third moon shone creamy white and crescent-shaped. The nightscape, both beautiful and strange, created an unexpected longing for Myrrh.

Light from the tent flap opening and the sound of soft voices warned him of company as Torgin, Esán, and Seval strolled in his direction. *The end of being alone.* He sighed and then smiled to himself. *It's time to celebrate, and that means food.*

Torgin's green eyes gleamed in the moonlight. "Let's find Brie. I think it is time for a meal, and I'm starving."

Esán and Seval chorused their agreement.

Ira gave Torgin a playful punch in the arm. "Race ya to Brie's tent." He sprinted across the sand, his melancholy mood a thing of the past.

Brie fell into bed after an emotional evening and slept the night through. She awoke feeling rested for the first time in ages, stretched, and stared up at the strangeness of the coned ceiling. *Where am I...oh, yes.* Closing her eyes, she filled her lungs with cool air and released it in a luxurious exhale. *It's nice to be quiet without the assault of remembering, of planning, of contriving...*

Memories, good and bad, flooded in. She sat up. Fingertips pressed against her temples, she tried to shroud their onslaught. A moment of blanketed stillness and then the chaos of impressions reformed. Hoping to stem the flow, she squeezed her eyes shut, slid her fingers past her hairline, and combed them through tangled curls until their tips touched at her crown. *Memories,* she thought, *are the stories we tell ourselves.* Her hands traveled down the back of her head, along the sides of her neck, and dropped like dead weights to rest on her thighs. *What are my stories?*

She slipped her legs over the edge of the narrow bed and pressed her bare soles into the soft weave of a goatskin rug.

"Who am I?" The whispered words floated on a shaft of sunlight streaking through the loose tent flap and morphed into a series of silent questions. *Am I a ConDria or a girl? Am I KcernFensian or RewFaaran or both?* She thought about her friends. *Esán, Torgin...Ira. What is missing in my memory? I know there's something I'm forgetting, something that would fill the emptiness I'm feeling here, alone in a tent in the middle of Fera Finnero.*

Eissua Oasis, becoming the ConDria, and feeling the shift for the first time filled her thoughts. Exquisite memories of water and flight changed confusion to wonder. She smiled and looked around the tent. *I needed this time alone to absorb all that's happened.*

Memories of last night's celebration filled her with awe.

Women, their long dark hair flying around them, danced to the intense, rhythmic music played by men on drums made from clay and tanned goat skin. Children sang and laughed. Everyone ate from tables laden with more food than Brie had seen in several sun turnings.

Through it all, WoNadahem Mardree sat at the fringe of the festivities, the red fox at her side. Her strange eyes captured the firelight and glowed like the rising moons of DerTah. The small, desert snake coiled on her shoulder, flicked its tongue, and hissed. The crystal dangling from a leather thong around her neck glowed different colors as the celebration progressed.

Brie enjoyed the festivities from a quiet, shadowed corner. Although the Atrilaasu allowed her the privilege of anonymity, their dark eyes found her often, and their smiles warmed her as much as the fire.

Nichi teased Seval into dancing a quadrille with three other couples. Ira and Torgin ate enough for six men before joining in the celebratory games. She grinned. *You'd think they've been a part of the Dansmen's culture forever.* The evening brought joy all around.

As the full saffron moon reached its zenith, WoNa rose, and the Dansmen grew quiet.

"Tonight, the ConDria od Atrilaasu and her companions honor us with their presence." The Oracle's alto tones sent a wave of anticipation through the tribe. She continued. "The dreaming place has shown me the will of the desert spirits. The ConDria and her friends are central to The Unfolding. We, the Atrilaasu, must adopt them and present them with the protective Vestments of Drango."

Brie exchanged glances with Esán, who had joined her earlier. Torgin, Ira, and Seval made their way to her side.

WoNa's eyes roamed the crowd and came to rest on her and her circle of friends. "All those who cherish this dreaming affirm it now."

Men, women, and children formed a circle around them, with WoNa at the center. A high, pure voice rose in song. Others joined in until the entire tribe sent their chorused tribute soaring into the night sky.

> *"ConDria rising in our time of need*
> *As foretold by the ancients who planted the seed.*
> *Today we are honored to welcome her home.*
> *She is Atrilaasu where e're she may roam."*

WoNa raised a hand. The Atrilaasu repeated the song a final time, and then silence enveloped the Oasis. After several moments, she raised her voice once again. "As tradition demands, I, WoNadahem Mardree, commit to stand as the TorPan of Brielle AsTar and Ira Raast."

Narrtep stepped into the circle. "I offer to be the TorPan of Esán Efre and Torgin Whalend."

Seval shot a frightened look at Esán. Nichi moved to his side. A tall man left the ranks and joined Narrtep and WoNa. "I, Strom, the father of Nichook, am honored to sponsor Seval and act as his TorPan."

A cheer went up.

Again WoNa raised her hand for silence. "In the ancient teachings, every tribal member must pass from child to adult at the age of Ettainni. The Ceremony of Drango accomplished this. The Oracle touched her heart. "Brielle AsTar, are you prepared to accept your responsibilities as an adult member of the Atrilaasu Dansmen?"

"I am, WoNadahem."

"Ira Raast?"

"I am, WoNadahem Mardree."

Narrtep repeated the question. Esán and Torgin each affirmed their willingness to be adopted as Atrilaasu Dansmen.

Strom posed the question to Seval. Brie watched the boy blush. His stuttered 'I am' was barely a whisper, but his eyes were shining as he smiled at Nichi.

A wave of WoNa's hand sent the Dansmen scurrying in several directions. Women hustled younger children off to bed. Men and older children faded into the night shadows. Strom and Narrtep remained with WoNa. A serious quiet settled over their faces. Brie felt Ira fidget behind her. Torgin rested a hand on her shoulder. Seval gulped and moved closer. Esán remained a steady presence beside her.

WoNa smiled. "You and your companions honor us, ConDria. I will explain the Ceremony of Drango. At the time of Ettainni, Dansmen receive drango tunics and boots. The DerTahan drango is an immense iguana-like creature. Its hide, though supple after tanning, is tough and almost impenetrable. Taccus needles cannot pierce it. Nor can the sting of a roscipon, Fera Finnero's most deadly insect. It will even deflect the blow of a knife. We create tunics for each individual initiate. Your

TorPan will sew you into it, praying with each stitch for your safety and well-being.

"The history of this ceremony is as ancient as the desert sands. When the time draws near, we prepare both boys and girls for the hunt. All Atrilaasu train as warriors to protect the tribe in times of need. Hunting a drango is part of the training for this adult responsibility.

"Once the hunters find the drango, the initiate must mount it. We used the knife of the TorPan for the kill. A quick thrust of the blade into the brain kills the creature instantly. Since time is of the essence, you will not join the hunt. The Unfolding presses us to move quickly."

Brie's daydreaming ended when Nichi stuck her head in the tent. "WoNa will see you soon." She placed a tray of food on the table and left.

Brie ran a brush through her curls, washed her face, and fastened her beaded headband in place. She shrugged into a cream-colored blouse and sleek pants, the soft green of water at first light. The wheat-colored tunic draped over a deep blue cushion awed her.

She held it up and inhaled its scent before slipping it over her head and shoulders. It molded to her upper body and slid smoothly over her hips. She picked up her boots and pulled them on. Pliant drango leather hugged her legs to just above the knee.

The final ceremonial gift—the knife used to cut the thread after the last stitch in her tunic—lay on the chair. A Drango hide sheath, dyed a dark, warm tan, attached to a leather belt that fastened with a rounded tooth. She grasped the satiny bone, carved to form the handle, and withdrew the blade. When WoNa presented it, she shared an Atrilaasu belief. *The gift of a knife is the gift of life. Wish I knew more about how to use it.* She replaced it and ran a hand over her tunic.

Sighing, she picked up a piece of flatbread and smothered it with taccus jelly. *Esán is with us, so a rescue is no longer needed. What is our next step? Somehow returning to Myrrh doesn't seem right.* She took a bite and stared into the distance. *Perhaps my meeting with WoNadahem Mardree will provide the answer.*

Esán learned at the celebration that an underground river fed the oasis. Now, standing on the lake shore, he admired its magnificence and observed the hustle and bustle of tribal life. Around the basin, the Atrilaasu people performed their various duties before the heat of mid-turning sent them inside. Women and children weeding gardens and irrigating; a potter working at her wheel in an open tent; another woman making soap; men sharpening knifes, making tools, and building household items—all were busy assuring that life at Eissua Oasis would prosper.

His attention shifted to the cascading waterfall and the misty rainbow shimmering above the lake's surface. The first rays of morning sunlight picked out individual droplets that sparkled like diamonds, then lost their distinctiveness in their splashing arrival in the plunge pool below.

He loved the peace of the early morning but knew it would not last. With luck, his meeting with WoNadahem Mardree would provide some much needed answers, especially for Seval. His instincts assured him she could help untangle the boy's mind.

He glanced down at his drango tunic and boots, touched the knife at his side, and smiled. After he and his friends had received their vestments, they pledged their loyalty to the Atrilaasu and to the successful conclusion of The Unfolding. *What an honor!*

A red fox exiting a dark opening in the outcropping stopped at his side and gazed at him. With a sharp yip, it trotted back the way it had come. Esán followed.

The fox led him down a short tunnel that opened into a cave about twice the size of the small one in Oche Cavern in the Dojanack Mountains on Myrrh. WoNadahem sat on a low, cushioned seat by a fire, the only light in the space. He realized with a start that her sight was impaired.

"Come closer, Esán." Her alto voice hummed like a melody. "Let my fingers learn your face."

"You're blind," he whispered.

The small snake curling around her wrist whistled. She smiled. "Only my eyes do not see. My heart, my spirit, my hands, my nose...they all provide what my eyes cannot."

He knelt. Her fingers traced his face, sensing, he felt sure, more than a sighted person would perceive. She touched his heart. The crystal on her forehead flared blue and settled back into the pale orange of early morning.

"Sit, Bearer of the Seeds of Carsilem. We have much to discuss." She ran a hand along the red fox's back. "Please, Yaro, guard the entrance."

Esán watched it depart, wondering at the miracles of life. "You know Yaro, the Pentharian?"

Her head turned the direction the fox had taken. "We spent much of the night talking. Pentharian are most interesting creatures, are they not?"

Esán waited for her sightless eyes to find him again. "WoNadahem Mardree..."

Her expression stopped him. The snake slithered up her sleeve and reappeared on her shoulder. She turned her head. Its forked tongue sniffed her lips. Firelight danced in her saffron and blue eyes. "I am called WoNa, Esán." She released a hissed breath. "Do you know you are from the planet of Tao Spirian?"

He started to shake his head and caught himself. "I did not know."

"You are a full-blood and carry dual seeds. You are the one long awaited by your people."

"What is the Seed of Carsilem? No one will tell me."

"They don't tell because words do not express it well. It is like trying to explain the spirits of the desert or the one Myrrhinian's call Emit. What I can tell you is that you, Esán, hold the potential for greatness. And it is not only the power you carry. Give me your hand." She took it in hers and ran a finger over the surface of his palm. "You suffer from a disease passed to you via the genetic patterns of your ancestry. An Arrenduca healer on your home planet of Tao Spirian holds the key to your healing." The finger drew a pattern on his skin. "You must not return to Thera. If you do, the disease will kill you." Her strange eyes closed. "Your power draws your enemies to you. You must find your father. He can protect you." She opened her eyes and placed her palm on his.

A current tingled throughout his body. An image formed...a blue heron in pursuit of... It faded. "How do I return to Myrrh, WoNa? My father is there. And the Evolsefil Crystal waits. I must return it to the Cave of Canedari."

"You must seek the portal on the shores of the Sea of Trinuge. Soldiers guard the one in Fera Finnero. Your friends must accompany you. Do not leave them. You are their savior, and they are yours."

The snake hissed. She dropped his hand. "Ah. Your friend, Brielle, will be here soon. One more thing, Esán Efre...Seval is in grave danger. If he regains his memory, it will increase his danger and yours. But it must be his decision. Bring him and your friends, Torgin and Ira, to me. Ask Torgin to bring his flute. As soon as Brielle and I finish working, we will meet together with Seval to help him decide his fate."

Brie followed the red fox along the shore to a cave entrance in the outcropping. Esán emerged as she arrived. A mix of emotions played on his face. He gave her a quick hug and stepped aside to let her pass. "She is quite amazing, Brielle. She's blind."

"I know. Don't tell Seval why the Oracle wants him to visit her."

Esán laughed out loud. "I can't keep any secrets from you." He sobered. "I won't tell him." He started to leave, then looked over his shoulder. "She says to call her WoNa."

The red fox yipped. She waved at Esán and looked down at the shifted Pentharian. "Lead on, Yaro."

When she arrived in the cave, it appeared to be empty. Standing still, she shut her eyes and allowed her senses to define her surroundings...the smell of smoke, the touch of air flowing in from outside, the sound of her own breath. She did not sense WoNa's presence, and yet...The Star of Truth tingled in anticipation and then began to throb. She opened her eyes. A hand moved into the fire's light. Tiny eyes gleamed red. A forked-tongue flicked her cheek. The snake hissed a series of wheezy syllables and withdrew beneath the sleeve of a teal blue kcalo.

"When I am seated, Brielle, please kneel in front of me." The voice, which sounded like the low notes Torgin played on his flute, moved around the fire. The tall Danswoman stepped into its light and lowered onto her cushioned seat.

Brie knelt and closed her eyes again. WoNa's fingers drifted over her face, tracing its structure—the eyebrows, the eyes, the length of her nose, the curve of her lips and chin—before they floated back to rest in her lap. Brie sat back on her heels and waited.

"So much to read in you and so little time. Sit here by my knee." WoNa patted a cushion beside her. "Many changes make you wonder who you are.

You are yourself, Brielle. You learned that on the Throne of ReNin RepPosu on Myrrh." The rich tenor of her voice filled the cave.

Astonishment rustled through Brie like a shift in the wind. "You know about ReNin RepPosu? I saw you and the sands of DerTah and the planet of RewFaar. Some of it terrified me. Some inspired me to do my best. Seeing the future..." She shuddered.

WoNa leaned closer. "Knowing the future is a tremendous responsibility. What have you learned, Brielle?"

Brie brought the palms of her hands together and pressed her index fingers against her lips. The fire crackled. She lowered her hands. "I think living in the future is as unrewarding as living in the past. It is vital you focus on this moment, or you will miss the richness of it."

The Danswoman's mouth curved into a smile. "Almiralyn would be proud. You know, of course, that our actions of today create the future. The future we see can change in an instant." Again, the snake contributed his hiss to the conversation. WoNa nodded and touched Brie's cheek. "We have things to do before we can help your friend, Seval. Please ask Yaro to join us."

29
DerTah

Grouchy from too little sleep and several nerve-wracking encounters, Nomed couldn't seem to turn off the list of grievances bouncing around in his mind. He didn't trust Lorsedi. Wolloh kept his game close to his chest. Nissasa was as dangerous as a Fire ConDra. And TheLise took too many risks. *Women are so shortsighted.* He paced across his room. *Not only that... Esán vanished with that young servant, Seval, and Wolloh appears unconcerned.* A scowl tugged at his scarred cheek. The High DiMensioner focused, instead, on the danger within his own domain.

Although he could not find fault with his mentor's desire to deal with Nissasa and Gidtuss, he chafed at not knowing the whereabouts of his nephew. Esán could take care of himself, but he was inexperienced.

Yanking the door open, he strode down the hall. He and TheLise had a date, one he dreaded. Lorsedi and Wolloh were prepared to sacrifice her to

Nissasa's evil intentions. He was not. In theory, their plan was a good one—but placing a woman in danger felt wrong. He almost laughed. *Since when have I cared about women?* Surprise flashed. *I care about TheLise. Da'amit all.* Life had taught him to keep everyone at arm's length, and then Esán came along, and then TheLise. *What's wrong with me?*

He glared at the Dreelas' door, schooled his expression and his mind to acceptance, and knocked. A brief pause and she stood regarding him, a half-smile playing at the corners of her mouth. Her sleek dress of coppery silk sported a neckline scooped low in the front and a back that was almost nonexistent. Sculpting every curve of her body, it left little to the imagination.

He kept his voice bland. "Are you ready?"

She stepped into the hall and closed the door. The smell of her perfume, the touch of her hand... His heart thumped. Disdain draping him, he offered his arm.

At the drawing room door, they paused. Her enchanting smile lit her face. He looked down at her and glowered under his raised brow.

"Really, Seyes, you are the most stubborn man I know." The smile had changed in an instant to a petulant pout. She tossed her head and strolled into the room. Every head had turned, and every male stared. She advanced toward Wolloh, her sensual beauty blazing with every step, every movement of her head or hips or luminous gray eyes. Gidtuss, the only male unaffected, glared with disgust.

Nomed had intended to follow, but found himself intercepted by Lorsedi and Nissasa. "Good evening, Seyes. It appears you annoyed the Dreelas." The Largeen Joram followed TheLise with his eyes. "She is lovely, you know."

"Lovely and a hothead." He, too, looked in her direction. "Do you ever wonder at the inability of women to understand the simplest things?"

Lorsedi laughed and turned to his son. "You've a way with the ladies, Nissa. Can you answer Seyes' question?"

The tall man narrowed his predatory gaze. Muscles rippled beneath his elegant jacket. He nodded toward the object of their discussion. "She is quite gorgeous. Are you involved?"

Nomed let himself appear obtuse. "Involved? As in lovers or friends?"

Nissasa's lazy smile did not touch his eyes. "As in either?"

"We apprenticed with Wolloh as young adults. You might consider us friends."

The man caught her eye and smiled. "And is she a staunch supporter of the High DiMensioner?"

Nomed laughed. "TheLise is a staunch supporter of TheLise. She plays her own game. If you'll excuse me, I must make my apologies to Wolloh for such a rude entrance." He nodded and sauntered across the room.

He reached Wolloh's good side as TheLise joined Baroh, Omudi, and two women from RewFaar.

Wolloh cast her an appreciative glance. "She is one fine woman." He looked back at Nomed. "It appears he's taken the bait."

Nomed scowled as Nissasa oozed his way to TheLise's side. He faced his mentor and changed the subject of conversation. "Who are the women with Baroh?"

"The older woman is the LaChett Roween Rattori, Nissasa's mother. The other is Tissent, SparrowLyn AsTar's aunt and her mother's twin."

Nomed angled his body so he could see them more clearly. "So twins run in the family." He glanced over his shoulder at Lorsedi. "And so does red hair."

Wolloh's smooth lips curved upward. "Tissent is a good woman. She gave up her life in KcernFensia to save it and the people she loved. Roween, on the other hand, is a schemer, part RewFaaran and part rattlesnake, with political aspirations for her son. She is as dangerous as Nissasa."

"I believe LaChett is a title, but I don't know its reference." Nomed glanced again at the topic of their conversation.

"It refers to a RewFaaran woman claimed by one man. Lorsedi tells me he chose Roween as a LaChett to keep her from stirring up trouble. Men on RewFaar may keep several LaChett at one time."

Gidtuss, descending on them, ended the conversation. Nomed dodged out of range, made his way to the bar, and ordered a glass of red wine. A casual turn of the head brought TheLise into view as Lorsedi's son had made his move. She laughed and pouted prettily. Nissasa smiled and guided her toward the patio door. Roween's hawk-like features flashed extreme satisfaction as she gazed after them. The game was well underway.

Corvus moved from guest to guest with a tray full of DerTahan delicacies, memorizing faces and gleaning information to help him protect Esán and the twins. Time at Shu Chenaro had taught him much. Lorsedi's arrival with his entourage cast a whole new light on the past few sun turnings and on the future. Until Wolloh and Lorsedi neutralized Nissasa Rattori, Corvus' charges remained in danger.

The Dreelas of Trinuge reached for an appetizer, caught his eye, and held it. He glanced away, pivoted, and offered the tray to Dreela Omudi of Geran Island, who scooped up several goodies without taking his eyes off the dark, angular woman beside him.

Corvus navigated the crowd, dodged a fellow servant, and ducked into the kitchen. *Dreelas TheLise's eyes flashed a warning. Does she know who I am? Impossible.* He frowned. *Dare I return to the drawing room?* He reviewed what he had learned. *Esán and the twins must be my priority. Being forearmed can only help. One more pass and I'm away.*

He grabbed a well laden tray and backed through the door. Working the periphery, he closed in on Wolloh. The High DiMensioner beckoned him forward. The group surrounding him included Nomed and Lorsedi. With a subservient demeanor, he offered the tray and prepared to move on. A clawed hand on his arm detained him. Corvus glanced at the scarred face.

Wolloh picked up an appetizer with his good hand. "What have you heard regarding your granddaughters, Lorsedi? Have you found them?"

The Largeen Joram bit into a puff pastry stuffed with taccus grubs. "Tasty. What is the filling?" He looked directly at Corvus.

"I believe it is—" The hand on his arm froze his response.

"Perhaps you would prefer to enjoy it." Wolloh popped one into his twisted mouth, chewed, and swallowed. "I doubt it is something one would eat on RewFaar."

Lorsedi sampled a piece of smoked noorgnaak, a desert marsupial, and nodded his appreciation. "My granddaughters seem to have disappeared, or at least they are in hiding. Their mother is on Thera. With luck, my men will find her soon." He helped himself to a glass of wine from a passing tray and raised it. "To reuniting my family."

The clawed hand released Corvus' arm. Wolloh lifted a glass from the tray. "Here. Here."

Corvus melted into the crowd. His time at Shu Chenaro had ended.

From beneath lazy lids, Nomed scanned the dispersing crowd. Wolloh's party had gone on forever. The sun's early light glowed along the horizon finally prompted his guests to drift toward their rooms.

His vantage point beside the bar gave him a covert view of TheLise as she gazed up at Nissasa. Her mysterious smile and seductive stance produced a lascivious grin on the man's hawkish face. He kissed her bare neck and whispered something that made her brush his lips with a fingertip. After taking leave of his mother, he slipped an arm around the Dreelas and escorted her from the room.

Nomed ground his teeth and shifted his attention to Wolloh, as Lorsedi shook hands with Baroh and Omudi. Tissent, a lone figure by the double doors into the garden, smiled as his gaze rested on hers. He made his way to her side. "I don't believe we have met. I am Seyes Nomed."

Tranquil eyes gazed up at him. "I am Tissent. You are The DiMensioner, are you not?" The gentle voice softened the edges of his anger.

"I'm not sure about *The* DiMensioner, but I've studied the art of DiMensionery."

Sea-green eyes bathed him in their coolness as she searched his face. "I believe you have met my great-nieces, Arienh and Brielle."

"Your great-nieces?"

She shifted her gaze to the desert garden and glided beside him through the open doors into the soft light of dawn. "I am their grandmother's twin. Lorsedi is searching for them. What are they like?"

Drawn in by her serenity, Nomed shared a little of what he knew about her nieces. When he had finished, they watched the golden rays of sunlight streaking the sky above the horizon. He couldn't help but compare her untroubled quiet to the always-electric energy of TheLise.

She stirred beside him. "Thank you for your kindness, Seyes. I worry about my sister and her family." Warm color touched her porcelain complexion, tinting her eyes a deeper green. "I would say goodnight, but..." She raised a graceful hand, bringing his attention to the beauty of morning.

He smiled down at her. "May I walk you to your room?"

"That would not be wise." She strolled to the double doors.

"RewFaaran rules regarding men and women are very strict, and we wouldn't want to raise any eyebrows, would we?"

He laughed and bowed. "Until we meet again."

Tissent responded with her gentle smile before she glided through the doors and out of sight. Nomed clasped his hands behind his back, his thoughts trailing after Tissent, his eyes watching the sun melting the night's shadows away. *That was quite interesting.*

A mental tug informed him that Wolloh awaited his arrival. *Will this night ever end?* He did an about-face and made his way to his mentor's sitting room.

The High DiMensioner od DerTah sat in his favorite chair. The pinched contours of his face and the way he held his body highlighted his fatigue.

Nomed sank into a comfortable chair opposite him. "Sleep might be a good idea, Wolloh. Even I'm tired. It's been a hard turning."

"It has indeed. Prior to retiring, however, you and I have important things to discuss. What I have to say won't make you happy, Seyes. But it is vital you and I understand the consequences of our actions." He turned his head and called softly, "Come in."

A hidden door slid open and Stebben entered the room. Nomed noted the lack of uniform and the somber expression.

"Please join us in our discussion."

Wolloh's Major Domo pulled up a chair, made himself comfortable, and nodded. "Good morning, sir. Nomed."

"Good to see you, Stebben." Nomed noted the subtle power emanating from the man. He also paid attention to the fact that Wolloh refrained from posturing for effect and held them both in a contemplative gaze.

The High DiMensioner cleared his throat. "I have something most serious to discuss with you, Seyes. I would appreciate your hearing me out."

Nomed couldn't remember a time when Wolloh had spoken with such candor. "I'll do my best to listen until you're finished."

Wolloh's face relaxed as he resettled his tired body. "Stebben and I have been doing some research. Our findings suggest that removing the Evolsefil Crystal from Myrrh will have disastrous consequences far beyond the destruction of Myrrh and Thera. Evolsefil is the Prima Crystal of a network of crystals placed throughout this solar system. Control of it gives its steward control of all the others. The Galactic Guardians chose

Almiralyn to protect Evolsefil because a need for power does not sway her."

Nomed forced down a retort.

Wolloh continued. "Nissasa has also discovered this potential. It is his goal to establish Thera and Myrrh as RewFaaran colonies and to use the power of the Evolsefil Crystal and the fountain, Elcaro's Eye, to gain dominance over this entire solar system. Your hatred of Almiralyn and Myrrh plays right into his hands. I understand your desire for revenge, and I pledge to help you with Almiralyn, but you must promise me you will set aside your lust for Evolsefil."

Nomed tried to wipe his surprise from his face with a frown.

"Yes, I know you planned to take it for yourself. Are you aware that its base is no longer quartz, but is now solid gold, and gold filaments thread the crystal spire? Its power has increased one hundredfold, Seyes. If removed, it will end life as we know it in the Clenaba Rolas Solar System and beyond." He paused, but maintained the serious intent in his gaze. When he continued, his tone became harsher. "Evolsefil's safety is vital to RewFaar, Thera, and DerTah, to all planets in the solar system."

Nomed felt the scar on his cheek start to pulse. The emotions boiling inside him propelled him from the chair and sent him across the room and back. He was a kid again, a kid with a shard of glass in his hand and anger twisting through him like a tornado. An image of Tissent's calm face emerged through the mist of fury and hatred. He inhaled and returned to his seat. His skills as a DiMensioner helped him to slow his heart rate. The anger abated. The emotional storm dissipated. With a long, exhaled breath, he placed steady hands on his knees and raised his eyes to his mentor's face.

"It is not Myrrh that I hate." He kept his voice low and controlled. "It is Almiralyn's treatment of me as a boy that makes my blood boil."

"I agree she was unfair and insensitive. We will deal with her after we take care of Nissasa. Can you promise to forget about Evolsefil?"

The image of the regal, clear quartz crystal with the six smaller sentinel crystals surrounding its base filled Nomed's mind. The majesty of it—the power, its ability to tap into the very heart of him—left him bereft of breath. *Which is more important—Wolloh or the Prima Crystal Evolsefil?* The understanding in his mentor's face made him wonder again at the emotional connections he was discovering. Shoving the thought away for a later time, he offered his hand. "I will never forget the crystal's magnificence, but I do promise not to pursue my desire to make it my own."

Wolloh's good hand clasped his. "Thank you, Seyes. I am so proud of the man you have become."

Nomed saw the pride shining in his good eye and felt the warmth in his handshake. Both were worth more than a hundred crystals. He released Wolloh's hand. "What's next?"

The marred face expressed a studied intensity. "Stebben, be so kind as to share what you discovered."

Nomed leaned forward to listen. Stebben was becoming more interesting by the turning.

30
Myrrh

Kieel returned to the evergreen branch to retrieve his walking stick and to meet with the boys. Ashor arrived first. The impish face, usually wreathed in smiles, was a portrait of discouragement. Before he could report his findings, Mumshu landed next to him. He, too, appeared downcast.

"What did you discover, boys?" Kieel kept his tone brisk and business-like. "We need to make our move soon."

Mumshu groaned and hung his hat on a twig. "What can we do against soldiers?"

"There are so many of them." Ashor chimed in.

With a supreme effort, Kieel restrained his impatience. "It doesn't matter that we are only three. It matters that we have the courage to try. If we plan well, we'll succeed. Tell me what you know."

"They tied Sibee to a tree. There's a soldier close by, but he doesn't seem very interested in him." Ashor's face had lost some of its pallor.

Mumshu nodded. "There are eleven medium-sized tents and one that is larger. Six soldiers guard the perimeter of the camp. Two men have climbed trees, the rest are on foot." As he made his report, he began to appear more confident. "There is also a cook tent and a kitchen fire near the center of the camp."

Kieel nodded his approval. "Good work. The commander of this platoon is called Tinpaca Mondago, and he intends to question Sibee after supper. I suggest we wait until the soldiers are eating. What are they using as a light source?"

Ashor scratched his head. "Don't be mad, Kieel. I explored a tent." He bit his lip. "Found lite-sticks with on and off switches."

Kieel ignored the disregard of his order to stay in the trees. "Good work. In the big tent, I saw a couple of candles. If we are lucky, they'll be lit."

"So we can start a smoky fire." Ashor's grin returned to his face.

"How will we free Sibee?" Mumshu fluttered to sitting.

"I can take care of that." Kieel held up his walking stick.

Ashor looked incredulous. "A walking stick?"

Kieel held it in one hand and with the other grasped the knobby top and pulled. A sword's silvery blade flashed into view.

Mumshu almost fell off the branch, beat his wings rapidly to stabilize himself, and stared. "I didn't know your walking stick was a sword."

The Nyti leader slid the blade into its wooden sheath and tapped Mumshu on the head. "You still have things to learn, boy. I'd better report to Almiralyn. You stay here. If anything changes, one of you let me know." Without waiting for a reply, he flew through the forest to the Tirips tree where the Guardian waited, told her what they had discovered, and outlined his plan.

Almiralyn's white feathered head gave an affirmative bob when he was done. Her sapphire eyes held a glint of frustration. Kieel knew how hard it was for her to stay hidden. "We'll be fine, my lady. Please stay here. As soon as Sibee is free, we'll let you know."

Again, the head bobbed up and down.

Ashor appeared next to them. "Dinner is about to be served."

Almiralyn flew higher in the Tirips tree to survey the scene. Two-man tents circled what had been her garden. The flag of RewFaar fluttered in the coolness of dusk above a large tent next to the pond. At the camp's center, soldiers gathered near the cook tent, chatting amongst themselves in subdued voices.

Their actions suggested they had no intention of leaving Myrrh soon. Chopped and split wood was piled behind the cook's tent. Four guard stations established around the camp would provide advanced warning of trouble. The soldiers had unpacked their gear and organized their tents.

She expected them to invade the Terces Wood in search of food. Streams packed with fish, herds of deer, and plenty of edible flora would provide them with enough to eat well for many moon cycles. The thought of these strangers tromping through the forest made her heartsick.

The soft flutter of wings alerted her to several Nyti. A girl with light brown hair shot through with green took the lead. "I'm Reana, my lady. Kieel sent us to check in with you. He's ready to free Sibee. We'll stay out of sight unless the diversion Mumshu and Ashor have planned fails. If it does, we'll create another one."

Almiralyn bobbed her feathered-head.

The girl held out her hand. A dragonfly landed, its luminescent wings a blur of movement. Reana smiled. "This is Ethor." The dragonfly gave a soft buzz and darted away. "It's time." Hidden within the trees, she and her comrades circled the camp.

Almiralyn flew to a higher branch, ruffled her feathers, and prepared to observe the Nyti at work.

Kieel watched Sibee's guard depart for dinner, then crept through the tall grass to the slender tree that served as the Wood Tiff's backrest. A single rope wound once around the trunk and looped around the Tiff's wrists. Another trussed his ankles. A gag covering his mouth would stop him from giving them away.

Darting around the tree, he hovered in front of him. Sibee's eyes rounded and his mouth tried to grin. Kieel put a finger to his lips and flew to his shoulder. "Not a sound. Scooch forward, and for Emit's sake, do nothing else until I tell you. Understood?"

Sibee nodded.

Behind him, Kieel braced his feet on the boy's wrists and withdrew his sword. The fine razor-sharp steel was small for the ropes holding the Tiff. Determination lending him strength, he began the hard work of sawing.

In the big tent, Ashor and Mumshu hid beneath a cot. A man sat at the table, a cigar clamped between his teeth. He puffed. The tip glowed red and sent smoke curling in a cloud around his head.

Ashor nudged Mumshu. "Tinpaca Mondago."

A soldier ducked into the tent and saluted. "Dinner, sir. Would you like me to serve you here?"

"I'll join the men."

"Yes, sir." The soldier marched from the tent.

After savoring a last draw on his cigar, the Tinpaca sat for a moment, rolling it back and forth between his finger and thumb. Exhaled smoke formed hazy wisps and dissipated. With a grunt of pleasure, he stubbed out the cigar, rearranged the papers he had been inspecting, and exited the tent.

Ashor picked up a lumpy bag, zipped to the tabletop, and plopped it down next to the ashtray. Since no candles were visible, he was glad this Human smoked.

Mumshu fluttered to his side. "I don't see any candles. What'll we do?"

"We'll use the cigar if it still has a spark." He scurried around the ashtray and peered at the barely smoking ash. "Nasty, but still hot. Mums, you take a draw on the cigar. I'll blow on the tip."

Mumshu grimaced. "You take a drag. I'm not."

Ashor stood up, hands planted on his hips. "We don't have time to argue."

Mumshu's features shaped stubborn as he folded his arms across his chest.

Aware of how contrary his friend could be, Ashor shrugged and darted to the end of the cigar. He waited for Mumshu to kneel and cup his hands around the tip before placing his lips on the sticky end. He sucked in and blew a Nyti-sized blast. Nothing happened. Mumshu peered up the length of the cigar and shrugged.

"Don't stop blowing, idiot." Ashor inhaled, exhaled, and put his mouth over the end. He took a deep drag. Smoke filled his mouth and burned out through his nose. Clutching his sides, he lifted off the table, coughing and choking. Mumshu doubled over with laughter.

Ashor spat and wiped his mouth and watering eyes on his sleeve. His stomach flip-flopped. He ignored it and peered at the cigar. "It worked. Find something to start the fire in." He flew around the table and hovered. "Mumshu, we got a bucket right here."

Kneeling, he picked up the corner of a piece of paper and began scrunching and crunching it into a misshapen orb. Mumshu followed his example, beginning at the opposite corner. Working in efficient silence, they crumpled several pieces. Together, they dragged one to the edge of the table and pushed. Peering over the side, they watched it hit the target.

Mumshu slapped him on the back. "We did it."

Ashor flitted back to the paper. "We have more to do, Mums. We can celebrate later."

After dumping several more into the bucket, they returned to the ashtray. Faint smoke still curled upward from the cigar's tip.

Mumshu gave Ashor a sly grin. "It needs another draw, Ash."

Ashor assumed his stubborn stance and shot his friend a fierce look. Mumshu scowled but flew to the tip. The ash flared to life.

"Good job, Mums." Ashor thumped his back while he coughed. "Always knew you were full of smoke, but no fire." Mumshu's coughing turned to laughter. "Can we just get this done?"

They rolled the smoking cigar across the tabletop and pushed. Like a miniature missile, it nose-dived into the bucket. Ashor grabbed his bag and dumped it and its contents in after it. "Sure glad Reana brought these fire poppers."

Mumshu zipped beneath the cot and retrieved a similar bag, which he also tossed in. "We'd better make our escape."

Ashor shot to the entrance. "All clear." With Mumshu close behind, he whizzed to the edge of the Terces Wood and landed on a branch in a tall pine.

Kieel cut through the rope around Sibee's wrists and stood watch while the Tiff untied his ankles. Laughter at the center of the camp enticed him to investigate. Hovering beside the cook tent, he peeked around the corner.

A soldier tossed his plate in a tub and stood up. "Better check on the Tiff."

Grateful it was well past sunset, Kieel whizzed to Sibee's side. "Sit still and look pouty." Quick as a shot, he tightened the knot Sibee had worked loose at his ankles and flew into the leafy branches of the tree.

The soldier marched to a stop in front of the small Tiff, snapped on a lite-stick, and flashed it from the ropes at his ankles to Sibee's face. "Bet you're hungry. You'll be glad your stomach's empty when the Tinpaca gets hold of you. A word of advice... Spill everything you know, and he might let you go."

A loud pop near the big tent was followed by a second. Shouts erupted from the opposite side of the camp. With a perfunctory glance at the Tiff, the man rushed toward the sound.

As soon as he was out of sight, Sibee untied the knots at his ankles and yanked the gag from his mouth.

Kieel flew to his side. "Run, boy. Stay hidden. Soldiers are guarding the woods.

"Thanks, Kieel." He dashed behind a beech tree. Ducking into high ferns and brush, he made his getaway.

Kieel, with Ashor and Mumshu close behind, zipped through the encroaching darkness and made their way to Almiralyn's tree.

From her vantage point, Almiralyn heard the sharp, sporadic pops and saw smoke billowing from the big tent. Tibin and Tuper hid close by. They would snag Sibee and escort him home. She felt certain his mother would confine the young Tiff to his TreeOm until the soldiers had departed.

A shout sounded the alert. "Hey, the prisoner's gone." Soldiers quickly spread out, combing the woods behind the tree where Sibee's ropes lay scattered. Reana's band of Nyti waited to lead them in the opposite direction.

As soon as Kieel landed on Almiralyn's bird back with Ashor and Mumshu, she swooped through the trees to the edge of Nemttachenn's clearing, where the Nyti dismounted. Shifting, she held out a hand.

Kieel zipped to her palm. "That was too close, my lady."

"I am grateful to you and your people, Kieel. Unfortunately, Sibee has put all the Wood Tiffs at risk. Tibin will keep everyone hidden until you deliver a message that it's safe to come out."

The Nyti leader tugged at his small goatee. "I will station Nyti around the camp and keep you informed about what's happening there. We are small to be your army, my lady. But we will do our best to be your eyes and ears."

"Thank you. As soon as Major Jordett and Allynae return from the Dojanacks, they can help. And there are two Pentharian hidden near Demrach Gateway."

"Are they the same ones who helped with the DiMensioner?"

"Yes. If you need help, find them. One is called Yuin, and the other is Jeet."

She held out her other hand and called out softly. "Ashor. Mumshu."

They flitted to her palm and chorused in unison, "At your service, my lady."

"You did well today, and I thank you. But you confer with Kieel before doing anything else. Do I have your word?"

Ashor's big smile lit his face. "Of course, my lady. I'm glad Sibee escaped."

"Me, too." Mumshu touched his head as if to remove his top hat, looked around frantically, and frowned. "I lost my hat."

Kieel laughed. "We'll find you a new hat, Mumshu." He darted into the air. "Come on, boys. We have things to do."

Almiralyn stood in the quiet of early evening. A breeze rustled the leaves and cooled her cheeks. *It's been a difficult turning. Thank goodness for the Nyti.* She sighed. *I feel so trapped. How can I protect my people when I dare not show myself? I miss Karrew. How is he faring...and Sparrow and Merrilea and One Man? And what about the twins and Torgin? Have they found Esán?* Morose feelings left her shaking her head. *I'm feeling sorry for myself.* She gave a quiet laugh. *Paisley will cheer me up.*

She ambled across the clearing. At the entrance to the tower, she paused. Two figures sat at a table, a chessboard between them. Paisley's hand hovered over the board. It retreated to rub his chin, then hovered again. He nodded to himself and moved a rook.

The figure opposite him chuckled. "You are a formidable opponent, Paisley James Tobinette." He looked at the black man, moved his queen, and grinned. "Checkmate."

Almiralyn smiled to herself. *So, Chee Trann, you have found a friend.*

31
Thera

From Voer's vulture back, Sparrow scoured the Demrach Valley far below. Head winds tugged at her hair, yanked the turmoil of chestnut tendrils behind her, and whipped tears to her eyes. The landscape blurred. She blinked. Demrach River came into focus, its meandering curves cutting the valley in two. They were almost halfway across.

She searched with her mind for One Man and found nothing. Her greatest fear—the Tabagie would become the hunter. Could Esán's father defeat it? She hoped he would not have to try.

Peering to her left, she strained to see Merrilea and Stee. The Pentharian had separated. If the Tabagie gave chase, it would have to choose. Tasseled strands of hair whipped across her line of vision. Impatient fingers yanked them away. She could just make out a vulture's shape in the dimming light. On its back, Merrilea was barely visible. It was her knowledge of the Central

Mountains that had gotten them this far. Soon, it would be Sparrow's turn to be the guide. But prior to traveling any closer to Singtil, they had to rid themselves of the danger that pursued them. She extended her senses, searching again for Esán's father.

One Man's blue heron form circled over the forest, allowing the sour tang of smoke to dictate his course. The Tabagie's reputation as a killer made him cautious; the creature's odd behavior made him wonder at its goal. Was it here to kill? One Man thought not. It was time to end the chase. He closed the gap, shot beyond the smoky form, and swooped around to meet it head on.

The oncoming cloud of gray dodged, soared higher, and streaked over the valley, headed straight for the women and the Pentharian.

The heron floundered in a sooty haze that left its throat burning, and its vision impaired. Swooping lower, it pressed its powerful wings against the air in an attempt to match the Tabagie's speed.

The sunset staining the sky with color left the land below shadowed and provided the Tabagie with the means to maintain its form and to hide from its pursuer. A breeze dispersed its scent and left the heron with no means of tracking it.

Aware the gap between it and the Pentharian who carried the women narrowed with each wing stroke, One Man landed in Human form and prepared to teleport. A quick mental search brought Sparrow's patterning into focus. She was almost at the river. *"Sparrow! Down by the water, now."* He squinted, peering through the fading light. *I can feel her. Why doesn't she answer? "Sparrow?"*

Intense heat sent sweat dribbling down Sparrow's brow and compromised her ability to concentrate. Afraid of what followed, she pressed her belly against her mount's back and clung to its neck. The power of the vulture's muscles straining to carry her to safety told her Voer knew the Tabagie had found them.

A faint mind touch dragged her from fearful imaginings. She forced herself to relax, focus on One Man's words, and positioned her head near Voer's ear hollow. "Down by the water, now."

Beak pointing earthward, the enormous bird swooped toward the river. A smoky cloud shot beyond them. The vulture landed. Sparrow slid to the ground, her eyes searching the dusky terrain. Voer materialized beside her. Out of the corner of her eye, she saw Stee pull Merrilea into a stand of trees a short distance away.

A sputtering hiss mingled with the sound of the river's lazy summer current. No birds sang. Nothing moved but a tower of billowing smoke, wafting and waning in the sun's diminishing light.

Voer's goal, as he placed himself between the smoky cloud hovering not five arm-lengths away, and the mother of Almiralyn's nieces, was her safety. His keen Pentharian sight picked out the amorphous body and kept in his line of vision.

The Tabagie floated closer. A sound by the shore halted its progress. It remained motionless, its glowing, ember eyes fixed beyond his shoulder.

"Don't move." The whispered words sent a thrill of relief through Voer. Sparrow's hand on his arm lost some of its tension. Thanking the gods of ReTaw au Qa, he took his eyes off the Tabagie od Ro-ec. One Man arrived at his side. Their eyes met briefly and returned to the undulating smoke.

One Man kept his voice low. "If it wanted us dead, we would be already. I believe it is here for some other reason."

Voer nodded. "I agree."

Sparrow joined the conversation. "I think we should approach it and ask what it wants."

One Man eyed the Tabagie. "I'll go. Stay here." He took several steps and stopped a short distance from the creature's oscillating form.

It crackled and sputtered. "I mean no harm. I am a messenger."

"Whom do you seek, Tabagie od Ro-ec?" One Man remained still.

"I seek SparrowLyn, the mother of twins, and also the father and aunt of Esán." Smoke puffed from its lipless mouth. Its ember eyes blazed brighter.

"Who would send a Tabagie to deliver a message?"

The smoky mass diffused and reformed. "Wolloh, High DiMensioner od DerTah is my master. For him I followed your scent, and for him I will fade when his warning is delivered." The tower of smoke billowed and doubled in size. "I swear on the heart of my creator and the Netherworld od DerTah that I will not harm you or yours in this lifetime or the next."

One Man's response filled the night. "I hear your oath and honor your presence. I am Somay, known as One Man, the father of Esán. Do I have time to confer with my friends?"

The creature shrunk to its normal size. "The fading will not begin until I have warned you."

Voer marveled at the exchange. *A Tabagie as a messenger...* He glanced down at Sparrow. Only her eyes were visible in the shadowy light.

One Man returned to his companions. "I believe it speaks the truth. What do you think?"

"I think we must listen." Sparrow nodded as Merrilea and Stee joined them.

"Wolloh is Seyes Nomed's mentor. How do we know we can trust him?" Merrilea shivered.

Voer glanced over his shoulder. "We don't. But if the Tabagie brings his warning, then he has gone to a lot of trouble."

"Are we in agreement?" asked One Man.

Nodding their assent, they faced the DerTahan messenger.

Again, One Man took the lead. "Tabagie od Ro-ec, we are of one mind and would hear your message."

Sparrow stepped to the front of the group. "I am SparrowLyn, the mother of the twins. By fading, do you mean you will die?"

"I do not know death as you know it, Mother of Twins. Tabagies disintegrate into nothing, leaving only their eyes behind. When I expire, you must keep mine. If you need my protection, place them in fire, and I will come." The hot coals in his eye sockets burned brighter. A hazy arm lifted, a fist formed, and a finger pointed at Merrilea. "You are the aunt of Esán?" The hand puffed out of existence.

"I am Esán's Aunt Merrilea. Do you have a name?"

"Not in the way Humans bear names." The Tabagie wheezed a series of sounds. "That is my calling." He faded in and out. "I grow weaker. Who remains unknown?"

Voer answered, "I am Voer, the Pentharian, and this is my comrade and blood brother, Stee. We are protectors and friends of these Humans."

The Tabagie drifted closer. Voer's nose twitched at the potent acid smell.

"It is good. Guard them well, for Wolloh has charged me to give these words." The Tabagie's raspy voice changed to that of a Human. "I, Wolloh, High DiMensioner od DerTah, send this warning. Beware Nissasa Rattori, the son of the Largeen Joram of RewFaar. Hide and protect the twins' mother and grandmother and the aunt of Esán. Fathers must find a way to DerTah if they are to save their children. But beware the portal at Fera Finnero."

The creature of smoke diminished as they watched.

Sparrow ran forward. "Thank you, Tabagie."

A faint voice replied, "I am honored to serve." When the sound of the last word had faded, Wolloh's messenger vaporized, leaving behind the tang of volcanic smoke in the cool dusk air and two glowing embers at Sparrow's feet. The glow dimmed to a pinpoint and blinked out.

She picked up the two porous black coals, and, with a sad sigh, returned to her friends to share his gift.

Merrilea touched one and shook her head. "I can't believe Wolloh would warn us."

One Man looked thoughtful. "We can't judge a man we don't know. What we can do is listen."

"He certainly sent a strange messenger." Stee tugged a long braid. "What now?"

Sparrow pocketed the coals. "We find Gerolyn and Standin."

Voer sniffed the air. "How far to Singtil?"

Merrilea pointed up the valley. "It's over that ridge. Less than half a turning's walk."

"If we fly, we can beat the sun." The tall Pentharian sounded pleased. "Arriving with the dawn's dim light will give us an advantage."

Stee stepped forward. "We also put more distance between us and the soldiers who pursue us."

"I don't know about anyone else, but I need a snack." Sparrow held up her backpack. "We'll think better after we've eaten."

Voer accepted a piece of fruit and smiled. "Snack is good. It has been long since our last meal." He walked to the river's edge and let the sound of water soothe his heart. When he looked ahead, he could not foresee the end of this adventure. *One turning at a time...* He gazed deep into the river. "*One turning at a time...*

The lengthy flight to Singtil ended at last. Sparrow and her companions touched down on the forest floor and crept to the edge of her parents' land. The Pentharian shifted to barn cats and prowled the perimeter, scouting the area for soldiers. One Man's blue heron flew above the farm and down the road toward the village. Merrilea leaned her tired body against a tree and stared into the predawn darkness, her fatigue emanating from her like an early morning mist. Sparrow understood. She stretched her aching limbs, wishing for a hot shower, hot food, and a comfortable bed.

A tabby cat's meow announced Stee's appearance in his natural form. "All is quiet. There's no sign of soldiers on the farm. The outbuildings and barn are both clear."

The dim light caught the fluttered movement of a large moth. Voer materialized beside Merrilea.

"Oh!" She clapped her hand over her mouth. "Sorry, Voer, you startled me. Weren't you a cat?"

Thin red lips curved into a smile. "I change form as needed, aunt of Esán." He grew serious. "All is quiet in the house. Man and woman sleep in separate rooms. I found no one else. I suggest we hide in the barn while Sparrow goes to wake her parents."

"What about One Man?" Merrilea's expression mirrored the worry in her question.

"He will join us soon. You and Sparrow keep low. Stee and I will be barn cats and stay close by." The Pentharian shifted.

Merrilea gasped. "I don't think I'll ever get used to shape shifting. Can you shift, Sparrow?"

"Never tried. Almiralyn says I can." She shrugged. "I guess I'll find out if a need arises. Better go. Ready?"

"Ready."

They dodged from tree to tree until they reached a hedgerow across from the barn. An open field stretched between them and their goal. Sparrow scanned the area. Nothing moved. "Stay close."

Side-by-side, they sprinted over the rough ground. Merrilea tripped, caught herself midway to her knees, and stumbled forward. Sparrow grabbed her arm and hauled her through an open door into the barn.

"Are you hurt?" Sparrow inhaled a rasping breath.

"No." Merrilea gulped in air. "Just out of shape."

Voer's tattooed face appeared from the dim interior. "All remains good."

Sparrow closed the door and allowed her eyes to adjust and her breathing to calm. She savored the sweet smells of fresh hay and saddle soap and longed for the peacefulness of her childhood. Voer smiled down at her. She met his gaze, gave him a small nod, and, hurrying between the stalls, led the way to the double front doors. Opening one enough to slip through, she squeezed Merrilea's hand. "I'll hurry."

Jogging the distance between the barn and the house, she rounded the corner and stepped onto the screened-in porch. The soft squeak of a hinge on the kitchen door sounded louder than a scream in the quiet. She froze. The open door framed a figure she knew and loved. Tears welled up. She hurried into her mother's arms.

32
Der Tah

Brie looked from the Atrilaasu Oracle to Yaro, who stood next to her. Butterfly wings in her stomach beat a warning of what was to come.

"Tell me about the Sebborr, Brielle." WoNadahem Mardree's strange eyes shimmered in the fire's light. Her mouth drew a stern line beneath her nose.

Brie gulped in a breath. "There were four. The leader had night-dark eyes that bored into mine like hot irons. He left his mark on my chest with the tip of his sword and claimed me as his own. It was awful. Nichi told me I couldn't be with another man, or I would die. Is that true?"

"We shall see." She extended her left hand. The small, red serpent coiled on her palm. "Show me the cut."

Fingers trembling, Brie lowered the neckline of her blouse and tunic to expose the thin, white zigzag. With unerring accuracy, the Oracle moved her hand to hover over the scar. Varied hisses sounded as the serpent's tongue sniffed the flesh.

"What healed the wound, Brielle?" The small snake slithered from sight.

"Almiralyn gave Ira a knife. He touched it to the cut."

"Efillaeh." The Oracle placed a hand on her heart. "The Unfolding moves faster than I realized. You are fortunate that Almiralyn is forward thinking. The knife has made it possible for me to undo the damage done by Dahe Terah, the leader of the Sebborr. It will be painful, but it is the only way to escape from his control. You must trust me fully, Brielle, or harm will come to both of us."

Brie ran a finger along the scar and swallowed her fear. "I trust you, WoNa."

The Oracle stretched her neck and tilted her head from side to side. "Yaro, if you can numb the area around Dahe's mark, the pain will be less."

The Pentharian's gold scales glistened as he moved around the fire to sit beside her. He placed a tattooed hand on hers and studied her face with his reptilian-like eyes. "I can do this, Brielle. I have both serum to numb and venom to kill. If you will trust me, I will rub my numbing agent around the scar."

"Thank you, Yaro. Will you stay with me?"

"He will hold you so you cannot jerk away. A cup is on the table, Yaro. Brielle, move closer. I must be able to reach you and the fire." WoNa shifted her cushion and pushed her sleeves back from her wrists.

Yaro retrieved the cup and knelt. "I'll drain my eyetooth into this and then rub the serum on your skin. It will not hurt, but the numbing will be instantaneous."

He placed his tooth over the side of the pottery cup. It lengthened and a clear fluid dripped from it, one drop at a time. When he removed the cup, the tooth retracted. With great gentleness, he smeared the sticky liquid along the scar.

When he finished, he turned to the Oracle. "Will my serum help you, WoNa?"

She held out her left hand. I would be grateful for some.

Yaro spread the numbing agent over her palm and set the cup aside. Sitting behind Brie, he pulled her close and wrapped his arms around her, pinning her arms to her sides.

"I will hold you and protect you, Daughter of KcernFensia and descendant of RewFaar. We are ready, WoNadahem Mardree."

When WoNa pressed her left hand against the scar, Brie felt nothing. The Oracle's sightless eyes closed. The snake's whistle shrilled.

Brie gasped. Only Yaro's powerful arms kept her from jerking away. Images of the Sebborr's face poured into her mind—the eyes, the beak-like nose, the cruel mouth twisting into an angry sneer. His howl of denial exploded in her ears. WoNa pressed harder. Brie's body arched in response to the sensation of her skin ripping. Waves of searing pain washed over her. Tears filled her eyes and streamed in a torrent down her cheeks. The Star of Truth added its tingled affirmation to the overload of sensory stimulus. A scream burst from her throat and bounced from wall to wall. Slowly, it melted into nothingness.

In the silence that followed, WoNa withdrew her hand. Emblazoned on her palm was the zigzagged scar, bright red and dripping crimson. Holding it over the fire, she whispered words that Brie could not understand. As each drop of blood exploded in the heat, the Oracle's face grew tighter and paler. At last, she removed her hand from above the flames. The serpent glided onto the scorched palm, licked the last blood from the wound, and once again hid in the folds of her sleeve.

WoNadahem Mardree of the Atrilaasu Dansmen opened her mouth in an agonized cry. Three times, she wailed, her naked pain beating against the walls of the cave. Three times, she brought the palms of her hands together —the sharp smack of skin on skin mingling with her screams. Teardrops splattered on the wounded palm, fizzled, and condensed into a vaporous mist. She closed her eyes, and curling her fingers, held the hand to her heart.

Although Yaro had released Brie's arms, she could not move. Grateful for his muscular chest against her back and the sound of his even breathing next to her ear, she fought to reorient herself. Terror for the Oracle overwhelmed her. She could only stare.

WoNa wiped the tears from her cheeks with her uninjured hand before grasping the hand at her heart. A deep inhalation brought the serpent out of hiding. Color rushed back to her cheeks. The rigidity in her body relaxed. Her eyes opened as she exhaled and held out her clenched hand. "It is done." She uncurled her fingers. The palm was unblemished.

Yaro looked at Brie's chest where the scar had been and smiled. "The mark is gone, Brielle. It is magic, and although I do not understand, I am glad to have been part of it."

WoNa opened her arms. "Come, child, you and I are now blood-bonded. We are family forever."

Brie put her arms around the Oracle's neck and sobbed. When her crying ceased, WoNa dried her tears.

"Dahe Terah can no longer claim you, but he will search for you. A second marking would make you his forever. Do you understand?"

"I understand, WoNa. I won't let him near me." She sat back on her heels. "You could have died, couldn't you?"

"I could have, but I did not." She stared into the distance. *We have more to do before we rest.* Her hand reached for Yaro. He took it in his. "Thank you, my friend. Your serum may have saved us both."

He touched the back of her hand to his forehead. "I am honored, WoNadahem Mardree."

"And I, Pentharian of ReTaw au Qa." She bowed her head. When she raised it, urgency filled her voice. *We have little time. Please bring the others to us, Yaro.*

The Pentharian disappeared, and the red desert fox trotted away from the firelight, leaving Brie to rest her head on the Oracle's knee and WoNa to run her fingers through her new daughter's red curls.

Nomed stood at the window, reviewing his conversation with Wolloh and Stebben. Absently massaging the scar on his cheek, he stared at the desert vista, where the sun's ascent chased a crescent moon below the western horizon. Today, the view he loved seemed filled with peril.

Stebben's report confirmed that Nissasa, a DiMensioner and probable member of the Mocendi league, was a formidable enemy. Nomed scowled. *If I hadn't missed the signs of his training, TheLise would not be bait in this dangerous game. Thank goodness Stebben has forewarned her.*

He ran his tongue over his lower lip and reviewed what else he had learned. Esán had taken Seval and disappeared into the desert. At least one twin had found her way to DerTah. And RewFaaran soldiers tramped through the Terces Wood on Myrrh. His nostrils flared. Lorsedi's plans were more benign than his son's. Capturing the twins, their mother, and grandmother was important to both. Nissasa's goal, however, was more lethal. He was also after Esán. The very thought of his nephew in Nissasa Rattori's hands made Nomed's blood run cold.

Lorsedi's oldest son had also contacted Dahe Terah, the tribal head of the Sebborr, a bloodthirsty band that terrorized the desert dwellers of Fera Finnero. Stebben's source did not know what Nissasa had promised them, but he was certain a takeover of DerTah and a reward for the Sebborr topped the list. Nomed shook his head in disgust. *Gidtuss and Thaer are playing right into his hands, the idiots.*

Nomed's concern for not only Esán, but for TheLise escalated. The more time the Dreelas spent with Nissasa, the more she increased her risk of discovery. Nomed doubted the man would hesitate to obliterate anyone who got in his way.

He had so many unanswered questions... *Where is Somay? What about Sparrow and her mother? Where is the other twin?* He stroked the scar on his cheek. *Why do I care? A short time ago, I would have sought Nissasa to discover what I might gain from joining forces with him. Now, I want to wring his neck.*

"*Nomed. Meet me.*" The intensity of the telepathic message propelled him to the door of his room. A careful inspection of the corridor informed him it was clear. Grateful for the late night festivities that were keeping the Dreelum and RewFaaran guests lingering in bed, he strode down the hall to the room TheLise had shown him a few sun turnings earlier.

He slipped inside and closed the door with a whispered thud. A quick survey of the empty room drove him to cross the stone tiles. He pressed the hidden indentation. The wall moved, the floor revolved, and he found himself in a small room. TheLise stood in the shadows, her back to him.

He noted the tear in her gown and forced stillness. "I'm here, TheLise."

She turned. Her hand held the neck of her dress in place. A bruise raged on her cheek, and her swollen lip showed traces of blood. One puffy eyelid drooped, hiding the gray iris beneath it.

Nomed's fists clenched at his side. His jaw ached from the strain of silencing the oath that wanted to explode from his lips. The scar on his cheek pulled his mouth into an angry sneer, which he wiped away as TheLise moved from the shadows and into his arms.

She pressed her injured body against his chest. "You should see the other guy."

"Does Wolloh know?"

"If we tell him, Seyes, it will only make matters worse." Behind them, the wall revolved. Wolloh Espyro stepped into the room.

"And if you don't tell, he will know and come to you again." Wolloh studied her injuries and ran a gentle finger over her cheek. "Nissasa will pay, you know. Of course, the coward has taken his leave." The High DiMensioner looked at Nomed. "I think we will risk teleporting to my private study." He put an arm around the Dreelas and linked elbows with Nomed. "Shall we?"

Their arrival in a room Nomed had not seen before, where Stebben waited with a medical kit beside an overstuffed chair. After easing TheLise into it, Nomed and Wolloh settled into chairs on either side of a square table.

While Stebben cared for the Dreelas, Nomed surveyed his surroundings. Unadorned, whitewashed walls contained no windows; nor could he see evidence of a door. A hutch with shelves and a cupboard underneath, a comfortable-looking brown sofa against one wall, and several chairs upholstered in varying shades of orange completed the décor. He glanced at Wolloh, whose gaze rested on TheLise's damaged face and torn clothing.

Stebben finished administering first aid and looked up, his expression grim but relieved. "She's bruised, but otherwise fine. No broken bones and no concussion."

TheLise laid an elegant hand on his arm. "Thank you, Stebben. Things could have been worse had you not interrupted Nissasa.

Wolloh placed a glass of brandy at her elbow. "Sip this, my dear. When you are ready, we need to know what you learned—what Nissasa gleaned from you."

Stebben replaced his supplies in the medical kit and leaned back in his chair. "Good thing you think on your feet, TheLise. Wolloh sent me to check on you by delivering a message to Nissasa. A man I instantly disliked answered my knock. Nissasa, he explained, was engaged and unable to come. When I refused to tell him anything, he shut the door in my face." He gave TheLise an appraising look. "I am finding RewFaarans to be irritants in many ways." She squeezed his arm. "After a short pause, Nissasa, a nasty scratch blazing a trail down one cheek, yanked open the door, thrust his rat-like face in mine, and demanded to know what I wanted. The unknown man stood behind him with a weapon drawn. I ignored him and presented Nissasa with the note from Wolloh." He glanced at the High DiMensioner. "Whatever it said must have shocked him because he turned white as a desert lily. The door slammed in my face. By then I knew you, TheLise, had made your escape. Nissasa's howl of frustration confirmed it. I hurried here."

TheLise held up her brandy. "Thank you for saving me from what could have been far worse." She took a sip and rested the glass on the arm of the chair. "Nissasa is a pig. He didn't beat me because he was after information. I refused to submit to him like some RewFaaran courtesan he had engaged for the night. He flew into a rage. I don't envy women on RewFaar if the men treat them the way he treated me. At some point, Gidtuss appeared in the doorway. Nissasa threw me to the floor. I pretended to hit my head and laid still. After he made sure I was unconscious, he demanded to know what Gidtuss wanted. The stupid man told him the Sebborr gathered ready to ride in search of Esán and that Nissasa's secret band of rebels was also ready. That's when you knocked, Stebben. Gidtuss snuck out the bedroom door. While Rikell, the dreadful man you saw, answered the sitting room door, Nissasa tried to wake me. I choose not to cooperate. As soon as they had both left the bedroom, I escaped." She touched her split lip. "You're right, Wolloh, he will pay."

Nomed refilled her glass. "The question is...what's our next move?"

The expression on Wolloh's disfigured face made Nomed hope he never deserved that look.

33
Der Tah

Esán walked beside Seval as they plodded through the sand to WoNa's cave, only half listening to the boy's barrage of questions.

"What if I don't want to see the Oracle? What did she tell you this morning? Why does she want us? Me?" Seval tugged at his tunic and kicked the sand as he walked.

Esán gave him a sidelong glance. "We're guests in her home. I imagine she's being a gracious hostess. She is the Atrilaasu leader."

Seval walked to the edge of the water. "I wish I..."

The words died away, leaving in their place the confused and haunted expression Esán had seen so often. "Don't worry, Seval. The sooner we get there, the sooner we'll know what she wants." He waved at Ira and Torgin, who stood at the cave entrance, and jogged to meet them. Seval followed, his steps hesitant and his expression filled with misgivings.

Torgin shook his head. "He's more afraid of stuff than I am."

Ira chuckled. "And that's saying a lot!"

Torgin's mouth twisted into a scowl. "Why are you always so mean?"

"I'm not mean, Torg, just honest. Hey, Esán."

"Hey, yourself, Ira." He winked at Torgin and grinned.

Seval joined them. Esán linked an arm through his. "Let's find out what WoNa wants, shall we?" He guided him into the cave, where they found Brie seated with the Oracle.

WoNa's luminous eyes blinked. She smiled. "Hello, Esán. Please bring your friends closer."

Brie slid to one side so the boys could kneel in front of the Atrilaasu leader. At first, no one moved. Brie caught Ira's eye. He knelt and dug his hands in his pockets. WoNa's delicately tattooed fingers explored his features. "You have many talents yet to discover. Be patient and they will manifest when needed. Your heart will always tell you the truth of a matter. Listen to it with care. I honor you, Ira."

"Thank you, WoNa. I am honored to be at Eissua." He retreated to the opposite side of the fire.

Yaro's fox nose pressed into Torgin's palm, urging him to go next. The tall boy knelt, his green eyes brimming with anticipation. "I am Torgin."

Sensitive fingers roamed his face. "You are a gifted musician, Torgin. Music is your life's blood. It will support the unveilings to come. You have a good heart. Let it guide you, and your fears will evaporate."

"I...ah...Thank you." He shuffled around the fire and plopped down next to Ira.

Esán touched Seval's arm. "It's your turn." He sat down near WoNa.

The boy's eyes darted from the Oracle to the twin.

Brie smiled. "It's alright, Seval. Esán will be right beside you. And he's not frightened."

A tremble shook the boy's shoulders. He started to speak, ran a hand through his dark auburn hair, and knelt next to Esán. Taking in a hiccuped gulp of air, he closed his eyes.

WoNa's serpent poked its head from beneath her sleeve. The tongue flicked, but no sound disturbed the kneeling boy.

"I will explore your face to learn you, Seval," the Oracle said. When she had completed her exploration, she moved her hands to his temples. "If you choose, I will tell you why you do not remember. But it may not be what you want to hear."

He gripped her wrists and fought back tears. "I want to know, but..."

His whispered words choked into silence. No one spoke. A log rolling to the side of the fire pit sounded like thunder. Seval jumped, released her wrists, and fought to calm his ragged breathing. WoNa folded her hands in her lap and waited.

He rubbed his eyes and sank down, fanny against calves. "Please tell me why my memories are only tattered fragments."

Saffron and blue eyes found his face. "This knowledge places everyone in this cave and in the Eissua in danger, Seval. If your response is adverse, you could create a chain reaction that will change life as we know it on DerTah, Thera and Myrrh, and on RewFaar. Think carefully."

Ira's expression filled with compassion as he squatted by Seval's side. "I understand." He remained quiet for a long moment. "Someone wiped your memories. That's why you can't remember, and that's why you're afraid."

Seval shook his head and scooted closer to Esán. "No...I..."

Ira reached out and squeezed his shoulder. "I understand, Seval. My memories were stolen, too. An empty mind is terrifying."

Seval's face changed as the realization dawned. He looked at WoNa. "Can I get back my memories—who I am—where I'm from—if I have a family?"

"With the help of your friends, we can repair much of the damage." The small serpent's head writhed back and forth at the end of her middle finger. "We cannot heal the pain in your heart. Nor can I foretell how you will react or—"

"I want to know who I am. I want to understand why someone did this to me."

The snake gave a long and insistent hiss.

Seval turned to Esán. "Please help."

Ira pressed his point. "It's not fair to expect him to know how he'll respond until he finds out who he is, and what they did to him." He locked his gaze on Seval. "I think you should do this. You deserve to have your life back, whatever it is."

Brie fingered the Star of Truth. "We will all help you, Seval."

He sat, eyes down, lost in thought. At last he looked up. "Please, WoNadahem Mardree, help me remember."

WoNa untied her kcalo and slipped it off her shoulders. "It is as you wish, boy. I will need the help of your friends. Esán, sit here in front of me so I may lay my hands on your shoulders. You must be my eyes. Seval, lie down with your head in Esán's lap. Brielle, kneel on his right. We will need the Stone of Remembering. Ira, remain on his left side with Efillaeh. Torgin, please take out your flute. We will need music. You will know what to play."

Esán looked from one friend to another as they took their places around Seval. Each brought a special gift to the proceedings. He smiled as Torgin pulled out the flute and ran his musician's fingers along its length. Esán found the flute comforting. His father had crafted it and given it to Torgin. One Man's love seemed to rise from it and wrap itself around him and his friends.

WoNa reached down to pat the red fox at her side. "Yaro, guard the door well. No one must enter for any reason."

The fox gave a small yip and trotted to the cave entrance.

The Oracle's hands on Esán's shoulders sent a shock shooting down his spine. "Seval, you are sure?"

"I am sure." He tipped his head back, his eyes searching for her face. "Will it hurt?"

"Only time will tell. You must be as still as possible. Your friends will hold you, Seval. Close your eyes, and we will begin. Torgin, please play."

Torgin positioned his fingers and pressed his lips to the silvery instrument. Notes gentle as the first rays of morning filled the cave. A sense of calm saturated the space and those gathered to assist the Oracle of the Atrilaasu.

Esán placed his palms on either side of Seval's head, shut his eyes, and concentrated on the boy's mind. Tattered webs of memory hung limp and gauzy in the desolate emptiness. Occasional flashes of gray light ignited and faded. To one side, a touch of color glowed, changing hue as Seval's emotions shifted. *Wow, that must be his recent memories.*

WoNa whispered, "Ira, place Efillaeh on his heart and hold him still."

Esán opened his eyes a narrow slit to watch Ira put the knife, point upwards, on the center of Seval's chest. An emerald haze floated from the blade to surround the boy's body from shoulders to feet. From the amethysts in the hilt, glowing strands of purple light encircled his head. Spiderweb threads of dull gray shivered. Esán gasped. As though a breeze had begun to blow, Seval's ragged memories filled with energetic wakefulness.

The Oracle's alto tones merged with Torgin's music. "Brielle..."

Again, Esán squinted. The Stone of Remembering glistened on Brie's palm. She balanced it on Seval's forehead. He moaned and tried to twist free. Esán squeezed his eyes shut. He gripped the boy's head and held it still. A stabbing pain tore through his brain. Seval's scream merged with his own.

Music soaked up the strident sound note-by-note until only the flute's beauty filled the cave.

Esán swallowed as electrical impulses flared in his friend's mind and skipped from synapse to synapse. Color infused Seval's memories and wove them into a rich tapestry depicting his life—the RewFaaran landscape, his mother's face, his father's laugh, and the joy that filled every moment. Hues muted. Darkness changed the mood. New images discolored the tapestry's weave—a brother's plot to kill—Seval's discovery of the plan—a rough covering pulled over his head, ropes around his hands and feet; a table, blinding light, metal straps binding him; searing pain, then nothing. A new image emerged in a pain-misted mind—a horse-drawn wagon, another long blank, and waking up in a room at Shu Chenaro.

WoNa raised her hands. Brie removed the Remembering Stone and Ira picked up Efillaeh. Torgin played a last series of notes—strangely dissonant and melodic at the same time—and lowered the flute.

Esán's mind blanked. The broken link left him bemused and bereft. He blinked and stared down at Seval's pale face.

The boy's eyes fluttered open. For a moment, he returned the stare. Struggling to sit up, he hugged his legs to his chest and rested his forehead on his knees. When he lifted his head, tears streaked his cheeks. With painstaking slowness, he stood up and walked to the cave entrance. His shoulders sagged, then squared. He turned. Emotions stampeded across his face like wild horses across a prairie.

Esán saw no fear or confusion. Sadness, frustration, wonder, and deep-seated fury followed one another in rapid succession. Soft facial features grew more chiseled. The forlorn look of a frightened child morphed into manhood that draped confidence around his broad shoulders. A hint of iron will shone in the once-sad eyes as they traveled from one person to the next and finally came to rest on WoNa.

He bowed. His voice when he spoke had deepened. "Thank you, WoNadahem Mardree, for the return of my life. My name is Desirol Telisnoe. I am the youngest son of Lorsedi Telisnoe, the Largeen Joram of RewFaar, and his chosen heir."

Brie gasped. "Lorsedi's my grandfather. That means we're related, Seval...I mean, Desirol."

He gave her a sharp look. "Then you're not safe either."

WoNa's hands tightened on Esán's shoulders. The snake's head appeared from her sleeve and hissed. The crystal on her forehead glowed crimson.

Esán stared at the boy from RewFaar. *I shared the return of your memories...none of us are safe, not even Torgin.*

Screened by a clump of palm trees near the base of the rock outcropping beside the desert lake, Corvus watched the red fox at the entrance to WoNa's cave. It raised its nose, sniffed the air, and disappeared inside. He scanned the oasis. He had visited Eissua several times. Today, he surveyed the layout with an eye to its defense. Perhaps WoNa and Narrtep would have some good ideas.

He had news for the Oracle, but his search for Esán and Seval had created the urgency of this trip. Some time ago he had seen them enter WoNadahem Mardree's cave with Torgin and a tall boy who looked enough like Allynae to be his son. *That must be Ari. That means Brie's here, as well.*

A kcalo-draped Dansman and the fox appeared at the cave entrance. Stepping from the trees, Corvus trudged down a gradual rise to meet them halfway. The sun-baked face broadcasted suspicion in the set of his mouth and the squint of his eyes. In his hand, an unsheathed knife flashed in the sun.

"Who enters Eissua without WoNadahem Mardree's permission?" The man's voice grated like sand on paper.

Corvus pushed back his hood. "It's me, Narrtep."

"Corvus! It's good to see you." Narrtep slid the knife back in its sheath and held out his hand.

Corvus grasped his arm at the elbow and touched his other hand to his heart. "It's good to see you, too, Narrtep. Please tell WoNa I have urgent news."

"She has asked not to be disturbed. I'll see how much longer she'll be."

Suppressing his desire to hurry things along, Corvus studied the landscape. Of all the places he had visited in the desert, Eissua Oasis was his favorite. It held a magic and beauty that appealed to his sensibilities. On top of that, WoNa was a formidable ally. Few outside the desert realized the strength and breadth of her power. He needed her advice and her help.

Narrtep reached the cave entrance. The fox trotted inside and reappeared almost at once. The Dansman sprinted back in his direction, his kcalo flapping around his legs. "She says come now."

Striding at the Dansman's side, Corvus felt a sense of relief that he would soon have the children under his protective wing. At the outcropping, the fox, not Narrtep, escorted him into the Oracle's cave. He smiled to himself when Yaro materialized beside WoNa and placed a protective hand on her shoulder. *I should have known.*

WoNa's snake whistled. She offered her hand. "Welcome, Corvus Difner."

He grasped it. "I am glad to be here, WoNadahem Mardree. I have news. It's not good, I'm afraid."

Tendrils of flaming hair writhed like living things as she inclined her head. The Oracle Stone on her brow glowed deep amber. "Join us. Esán, please introduce your friends."

Esán flashed him a relieved grin. "Corvus. Am I glad to see you! These are my friends from Myrrh...Yaro, the Pentharian, Torgin, Ira, and Brielle. And this is Desirol Telisnoe, Lorsedi's youngest son."

"Esán has told me about all of you. I know he is glad to have you here." He studied the former Seval, intrigued by the changes. "Hello, Desirol. I am pleased that you have regained your memory."

"Who are you?" Desirol demanded, suspicion vibrating through each syllable.

"He is a friend." WoNa greeted Corvus with a gentle smile. "It is good you have come. We must hear your news."

While the group resettled to make room for him beside her, Corvus studied Lorsedi's youngest son. His news would be especially difficult for Desirol to hear.

34
Myrrh & Thera

Sparrow clung to her mother like a drowning woman to a lifeline. It had been fourteen sun cycles since they had last seen each other. Fourteen sun cycles since...

Her mother held her at arm's length. Weary eyes brimming with tears regarded her with concern. "You'd better tell me why you're here." She guided her into the big country kitchen and closed the door. "I know others are waiting in the barn, but..."

"Lorsedi is looking for us...you, me, and the twins. Almiralyn sent my friends and me to bring you back to Myrrh, so we—"

Color flooded her mother's weathered cheeks. The lackluster green of her eyes deepened to emerald. Facial lines faded into porcelain smooth skin. Dull brown hair sprinkled with gray turned a deep chestnut brown and slipped from its restrictive bun to hang in loose shoulder length curls.

Sparrow gasped. "Mother, I..."

In the blink of an eye, the older woman with her sad, haggard expression stared back at her. "I'm sorry, Sparrow. You caught me by surprise. I lost control." She sank onto a chair and covered her face with the calloused hands of a farmer's wife.

Gerolyn's demeanor when she lowered them was business-like, and her tone, brusque. "Fetch your friends. I'll wake up, Standin."

"No need, Gero. I'm here." A slender, stooped man stood in the doorway.

Sparrow threw her arms around him. "Father, I am so glad to see you."

His hug was gentle, his smile wistful. "It has been a long time, girl. You'd best do as your mother asked. We may not have much time."

She hugged him again, skirted the table, and dashed from the kitchen.

Her mother's voice drifted after her. "How long were you there, Standin?"

"Long enough."

"I'm so sorry..." The closing door cut the sentence short.

Sparrow hurried across the yard, her thoughts in turmoil. *Mother still loves Lorsedi. Poor Standin.*

Voer waited with the barn door ajar. After a quick explanation, she led her companions to the house. Her mother greeted the Pentharian with the grace of one used to aliens in her kitchen. Standin blanched and stuttered an awkward welcome.

Gerolyn refused to talk until everyone had eaten. Soon, plates heaped with crisp brown toast, scrambled eggs, and country ham sat in front of each visitor. Conversation remained casual while they enjoyed their meal. Gerolyn charmed the Pentharian by asking about their home. Merrilea's questions about the farm penetrated Standin's natural shyness.

Sparrow ate in silence and studied her parents. Gerolyn's face, animated with interest, held a hint of the younger woman. Standin had aged in the past fourteen sun cycles. His pale, wrinkled face wore sadness like a second skin. Once-broad shoulders hunched forward. Hands crippled with arthritis trembled when he lifted a fork to his mouth. He caught her eye. Her loving smile seemed to temper the sorrow in his express.

After morning meal, Sparrow shared a condensed version of what had occurred during the past few weeks. She began with the DiMensioner's desire for revenge and his disappearance with Esán and finished with

Lorsedi's soldiers in the Terces Wood and the Tabagie's message from the High DiMensioner od DerTah. "That's why we came. You can't stay here."

A postural change in Voer's body stopped conversation. Anxious faces turned his direction. His expression telegraphed a warning as he and Stee moved to stand on either side of the door.

Sparrow's senses reached beyond it. "It's One Man, and he's not happy." Voer pulled the door open.

One Man slipped into the room. "Soldiers will arrive in Singtil on the morning train. We have to leave soon. Do I smell food?"

Gerolyn offered him a heaping plateful. "I expect you'll need this. I'm Sparrow's mother, Gerolyn, and this is her father, Standin."

One Man accepted the plate and sat down. "Good to meet you both. We'd better make plans while I eat."

Voer and Stee returned to the table. "I dislike the idea of returning to the Demrach Gateway. Many soldiers are on the lookout. It is not safe." The blue Pentharian gazed at his companions.

Stee nodded. "We also must decide how to travel with this many people." He looked at Gerolyn. "Can you shape shift?"

Standin interrupted. "You don't need to go back, nor does Gero need to shift."

One Man's fork stopped midway to his mouth. "We can't go through Idronatti, if that's what you're thinking." He chewed a mouthful of ham, ate the last of the eggs, and wiped the plate clean with a scrap of toast.

"There's a gateway much closer than either Idronatti or Demrach Falls." Gerolyn's voice held a note of anticipation.

Interest around the table intensified. Sparrow studied her parents. "I don't know about another portal. Where is it?"

Standin ran a trembling hand through his sparse white hair. "In the barn."

"Our barn?" Sparrow stared at her father. "You never told me about a portal in the barn. What's its destination point?"

Her mother answered. "It will take us either to Almiralyn's barn or to Nemttachenn Tower, depending on the Key used to open it."

"Nemttachenn is our best bet. Voer and Stee know the Key." One Man carried his dishes to the sink. "I suggest we use it sooner than later. The soldiers have already disembarked in Singtil. And we'd better not leave these dishes."

Standin stood. "I'll do those. You'd best go."

"Standin, you can't stay here." Gerolyn's voice held a note of panic as she hurried to his side. "You know the portal will only support one trip. It will seal as soon as we're all safely in Myrrh. Please come with us."

Voer cleared his throat and pushed back his chair. "Stee and I will scout the road. We'll meet you in the barn."

The Pentharian placed their dishes in the sink and slipped out the door. One Man and Merrilea urged Standin to move aside and busied themselves washing dishes.

Sparrow took her parents into the living room. "Please, Father. Come with us."

Standin touched her cheek with a crooked finger. "Girl, I love you, and I love your mother, but I'm staying here."

Gerolyn started to speak. He hushed her with a sad smile. "You, of all people, know I can't leave the farm, Gero. It's my home, and I mean to die right here." Pain-filled eyes focused on Sparrow. "I've very little time left, Daughter. Take your mother and keep her safe."

"But, Standin—"

"Please, Gerolyn. You're my dearest love, but we knew from the start that I'd leave this life long before you. The farm is where I belong for however long I've left. Go. Collect whatever you need to take while Sparrow and I say our goodbyes."

Gerolyn spoke through her tears. "You'll come with us to the barn?"

"Of course. Be quick, Gero. I want you away and safe."

Sparrow remained quiet as Standin watched the woman he had protected for thirty-two sun cycles hurry down the hall. The weight of his shattered heart made him sag inside his tired, old body. Moisture glistened in the corners of his eyes. Sparrow suspected he loved her mother more deeply than Gerolyn realized.

"Father, are you sure? We both love you and want you with us."

He gathered her in his arms and spoke next to her ear. "You and your mother have lives to live that don't include me. I've done what I promised Almiralyn I'd do. My only regret is not meeting Ari and Brie." He kissed her on the cheek and released her. "Promise me you'll get your mother to safety."

One Man appeared at the door. "Voer and Stee are back. We have to go."

Sparrow hugged the only father she had ever known. "I promise."

Esán's father rested a hand on Standin's shoulder. "I'll take care of them both, Standin. Also, I've put an illusion around your land. The soldiers will only see an aged farmer. I primed the villagers to say you have been living alone out here for several sun cycles. Is there anything else you need?"

"I need y'all to be gone before it's too late." He herded them through the house and onto the back porch.

Voer waved from the open barn door. "Hurry! They're almost here!"

Breaking into a run, Sparrow and One Man headed for the barn. Standin limped after them.

Inside, Gerolyn summoned the portal with the Key Almiralyn had given Voer and Stee. The Pentharian and Merrilea clustered around her. Breaking from the group, she kissed Standin's cheek. "I'll never forget you." She hugged him one last time. "I love you."

One Man gathered everyone together. "We need to travel in two groups. Voer, you take Gerolyn and Sparrow. Stee, you come with Merrilea and me." His gaze flashed to the barn doors.

Voer didn't hesitate. Sparrow felt his firm grip on her arm. The next thing she knew, they were running forward. She caught her mother's eye as they jumped into the portal.

Paisley's laugh filled Nemttachenn. "I demand a rematch." He gave CheeTrann a challenging look from under black, bushy brows. "I realize you've played chess for more sun cycles than I can even imagine, but..."

A deep chortle rolled up from CheeTrann's belly. "I accept, my friend. You are a tough opponent, and I like that. Ahh." He rose and performed a regal bow. "My lady, welcome."

Almiralyn's silhouetted figure stepped into the tower's diffused light. She smiled at the Sentinel of Myrrh. "Nice to *see* you, CheeTrann. It's been a long time since you put in an appearance." She crossed the granite floor to the table and studied the chessboard. "I'd say Paisley'll be a match for you in no time, my friend. I gather Alli and Jordett have not returned from the Dojanacks?"

"No, my lady. All has been quiet."

She walked across the tower to view the heart of Myrrh, shrouded in gray. "You have hidden Evolsefil well. Even I wouldn't notice it if I didn't know it was here."

The Sentinel nodded. "Wove a spell of invisibility around it when I learned there were RewFaaran soldiers in the Terces Wood."

Paisley joined her and tried to distinguish the crystal from the granite wall. "I wondered where it was. You're good, CheeTrann."

"I am, aren't I?" The big man executed an elaborate bow and then straightened, peering intently at the tower's center. A deep rumbling made him frown. "Who do you suppose is coming through?"

As he spoke, the floor melted away. Almiralyn strode to the perimeter of a yawning hole. "This is not the normal gateway. It has to be the one from Standin's farm."

The Sentinel loomed beside her and pointed at a wobbled-movement that distorted the circumference of the portal. "There's an abnormality in its spin, my lady."

"Help me stabilize it, CheeTrann, or we'll lose whoever's jumping." She edged closer.

CheeTrann threw his arms wide. Blue light encircled the portal as the Guardian recited the steadying verse.

> *"Vortex spinning through Dimensions*
> *Ease your turning, timing, tensions.*
> *Stabilize and create bumpers*
> *To protect arriving jumpers."*

The jagged swirl of colors smoothed to a systemized pattern. Voer, Sparrow, and a woman, Paisley felt sure was Gerolyn AsTar, arrived in the tower.

Voer hurried the women away from the vortex and turned to Almiralyn. "One Man, Merrilea and Stee are right behind us."

The deep tunnel-like opening wavered. Turbulence shook its center.

Roaring winds pressed the tower occupants against the walls. CheeTrann's blue light dispersed and reshaped as he fought to contain the dissipating vector field. Almiralyn levitated upward and hovered above the portal. Clothes slapping and hair flying, Sparrow and Gerolyn shot to her side and joined hands to form a circle. They blurred into an indistinct collage of faces and bodies that left Paisley straining to distinguish them one from another.

CheeTrann's deep voice boomed through the tower. "Stabilize Nemttachenn Portal. Safeguard the incoming mortal." Blue light blasted the height and breadth of the tower. Evolsefil's shimmering luminescence broke through the barrier of gray. The Prima Crystal hummed.

As the women touched down beside the crystal, the wind ceased as suddenly as it had begun. Stee and Merrilea emerged from the gateway. Esán's aunt pointed at the vortex. "One Man..."

The sound of the portal walls collapsing, crunching, crashing together shook Nemttachenn. A flash of white light from Evolsefil stayed the closing vortex. One Man arrived in the center of the tower, fighting for breath, his face streaked with blood. The opening slammed shut. He staggered and fell to his knees.

Merrilea was at his side before anyone else could move. "Somay?"

One Man, eyes filled with tragedy found Sparrow and Gerolyn.

"Standin?" Gerolyn said, her tone heavy with knowing.

Sparrow put an arm around her mother. "Tell us what happened, One Man."

His shoulders sagged as he rose. "Two soldiers burst into the barn as you disappeared. Stee grabbed Merrilea and pulled her with him into the vortex. Standin picked up a pitchfork and shouted, 'You're trespassing. Get off my land.' A soldier pulled a weapon and fired. Standin flew backwards into my arms, a gaping wound in his upper chest. As I dragged him toward the portal, he broke free and, with superhuman strength, shoved me into the vortex. The last thing I saw—" His voice broke. "He fell to the ground. I tried to save him, Gerolyn. I'm so sorry."

Gerolyn laid a gentle hand on his shoulder. "Standin was dying, One Man. We've known for some time he could pass away any moment. At least he died fighting for what he loved."

Sparrow sobbed. "We don't know if he's dead, Mother."

"I know, SparrowLyn." Gerolyn, tears streaming down her face, put her arms around her daughter. "My heart aches with the loss of him."

"Who will take care of his memorial service? And the farm? And..." Sparrow gazed at her mother. "He raised me like his own, and I loved him with all my heart." She buried her face on her mother's shoulder and cried.

"We arranged everything, dear one. The villagers will take care of him. A young couple who have helped us for the past two sun cycles will inherit the farm. We made plans as soon as we learned how sick he was."

Paisley moved away from the group. Sparrow's intermittent sobs echoed through the tower. Almiralyn's eyes filled with tears. Merrilea leaned her head against One Man's shoulder. Her drawn expression mirrored the Guardian's solicitude. The Pentharian slipped from the tower and stood framed within the entrance outline, their strange faces somber with regret.

Paisley understood loss and the deep hole it left in one's heart. He pulled at his mustache and pressed his lips together. Old memories—the death of his mother, the father who had left and never returned—made him shift uneasily and look away. His gaze found CheeTrann. The ghost-like figure floated near Evolsefil, reweaving the grayness that hid the crystal from enemy eyes. He wondered if the Sentinel could shroud a wounded heart.

Sparrow stirred in her mother's arms. "I loved him, you know."

Gerolyn kissed her forehead. "So did I. And we will both miss him." She released her. "But now I suggest we consider what's next. Lorsedi's soldiers will soon know we're here."

Almiralyn's jaw tensed. "They already do."

Paisley stared at the two women from KcernFensia, marveling at their ageless beauty. Gerolyn, who had emerged from the vortex a haggard older woman, now appeared sun cycles younger, her chestnut hair gleaming around an elegant, aristocratic face. The power emanating from her almost rivaled that of the Guardian. They faced each other, sea-green eyes staring into sapphire blue. *They are beautiful.* He pursed his lips. *Beautiful and formidable.*

35

Der Tah

WoNadahem Mardree savored the quiet of her emptied cave. Her young guests had collected their things. Corvus had met with Narrtep and the men of the tribe to warn them regarding Dahe Terah and Nissasa Rattori. Soon, a systematic evacuation of Eissua Oasis would begin. Women and children already hid in the catacombs beneath the rocky outcropping in a secret cavern. It would be their haven for as long as needed.

To prepare for the upcoming tempest, she would summon a sandstorm as a diversion for her enemies. If the onslaught of Sebborr and RewFaarans warriors found Eissua, only emptiness would greet them. The tribal men worked to secure the animals in corrals in the catacombs; emptied tents; and removed tools, food barrels, and other necessities to a safe spot. Her snake hissed in her ear. She frowned. Despite her best efforts, Dahe might navigate the storm. He had the instincts of a Fire ConDra.

An Oracle of unbounded talent, she had foreseen the coming of a bearer of dual Seeds of Carsilem, the rising of the ConDria, and the coming of a war spanning three planets. She had seen the Star of Truth, the Compass of Ostradio, Efillaeh, and the Stone of Remembering arrive in the Desert of Fera Finnero. Her visions included Wolloh and the DiMensioner, Seyes Nomed, and the Dreelum od DerTah. She watched Corvus arrive at Shu Chenaro at the appointed time. And she met the gold Pentharian from the planet of ReTaw au Qa. She had dreamt and recorded them all.

The greatest unknown was Desirol Telisnoe. He had presented himself in the place of dreaming, but his reaction to his situation remained uncertain. She wouldn't know about it in time to be involved. The spirits provided what she must know, not what she wanted to know.

Although time was of the essence, she sat lost in thought— remembering...

"WoNa, see with your senses." Her mother speaks softly. WoNa is only three sun cycles. Already she has learned to read the faces of those who visit with her sensitive fingertips. The family's tent is as familiar as her child-sized palm. Today, Mamman is reinforcing her lesson of yesterday. WoNa sits cross-legged on a rug. She listens, smells the air, sticks out her tongue to taste it, and extends her chubby arms out to her sides. Others besides her mother occupy the tent. She closes her sightless eyes—the ones her mother tells her are the color of two of DerTah's moons, the ones that mark her as special.

"Tell me what you see." Her mother sits across from her. WoNa smells the spicy aroma of her skin, the mint she uses in her hair. She hears the way her breath enters and leaves her body and the rustle of her belted skirts. "You are here, Mamman."

"Tell me something I do not know, dear one."

WoNa smiles. She loves the sound of her mother's voice. "Tork, the goat, is by the door. A chicken pecks at seeds nearby. Narrtep is hiding behind the bed." She frowns. "I sense something I do not know."

"A present for you, WoNa, but you must find it."

WoNa tips her head to listen. A soft scrape informs her where to search. On hands and knees, she crawls toward the sound and stretches out on her belly. Her nose wrinkles as she sniffs the air. Something tickles her cheek.

Her fingers discover a slender, round object that wiggles beneath her touch. She places her hand palm up beside it. Hissing sounds move with it as it slithers up her arm. She hears in its hiss the syllables of her name. Her face turns in its direction. Something flicks, tasting her lips. She giggles, delighted with her gift.

"A serpent." She sits. "Is it mine?"

Her mother laughs. "It will help you to see, my daughter. Go. Get to know your new friend."

That night, the dreams begin.

She is eleven cycles when the dreamings coalesce into comprehensive visions. No longer vague wanderings, they presage events to come. The ancient ones of the tribe tell her she must write them in a book. They train her to understand the symbols for language by teaching her to shape them in the sand. Soon, she can see them in her mind. Now she writes in journals with blue-black dye, the same dye used for her tattoos.

Time moves through its cycles. She is sixteen and wears the Oracle Stone on her brow. Revered by her tribal leaders, they allow her to live in the cave beneath the outcropping. Here, she dreams her dreams and records them. Life at Eissua is hard. Although it is not her fault, she feels responsible for the famine that kills livestock and starves the tribe. Losing her mother and father to a disease that leaves the Dansmen fewer and sadder and a younger brother stolen by the Sebborr mark her heart forever. Still, the power grows stronger, though only the ancient ones guess its full potential. In time, she earns her place as WoNadahem Mardree, the Headwoman and Oracle of the Atrilaasu.

The serpent's whistle ended her reveries. Recent sun cycles had brought prosperity to the tribe. Narrtep, her protector and friend, remained at her side. But things were changing. She had dreamt The Unfolding and knew her young guests were the key to a successful outcome.

Moving with effortless grace to the cave entrance, she lifted her face to the sun. It was high above the oasis. With confidence born of seeing from within, she made her way to the tent where the boys gathered their possessions.

Esán stuffed the last item in his pack and fastened the straps. Behind him, Ira and Desirol were having a heated argument.

"I don't want to sneak away." Desirol's voice rose, high-pitched and angry. "I want to look Nissasa in the eye. I want to condemn him to his face before—"

"Before you what?" Esán kept his voice calm. He glared a 'don't-you-dare,' as Ira started to speak. "Didn't you hear Corvus? The Sebborr are joining forces with your brother and his men—at least sixty in all. Nissasa is powerful, ambitious, and even more dangerous than you realize."

Ira looked daggers back at him and shrugged his pack on over his kcalo. "You can stay Desirol, but I'm not. I intend to live another turning and not as a slave to the Sebborr."

"Your brother didn't kill you." Esán paused. "Have you asked yourself why?"

"No, but..."

"Because," said Torgin, "he needs you for something. That's the only reason he let you live."

Ira clapped his friend on the back. "Good work, Torg. You're getting smarter by the moment."

"Sarcasm doesn't become you, Ira." Brie strode into the tent. She transferred her attention to Desirol. "I'm sure your father would prefer that you return to him alive."

Desirol's response became even more combative. "I am not leaving. You go. Run with your tails between your legs."

WoNa appeared in the tent opening, the landscape of Eissua Oasis stretching out behind her. "What does Nissasa desire above all things, youngest son of Lorsedi?"

"He wants to rule RewFaar." Desirol's hatred gleamed in his eyes.

"Then take the option away from him, stay alive, and out of his control. He needs you for something, or you would already be dead. Torgin is correct."

"He doesn't need me. He sent me away." Desirol curled his hand into a fist. The impetus of it hitting his left palm drove both hands against his heart. The smack cracked the air. Defiance painted his face crimson. He turned away.

No one spoke or moved. Dark auburn hair formed a screen that hid his face. He clenched his hands into balls at his sides. His chin lifted. A release of tension proceeded down his neck and spine. Fisted hands relaxed. He tucked his hair behind his ears and rotated slowly. Comprehension had erased the hurt and anger.

"If I am captured by Nissasa, he will use me to hurt my father. For the sake of my world and its leadership, I must not let my brother's deceit make me forget my duty as the next Largeen Joram of RewFaar."

Ira marched to the door. "Since that's settled, can we please get moving?"

WoNa blocked the way. "You are impetuous, Ira. I believe some planning might be important, don't you?" She held out her arm. "May I sit?"

Esán thought his friend would balk and started forward. Ira shot him a dirty look, took the Oracle's arm, and led her to a chair. Everyone but Ira sat on the ground around her.

WoNa waited. Her small snake, posed like a miniature cobra on her shoulder, flicked its quick, little tongue. "Ahh." The exhaled response brought her eyes to Ira. "Won't you join us, Ira? We have some important things to discuss."

Looking arrows at everyone in the tent, Ira dropped his pack with a plop on the ground and sprawled beside it.

She smiled. "Thank you."

Torgin glanced around. "Where are Corvus and Yaro?"

"They are keeping watch. I have sent my people into hiding. Only Narrtep remains to help me once you are gone. Corvus, Yaro, and I discussed many options. I will share two, and you may decide which feels the best."

Ira squirmed. "They aren't the only ones who know stuff. What if we have ideas of our own?"

Brie moved next to him and put an arm around his back. "I suggest we hear WoNa's plans first. Then if we think of something better, I'm sure she'll listen."

Ira shook off her arm and scooted out of reach. "Leave me alone, Brie. Go sit with your best friend, Esán." He folded his arms across his chest and glared at the ground.

An uncomfortable silence settled over the group. Ira bit his lip. "Sorry. I don't know what's wrong with me. I just want to hit something."

WoNa fingered the small crystal hanging on a leather cord around her neck. "You and I will talk, Ira, but first I must explain how we are going to fool your enemies."

Ira nodded, looking miserable. "Sorry, Brielle." His whispered apology was filled with sadness.

Esán wondered at Ira's behavior. Ari, as Ira, was even more irascible than usual. *Perhaps he misses his companionship with Brie.*

"Esán?" WoNa's voice caught him unawares.

He pushed his thoughts to the back of his mind. "Sorry, WoNa. What do you need?"

Ira scowled. "You, too, pay attention." He choked. "Sorry..."

A flash of understanding lit the Oracle's unusual eyes. "Perhaps it would be best if we talked first, young Ira. Please, Esán, take the others outside and close the tent flap."

Feeling abandoned and apprehensive, Ira fought the urge to bolt after his friends. The serpent's hissing recalled his attention. "I like your snake." He swallowed the gruffness in my voice.

"I like him too, Ira. He is my eyes. Please come closer."

Rebellion welled up in his throat. Biting his tongue, he shuffled forward on his knees. He stiffened as her fingers roamed his face. An impulse to slap her hand away vanished in a gasp of surprise. The hand he raised grew smaller and more feminine. His body changed.

"What the... Oh!" The syllable expressed it all. Ari looked up at the Oracle. "I forgot." Tears streamed down her cheeks. "I am Ari, Brielle's twin. I miss her so much." She ran a hand through short-cropped hair and smiled a crooked smile. "We cut it so I wouldn't need to worry about it." The smile faded into a frown.

"Do you remember why you must remain in your Ira form?"

Ari thought back. "I do, WoNa. Can you tell me why I'm so angry?"

"You left Myrrh in a hurry. Almiralyn didn't have time to teach you about the effects of shape shifting, especially staying for an extended time in your shifted form."

"Lorsedi's soldiers were in the Terces Wood. She barely had time to finish her work with us. Is it being Ira for too long that makes me so darn mad?"

WoNa nodded. "It is. Once you become accustomed to being Ira, it will happen less. You know you must return to that form?"

Ari stared at her hands. "I do. Will I forget who I am again?"

"You will forget again, but I will provide a trigger to help you resume your natural form when your anger becomes too great. You know that Brielle and I are blood-bonded?"

"She told me."

"You and I will now share that bonding. Please take out Efillaeh. I need you to cut the tip of my finger and the tip of yours. Can you do that?"

The knife slid from its scabbard. Ari held it up. Amethysts in the handle flared. "I can." She made a tiny cut on the tip of her index finger and one on WoNa's.

"Hold the knife in your other hand and place your finger on mine. Repeat after me,

> *"Bonded forever, family as one.*
> *Sharing our blood, this gift is begun.*
> *Tie us together, emotions and heart;*
> *Bind us forever so we may not part."*

As Ari repeated the words, heat flowed through her body. Efillaeh emitted a soft hum and pulsed in her hand. For a long moment, complete darkness robbed her of sight. A surge of panic filled her belly. The snake whistled, then hissed a series of sounds. She gasped as the blackness dissolved. Her eyes darted to WoNa's face. Tears glistened on the Oracle's cheeks.

"Thank you, Ari. You gave me the gift of sight, if only for a moment." She touched a tear and tasted its saltiness. "I will never forget your face, my dear."

Ari looked at the tip of her finger. The cut had healed. Gladness filled her as she replaced Efillaeh. "I think it was the knife, WoNa."

She smiled wistfully. "Perhaps. Listen closely. When the anger becomes too great, my blood will pulse in the tip of your finger. You will know to seek solitude. Your shift will be quick, only long enough to disperse the anger. Then you will return to Ira with no memory of Ari. Never forget, Daughter of KcernFensia, you are unique in all the universe." She snapped her fingers.

Ira shook his head. A moment of confusion faded. A sense of peace unlike anything he remembered knowing infused his mind. "What just happened?"

WoNa kissed his forehead. "You found yourself." She straightened, her face alert and watchful. "Call your friends. We have little time."

Ira scrambled up and strode to the tent entrance. Flipping the flap aside, he peered at the sunlit oasis. Brie, Esán, Torgin, and Desirol gathered around Yaro. The Pentharian caught his eye and herded his friends to the tent. He stepped aside to allow Yaro to enter.

The Pentharian ducked past him and hastened to WoNa's side. "Time is of the essence, WoNadahem Mardree."

The Oracle raised her chin. Lids half hid the saffron and blue of her eyes. "It seems my desire to let you choose is no longer an option. The choice must be Nesune Ruins. It is on the far side of Fera Finnero. You will teleport there."

Torgin's voice cracked. "I can't tele..."

Desirol frowned. "Where's Nichi? I'm not leaving without her."

"She is with her family, Desirol." WoNa's eyes glinted. "Her journey is not on your path."

"But I want her with me. I demand that she come." The boy's tone held more fear than anger.

WoNa's response held a note of sympathy. "Nichi has her own destiny. Who knows...she may cross paths with you in the future."

Corvus pulled the tent flap aside. "Nissasa and Dahe have almost closed the circle. They are moving fast."

The tent filled with a flurry of activity. Torgin tied his kcalo over his drango tunic, settled the flute in its case across his chest, and shrugged his pack onto his back. Ira helped Brie position her backpack and bedroll, then grabbed his own and hoisted them into place. Desirol hesitated. Esán tossed him his gear.

"Move it, Des. We don't have all turning."

WoNa raised a hand for silence. "Please listen. When you arrive at the ruins, you will see nothing but sand. Stay still. Listen and watch. The desert will guide you. Torgin, take out your compass. Ask it to show you Nesune Ruins. Esán, hold the compass with him. Everyone else form a circle. Place one arm around your neighbor and one hand touching either Torgin or Esán."

She sniffed the air. "Yaro?"

"Here, WoNadahem Mardree." He joined the circle next to Torgin.

"Keep them safe, Pentharian of ReTaw au Qa."

"I will do my best."

When Corvus remained outside the circle, Ira stared. "Are you coming?"

"I remain with WoNa and Narrtep. I promise to join you as soon as I can."

Desirol stepped away from the circle. "If he is staying, so am I."

Ira grabbed his arm and drew him back. "Steady, Des. It's not the time to make a poor decision. WoNa knows what's best."

The RewFaaran tensed. Ira's grip tightened. He glanced at the Oracle. Her attention focused beyond the tent.

"Go. Now!" She rose. "I will call upon the wind and the sands of Fera Finnero to scatter the enemy."

Torgin's eyes held Esán's gaze. "Nesune Ruins." He pronounced each word with care.

The needle blurred in its circular spin and stopped, pointing north. A picture formed—red sand stretching forever. Ira squeezed his eyes shut.

36
Der Tah

Nomed and Wolloh relaxed in the High DiMensioner's sitting room, sipping ice-cold punch from chilled crystal glasses and awaiting Stebben and Lorsedi. TheLise was tucked in bed to recover from Nissasa's assault, with a guard posted for her protection.

A soft knock and Stebben pushed the door ajar. Wolloh waved him in. Stepping aside, he allowed the Largeen Joram to precede him. After pouring two glasses of punch, the Major Domo reclined in a chair near the door.

The Largeen Joram sat opposite Wolloh, savoring an occasional sip of the refreshing drink, as he listened to a digest version of all that had occurred. Wolloh finished with a description of what Nissasa had done to the Dreelas. Lorsedi, his fury reddening his fair complexion, rose from his chair like a whale surging upward from the sea. Loathing filled his deep-set eyes. The raptorial danger sharpening his features reminded Nomed of a vulture preparing to devour its prey.

Controlled anger carried him to the window. When he turned, his rage had altered to that of the calculating huntsman. "Only small men vent their anger on those less powerful. Nissasa is small and stiff-necked. His cruel nature clouds his judgment. If we lay our plans well, he will trip on them. *And*...he will be ours."

Wolloh's tortured profile nodded. "Do you have a plan in mind?"

Lorsedi returned to his chair and repositioned it to face both Nomed and Wolloh. "Here are the issues as I see them. One... I have split my troops between Shu Chenaro, the portal in Fera Finnero, and Myrrh and Thera. Consolidating is a must, or I cannot counter Nissasa and his group of traitors. Two... Nissasa has spies watching our every move. His mother tops that list. I brought her here to monitor her. We must neutralize her and discover Nissasa's other moles. Three... We need to reorder our priorities. Almiralyn, as an enemy, is compounding our problems. I suggest we send her a message that we would like to join forces against our common foe."

Nomed's eyebrow arced as the Largeen Joram's piercing gaze fastened on him. "Our priority..." Lorsedi's features chiseled into a tenacious mask. "... is to find your nephew, Seyes, and my granddaughters. If Nissasa finds them first, he gains bargaining chips that could cripple us."

"And what of Elcaro's Eye and the Compass of Ostradio? I'm sure the Guardian will not hand them over." The arched brow descended.

"It seems they are also important to Nissasa. Almiralyn will need all the help she can get to keep them safe. Perhaps she and I can come to some agreement at a later date. For now, I must let my personal desires take a back seat."

Nomed scrutinized the man across from him. Reasons for not trusting him surfaced and fell away. What he'd learned from the past few sun turnings and what Wolloh had shared replaced them. A good judge of character himself, he still respected Wolloh's ability to discern fact from fiction. Lorsedi's astute evaluation and willingness to revamp his plans to deal with the fast-developing situation impressed him. He offered his hand. "I believe I may have misjudged you. I hope you will accept my apologies."

Lorsedi clasped it warmly. "We have much to learn from each other—and much to do."

Wolloh observed them with the satisfied expression of someone who had won a strategic prize. "It is good that we work together. I suggest we take immediate action where we already know problems exist. Lorsedi, I don't need to tell you what you must do. Nomed, please check on TheLise. See if she can remember anything else that will help us. Also, advise her of the changes in our strategies. Stebben, contact your sources and have them find out who Nissasa's cohorts are here at the ranch. Also, put Roween Rattori under surveillance. Pick good women. Nothing must alert Roween that we're focusing our attention on her or her son."

Lorsedi nodded. "Speak with Tissent, Stebben. Explain the situation and ask for her help. Tell her it is my wish and why."

Wolloh's lopsided smile flashed. Stebben prepared to depart. At the door, he turned and gave his master a shrewd look. "And?"

"Get word to Corvus that we need to parley."

The Major Domo bowed and left.

Nomed waited until the door had closed. "And who, may I ask, is Corvus?"

The High DiMensioner picked up his glass and drank deeply before setting it back on the table. "Who is he, indeed?"

"I gather you don't intend to share." Lorsedi clinked the ice in his glass.

"Only when I am positive about my answer." Wolloh moved in the chair. "I think I must rest this body. Meet me here this evening. Perhaps after dinner."

The Largeen Joram set down his glass and pushed his chair back. "Until later, then."

Nomed finished his punch as the door closed and looked at his mentor. "Do you believe him?"

"He is a master strategist. Compromise is part of the game. If anyone in this solar system knows how to cut his losses, it's Lorsedi. You're not the only one being asked to give up something, Seyes."

Nomed stood and looked down at his mentor. "Get some rest. I'll check on TheLise. By the way, I like Stebben. He's a good man."

"I trust him, which is more than I can say about most people. Keep your wits about you, Seyes. This is a deadly game."

Nomed gave him a cryptic smile and stepped into the hall. His hand lingered on the doorknob. He couldn't remember the last time he had seen Wolloh looking so worn. *Thank goodness he has Stebben.*

The empty hallway told him life at Shu Chenaro continued to be quiet. He made his way to TheLise's rooms. Unsure whether she was awake, he hesitated outside her door. It opened and an older woman carrying a tray smiled up at him.

"The Dreelas would be happy to see you, sir." She stepped past him and hurried away down the hall.

He entered the sitting room and waited for his eyes to adjust to the cool dimness before crossing to TheLise's open bedroom door. Draped in the folds of a rose-colored robe, she sat propped up on pillows. As she turned toward him, he noticed the swelling over her eye had reduced. He doubted the bruising would disappear so quickly.

"Come closer, Nomed, and tell me what has occurred."

He pulled a chair next to the bed and perched on the edge.

"You look uncomfortable, Seyes—ready to take flight. Am I so ugly you can't stand to look at me?" Her smile lit the one eye he could see, and her tone informed him she was on the mend.

"You could never be ugly, my dear. How are you feeling?"

The smile vanished. "Angry."

Her tone intrigued him. "Angry, and what else?"

Slender fingers pressed a crease into her robe. "Angry and frustrated at myself for allowing that man to hurt me. I thought I could control him. I misjudged him and me." She hugged herself. "It won't happen again." The dangerous edge to her voice left no doubt about her determination.

Nomed settled more comfortably in his chair and began a recitation of what had occurred after she had gone to bed. "And when Corvus—"

"Corvus? You mean the dark-haired man who takes care of the raptors?"

"Yes. You know him?" He leaned closer.

She looked thoughtful. "I hear he is remarkable with wild birds. My man who works in the stables says he has seen nothing like it."

"I think I might like to have a chat with your man." Nomed kissed her cheek. "Rest. I'll stop by later and let you know what I discover."

She put a hand on his. "Thank you, Seyes, for not scolding or telling me how silly I was to think I could deal with Nissasa."

"You, my dear, are harder on yourself than I could ever be." He smiled at her. "Do you know Tissent?"

"The quiet woman from RewFaar?" Her brow furrowed. "No."

"She's the twins' great-aunt. I think you might find her soothing. And interesting." Without waiting for a response, he departed.

Corvus crouched behind a tall taccus tree on the outskirts of Shu Chenaro. Behind him in the desert, a sandstorm raged. WoNa's diversion had given the children time to teleport out of harm's way. Watching them disappear had left him wondering if he would ever get them back under his watchful eye. *At least they wear the hide of the drango. That will help to protect them.*

Unwilling to step into the open just yet, he contemplated what had followed their departure from Eissua Oasis.

Narrtep ducked into the tent and stopped beside him, midway to the Danswoman.

WoNa shook her head. The red of her hair flamed brighter; the crystal on her forehead blazed deep cobalt. On her shoulder the small snake swept its head back and forth, its tongue a whip cutting the air, and its insistent hiss demanding attention.

Narrtep's hand on his arm arrested his instinctual need to go to her. "Wait, Corvus."

WoNadahem Mardree sat so still, Corvus wondered if she even breathed. Light from the open tent flap shimmered around her. Her eyes— startling orbs of vibrant color—widened. At last, she let out a breath. The serpent whistled. She left her chair and walked to Corvus' side. "Wolloh sends a message. He would like to meet with you. It is important. You must go."

Outside the tent the sun, a furious ball of red, hung low in the sky, almost hidden by the surging sands of DerTah. Corvus knew a raging storm obliterated the oasis from view. Narrtep and WoNa followed him into the open, said their goodbyes, and hurried toward the cave in the outcropping.

Remaining motionless, Corvus observed the haunting stillness of the oasis. Like the eye of a hurricane, nothing moved, no sound disturbed the oppressive silence. Further out in the desert, winds roared. The sand rose in a curtain of red granules that could tear a body to pieces. But Eissua Oasis floated, protected in a bubble of absolute calm.

Corvus scanned the outbuildings and gardens at the western edge of Wolloh's ranch and wondered at the High DiMensioner's game. When he arrived at Shu Chenaro, his initial impression of Nomed's mentor had not been favorable. As he looked beyond the maimed body, the posturing for effect, and the seemingly over-large ego, he discovered an intelligent man with unimaginable depth and a unique understanding of the Inner Universe. It had surprised him when Wolloh sent a Tabagie to warn One Man about the Largeen Joram's eldest son. Shrewd and aware of the undercurrents all around him, Wolloh had also warned Esán to leave with Seval before Nissasa and Gidtuss could make a move. *What of Lorsedi? Where does Nomed stand in all this? He's changed since my arrival in DerTah. That doesn't mean he's given up his desire for revenge.*

The sun's descent to the horizon cast long shadows across the landscape. It was time to move. WoNa had told him this meeting would be a tipping point. He hoped she was correct. He laughed to himself. *When has she ever been wrong?*

Glad for the camouflage provided by his dark kcalo, he jogged from one slashed strip of shade to the next until he arrived at the raptor center. A DerTahan hawk swiveled its head, the green-gold of an eye sparking. Corvus reached through the bars of its cage and ran a finger down its back. The bird responded with a deep crooning sound. He withdrew his hand, skirted the building, and dodged into the barn.

Voices nearby him made him divert into the tack room. Stebben appeared in the doorway and beckoned. Corvus followed him between several buildings to a spot close to the ranch house. Maintaining his silence, Stebben pointed ahead at a door almost hidden in taccus and desert shrubs. Corvus nodded. He had used it often when visiting Esán. His companion's height screened him from view as he hastened toward it. Stebben ushered him inside, where Wolloh waited.

The High DiMensioner offered his arm. Corvus took it. The next instant, they stood in the middle of a comfortable sitting room.

Offering a chair, Wolloh lowered his twisted body into one opposite. "Thank you for coming, Corvus. I realize this isn't the best time."

Corvus sat down. "What is so important, sir, that you would use WoNa as a messenger?"

Wolloh rubbed a finger along the ridges on the scarred side of his face before his good eye focused on Corvus and narrowed. "We need you to get a message to Almiralyn."

The statement hung in the air between them, each syllable dropping into the silence. Corvus caught them one by one. "And what makes you think I can do that, sir?"

The smooth lips on the High DiMensioner's handsome side shaped a knowing smile. "I believe you are a man of many talents. May I explain our need?"

"Please do."

Wolloh recounted his earlier discussion with Lorsedi and Nomed. When he had completed his description, he leaned back in his chair, his smooth profile relaxed, his expression one of openness and respect.

Corvus tilted his head to one side. "If I understand you correctly, sir, Lorsedi will give up his hunt for Elcaro's Eye; help defend Myrrh against his son Nissasa; and help protect our young people, as well as the twin's mother and grandmother."

Wolloh affirmed his statement with a blink of his good eye. "You have no reason to trust me, Corvus. I believe, however, that you understand more of me than most."

"And what about Nomed's desire for revenge and for acquiring the Prima Crystal?"

"I think you'll find Seyes Nomed is maturing in ways that have allowed him to step back from his own agenda to embrace the greater good. What made him hate the Guardian is between him and her. I hope that, if addressed by them, the situation can be resolved. Will you help?"

Corvus studied the man's face. *He knows much more than he lets on. Can I trust him? Lorsedi? Nomed?* Relaxing back in his chair, he let his quick intelligence and refined instincts go to work on the problem. When he had a clear picture of the situation and the potential success of joining forces, he returned his gaze to the High DiMensioner's face.

"I can't promise anything, Wolloh. Getting a message to the Guardian of Myrrh is a tricky business. I will do my best. How much time do I have?"

"As you know, Nissasa is already on the move. We should follow suit as soon as possible."

Corvus pushed back his chair. "Whatever happens, I'll try to return here later tonight." With mixed feelings, he headed back to the raptor center. A raven followed his movements with an ebony eye, cawed, and flapped its blue-black wings. He reached through the bars of its cage and scratched beneath its beak. *A message to Almiralyn from the High DiMensioner od DerTah...*

37
Myrrh

Almiralyn led her band of supporters to the Intersect entrance near Nemttachenn. The journey to the Dojanack Caverns via the Intersect, surrounded by moon and stars, the dangling roots of the Terces Wood, and the geode-encrusted underbelly of the mountains, left them awestruck.

Yookotay, the ReDael of the DeoNytes, and his son, Zugo, met them in Meos and welcomed them to their community and their home. Allynae and Sparrow embraced and then, her radiant smile speaking volumes, she reacquainted them with her mother.

As they spoke together, Jordett crossed the square. Merrilea's face, when she saw him, lost its pallor. Gentle words and tenderness from the major erased her last traces of fear. Almiralyn smiled...another romance in the making.

Yookotay escorted them to the council chamber where they gathered around the round table to share the details of their individual adventures. Almiralyn listened with intense interest and a touch of surprise. Wolloh's warning via a Tabagie topped the list. News of Nissasa's defection was deeply disturbing. But it was the death of Standin that troubled her the most. He had given up everything to protect a woman he could not wed and her daughter.

At the end of the discussion, they dispersed to their quarters. Almiralyn sighed and looked around the spacious cave prepared for her by Owae. Soft light from oil lamps positioned on a continuous ledge that followed the curve of the salmon walls bounced off flecks of quartz crystal. Forest green rugs woven from some type of hair or fur covered the stone floor. Carved in the wall across from her, a bed fitted with a thick mat and a dark orange comforter beckoned. A bench made from white stone decorated with green and carnelian cushions and a sturdy wooden chair provided places to sit. An obsidian pitcher and chalice sat on the bedside table, and above them hung a small mirror made from a reflective material.

Almiralyn stretched out on the bed and let the soothing atmosphere in the cave calm her tired nerves. For the first time since Lorsedi had appeared in Elcaro's Eye, she had time to review the past few sun turnings and to formulate her next step.

Peaceful solitude lulled her tired body and soothed a mind too full of questions. She woke with a start some time later, surprised that she'd actually slept. The moment her eyes opened, her brain buzzed with a long list of 'what ifs.' Yawning, she shoved them away, allowed herself a luxurious stretch, and sat up. *I sure could use Karrew's steady practicality.*

She smoothed sleep scattered wisps of silver blonde behind her ears and re-braided her long hair. The rhythmic flick of her fingers eased her returning agitation.

The small bell at the cave's entrance chimed, and the thick curtain covering it rustled. Allynae's head appeared. "May I join you? I have something I think you might be interested in."

She flipped her braid over her shoulder. "Of course, Alli, come in."

He grinned and whipped the curtain aside. Almiralyn sprang to her feet. "Karrew! How did you know I needed you?"

The raven flew to her shoulder and nuzzled his head against her cheek.

"I always know what you need." He hopped onto her offered arm. "I have a message from the High DiMensioner od DerTah."

"Wolloh?" Allynae's expression froze midway between curiosity and suspicion. "What could he want? And how do you know about it?"

Almiralyn sank down on the bed and waited for her brother to pull up the chair. He straddled the seat and rested his arms on the back. "Karrew's been doing some spying for me, Alli." She lifted her protector to eye level. "What's the message?"

While Karrew outlined Wolloh's proposal, provided an account of Lorsedi's response and Nomed's, and brought her up to date on the children, she watched her brother's face. Disbelief registered in every feature.

Karrew ruffled his feathers and cocked his head. "Wolloh is not what he seems, Mira. I don't know his game, but I know he has made every effort to protect Esán, Desirol, and the twins."

"What about Nomed? Why is he so bent on revenge?" Allynae's nostrils flared with dislike.

"Wolloh feels that is between the DiMensioner and Almiralyn." Karrew hopped to her shoulder.

Her brother leaned toward her. "What happened between you two when he was a boy, Mira? What would make him hate you enough to want to destroy you...and Myrrh?"

Almiralyn stared at the flickering crystal flecks on the opposite wall and cast her mind back to Nomed's time in Myrrh.

Davin Farlow, his given name, had been a problem from his first visit to Myrrh. He was an angry boy who bullied smaller children and hurt animals whenever he could catch them. She had warned him on repeated occasions that if he didn't change his behavior, he could no longer visit Myrrh. He always promised to do better. She had always relented, not for Davin but for his shy younger brother, Somay.

His last visit to Myrrh, Davin had arrived seething with rage. Somay's red, swollen eyes were fear-filled and teary. His cry of dismay had brought her into the sitting room. Davin, his anger roiling, clutched a small gray kitten in an up-raised hand. With a snarl, he threw it against the wall. The limp gray body slid to the ground, its neck twisted, and its life gone. She had banned him from ever returning to Myrrh.

What did I miss? What did my anger at the death of an innocent kitten keep me from seeing? Davin's image formed in her mind. Dark hair framed a face that was already well on its way to handsome. Huge, hazel eyes...a patrician nose— She inhaled a sharp breath. —a bruised cheek, and a blackened eye. *The boy was beaten. How many times had he come from Idronatti with his younger brother in tow to escape abuse?*

She opened her eyes. "I am to blame for his hatred."

Allynae started to protest. She stopped him with a shake of her head. "I am not the sole cause of it, but I was the adult. I failed to see a battered boy, and I sent him away to be battered further. No wonder he hates me. If I am to make amends, I must speak with Somay. He can help me understand Nomed's background. But first, we have other decisions to make. Someone has to go to DerTah and meet with Wolloh, Lorsedi, and Nomed."

Allynae stiffened. Mira, this is a bad time to leave Myrrh. I can't even begin to imagine what would happen if our enemies captured you."

Karrew flapped his wings and cawed. "I can meet with them."

Almiralyn shook her head. "I need you to continue as we planned, Karrew."

The entrance bell jingled. Allynae's brow creased. "Whose there?"

Gerolyn pulled the curtain aside. "I believe I can help."

Almiralyn gave her a knowing smile. "Of course, Gerolyn. You're the perfect person to act as my emissary."

Sparrow needed to paint. She hadn't picked up a brush since Nomed had disappeared with Esán. When she painted without limitations, her art could be most informative. She pressed a finger to her lips. *I might learn more about the twins.* Her mouth worked around a frown. She didn't know if the materials she required to paint were even available in Meos. The frown turned to a tentative smile. The best way to find out was to ask.

A quick glance in the mirror above the washstand trapped her into a staring match with her reflection. *Do Mother and I look alike?* She studied her face from different angles. *We have similar hair. Our faces are the same shape. I feel like I've lost something?* Mystified by her feelings, she stared at the wall.

As soon as they had reached Nemttachenn Tower, Gerolyn abandoned her farmer's wife façade. Her younger, more vibrant self bore only a slight resemblance to the mother of her childhood. Sparrow felt a wave of confused discomfort. Without wrinkles and the ever-present sadness, Gerolyn seemed like a stranger.

Regal elegance replaced the slouched fatigue Sparrow knew from the time she had spent with her and Standin on the farm. She radiated confidence and self-assurance. Her voice had lost its Singtil drawl and taken on a fluid, almost melodic tone. *Like Brie's.* She sighed. *I feel as though I've lost both parents.*

She studied her reflection. "She is your mother, no matter how she looks or acts. Don't distance yourself from the woman who birthed and raised you because she has become who she truly is."

"Wise advice, daughter." Gerolyn smiled from the entryway. "I am still the same woman. My love for you has not changed." The curtain swished into place behind her. "I should have shared more about your ancestry with you, but I couldn't risk it. If the PPP had questioned you…"

Sparrow could fill in the blanks. Careful to keep an accusatory tone from creeping into her voice, she asked the question tugging at her heart. "Did you ever love Standin?"

"I loved him, Sparrow." Her mother's expression reflected the depth of her feelings. "Not the way you love Allynae, but I loved and respected who he was. I understood what he willingly gave up to protect us. He made a hard choice, and I will always hold his memory in my heart. He loved you like his own daughter. Know that."

Tears welled up in Sparrow's eyes. "I know. He will always be my father. I wish I had known he was ill. I would have tried to come home sooner."

"He wouldn't let me send word to you. Standin was a very private person. He also understood the dangers involved in being on the PPP Watch List. When things settle down, we will have a special ceremony for him. Almiralyn has said we can put a marker in her garden."

Sparrow took a step. Her mother met her halfway and wrapped her arms around her. Sparrow sighed. *Mother and daughter forever.*

Gerolyn broke the embrace and drew Sparrow with her to sit on the bed. "I have some things to share. I am leaving for DerTah with Karrew. The

High DiMensioner has sent word that he would like to join forces with Almiralyn to protect Myrrh, the twins, and Esán."

"But I don't want you to go." Sparrow realized she sounded like a young Ari. "I mean…I have had so little time with you. Can't Almiralyn go?"

Her mother took her hand and sandwiched it between her smooth palms. "You know she can't leave. I want to go. I am trained in the art of negotiation and schooled in the detection of subterfuge. Almiralyn took me in when I was pregnant with you. She found Standin and set us up on the farm in Singtil. I owe her for our lives. SparrowLyn, it is time for me to see your birth father. Tissent is there, as well. My heart aches to hold my twin in my arms."

"Ari and Brie are there. I'll go with you."

"You have paintings to paint. Almiralyn can't use Elcaro's Eye, so she needs your gifts to help her foresee what needs to be done. I will be gone just long enough to discover if Wolloh is honest in his intentions and how to protect Myrrh and find our girls, if he is."

"How will you get there? Aren't the gateways guarded? What about Fire ConDra?"

Gerolyn patted her hand. "I will shape a raven and accompany Karrew. Ravens mate for life. It will not seem odd for two to travel together."

"How soon?"

"When I have finished explaining the situation to you." She stood and pulled Sparrow with her. "Come. Karrew grows impatient."

"*He sent you a telepathic message, didn't he?*" Sparrow hugged her mother. "I understand."

Her mother held her at arm's length. "*You are your mother's daughter!*"

Allynae stuck his head into the room. "You ready?"

Gerolyn hugged her one last time. "We are. Do you know where we're going?"

He moved to allow them to pass. "I don't, but Zugo does."

Yookotay's son looked from one to the other and smiled. "You look alike, except for your eyes. Sparrow's are the same color as the twins." He fell in step beside Gerolyn.

Allynae linked his arm through Sparrow's. "He's right, you know. There's no doubt you and Gerolyn are mother and daughter." His tone grew serious. "I know you don't want her to go."

"I don't, but I understand why she needs to and why she is the perfect person to represent Almiralyn." She looked up at his craggy face. "Promise you won't leave me."

"It would be foolhardy to make a promise I might not keep." He guided her along the tunnel. "Let's make the most of whatever time we have together."

They arrived at the Nervac Gateway, where Yookotay listened while Almiralyn gave Gerolyn her final instructions. "This portal has its own set of Keys. The one for DerTah, Tres ed Esti, will take you to the Fera Finnero destination point. You'll need to be careful, or the guards will spot you."

"It will be night when we arrive." Karrew alighted on the Guardian's shoulder. "We'll exit and angle upward. Don't worry. I will take care of Gerolyn. It's time."

Almiralyn stroked her raven's chest. "One last thing, Gerolyn. A man named Corvus will assist you when you arrive in DerTah. You can trust him implicitly."

Sparrow caught her mother's eye. "*I love you.*"

Her mother smiled and nodded. "See you all soon."

Two ravens shot into the spinning portal.

38
Der Tah

Brie's breath caught in her throat. Searing heat blasted the moisture from her lungs. Bright light burning through her lids made her squint to pick out Esán's back and the sun-drenched side of Torgin's face. To his left, Yaro sniffed the air. A slight angling of her head brought Ira and Desirol into sculpted relief against the red sky. Although the area where they stood was hauntingly still, a short distance away, the sand formed a swirling curtain of red all around them.

WoNa's instructions were explicit…Be still, and the desert will show the way. Brie sent a telepathic message. *"Esán, did we make it?"*

He scanned the area. *"I don't know. All I can see is sand."*

Torgin stared at the compass. "The picture is gone. Usually, when it disappears, we're at our destination. What do you think, Yaro?"

"We're in the middle of nowhere." Desirol grimaced. "I told you we should stay at Eissua." The words, hissed between bared teeth, sounded far too loud in the immense silence.

"Easy, Desirol." Yaro searched the terrain. "WoNa called it the unseen ruins, didn't she?"

Ira gasped and pointed. "There!"

At their feet, a faint strip of shade vacillated in and out on the hot sand. Brie slipped her hand into Esán's. Torgin clutched the compass and moved closer to Yaro. Ira and Desirol crowded behind them. A faint path solidified and widened at its far end. The air shimmered and steadied. An entrance, framed in an arch of multi-hued sandstone, yawned wide and dark against the whirling sea of red.

"I guess we found it." Torgin gulped and tucked the compass beneath his shirt.

Yaro studied the arch and scanned the surrounding terrain. "I'll take a look." He strode to the entrance and peered inside. Changing to a panther, he pressed his nose into the darkness, sniffed the air, and leapt through the archway.

Torgin stared after his heart brother. "I think we should wait."

Ira caught his eye. "If we listened to you, Torg, we'd be sitting in Idronatti, scheduled to the chron-click by the PPP."

Torgin scowled. "You make..."

Brie gasped. All eyes turned her direction. She rubbed the Star of Truth and glanced at Esán. "*We need to move.*"

He nodded. "*We have company headed this way. We'd better tell Yaro.*"

Ira's gaze darted from one to the other. "Wish you two would speak out loud. What's up?"

The panther appeared in the arch and shifted. Yaro waved them forward.

Brie ran to his side. "There's something out there tracking us."

Esán joined them, with Torgin, Ira, and Desirol at his heels. "I feel it, too, Yaro, and it's traveling fast."

Yaro looked grim. "A walkway runs through the middle of the temple. I suggest we stay on it. Brie, you take the lead. Esán and I will be the rear guard."

Desirol shot the Pentharian a black look and folded his arms across his chest. "Who made you the commander, Yaro?"

Esán answered in a soft but firm voice. "Yaro has more experience in battle than anyone here. WoNa also charged him with keeping us safe. If you want to stay out here, Desirol, go ahead. However, I'm willing to bet the entrance will disappear once we're inside, and you'll be out here on your own with whomever or whatever is tracking us. Go, Brielle."

Not waiting for Desirol's response, she took a cautious step into the darkness and let her eyes adjust. Cool, damp air filled her lungs. A muted, greenish glow highlighted four steps leading to a stone walkway. Tentative but curious, she descended the stairs and proceeded down the path. She glanced over her shoulder as Yaro, the last to enter, passed under the arch. The sunlight began to dim. Like the shrinking of an eye's pupil, the arch grew smaller and smaller until only a tiny dot of light remained. The bright dot snapped to black, leaving them in Nesune Ruins with no visible way out.

Nissasa huddled on the lee side of his rehos beneath the folds of his kcalo. Anger as fierce as the storm that had brought his troops to a standstill churned in his gut. Wind ripped the sand away from the desert floor and hurled it skyward to pelt down from clouds like a driving rain. The Atrilaasu Oracle used the forces of nature to hold him at bay. Incensed, he hunkered down to ponder the news he had received prior to leaving Shu Chenaro.

Desirol and Nomed's nephew have disappeared from the ranch. He scowled. *Why didn't I have the boy watched?* The wind's howling echoed his frustration. *I misjudged Wolloh Espyro, an error I will not make again.*

His spies had also discovered one of his father's granddaughters had arrived in DerTah several sun turnings ago. He tugged his kcalo tighter. Her friend with the compass could be with her. He wanted her; he wanted Desirol and Esán; he wanted that compass.

Wind, wailing like a hungry ConDra, caught the edge of his kcalo. The woven cloth slapped at his body. He yanked it down and tucked it beneath his legs. A narrow gap in the folds of his scarf gave him a view of sand, sand, and more sand. It seemed determined to bury him alive. Fighting against the wind, he retied his scarf to better protect his face and eyes.

TheLise's sultry, charismatic smile stole into his thoughts, reminding him of the smoothness of her skin, her gold-spattered gray eyes, her passion and fire. Had she cooperated, he would not have hit her. He rubbed the knuckles of his right hand, remembering the impact as it contacted her cheekbone. A finger touched the scarf, hiding deep scratches on his face. He had been unprepared for a fight. Women in RewFaar would never have dared to spurn his advances. When he got his hands on her again, she wouldn't either. She would be his, a trophy to flaunt when he returned to his home planet as the new Largeen Joram.

He lowered the scarf enough to peer at the storm. It showed no signs of abating. Settling more comfortably against his rehos, he contemplated his ancestry and the events that had brought him to this point in his life.

RewFaaran soldiers kidnapped his grandmother, a country girl from KcernFensia, transported to their home planet, and placed her in servitude. At eighteen sun cycles, the child's father, a soldier in RewFaar's military, abandoned her and her infant daughter, Roween. Alone and disheartened, she abandoned the baby with a note explaining her parentage in the chapel in LaTenge Famele and disappeared. The Largeen Joram, Lorsedi's father, arranged for Roween to be adopted into the household and raised by RewFaaran women. Intelligent, scheming, and shrewd, she had made sure Lorsedi bedded her. Overjoyed with the birth of their son, she planned for his future. He would be the next Largeen Joram. When Lorsedi selected Desirol to inherit his position instead of Nissasa, she was furious. In secret, she had arranged for his training in the arts of DiMensionery, the one thing that might give him an edge over his father. Self-satisfaction made him smile. *I will soon be the most powerful man in the Inner Universe.*

He cast his senses outward. Had RiKell reached the oasis before the storm? Nissasa was certain his quarry would teleport to some distant spot. RiKell's job was to find their trail, track them, and lead his master right to them. His prize for success—Desirol. A sneer pulled at the fabric of the scarf. *Wolloh, High DiMensioner od DerTah, you do not know with whom you are dealing.*

Curious about the dim light filtering through the ruins, Torgin pushed the hood of his kcalo back and strode along the path. *Clearly, Nesune is buried beneath the desert, so where's the light coming from?* Not far ahead, a radiant sparkle caught his attention. Angling between two raised mounds, he stepped off the walkway. Icy darkness creeping up his drango boots stopped him. A shock wave raced through his body. Air gushed from his lungs, leaving him breathless.

"Torgin, grab my hand." Yaro's guttural command cut through his fright.

He executed an off-balance pivot, grabbed for his heart brother, and missed. Darkness sucked him lower. Hysteria powered his body forward. Strong fingers gripped his wrist. Still, he sunk deeper. His wet kcalo wrapped his thighs like a swaddled baby. He could not move. Creeping cold reached his hips. Flashed memories of the death shadow sent him spiraling toward panic.

Esán appeared beside Yaro. "I can help. Torgin, concentrate on me. Don't think about the death shadow. Yaro, when I say go…"

Torgin forced Wodash od DerTah's hideous image from his mind and focused on Esán. He stopped sinking. Little by little, the dark receded to mid-thigh. He could see the strain building on Esán's face and fought to keep his panic from resurfacing.

Brie placed a steadying hand on Esán's shoulder as he sank to his knees and took a deep breath. "Go."

Yaro's powerful pull hauled Torgin from the muck. The instant his foot touched the white stone, the darkness let go. He staggered, tripped on his kcalo, and fell to his knees beside a panting Esán.

Yaro peered down at him. "It is good we followed, heart brother, or we might have lost you."

Torgin gulped. "Thanks, Yaro."

Ira clapped him on the back. "By the Fathers, Torg, did you step in a hole or something?"

"It looked like you were sinking." Desirol stared at the flat black bordering the walkway..

Brie knelt beside him. "Are you alright, Torgin?"

"I'm fine." He put an arm around Esán's shoulder. "I don't know what you did, but thank you."

"I used telekinesis to lift you. Whatever is down there fought like mad." He stood up, offered a hand, and helped Torgin to his feet. "You're lucky Yaro was so close."

Torgin stared into the darkness stretching to the far wall and shivered. "I'm lucky you were *both* nearby."

Yaro herded the group further into the temple. "I suggest we stay on the walkway. We don't want to discover what happens when the dark engulfs a whole body."

Esán held up his book on DerTah. "I suggest we rest while I review the information on Nesune. We need no more surprises."

Torgin peeled off his soggy kcalo and draped it over his arm. Staying near Yaro, he studied what was visible of the ruins. The stones forming the walkway appeared to be white marble. The walls, at least what he could see of them, were sandstone. At first, he assumed they were built of quarried blocks like the entrance archway, but it soon became apparent that they were solid, smooth, and unblemished—no blocks and mortar. *Could this be a natural cavern?*

The walk ended in a large circular area. A narrower marble pathway defined its circumference and encircled an intricate, inlaid design depicting a four-petaled flower. At its center, a three-dimensional replica of a desert lily, crafted from silver, glowed around a gleaming quartz crystal the size of Paisley's enormous fist. Benches carved from a moss green jade-like mineral sat at measured intervals on two sides of the circle. Across the back, four man-sized statues sculpted from the finest selenite gazed from gleaming gemstone eyes at the temple entrance. Each offered a bowl—one of obsidian, one of golden citrine, one of rose quartz, and one of clear quartz—from which water streamed into a rounded marble trough and swirled down into gold-covered drains.

He glanced over his shoulder. "Where are we?"

Esán shrugged off his pack, selected a bench, and began to leaf through the book on DerTah. "That's what I'm trying to find out."

Brie searched around in her pack, pulled out a lite-stick, and slid onto the bench beside him. Ira sprawled on the ground at his feet. As Desirol plopped down beside him, his kcalo flipped open.

Torgin frowned. "Hey, Des, where's your tunic?"

Desirol yanked his kcalo closed. "I left it at Eissua. I am RewFaaran, not Atrilaasu."

Ira made a contemptuous face. "How stuck up can you get?"

The RewFaaran was on his feet in an instant. "I am the son of the Largeen Joram. Adoption into a tribe off planet is not appropriate."

"What about Nichi?" Ira's hands rested on his hips.

A flush infused Desirol's fair face. He looked away.

Torgin draped his wet kcalo over the bench to dry. "Come on, Des. I don't care if you kept the tunic or not. I want to learn more about Nesune." He dropped to the ground next to Ira.

Desirol scowled, moved apart, and sat down.

Yaro remained standing, his alien eyes alert.

Esán began to read. "The ancestors of the Atrilaasu Tribe built the Temple of Nesune. Buried in Fera Finnero for over a century, it was one of the most beautiful and revered temples on DerTah. Constructed to honor NesDu, the desert god of the sands, and RyPhez, goddess of the desert winds, it had at its heart the HeLew od Meti. The four Statues of Sinnttee lined the eastern end of the temple, offering the gift of their water. Created within a natural cavern at the center of what had once been a magnificent series of sandstone cliffs, Nesune's marble walkways symbolized the path of life. The darkened areas to either side of the path represented the Realm of SeDah. Those who wandered off the walkway are said to disappear into the Abyss of the Dead."

Torgin shuddered and looked at Yaro. "Thanks again, my brother."

The golden Pentharian placed a hand on his heart and bowed his head.

"Does it say anything about the HeLew od Meti and the statues?" Curiosity gleamed in Brie's brown eyes.

Esán flipped a couple of pages. "The HeLew od Meti embodies the four phases of Human life...childhood, youth and young adulthood, the middle sun cycles, and old age. At its center, the desert lily represents the culmination of the four phases and the ascendance into VeeNah, the home of spirit and light." He turned another page. "The four statues, Ceeconni, Manitullie, Sorttince, and Tutsasseen, personify the most significant virtue of each phase of life. It is said that drinking water from one of their bowls instills that virtue in the recipient."

Torgin got to his feet and stretched. "I want to examine the HeLew od

Meti. I think it's laid out in line with compass points." While he talked, he pulled out his compass and went to stand at the opening in the circle. Holding up Almiralyn's gift, he adjusted his angle until the needle on the face settled.

Just as I thought. The designers aligned petals with the four directions on the compass. How fascinating. He tucked it beneath his kcalo and studied the southern petal.

Brie joined him. "I sure wish I understood the symbolism." A gentle nudge from her elbow made him angle his head to see her better. She touched a finger to her lips and slipped a small book in his hand. "Put this in your pocket. It's a replica of the one Esán has. Don't let Desirol know you have it."

He wanted to ask questions about it and Desirol, but the RewFaaran strolled toward them. "Hey, can I see your compass, Torgin?"

Yaro's tattooed fingers clasped around Torgin's wrist. "I have something to show you, brother of my heart." He guided him toward the Statues of Sinnttee.

Torgin cast a furtive glance over his shoulder. Desirol's eyes drilled into his.

39

Der Tah

Karrew and Gerolyn shot through the Nervac Gateway's swirling entrance. The portal's dimensional void, where sound was nonexistent and flashes of color left their retinas in shock, enclosed them. When suspended in time, Karrew always believed a jump would last forever. He knew better. Holding his wings steady, he shot toward the DerTahan night.

A blast of fresh air alerted him to the end of the journey. The destination point rushed closer. The night sky snapped into focus. With Gerolyn's raven form beside him, he streaked straight for the huge saffron moon and landed at the top of a high red dune. Nothing in the RewFaaran camp at its base suggested the guards had noted their arrival.

Hidden from enemy eyes by a curtain of night, Karrew led Gerolyn straight to Shu Chenaro's raptor center, swooped through an open window, and landed on a wooden perch. Gerolyn settled beside him, her head cocked to listen.

He ruffled his feathers. *"Stay here. I'll scout around."* Unfurling his wings, he took flight. Conscious of Nissasa's spies and their seeking eyes, he inspected the barn and the surrounding area until, satisfied Gerolyn was safe, he flew in search of his contact.

Wolloh stared at an oil painting on the wall in his sitting room. While his good eye picked out the details of the lush Trinugian forest, his mind wandered. Lorsedi and Nomed had stayed after Corvus departed, discussing strategies for limiting Nissasa's power. Lorsedi's inclination was to kill him outright. Something kept Wolloh from making death their goal. He preferred to let time provide the correct outcome.

After they left to rest, he sank into his favorite chair to enjoy the solitude and the opportunity to doze. Thoughts of Corvus roused him from a vague dream in which darkness roiled and men screamed. Banishing its dread-filled aftermath, he fixed his attention on the only man he knew capable of delivering a message to the Guardian of Myrrh.

Corvus Difner, a fascinating enigma, arrived at the Shu Chenaro at approximately the same time as Nomed and Esán. A coincidence? Wolloh doubted it. He had sensed the man's presence like a splash of cool water and knew at once there was a connection between him and the nephew of his former apprentice. Attempts to read Corvus' mind had increased Wolloh's curiosity. The subtle nature of the shields blocking his probe had given him a glimpse of a simple man with simple tastes. He knew better. Intrigued, he had remained watchful. Stifling a yawn, he continued his reverie. Two turnings ago, Corvus had given him a small opening. When Wolloh needed to reach Almiralyn, he knew where to turn.

Stebben's silent entrance pushed drowsy thoughts from his mind. The Major Domo placed a tray on the table next to him and poured a cup of strong tea from an elegant porcelain teapot. "Corvus is here with a response."

Wolloh cradled the cup, allowing the heat to soothe the damaged fingers of his left hand. "Give me a moment and then show him in. Please stay to hear what he has to say."

The tall man bowed and withdrew. Wolloh's appreciation for his Major Domo teased a smile at his lips. He raised his cup to the closed door; took a sip of tea; set it back on its delicate, white saucer; and prepared to receive his visitor.

The need to meet with Corvus alone had been part of his reason for sending Nomed and Lorsedi to rest. Corvus would have information for his ears only. The door opened. Stebben ushered him into the sitting room.

Wolloh angled his good eye in his direction. "Stebben will pour you a cup of tea, and you can tell us what you have learned." He raised his cup to his lips and scrutinized his guest over its fragile rim.

Exuding the watchful confidence of a wild bird, the man perched on the edge of his chair and accepted the steaming infusion. Stebben took his usual seat by the door.

Corvus inhaled the fragrance and smiled. "My favorite." He relished a sip. "I won't waste your time. My source reached Almiralyn with your proposal. She has sent an emissary to represent her and to negotiate terms amenable to all parties concerned."

Wolloh kept his eye on the man's face. "I had thought you would act in this capacity."

"Sir, the person the Guardian has chosen is a much better choice. I don't believe you have met her in person, but you know of her." Corvus' expression was pleasant and direct.

"Her?"

"Yes, sir...the twins' grandmother, Gerolyn AsTar. She trained in the art of negotiation on her home planet of KcernFensia."

Tempted to posture his scarred side to the man, Wolloh chose instead to face him directly. One good eye and one vacant one held his gaze. "Gerolyn is here, in DerTah?"

"Yes, sir. She would like time to meet with her twin and change clothes before she comes to you."

Wolloh narrowed his eye and stroked his feathered brow. "No one but Tissent must see her until I give the word."

"Consider it done, sir." He finished his tea and left the room.

Stebben took his seat. "Events move in a new direction."

Wolloh relaxed back in his chair and massaged his clawed fingers. "Yes, they do. I believe it is time to awaken Nomed and Lorsedi. Ask them to join me in the study in one chron-circle."

Stebben arranged the tea things on a tray and left. Wolloh savored the silence, cocooning the buzz of thoughts in his mind.

Corvus had introduced himself to Gerolyn and now stood outside her twin's door. When Tissent opened it in response to his knock, he gave her a moment to size him up. "I am Corvus Difner, an employee of the High DiMensioner." He offered a note from Gerolyn. Please read this. I will wait for your reply."

Tissent accepted the note. "Please come in and have a seat."

He remained standing and with a touch of surprise registered how much alike she and her sister appeared—identical like Brie and Ari—but also different. Tissent's quiet serenity contrasted with Gerolyn's more dynamic personality. Her concentration as she opened her twin's note was absolute. A hand went to her heart. Cool green eyes darted over the note a second time. "Is this true?" Her whispered question quivered. "Is she here at Shu Chenaro?"

Words seemed inadequate. He nodded.

"Bring her here. Of course, I will see her." Her hand gripping the doorknob held him still. "Let no one see her. Can you manage that?" A small smile lit her eyes. "Of course, you can. Hurry! I'll be waiting."

The note trembled in her hand as she moved aside. He slipped into the corridor and walked with dignified calm to the central garden. After assuring himself he was unobserved, he took a breath and arrived outside the raptor center where Gerolyn waited.

Even as noiseless as his appearance was, her eyes, so like her sister's, found him before he crossed the threshold.

"You saw her?" A tremor in her voice confirmed the importance of seeing her twin. "It has been a long time since circumstance separated us. How is she?"

"She is, like you, eager to be reunited. If you approve, we'll teleport to her room. It's important to keep your presence and mine a secret."

She rested a hand on his arm. "Whenever you're ready."

The energy of their arrival in Tissent's room stirred the filmy curtains at the window where she stood, staring at the moons of DerTah. Corvus stepped away from Gerolyn as her sister turned. Their eyes met, and they were in each other's arms, dark chestnut hair hiding their faces.

Feeling like a voyeur, he turned to study a large painting of a landscape. Its subtle colors soothed his nerves and allowed the women a private moment. He cleared his throat and turned. Identical radiant expressions beamed back at him. And then they surrounded and embraced him; kissed him, one on each cheek; and stepped back, their arms around each other's waists. Tissent's smile, in the past touched with sadness, projected only joy. Gerolyn's fatigue from her recent journey had vanished.

He returned their smiles. "I'll leave you, but I'll return at the chroncircle plus half. I am so happy for you." He didn't wait for a reply, but teleported to the barn and the company of the birds he loved.

Nomed stared at his bleary eyes in the mirror. Too short a nap had left him feeling hazy. He cupped his hands and scooped water from the washstand. The cool splash of it on his face chased the last vestige of sleep away. He whipped a towel off the rack and scrubbed his face and neck dry. As he lowered it, his mirrored eyes lingered on the scar on his cheek. *Will I ever move beyond that incident?*

With a purposeful pivot away from the mirror, he strode into the bedroom and slipped on a dark green shirt. *What has Corvus discovered? Will Almiralyn work with Wolloh and Lorsedi...and me? How is TheLise?*

He knocked on the Dreelas' door. When it opened, he could only smile. As lovely as ever in sleek black pants and a long, flowing, white blouse, TheLise gave him no time to comment. "I'm coming with you, Seyes. No. Don't raise that eyebrow at me. I've decided."

Since arguing would be fruitless, he offered his arm. "Allow me to escort you."

She rewarded him with a warm smile. He noted the artfully applied makeup that hid most of the Nissasa's damage. Only minor swelling above her eye hinted at something amiss.

When they reached Wolloh's study, Stebben nodded them into the room, where Lorsedi and the High DiMensioner sat near the fireplace, conversing in quiet tones. TheLise's entrance brought the Largeen Joram to standing.

Wolloh scrutinized her face. "I see you are on the mend, my dear. Thank you for joining our little conclave."

She inclined her head. "I wouldn't have missed it." Smoothing her blouse beneath her, she eased onto the chair Lorsedi had positioned for her and smiled up at him. "Thank you."

He remained serious and attentive. "I must apologize for my son's behavior and for putting you at risk."

She patted the chair beside her. "Please sit, Lorsedi. I agreed to play the game. You are not at fault."

He bowed his aristocratic head. "You are most gracious, Dreelas."

Stebben waited for Lorsedi to sit before he stepped into the hall. A soft exchange, indecipherable in the study, preceded Corvus' appearance.

The suspense building in the room made Nomed glance at its occupants. Corvus and Wolloh appeared unaffected. Lorsedi watched the man with hard eyes. TheLise wore a curious smile. Stebben maintained his ineffable calm.

The tension heightened as Wolloh spoke. "Good evening, Corvus. We are eager to know what you have learned."

"Almiralyn, the Guardian of Myrrh, asked me to tell you she understands the need to join forces. She has sent her emissary to meet with you." Corvus bowed and left the room.

Nomed felt a wave of disappointment. *An emissary? Why didn't she come herself?*

Gerolyn dressed with care. Tissent's wardrobe, packed for the formalities of a state visit, had provided her with the perfect dress. Simple and elegant, the fitted bodice flowed into a soft, floor-length skirt. The color, a deep teal blue, made her eyes shimmer with light. Her chestnut hair piled high on her head stressed her long neck and fair skin. She wore gold studs in her ears and around her neck a gold chain with a solitary diamond given to her by the one man in the universe she had truly loved.

She couldn't deny her nervousness or the anticipation tying her stomach in knots and wished Corvus would hurry. When he appeared in the hall, she wanted to run. Instead, she wrapped the dignity of her training around her and walked beside him to the meeting place. He opened the door and stepped aside. She glided past him into the room.

Although five heads turned toward her as she entered, she saw only the dark, hooded eyes of the Largeen Joram of RewFaar. With a gracious smile, she switched her focus to the man who leveraged his body from his chair and hobbled around the table. She knew from Tissent's description that this was the High DiMensioner od DerTah.

With none of the posturing her twin had described, he turned his full face to her, the intelligence in his good eye meeting her gaze. "It is a pleasure to see you, Gerolyn AsTar. Welcome to Shu Chenaro."

Struggling to keep from seeking the only person in the room that mattered, she took the hand he offered. "I am delighted to be here, Wolloh. Thank you for your hospitality." The steadiness of her voice pleased her. The tightness in her stomach eased.

"Allow me to introduce my colleagues." He nodded at the woman on Lorsedi's left. "TheLise, Dreelas od Trinuge."

The Dreelas gave her a genuine smile. "Welcome to DerTah. We look forward to hearing about Myrrh."

Gerolyn noted the makeup and the puffy eye. "Nissasa." The telepathic message surprised her. She kept her face neutral and her voice even. "It is a pleasure to meet you, TheLise. I understand your homeland is most beautiful."

Wolloh directed her attention to the man next to her. "The DiMensioner, Seyes Nomed."

He gave her a moment to appraise the face of One Man's brother, the scar on his cheek, the hazel eyes that glowed with appreciation and a touch of distrust. She inclined her head and followed Wolloh's gaze to a tall, well-built man standing behind him.

"Stebben, my Major Domo. And last but not least, Lorsedi Telisnoe, the Largeen Joram of RewFaar."

Across from her Lorsedi rose with agonizing slowness, his face an inscrutable mask, his jaw set in stone.

Wolloh limped to the door and leaned on his cane. "Please everyone, I suggest we give Gerolyn and the Largeen Joram some time alone."

Chairs scuffing against the tile floor, footsteps moving around her, a door closing, and a silence heavy with feeling occurred like the amorphous background in a dream. She held her breath and wondered if Lorsedi would stay on the opposite side of the table. When he finally walked around it to look down at her, she could see the young, handsome face she remembered beneath the lines etched by his successes and failures. Fine wrinkles around the eyes looked carved into the fair, freckled skin. The unforgettable features hardened, then melted into a flood of mixed emotions.

A hand reached out. His finger skimmed her cheek and trailed down her neck. He fingered a wayward curl, touched the diamond at her throat, and lowered his hand. His voice, when he spoke, carried an unexpected harshness. "Why did you leave KcernFensia without sending word? I would never have allowed my father to hurt you or our child."

Her heart pounded in her ears. The air she had held in lungs since the room emptied whispered away. She felt herself falling...

40
Myrrh

Kieel and his Terces Wood Nyti maintained a constant patrol of the RewFaaran camp. Nothing worrisome attracted their attention until well past middle night when he noticed movement on the forest side of the camp. Hidden within the interior darkness of the woods, he flew to a better vantage point and peered between the leaves as a man stepped from the cover of the tents and crept toward the trees.

In the upper branches of an old maple, Kieel found Mumshu fighting to stay awake. "Trouble." He explained the situation in a whisper. "Find Ashor and keep watch. I'll be back as soon as I can."

Zipping between trees, he followed the soldier along the trail to Allynae's cabin. His silent tread and the way he kept stopping to listen and peer into the darkness told Kieel he was on a clandestine mission. At the perimeter of the cabin's clearing, the soldier hung back, hiding behind a large-trunked oak.

Glad for a dim crescent moon, Kieel circumvented the outbuildings landed on the roof of a shed. The soft whir of wings alerted him to Reana and her dragonfly, Ethor.

"There are two more soldiers over there." She pointed at a spot near the main trail. "What do we do?"

Kieel nudged her deeper into the shadows as the soldier he'd followed dashed to the cabin. The man bound up the steps and pressed his back against the wall. A quick sidestep brought him to the door. As still as a cat stalking prey, he pressed his ear against the wood grain, pushed the door open, and slipped inside. Moments later, he reappeared. "Hoot, Hoot." The arranged signal brought his two comrades skulking to the cabin. Once they were all inside, the first soldier scanned the clearing and followed.

"Now what?" Reana asked.

"I go in; you stay here. Send Ethor to warn me of trouble." Kieel gripped his walking stick. "Be careful, granddaughter." He darted away. Behind the cabin, he fluttered to the sill of an open window. Inside, the soldiers sat in a tight circle around a single lite-stick.

On silent wings, Kieel zipped to the top of a bookcase and knelt on the edge closest to the group. With a jolt, he realized Cantruto, the adjutant to Tinpaca Mondago, was in charge.

The discussion confirmed the men were traitors. The name Nissasa Rattori came up several times as the group discussed ways to get a message to him. They need reinforcements. Tropal Gateway near the cottage acreage had proved ineffective. Gaining control of the Demrach Gateway was their goal.

Cantruto shot a furtive glance around the cabin and leaned in to his comrades. "The package has arrived at its destination. A message for the Guardian is on its way. It will bring her out of hiding, and we'll grab her. Once she's in our hands, Evolsefil and Elcaro's eye are as good as ours. And she'll tell us the whereabouts of SparrowLyn, the twins, and the boy, Esán."

"And if she doesn't?" The youngest man scowled.

The ruthlessness in Cantruto's expression provided an answer. Kieel shuddered.

The men leaned even closer together. Their faces, illuminated by the glow of the lite-stick, only exacerbated Kieel's growing sense of dread. Cantruto wore cruelty like a second skin. The other two magnified it. Kieel's blood ran cold as they developed a barbaric plot to murder Mondago. Nissasa wanted him dead before the messenger arrived. The assassination would take place as soon as they returned to camp. A shuffle of feet announced the end of the meeting. The men slipped from the cabin into the forest.

Kieel zipped down to a windowsill, his mind in turmoil. Reana whizzed through the open window and landed beside him. A large dragonfly followed. Kieel clutched the knob of his walking stick. The dragonfly was *not* Ethor. A blue Pentharian materialized in its place. The warrior's sudden appearance left Kieel at a loss for words.

Reana filled in the gap. "This is Voer, Grandee. He followed the other two men. We listened from the window."

Relaxing his grip on his small sword's wooden sheath, Kieel lifted into flight and hovered at the height of the Pentharian's tattooed face. "Almiralyn only told me of Yuin and Jeet..." He let the words hang in the air like a question mark.

"My comrade, Stee and I, were in Thera with the mother of the twins and One Man, Esán's father. We returned a short time ago. Almiralyn asked us to help you monitor the RewFaaran camp. When I saw you follow the one called Cantruto, I followed the other two. Reana offered to introduce us." Voer's stance and his explanation were open and friendly. He held out his hand, palm up. "I am honored to meet the Matrés of the Nyti."

Kieel flitted to the upturned hand. "I am honored to meet you, Voer. How much did you hear?"

"I arrived as you entered the cabin."

"Then you heard everything?"

"Yes. I have a message for you from Almiralyn. The Guardian has sent an emissary to the High DiMensioner od DerTah to negotiate a plan to join forces against Nissasa Rattori."

Kieel tapped his walking stick on Voer's palm. "Then we must warn the Tinpaca of Cantruto's duplicity."

A dragonfly flashed through the window and hovered near his granddaughter. She listened, then nodded. "It's all clear. The men head back to camp."

Kieel lifted off Voer's palm. "I suggest we arrive first." He shot out the window with Reana at his side. The two dragonflies streaked ahead of them. He hoped they would make it to the camp in time.

One Man slipped away to his quarters in Meos, shook his long hair loose from its braid, and sank onto his stone bed. Resting his elbows on his knees, he dropped his head in his hands. He sighed, knowing his solitude would be short-lived. *Sometimes I wish my acute senses would take a rest.* He shook his hair back from his face and crossed to the entryway as the small bell rang. Knowing Almiralyn waited, he pulled the curtain aside.

Her attempt at a smile melted away as quickly as it appeared. "I don't want to intrude, Somay, but I need your help."

"I've been expecting you, Almiralyn. Please come in."

He guided her to a chair and sat on the bench facing her. "I'll help in any way I can. What is it that has upset you?"

Her hands slid down her upper thighs and gripped them above the knees. Her elbows locked, and her shoulders hunched forward. She closed her eyes and inhaled a deep breath. As it released, she searched his face. Apparently satisfied with what she saw, she relaxed back in the chair. "It is important that I make peace with your brother." She swallowed. "I need to understand your history and his—how you came to Idronatti—what happened to him when you were children. Anything that will help me understand how I hurt him enough to make him want to destroy Myrrh and me."

He had wondered at her use of his given name, Somay. Now he understood. Knowing her as he did, he did not doubt her sincerity, nor that her pain matched Davin's in its depth and breadth. He, too, felt a need to bridge the gap between his brother and himself. Sharing their family history with Almiralyn would help them both understand what drove the DiMensioner. The time had to stand united against a common threat.

"You know he is my *half*-brother, right?" When she nodded, he continued. "And you know his true name is Davin Farlow. For this discussion, I will refer to him by this name. If you have questions, ask. I will share what I have pieced together from my mother and, with the help of the Seed of Carsilem." He inhaled a deep, calming breath.

"Our father, Koewin Farlow, was Idronattian by birth and a ranking member of the PPP's Unit 22, an elite group of scientists hand-picked for planetary exploration. While in Tao Spirian on a secret expedition, he met our mother, Sancia. It was love at first sight, at least for him. Sancia could not love a man from another planet.

"On Tao Spirian, in a ceremony celebrating one's transition to life, the high priest and priestess select the person one will be mated to when one achieves the Age of Latdus. Sancia had only a moon cycle left before she would Join with her lifemate, Eitan. She did not return Koewin's feelings.

"One night, in a fit of anger, he followed her home from work. When she refused to bed with him, he took her by force. What follows is the story Koewin related in a letter he left behind when he disappeared from Idronatti. I heard it so often that I long ago committed its contents to memory.

"Sancia, I never spoke of the events following the evening that I took you by force on Tao Spirian. I would like to do so.

I woke up with no recollection of where I was. My accommodations included a cot, a latrine, and a chair. One window allowed me to watch the moon cycles pass.

"For six moon cycles, the only person I saw was the boy who brought my food. One morning, a priest unlocked the cell and escorted me to a shower. When I was clean and dressed, he led me to a room where three men waited. I was told to sit with them at the table.

"A slender man, whose name sounded like a series of musical notes, explained the seriousness with which Tao Spirians looked upon my crime. When I denied my actions and tried to blame you, Sancia, the man reminded me that the type of behavior I had exhibited was unheard of on the planet. He explained that all Tao Spirians citizens maintained an empathic connection to one another that is enlivened during times of pain or suffering, one that began at birth. The entire population of the planet had experienced my abuse of you.

"The information shocked and shamed me. Punishment for my crime was total isolation for the rest of my life. A prison official informed me you,

Sancia, were pregnant with Davin. He gave me time to think, then offered me a means to make amends. If I agreed to their plan, we would remain on Tao Spirian for two additional sun cycles. You would, during that time, fulfill your commitment to Eitan. Then we would be Joined in the ways of Idronatti, and you would return with me to Thera. Shortly after our arrival in The City, you would give birth to a second son by your lifemate, whom I would claim as my own. I was to raise both boys. If I did this, the Tao Spirian council would not report my behavior to the PPP. I swore an oath not to harm you or the boys. They told me not to tell anyone about the deal. The idea of isolation terrified me even more than incarceration in Tower Five, so I agreed.

"The rest of the letter contained remorse for his actions and an apology. What I am about to tell you, I distilled from conversations with my mother regarding their life in Idronatti.

"When Koewin and his family returned to Thera, his Joining with a Tao Spirian met with disfavor in the PPP. They downgraded his job, and placed him in housing in Domlenah Lower Blue, a poor substitute for his former Uptown Blue apartment. Fury at the hopeless situation he had brought upon himself boiled over. He blamed our mother, but he dared not hurt her or her Tao Spirian son. No one could tell him what he could or couldn't do to his own son. When Davin turned five sun cycles, he became the target for our father's anger."

One Man paused. The memories made his heart ache. He glanced at Almiralyn, saw the understanding in her eyes, and continued.

"I remember the constant tension in our home—my father's yelling—Mother's gentle response. When she refused to retaliate in anger, Koewin would beat Davin. Afterward, he would leave for long periods. Our life was wonderful without him. When he returned, the cycle of anger and abuse began again.

"At home Davin was stoic. At the Education Center, he was always in trouble. Myrrh was the one place he felt safe. The turning he broke the kitten's neck, Father's beating had been brutal. When you banned him from Myrrh, he swore he would make you pay.

"Prior to his fourteenth Sun Cycle Celebration, he ran away so they could not expunge his memories of you and Myrrh. Everything that went wrong in his life, he blamed on you, even the fact that Tianna, Esán's mother and my lifemate, did not love him."

"Somay, I am so sorry." Remorse filled Almiralyn's features as she shook her head. "How did I miss the signs? Why I was so thoughtless? I have no excuse for behavior so unbecoming a Guardian."

The empathy of his race kept him quiet while she sorted through her dismay and self-reproach. Finally, he touched her knee. "Almiralyn, we all make choices that are contrary to our nature. Learning from our errors is what's important. Isn't that part of the impetus for The Unfolding?"

She wiped a tear from her chin. "You mean facing the shadow parts of ourselves and growing beyond them?"

He smiled. "Yes. I realize that's only a small part of it, but it is important."

The Guardian of Myrrh smiled her agreement and squared her shoulders. "How can I make this up to Davin?"

"You may have to accept you can do nothing. Once you have spoken with him, it will be his responsibility to find space for forgiveness." He handed her a handkerchief.

"Thank you, Somay. I appreciate your willingness to share." She dried her tears and returned it. A quick hug and she took her leave.

In the quiet that followed, he refolded the handkerchief and pressed it to his heart. The tears of a Guardian were a gift of love. He tucked it carefully away and returned to his chair, his hair tenting his face once more. The memories had stirred up emotions he preferred to keep hidden. *Memories, stories of our pasts—* He shut his eyes, wishing Tianna were in the room, wishing he could talk to her, wishing he could share his concerns about Esán.

Sparrow gazed around the artist's studio deep in the Dojanack Caverns. Almiralyn had made sure she had what she needed to paint in Meos. Yookotay had ordered the studio prepared and arranged for special illumination that replicated natural light. Clean canvases stacked against the wall waited for her to cover their pristine whiteness with color. Merrilea had put a drop of her Myrrhinian blood in each jar of paint as Almiralyn had instructed when they first arrived in Myrrh several moon cycles ago. Sparrow had learned while painting the events of the DiMensioner's revenge to respect this wish. Her work had become prophetic and alive. Ready to begin, she centered herself and picked up her palette.

The canvas on the easel called her to splash it with a pale blue wash. She dipped her brush in the blue on her palette, mixed it with a dab of white, added a touch of water, and began. The pictures in her head merged and flowed from brush to canvas. Her concentration was so complete she barely noticed Allynae enter and walk to her side. One color after the other, a shadow, a highlight, a touch of texture until she dropped her brush in a jar and stepped back. The shock of the image shook her from her creative trance and left her trembling. Allynae's arm around her waist steadied her. His silence caressed her, calming the emotions that sent tears rolling down her cheeks.

She stared at the two figures on the canvas. Her mother, in a long dress of teal blue, her hair piled high on her head, a single diamond on a gold chain around her neck, looked up at a man with an abundance of red hair and a sprinkling of freckles. He was tall and well-built with a strong profile. Authority robed him like a priest. "It's him—the Largeen Joram of RewFaar."

"He's your father, Sparrow." Allynae's arm tightened as she wavered.

"I know." She leaned into the comfort of her life-mate's presence and sobbed.

41

Der Tah

Rikell trotted over the desert sands, unaffected by the heat or the lack of water or the dust billowing around it. It had cast off its Human form in favor of its own more adaptable body. Its lanky, loose-limbed frame with its leathery skin and bear-like, skull brought cringes of distaste and often terror from those not of its origin. It laughed out loud. "I am a Mindeco from the Trutore Mountains on RewFaar. I am Mindeco, Mindeco, Mindeco!" The bellowed words roared above the wind's fury.

Lumbering to a standstill, it inhaled. Wide nostrils opened and closed and opened again. Teleportation's unique scent, dispersed by the howling tempest, had grown less prevalent. It crouched, scooped up a handful of sand, and let it slip between its talon-like fingers. Nose to the ground, it loped along on all fours. Speed, one of its greatest assets, excited it almost as much as the kill. The exhilaration of blood pounding beneath its skin, the scorching air licking its face, the sand bouncing off its thick hide filled it with delight. With the black emptiness of its single, centered oculus fastened on the terrain and the fast-fading trail, it sped up.

Thoughts of Nissasa Rattori, the only Human ever to bind it, made it snarl and gnash its teeth. It hated and feared its RewFaaran master. No Human could cause its demise, but Nissasa Rattori could make its time outside the Trutores unbearable. Only success would insure Rikell's ability to remain free, only success would provide it with its next Human body.

Again, it paused. Hunching low, it pressed one nostril closed and then the other and blew. Once its nose was clear of sand, it resumed its fast-paced gallop. *Too bad Nissasa wants the objects of this search alive. If a healthy kill awaited me, I'd speed up. Why he needs me to do this job is a mystery. I'm only after a couple of children. How difficult can it be?*

Esán had read all there was to read regarding the Temple of Nesune and its ruins. Ira and Desirol slept, curled up on a bench with a pack for a pillow. Yaro and Torgin sat together near the Statues of Sinnttee, talking in whispers. He tucked the small, leather-bound book in his pocket and made a slow and studied circuit of the HeLew od Meti. When he reached Brie where she knelt at the eastern petal, her lite-stick illuminating the ornate image, he crouched beside her. "Beautiful, isn't it?"

"It's fascinating. I wish we had time to study it." She shot a worried glance at the entrance. "Whatever is following us is closing the gap. Can you feel it?"

He let his gaze roam the petal's design and sent a telepathic response. *"It is unlike anything I have ever known—worse than the death shadow. I tried a mind probe, but its shields..."* He shook his head. *"At this distance, I couldn't break through."*

"It's tracking the energy trail left from teleporting, isn't it?" She hurried on. *"We can't teleport again, can we?"*

He pulled her to her feet. "We'd better talk to Yaro. Maybe he'll have some ideas."

Choosing not to disturb Ira and Desirol, they circled the HeLew and approached the Statues of Sinnttee from the opposite side.

Torgin patted the bench next to him. "Have a seat. Aren't the statues exquisite?" He flexed his musician's fingers and rubbed his palms along his pant legs. "I know that look, Esán. What's wrong?"

Brie sat down next to Torgin. Esán explained the problem.

"Worse than the death shadow?" Torgin groaned. "What do we do?"

Yaro stood up. "Brie, wake the boys and explain the situation. We'd better be ready to move at a moment's notice."

The Pentharian fingered a gold earring. "I wonder if the ruins' arch opens to everyone? Does your book say anything, Esán?"

"No. It only describes the temple and its symbolism."

"I suggest we teleport somewhere else." Desirol sauntered into the group.

Esán shook his head. "It follows the energy trail left behind by teleporting."

Ira nudged in next to the RewFaaran. "What do you suggest, then? At least if we teleport, it will give us more time."

"By the Fathers!" Torgin pointed.

Everyone turned, eyes riveted to the end of the marble walkway, where a spot of light shimmered, faltered, and began to grow. The arched entrance took shape. A shaft of sunlight shot along the marble path, spotlighting the HeLew od Metis. Its crystal center burst to life. Sparkles of light leapt around the temple.

In the distance, a dark form pounded toward them. Small at first, it grew bigger and bigger until it crouched, a silhouetted-figure beneath the sandstone arch.

As it began to straighten, Desirol gulped in air and gripped Esán's arm. "A Mindeco." The whimpered word held such hopeless terror that it left everyone but Yaro trembling. Features still obscured in shadow, the creature's gangly figure lumbered down the walkway. Long arms swung at its sides. A flare of light from the HeLew lit the hideous face. A cry of horror exploded from Torgin.

His eyes fixed on the advancing form, Yaro motioned his charges behind him and spoke in an undertone. "Esán, are there any other chambers where we could hide?"

Brie answered. "There are several. But I don't remember where they're located. We don't have time to look."

Esán pulled the book from his pocket and thrust it into her hands. "I can hold it off for a while. Find a hiding place. Put the telepathic picture in my head. Everyone hold on to me." He put a hand on Yaro's shoulder and an arm around Brie's waist, shut his eyes, and pictured shields forming around them. Focused on the energy he had used to ward off the projectiles thrown at him during his assessment with Wolloh, he prepared to repel the Mindeco.

In the recesses of his mind, he was aware of the silent flipping of pages. Fear emanating from Torgin, Ira, and Desirol almost suffocated him. Brie held hers in check. Yaro remained a shield in front of him, solid and calm—prepared to risk his life for theirs.

The beast slammed into the shields, stumbled backward, and let out a deep-throated growl. Mammoth fists pounded against the barrier. Esán's friends pressed closer, their sweat smelling of fear, their breath hot on his neck. A roar of frustration shook the ruins. The stench of rancid meat washed over them. On all fours, the Mindeco prowled the perimeter of the shields. It completed the circle and straightened.

"I am here for the brother of Nissasa, the boy, Esán, and the twin, Brielle. Give them to me with the Compass of Ostradio, and I will not harm the rest of you."

It planted its powerful body where they could see its heinous features. Its singular eye picked them out one by one. "If you choose to protect them..." It loomed taller. "I will kill all of you."

The voice, so deep it sounded like the booming return of the surf in a storm, shook the barrier Esán fought hard to maintain. Another roar broke like a tidal wave, pounding the shields again and again until Esán felt his control beginning to weaken.

"Esán!" Brie's voice infused him with strength. The shields steadied. The blurred image of a room formed in his head. He focused. It stabilized.

Screeching a series of profanities, the beast, a battering ram of muscle and sinew, hit the barrier with the full weight of its enormous body. Pain ripped through Esán. He crumpled to his knees. The splintering shield tossed the Mindeco into the air like tumbleweed in the wind. It landed halfway up the walkway, a growling heap of angular bones.

Gasping for breath, Esán scrambled to his feet. In front of him, Yaro shifted to panther and crouched. The Mindeco regained its footing and lurched toward them. Esán flung himself on the panther's back. It lunged at the oncoming beast. Their collision in mid-air provided the contact needed to teleport them away from his friends.

Darkness, as black as tar, enshrouded them. Esán pitched through the air, slid over the floor, and rolled into a crouch. Thwack, smash, groan—the sounds of battle bouncing off the walls told him the room was not big. A combatant brushing his arm forced him backward until the wall halted his progress. He swung his pack from his back, found his lite-stick, and thought it on.

The Mindeco towered above him. A powerful hand slapped the lite-stick from his grip and sent it arcing across the space until it hit the ground, skittered to a stop, and lay glowing. In the instant before the creature's enormous foot smashed it, Esán saw Yaro's panther form, already lathered with blood, ready to spring.

His thoughts racing, Esán reviewed his options. *What can I do to help? The lite-stick's worthless. How can I see in this?* He sliced the blackness with a hand. *Simmer down, Esán. Pull yourself together so you can think.* Closing his eyes, he slowed his breathing and let his senses bring an image of the two battling creatures into focus.

In the center of the square chamber, massive Mindeco hands encircled the panther's neck. The big cat shifted. A snake writhed around the Mindeco's wrist and sunk its teeth into the leathery flesh. Howling in rage, the RewFaaran creature flung the snake through the air. Another shift and the panther landed and pounced, sending the Mindeco crashing against the wall. It shook its ugly head, sucked its wrist, and spit. Its roar shook the chamber as it hurled its body mass at the prowling panther.

Esán threw up a shield around Yaro. A grunt of frustration escaped the Mindeco as it smashed into the barrier and slid to its knees. The dark pool of its single eye found Esán. In one long stride, it crossed the space between them. Its massive fist plowed through the air, grazed his temple, and sent him tumbling into oblivion.

Distant sounds of conflict dragged Esán to the surface. He struggled to sitting. A panther's scream slammed his memory into place. He squeezed his eyes closed to erase the darkness. Images formed. Yaro, in his natural form, sprawled on his back in front of the Mindeco. The RewFaaran beast raised its fist for the killing blow and threw back its head, a howl of triumph issuing from opened jaws. Esán flung himself across the Pentharian's body.

Torgin stared at the spot where Yaro and the Mindeco had collided. Breaking free of the paralysis that had rendered him motionless, he ran forward. "Where are they? Yaro? Yaro? Answer me!"

Desirol seized his arm and yanked him around. "They're gone, you idiot. Stop yelling."

"Take your hands off me." Torgin pulled away and poised his fists ready for battle. "Yaro's my heart brother—"

"And how stupid is that?" Desirol poked him in the chest with a finger. "He's a mercenary who sells his services to the highest bidder." He poked again. "So, who's paying him to take care of you?"

Anger propelled Torgin's fist toward the RewFaaran's sneering face. Ira grabbed his wrist and glared at Desirol. "You're out of line, Des. I can't believe you said that. Apologize."

Brie stepped between them. "Please. We're in major trouble, and you three are fighting."

Torgin snatched his wrist from Ira's grasp. Focused on regaining control, he marched back to the Statues of Sinnttee. Tutsasseen, the Goddess of Wisdom, gazed down at him. The understanding in the carved face made him cup his hands beneath the water cascading from her clear quartz bowl. He gulped a deep drink. Cool wetness sliding down his throat quenched his thirst. But that was not all. His anger subsided, and compassion blossomed in its stead.

As he returned to his friends, he met Desirol's angry gaze. "I don't need an apology. I'm sorry your brother betrayed you, Des. Yaro is not like Nissasa. When you have known him longer, you will understand why he means so much to me."

"I didn't mean..." His cheeks flooding with color, Desirol pressed his lips together.

Torgin stopped him with a shake of the head. "It's done. We have other things to worry about."

Brie's smile rewarded his efforts.

Ira spoke up. "Like, where did they go, and what do we do now?"

"Esán teleported them to the chamber I found in this book." Brie held it up. "The question is whether Yaro is still alive."

Torgin wanted to scream but kept his voice calm. "He has to be."

Desirol sank down on a bench. "You cannot kill a Mindeco, not by ordinary means, anyway."

"Tell us about them." Ira joined him. "What is a Mindeco?"

The RewFaaran shuddered. "It is the monster that creeps through your nightmares and rips your heart out. It is pure evil, and it thrives on killing. Mindeco are only found in the Trutore Mountains on RewFaar. Nissasa must have bonded this one and brought it with him, which is terrifying."

"Why?" Torgin sank to the ground in front of him.

"Binding one is almost unheard of on my world. You must be more evil and more powerful than the Mindeco to gain control."

Ira grimaced. "For sure, none of us wants to fall into your brother's hands."

Torgin shuffled through his confusion. "I still don't understand what it is, or why it's so powerful." He looked at Brie, who stood nearby, staring into the distance. Her body shuddered from head to foot. Scrambling up from the ground, he hurried to her side. "What do you see?"

"They're still fighting." Her voice trembled. "Yaro is…"

A light flashed. Esán appeared in front of the statues, with Yaro in a crumpled heap beneath him. Blood-soaked braids tumbled around the Pentharian's colorless face. One leg twisted at an odd angle.

Ira helped Esán up and assisted him to a bench while Brie knelt by Yaro and pressed an ear to his chest.

Torgin choked and tried to force his legs to move. His reality wavered. Esán's shaky voice as he described the battle sounded like static on the V-Screen in Idronatti.

"I had to wait until the Mindeco wasn't touching him to teleport him back. I tried to help by putting a shield around him, but the Mindeco knocked me senseless. When I came to, Yaro, in his true form, lay at his feet, unmoving. The Mindeco stood over him howling. I threw myself over Yaro's body and teleported him here. I'm so sorry, Torgin."

Reality rushing back into focus left Torgin unable to control his legs. He dropped to his knees and touched the still face. "Yaro, speak to me. Open your eyes." He struggled to make sense of what he was seeing. Even in the dim light of the ruins, he could make out the gashes running the length of his friend's tattooed torso. Blood oozed from the torn flesh on his gold-scaled legs. Drops fell from a cut on his arm, forming a spattered patch on the temple floor. Torgin rocked forward. "You can't be dead." He withdrew his hand and stared at his blood-covered palm. "We have to do something. Ira?"

Brie knelt beside him, tears streaming down her cheeks. "He's gone, Torgin." She laid a hand on the Pentharian's chest. "He has no heartbeat and no breath."

He gathered his heart brother up in his arms and sobbed.

Ira felt Torgin's sorrow as though it were his own. Yaro was his friend, too. He fingered Efillaeh's handle, withdrew it from its scabbard, and balanced it on the palm of his hand. *Will it work?* He looked down at Yaro's battered body. *I won't know unless I try.* He glanced a question at Brie.

Blinking back her tears, she nodded and touched their friend's arm. "Help me lay him flat, Torgin, so Ira can place Efillaeh on his chest."

Torgin moved until Yaro's head lay in his lap. Brie and Desirol straightened the Pentharian's broken limbs and knelt on either side of him. Esán joined the group. Pallor hallmarked the toll his battle to save Yaro had taken on his fragile strength.

Ira knelt across from Esán, his resolve strengthened by the hopeless pleading in Torgin's expression. Grief, shock, and horror had leached the color from his friend's cheeks. Tears glistened in eyes filled with dread.

This has to work. Ira held the knife up in a plea to the Statues of Sinnttee. "Please, help Efillaeh. Please help our friend." Steadying his shaking hands, he placed the knife on Yaro's bloodied chest.

42
Der Tah

Gerolyn opened her eyes to find the Dreelas od Trinuge seated by her side on a settee. Wolloh's sitting room was quiet but for the sound of voices murmuring beyond the door.

The Lise felt for her pulse. "How are you?"

The soft timbre of the woman's voice eased Gerolyn's agitation. "What...oh...I fainted." The memory of the man she had never stopped loving overwhelmed her. "Lorsedi?"

"He thought you needed time to recover. I'll fetch him when you feel ready to see him." The Dreelas shifted to the end of the settee.

Gerolyn eased herself to sitting, and, tucking a loose curl in place, studied the woman next to her. "Nissasa did that to your face?"

"He has quite a temper when he doesn't get what he wants."

"I hope you managed some damage of your own."

TheLise's slow smile provided the answer. "Can I get you anything before I call Lorsedi?"

"Water, if you wouldn't mind."

"As it happens, Stebben brought a pitcher." She poured a glass and passed it to her.

Gerolyn sipped while she sorted her thoughts. When she felt equipped to deal with the situation, she set the glass on the table and stood up, smoothing the wrinkles from her skirt. A relieved smile flashed. "The room has stopped spinning. I think I'm ready to see him. Thank you, TheLise."

The woman gave her a studied look. "We are involved in a battle of wills, Gerolyn. Stay alert. If I can help, please ask." She rested a hand on her arm. "Take care. I'll wait outside."

The murmuring paused as TheLise stepped into the hall. Gerolyn touched the diamond at her throat as Lorsedi entered and closed the door. Concern flickered in his dark eyes. She held out her hands. He took them in his and held them to his heart. "You have recovered?"

She could only smile and nod.

He embraced her and rested his cheek on the top of her head. "I never want to lose you again."

Allowing herself a moment to enjoy his presence, she relaxed. The awareness of his heartbeat and the rise and fall of his chest made blood rush to her face. She sighed. "We have responsibilities, Lorsedi."

He held her at arm's length. "You're sure you're alright?"

"I'm fine. Seeing you after all this time..."

He brushed her lips with his. "I know. We'll talk later. I suggest we take care of business first." Another light kiss and he left her side to invite their cohorts to return.

Stebben waited alone outside the door. "Wolloh would like you to join him in the conference chamber."

With mixed feelings, Gerolyn laid her hand on Lorsedi's arm and glanced up at the erect, authoritative figure of the man she loved. "I hope the decisions made here don't put us on opposing sides. I am bound to act in accordance with Almiralyn's wishes and what's best for Myrrh."

A solemn smile curved his lips. "I must do what I believe is right for RewFaar."

She nodded her agreement before they hurried after Stebben.

Efillaeh lay dormant on Yaro's chest—no green or amethyst mist—no change in Yaro. Brie could feel Torgin's fear building. Desirol's expression showed only curiosity. Across from Ira, Esán knelt with his hands resting on the Pentharian's arm. She sent him a telepathic message. *"Mindeco?"*

"Still in the hidden chamber. Hurry."

She considered the knife. *Why isn't it working?* A fleeting image of Efillaeh positioned a different direction flashed through her mind. The Star of Truth sent a tingling sensation up her neck.

"Ira, place the knife crosswise with the point over the heart." While she spoke, she pulled the velvet pouch from beneath her shirt and tipped the Stone of Remembering onto her palm. After placing it above Efillaeh on Yaro's breastbone, she sat back.

At the center of the stone, soft blue light began to glow. Like the wafting of mist above a lake at dawn, it floated over the bloodied body and gathered in an opaque cloud around the sacred knife. Rays of emerald light shot through the blue mist. Amethyst pools formed over each wound. Slow, methodical healing started on Yaro's face and head. Lacerations on his shoulders and arms began to knit together. His brutalized chest healed one wound at a time. Where tattered flesh smoothed into wholeness, Yaro's tattoos reformed. Broken limbs trembled and straightened. The deep slash on his right thigh healed last, leaving the only visible scar. Color rushed back to his face. A deep, rasping breath shook his body. The stone and the knife lay dormant once more.

Torgin leaned over the still face. "Yaro? Wake up. Yaro?" His heart brother's lack of response left him gasping for breath. "Why isn't he waking up? What did you do wrong?"

Ira handed Brie the Stone of Remembering and picked up Efillaeh. "We did what we know to do."

Desirol reached for the knife. "Can I see it?"

"No." Ira put it in the scabbard.

"Come on, Ira. Let me see. I'll give it right back." The RewFaaran reached across Yaro's quiet body.

Ira scowled. "You hard of hearing? I said no."

Desirol sprang to his feet. "I'm Lorsedi's heir. I demand to see that knife."

"Demand all you want, Des. I don't care who your father is."

Brie glared at Ira and then at Desirol. "Stop it! This isn't the time to fight. Yaro needs our help. The Mindeco will not stay trapped forever."

Desirol rounded on her, sneering. "You're always the little peacemaker, aren't you?" He whipped around and scowled at Ira. "I want that knife. If you won't give it to me, I'll take it from you."

A sarcastic laugh accompanied Ira's walk away from Yaro. "You want it... come get it, Lorsedi's *baby* son."

Esán pointed. "Look at the entrance!"

Everyone whipped around. The emerging stone archway solidified, outlining the figure of a man.

"Now what?" Desirol snarled.

"Get behind me." Esán eased to standing, his attention fixed on the approaching figure. "I'll put up a shield."

Like a worried sheep dog, Brie herded their friends into place. The shield shimmered and steadied. She could feel its tingling energy and the intensity of Esán's concentration.

The man advanced down the walkway. In the dimming light at the end of the single path, he paused. "I believe I can be of service."

Esán let the shield drop. "Corvus, I am *so* glad to see you!"

Brie hurried to his side. " Yaro won't wake up, Corvus, and, soon, the Mindeco will find us.

Corvus put his arm around her shoulders and guided her back to the prone body. "I will check on Yaro first. Then we'll decide how to deal with your Mindeco."

Corvus knelt and laid a hand on the tattooed chest. He frowned and shut his eyes. Finally, he looked at Torgin. "Only you can save Yaro, but it will take great courage."

"What do I have to do?" Torgin wrapped his arms around himself as though it would steady his shaking voice.

"Yaro floats in a place between worlds." Corvus' gaze remained steady. "In order for him to survive, we must release him. You are his chosen brother, Torgin. You must take Efillaeh and pierce his heart. If you do not, he will remain as he is for eternity."

Brie winced as horror flood her friend's face. On the back of her neck, the Star of Truth tingled its message of rightness. To save Yaro, Torgin must do the unthinkable.

Nomed sat at the table in the conference chamber to the right of his mentor, reminiscing about the afternoon he had introduced Esán to the Dreelum. The tan and cream tile floors and pale adobe walls, the abstract artwork, the lamps above the table made from the horns of a zeegall from the TheDa Mountains had not changed. Everything else had. *So much has happened since that first sun turning.*

Wolloh's good eye blinked. "Change, my dear Seyes, is all we can count on. And there is more to come."

Nomed leaned back in his chair and folded his arms. Across from him, TheLise sat with elegant calm, her face impassive.

Stebben entered and paused by the door. "They're right behind me."

Wolloh's gaze flicked to the place next to TheLise. "Join us."

As Stebben complied, Lorsedi ushered Gerolyn ahead of him into the room.

Nomed studied her. *Can she truly negotiate terms for Almiralyn when it's clear that she loves the Largeen Joram?* He shifted his attention to Lorsedi's face as he held out a chair for her at the opposite end of the table from Wolloh. The solicitude in his expression said it all. He loved her. Where did that put the RewFaaran leader and *his* loyalties? *This meeting becomes more and more interesting.*

TheLise caught his eye. His crooked smile formed an opposite curve to his eyebrow. A twinkle of laughter flew back at him from beneath a half-lowered lid. With a soft chuckle, he returned his attention to Wolloh.

The High DiMensioner's good eye gleamed. He looked from one guest to the next until his gaze came to rest on Gerolyn. "I believe you may have information to share before we begin to shape our plans."

She nodded and rose. "Almiralyn has asked me to act as her emissary. Her concerns rest not only with the safety of Myrrh but also with the safety of her nieces, Arienh and Brielle AsTar, their mother, SparrowLyn AsTar, and the boys, Esán Efre and Torgin Whalend. She asked me to clarify that the Galactic Guardians of the Fourth Galaxy selected her as the steward for the Prima Crystal Evolsefil *and* Elcaro, The All- Seeing Eye. Only the Guardians can change their stewardship. Also, the Compass of Ostradio is not a bargaining chip. With these stipulations in place, we may begin negotiations. Unless you have questions, I have two concerns to share."

Wolloh allowed a moment for other members to ask questions. When they put none forward, he continued. "What do you wish to share?"

"The Guardian is concerned that the difficult relationship between Seyes Nomed and herself will create problems unless they resolve it. She is ready and willing to meet with the DiMensioner." Gerolyn's deep green eyes sought Nomed's face. "She asked me to tell you, Seyes, that she accepts responsibility for her lack of sensitivity and wishes to apologize to you in person."

The unexpected statement left him momentarily numb. The occupants of the room blurred. Fighting to steady his jangled nerves, he gripped the table. Sun cycles filled with anger and hurt sent a backwash of emotions pouring through him. He floundered, a small boat capsized in a storm of fury and pain. When the roar in his ears ceased and his vision cleared, he could only stare at his whitened knuckles. The urge to leave the room and all the hurt behind held him rigid.

His aching fingers relaxed, and he lowered his hands to his lap. "My relationship with the Guardian of Myrrh will not influence my response to the needs of all of us." Wolloh's good hand squeezed his arm. Nomed saw only compassion in his mentor's expression. He let out a slow breath. "Thank you, Gerolyn, for delivering the message."

"You are most welcome, Seyes." Her solemn smile warmed him before her attention shifted to Wolloh and then to Largeen Joram. "This is the other concern, Lorsedi. Corvus asked me to tell you that Desirol is here on DerTah."

A mask dropped into place, wiping all expression from Lorsedi's face. "Please explain." The two words, cold as steel, rolled off his tongue with controlled precision.

"I believe Wolloh or Stebben will provide the most informed explanation." She took her seat.

At the Nesune Ruins, Torgin looked from one friend to the next and swallowed the bile, threatening to choke him. "I c-c-cannot s-s-stab Yaro."

"It must be your choice, one only you can make." Corvus' words, spoken with understanding, helped him to regain a semblance of calm.

Brie went to her knees beside him. "Do you remember when I sat on ReNin RepPosu?"

The adult Brie on the pink tourmaline throne formed in his memory. He nodded.

"Knowing the future carries with it a tremendous burden. I understood that when I sat on the throne and always struggle with the information I received. Esán's illness has shown him the face of death. Ira and Desirol have had their memories stolen and had to fight for their return. These events are turning points...times when we must die to parts of ourselves in order to grow. This is a turning point for you and Yaro."

He clutched his hands in his lap to stop their trembling. "How do you know so much, Brielle?"

"The throne, WoNa, all of you..." Her smile included everyone gathered around the still body.

Although her calm reply helped, the choice continued to unnerve him.

Ira squatted, bringing the cool blue of his eyes level with him. "Remember, Efillaeh is not an ordinary knife. It is a sacred healing blade. It's the only way or Corvus wouldn't ask you to do it. We'll be right here with you."

"I know what you say is true." He gulped down the lump in his throat. "I don't think I have the courage to do it."

Esán touched the Pentharian's tattooed chest. "Torgin, if this were you instead of Yaro, what choice would he make?"

"If it meant saving me, he would do what must be done." He pressed a hand to his churning stomach.

"How do we know you're right, Corvus?" Desirol glared. "You just keep showing up and leaving again."

Ignoring him, Ira held out Efillaeh. "Look. The hilt's glowing. It's telling you it's the right thing to do, Torgin." He placed the sacred knife in his hand.

Desirol started forward. "You wouldn't let me see it, and now you hand it to him?"

Torgin gripped the knife. His doubts dissolved. "Stop it, Desirol. This is about life or death." He slid his leg from beneath Yaro's head and stood up. "Tell me what to do, Corvus."

"Please kneel across from me, Torgin. Brie, kneel by Yaro's head. Ira, place yourself at his feet. Desirol, join me on this side. Esán, please kneel next to Torgin."

When everyone was in place, Corvus pointed at a spot between two ribs. "Thrust the knife into his chest here, all the way to the hilt. Don't withdraw it until I give you a sign. Do you understand?"

Torgin stared at his heart brother's quiet face. Love for the Pentharian brought tears to his eyes. The knife in his hand pulsed against his palm. "You have come to my rescue so many times. Now it's my turn."

He placed Efillaeh's glowing tip above Yaro's heart. A throb of fear ripped through his mind. He shoved it away and plunged the slender silver blade between the ribs.

Shock left him trembling. The impulse to withdraw the knife almost overwhelmed him. Then Efillaeh began to vibrate. Crackling electricity encapsulated Yaro's body. Tingling current shot up Torgin's arms to the center of his chest. Hair on the back of his neck stood on end as energy pulsed through his entire body. The amethysts in the knife's gold hilt blazed the color of rubies, staining his hands and Yaro's chest deep crimson.

Across from him, the Statues of Sinnttee grew to ten times their normal size. Water from their bowls cascaded into the marble basin at their feet and flowed from each end into a channel that traced the outer edge of the circle surrounding the HeLew od Metis. One by one, the petals sprung to life, their images vibrant with color. A shaft of light from the central crystal shot upward and formed a rainbowed arc that culminated at the spot where Efillaeh entered Yaro's heart.

Thunder quaking and zigzags of blue-white light flashing through the temple blinded Torgin. The ruins, his friends, the statues, all ceased to exist, replaced by the spectacular vastness of space. Stars and moons, suns and galaxies sped across the boundless universal canvas. The magnificent diorama tipped and went dark.

Like a butterfly emerging from a cocoon, Torgin struggled to attune to his surroundings. A held breath rushed from his lungs. Memory tossed him back to the present and the body of his heart brother impaled by his hand on the sacred knife. His eyes flew to Corvus' face.

The man held his gaze. "Remove it now."

He lowered his eyes and withdrew the blade, blood-free and shining. Corvus took Efillaeh from his shaking hands and passed it to Ira. On Yaro's chest, a tiny wound healed without a trace. Again, Torgin looked at Corvus. "Why isn't he waking up? Did I do it wrong?" His anxious gaze scanned the Pentharian's face.

No one in the group breathed. Their attention remained riveted to Yaro's prone form. Torgin sent Brie a pleading look.

She started to shake her head, then gasped.

Strong fingers wrapped around Torgin's wrist and squeezed. Eyelids fluttered. Lizard-gold eyes opened. "My heart brother," Yaro whispered, "I thank you."

43
Myrrh

Hidden from view in thick trees and ground cover near the enemy camp, Kieel perched on Voer's shoulder and peered through a narrow tunnel formed by ancient tree trunks. The RewFaaran tents created a haunting montage in the flickering glow of several campfires. Beyond them, he could see the silhouetted sunflowers camouflaging the Tropal Portal where Stee and Reana kept watch. Ashor and Mumshu hid at the edge of the trees, ready to signal if anyone stirred.

"Time is short." Kieel hovered close to the Pentharian's ear. "Are you sure Tinpaca Mondago will cooperate?"

Voer brought a golden eye in line with Kieel. "If he doesn't, I'll put him to sleep."

Ashor zipped into view and landed on the Pentharian's palm. "All's clear. The guard patrolling the perimeter is on the other side of the camp.

The circuit takes about a quarter turn of the chronometer." He didn't wait for a reply, but whizzed out of sight between the trees.

Kieel soared upward, Voer shifted to a dragonfly, and they darted through the woods to the top of a tent across from the Tinpaca's. Nothing stirred. The only sound was an occasional snore. The dragonfly shot into the tent and reappeared. Kieel followed him inside and kept watch by the entrance.

Mondago lay on a cot, sleeping the light sleep of a trained soldier. Voer materialized beside him, placed an arm across his chest, and a tattooed hand over his mouth. Mondago's eyes flew open, flashed astonishment, and darted to his weapon, where it rested atop the table. He struggled to rise. The strength of Voer's forearm kept him prone.

The Pentharian whispered next to his ear, "I am Voer. I have important information for you, information that will save your life. Can I trust you to be quiet and listen?"

Mondago tried to speak, then nodded.

"One false move and I *will* silence you. Understood? One wrong move..." Voer warned again and straightened.

Mondago threw back his blanket, swung his legs over the side of his cot, and stood up. "I've heard rumors that Pentharian were abroad in Myrrh. I didn't believe it." He modulated his voice to an undertone.

Voer didn't waste time. "You're in danger. Cantruto is here as a spy for the Largeen Joram's oldest son. Tonight, he and two other soldiers are planning to execute you. They're on their way here now."

"How do I know I can trust you?"

Voer's blue tail twitched. "Do you have a choice?"

Alerted by a movement near the camp's border, Kieel landed on Voer's shoulder. "Trouble headed this way."

Mondago flashed a look of surprise in his direction, and then he was all business. "I've known Cantruto was up to something." As he spoke, he bundled clothes and a pack under his blankets. "Are you willing to help?"

"I am here to do so." A dragonfly landed on his palm. "And so is Stee." It vanished, and an emerald green Pentharian appeared.

Mondago's eyes widened, but he maintained his soldier's stoic demeanor.

"We have serum to knock out our prey." Stee tapped his eyetooth. "Better than killing if you want information."

The Tinpaca squeezed the bridge of his nose. "Serum sounds good." He lowered his hand. "Can you manage not to be seen? I'd prefer to keep your presence between us."

"This can be done." Voer held out his palm as Reana darted into the tent.

She touched down. "Almost here."

Kieel landed beside his granddaughter.

Voer held the Nyti at eye level. "Take Reana back to the woods. We'll let you know when it's safe."

Wanting to stay but unwilling to put Reana at risk, Kieel grabbed her hand and hurried her away.

Almiralyn traversed the Meosian Central Square on her way back to her quarters. A turn down a dim tunnel brought her to her curtained entryway. Once inside, she reviewed her conversation with One Man. Feelings of guilt nagged. *How did I miss the signs of abuse? They were all there...the bruises, the angry outbursts, and the stubborn refusal to change his behavior. Davin...* She paced across the cave and back. What had turned her usual sensitivity to frustration? She searched her memory. A kitten's death sprang to mind. She fingered the woven pattern of her braid. *That does not excuse my lack of awareness.*

The entry bell chiming interrupted her persistent pacing. "Who's there?"

Jordett stuck his head in the room. "Better come with me. I have something of interest to show you." He didn't wait for a reply, but strode away down the tunnel.

She followed, her active mind listing possibilities. Jordett motioned her into a cave, where Sparrow worked with total concentration on a large canvas.

Almiralyn hurried to her side. The painting—a black panther in midair, with Esán clinging to its back—brought her up short. Its target stopped the breath in her throat. How had a RewFaaran Mindeco found the children on DerTah?

Merrilea entered the cave and gasped. "What on Thera is *that* thing?"

Allynae appeared behind her. "That isn't what I think it is, is it?"

Almiralyn spoke over her shoulder. "It's a Mindeco. Someone find One Man..."

"I'm here." He strode to Allynae's side, his eyes fastened on the painting.

"What is a Mindeco, Almiralyn?" Merrilea slipped her hand into Jordett's.

"It's one of the most malevolent creatures in this solar system. Although it can assume various forms, it prefers to steal a body to manifest as a Human. The victim's mind retains its memories, and the body remains alive, but the victim's humanity, that which defines it as a sentient being, dies in the first moments of takeover."

Sparrow wiped her hands on her shirt and hugged herself. "What happens when the Mindeco sheds the body?"

"Decomposition is immediate."

Jordett frowned. "Where did it come from?"

"Legend has it that in ancient times, tribes on RewFaar conjured up the Mindeco to serve them as slaves. Those tribes faded out of existence. However, the Mindeco remained hidden in the Trutore Mountains. Only a Human who is more vile in intent and purpose may gain control of one."

Allynae studied the painting. "Who control's this one?"

"I feel certain it's controlled by Nissasa. If it captures the children, we face a calamity beyond anything any of us can imagine." Almiralyn fought to control her escalating alarm.

One Man cleared his throat. "Alli and I can't wait any longer. We must go to DerTah. The Tabagie told us that only the fathers of the children can save them."

"And how do you propose we get there?" Allynae scrubbed his mustache with a finger.

Almiralyn put a hand on her brother's shoulder. "You'll have to use your talents and your training, Alli. You are as powerful as I am."

Her brother stared into her eyes, swallowed, and wrapped his arms around Sparrow. "To save our daughters, Esán, and Torgin, I'll set aside my dislike of DiMensionery. I haven't used it in a long time, but I expect necessity will refuel my memories."

Almiralyn heard the matter-of-fact statement and expelled a held breath. Unbidden, tears welled up in her eyes. "Thank you, Alli." She blinked them away and looked at his companion. "Sparrow, I've never expected you to paint to my need or purpose, but it is time. Without Elcaro's Eye, I must ask you to tap into your innate wisdom and show us where the children are. The chances of Yaro winning a battle with a Mindeco are slim. The sooner One Man and Allynae find them, the better."

Jordett removed the finished canvas from the easel and leaned it against the wall. One Man replaced it with a new one. Sparrow cleaned her brushes. She drank mountain water from a flask and returned it to its hook on the easel. *"I'll call you when I'm done."*

Almiralyn smiled at the telepathic message. *"Good to 'hear' you. I'll be waiting."* She herded everyone from the cave.

Kieel sent Reana, Ashor, and Mumshu to patrol the camp. They would also watch for other soldiers who appeared to be involved in Cantruto's plans. His desire to help, if needed, sent him zipping from shadow to shadow to Mondago's tent. After a quick look around, he slipped under the edge, flew to the tent's peak, and hovered in the dimness.

Voer and Stee shifted, one to a small bat clinging to an upper tent seam and one to a snake made invisible by the grassy ground. Kieel knew they would shift as needed to achieve their goal. Mondago crouched in the darkness.

A soft hoot sounded. A man's figure hunkered down outside the entrance. Kieel landed on a cross member, his hand on the knobby head of his walking stick. A second hoot whispered through the night. A man skulked into the shadows across the way.

The first man crept into Mondago's tent and dropped to his knees by the table. A small bat landed on his shoulder. He crumpled to a silent heap. Mondago dragged him to one side and crouched in his place.

Soldier number two arrived at the entrance. Cantruto peered over his shoulder. Creeping forward, the soldier crouched opposite Mondago.

Cantruto drew his knife and tiptoed toward the cot. A snake slithered up the pant leg of the second soldier. He melted to the ground as Cantruto lifted the knife and plunged it into the mound on the cot. Yanking the blade free, Cantruto gave a frustrated growl and pulled back the blanket.

Mondago straightened. "You looking for me, Cantruto?"

The man swung around, his knife raised for the kill.

"Not a good idea." Mondago lifted his firearm, the barrel at the level of his adjutant's heart.

Cantruto lunged for Mondago, caught him in the chest, and pitched him backward. The weapon flew across the tent. The knife flashed as the men rolled. Blood oozed from a cut on Mondago's upper arm.

Kieel scanned the tent for a Pentharian. The men rolled again. Cantruto straddled the Tinpaca's chest. Holding him by the throat, he poised the knife for the kill. A bat shot from the shadows. The adjutant crumpled. Mondago groaned under the sudden weight of Cantruto's collapsed body. Voer materialized, rolled the unconscious man aside, and helped Mondago to his feet.

Mumshu darted through the entrance as Kieel landed on Voer's shoulder. "Soldiers are stirring. Two head this way."

"We'll be close by." Voer shifted.

Kieel took Mumshu by the hand and escorted him from the tent. Mondago had the Pentharian to keep him safe.

Sparrow glared at her canvas. The sudden temptation to fling her brush across the cave made her shake her head. Paced steps carried her to the cave entrance. *Trying to paint on demand is tying me in knots. I can't think. And I can't create anything.* She turned, approached her easel, and grabbed a paint-splattered cloth. Eyes narrowed, she stared at her unsuccessful attempt to meet Almiralyn's urgent need. The painting blurred. A childhood memory stirred.

Her father smiled down at her. "Happy sixth Sun Cycle Celebration, dear daughter." His gift, a set of paints, began her journey in the arts. A wistful smile tugged. *I loved the splash of colors on paper, I loved the feel of the brush in my hand, and I loved the smell of the paints. From the first brush stroke, I was hooked.*

She pursed her lips in thought. Training at the Art Institute in Idronatti had honed her skills and challenged her to grow. But the discovery of the depth and wonder of her creative talent began with the twins' trip to Myrrh with Torgin.

Absently, she set down her brush and cloth and pushed her hair behind her ears. *Painting can be tiring and rewarding, frightening and enlightening.* Her completed canvases filled her thoughts. The memory of them lined up in the cottage studio made her smile. *They merged into one another and changed as though they were alive. I painted them by letting my talent and creativity do the work. I painted them by letting go!*

She blinked and stared at her less than successful first attempt. Replacing the canvas with a new one, she picked up a brush, wiped it clean, and closed her eyes. Everything fell away into a deep and absorbing silence. The gradual emergence of an image brought her mind to an alert standstill. She envisioned the image becoming sharper. An almost audible snap brought it into focus. Another snap left her mind grasping for the memory.

Her eyes flew open. She dipped a brush in a blob of paint on the palette. *Get out of your way, silly.* Her blanked mind filled with color. A reddish wash filled the background with color. A sandstone arch outlined an entrance where pale greenish light illuminated four steps leading to a white stone path that vanished in blackness.

She sent a telepathic message to Almiralyn and backed up to ponder her work. *Painting always transports me to another level. Mixing colors, creating highlight and shadow, adding texture and detail...all of it makes me feel whole and gives me a reason for being.* She sighed, rinsed her brush, and wiped it on the paint cloth. Her eyes bright with tears, she hugged herself. *I'm so grateful for this gift.*

Almiralyn entered the cave and crossed to the canvas. "Well done, Sparrow. I felt sure you could help."

Sparrow shook her head. "It was touch and go. For a while, I thought I'd fail."

"But you didn't. We now know where to find our young ones."

Allynae preceded One Man through the entryway. "It's in the desert. What is it?"

"Nesune Ruins in Fera Finnero." Almiralyn stepped to one side so One Man could look closer. "You'll need to visit Eissua Oasis and meet with WoNadahem Mardree. She'll be able to tell you how to find it."

One Man's face lit up. "The Atrilaasu Oracle. She's one powerful lady. We'd appreciate her help."

Allynae wrapped his arms around Sparrow and rested his chin on her head. His usually good-natured expression grew serious. "How do we find the oasis?"

"When it's time, you'll use the desert portal." Almiralyn paused as Jordett and Merrilea arrived, accompanied by Yuin, the ruby red Pentharian. She faced the semicircle of comrades. "I'm glad you're all here. Before we make any more plans, I'm going to awaken Elcaro's Eye. It's unfair to expect Sparrow to be our sole source of knowledge."

A young DeoNyte male strode into the cave and marched straight to her. His stance and the set of his jaw suggested stubborn resolve. "I want to go to DerTah to find my friends." He stood taller. "I know I can help."

"Zugo, you cannot go to DerTah. The desert heat would kill you. Your parents would never forgive me."

He dropped his hands from their resting place on his hips, but kept his pale eyes on her face. "I have to do something, Almiralyn. While they are in danger, I can't just sit here.

"I understand. Right now, however, I have an important job to do. When it's accomplished, I'll tell you how you can help."

He sighed. "Yes, m'lady. Father asked me to tell you food is prepared."

"Thank you, Zugo. Tell Yookotay we'll join him shortly."

She waited until he was out of earshot before turning to Allynae and One Man. "There is a decision you must make."

"And what's that?" Allynae sounded anxious.

"I'm torn between asking you to wait to leave for DerTah until Elcaro's Eye is functional or sending you now. I don't know what you'll run into there. The fountain can tell us what we need to know to keep you safe. What I am certain of is that events are moving far too fast."

One Man took a step toward the door. "We must go now. Whatever problems we are to face will manifest when they will. Esán, Torgin, and the twins are in danger. Waiting won't make them any safer."

"But it might keep you safer." Merrilea kept her voice steady, but her eyes betrayed her concern. "You can't help the children if something happens to you."

Allynae studied the painting. "I agree with One Man. Let's go."

Sparrow started to speak. He stopped her with a hug. "We'll be careful. I think we should eat before we leave."

As the group dispersed, Sparrow took one last look at her painting. "Nesune Ruins..." She joined Allynae by the cave entrance. "Our daughters are there, Alli. Promise you'll find them and keep them safe."

He cupped her hands in his and pressed them to his lips. "I'll do my best, SparrowLyn. That's all I can promise."

She kissed him. "Your best is all I can ask."

Almiralyn watched them leave the studio, grateful for Allynae's willingness to forsake his dislike of DiMensionery in order to help. She gazed at the painting. Food would have to wait. She had more important things to do.

44

Der Tah

Torgin couldn't take his eyes off Yaro's face. Only moments before, its pallor had intensified his facial tattoos. Now the skin, infused with its natural golden tan, softened their dramatic effect. His Reptilian eyes, gleaming with life, held only a shadow of his recent brush with death. Blue lips had regained their natural red tint. Even his gold-brown braids glistened with health.

As their companions dispersed to give Yaro time to reorient, Torgin helped him to sit propped against a bench. Sitting back on his heels, he examined his heart-brother's tattooed chest where the Mindeco's claws had shredded the skin and torn the flesh beneath. The healed injuries had left no disfigurement. Sculpted muscle under smooth skin covered with intricate designs gleamed with health. A thin red scar, the only outward sign of the battle, ran from below his right hip to above the lizard-like joint at his knee.

A smile lit Yaro's face. "You saved my life." His hand rested on his chest. "I honor you, my brother and comrade."

Torgin's face grew hot, but he kept his gaze steady and touched a hand to his heart. "I, too, honor you, brother of my heart."

Corvus offered his hand. "You have much courage, Torgin. I am privileged to call you my friend."

Torgin clasped it. "Thank you for coming when you did. Your knowledge saved Yaro."

His friends surged forward. Brie hugged him. Ira clapped him on the back. Esán's handshake, and the respect in his eyes, made Torgin stand taller. Even Desirol joined in what Torgin felt was a celebration of Yaro's healing, but also of his part in it...of his bravery. His heart filled with a rush of feelings unlike anything he had ever experienced...humility, pride, a sense of belonging. More than that, he felt confident and unafraid. He knew he could deal with life's challenges, whatever they were.

It was time to look ahead. Corvus and Yaro conferred together while Ira and Desirol sat on a bench and listened. Brie and Esán moved to the side, deep in conversation. Torgin wandered back to the Statues of Sinnttee. He studied the selenite faces, amazed at the artistry and the individuality of each one. Although he liked them all, Manitullie, the god of youth and young adulthood, appealed to him in a way the others did not. *I didn't think I was special*. He watched the light change on the statue's face. *But perhaps I am.*

"Magnificent, aren't they?" Yaro smiled down at him.

"They are. What did you and Corvus—"

"Give that back, Des. It does not belong to you." Ira's irate exclamation turned to anger. "I mean it. Give it back."

Torgin swung around to find him wrestling with Desirol for the knife, Efillaeh. A violent push sent Ira stumbling. Corvus lunged for the RewFaaran and sent him bouncing across the floor. Desirol jumped up, shoved Esán away from Brie, and pulled her against him. "Stay back, or I'll hurt her." He wrapped an arm around her throat as Esán started to move. "She means nothing to me, Esán. But this knife does. I must take it to my father." He angled his body toward the statues and waved the knife at Yaro. "If you move, Pentharian, she will pay." Bright, wild eyes darted to Torgin. "Give me the Compass of Ostradio, Torgin, or Brie will suffer."

Torgin did not move. "Are you sure you want to do this? We are your friends, Desirol."

Mixed emotions did battle on the youthful face. He appeared to waver. A fanatical gleam wiped away the moment of weakness. He pulled Brie closer. "I must go to my father. Give me that compass. And Esán will take us to him." He held the knife to her throat. "Right, Esán?"

Wariness replaced the cooperative atmosphere in the conference chamber as Lorsedi rose, the authority of his rank and position enveloping him. "Desirol is on DerTah?" Eagle-sharp eyes dissected the members of the group seated around the table.

Long accustomed to dealing with delicate situations, Wolloh watched him with total calm. "Please, Lorsedi, sit and allow us to explain. We did what we did with the best of intentions. Stebben will share what has brought us to this place."

Lorsedi's eyes, like hot coals, raked Stebben's face. "What have you got to do with this?"

"Desirol's mother, Chyneria, is my sister, sir."

"Chyneria..." The Largeen Joram's hostility lessened. "Please explain." He lowered to sitting—back stiff and expression inscrutable.

Stebben cleared his throat. "I think it would help if I shared a bit of our history." He paused a moment, then began. "Chyneria and I were born on Roahymn. When I was twelve sun cycles and Chyneria was eight, our peaceful life there ended abruptly. A Mocendi DiMensioner came for me. He killed our parents. I escaped with Chyneria. The only way off the planet was aboard an intergalactic slave ship. A friend of my father's sold us to the slave master, who took Chyneria to RewFaar and sold her to the man who supplied women to your household."

He faced Gerolyn, his bowed head in respect. "I learned that your sister, Tissent, took Chyneria under her wing and prepared her for life on RewFaar. I will be forever grateful." He returned his attention to Lorsedi. "The slavers brought a group of us to DerTah, where I escaped. Wolloh found me in the Towne of TiCeed on Geran and brought me here. He raised me like a son, taught me the art of DiMensionery, and at the age of

Tulad, manhood, gave me the choice to pursue my own desires or to remain here as his Major Domo."

Resting his arms on the table, he intertwined his fingers and continued. "When I was old enough to handle the news, Wolloh informed me he had found Chyneria. She and I had been in touch about ten cycles when she sent word Desirol was in danger. He had overhead something—a plan Nissasa was developing—and had vowed to stop him. The next message I received was a plea for help. Nissasa had kidnapped Desirol, expunged his memories, and with the help of Gidtuss, installed him here at Shu Chenaro. The plan was to drive a wedge between Wolloh and you, Lorsedi.

"I immediately sought Wolloh and discussed the situation with him. We decided the best thing for Desirol was to keep him here, where we could protect him."

Wolloh took up the story. "I did not tell you, Lorsedi, because Nissasa had gathered quite a following. Telling you would have alerted him. He and Roween would have murdered you forthwith. I wanted you alive. Your military expertise is respected and valued in this solar system. More than that, the Inner Universe needs your leadership. Giving you a reason to visit DerTah without raising Nissasa's suspicions was the challenge. Elcaro's Eye provided the means."

Lorsedi ran a hand through his thatch of red hair. "You helped me to establish the connection to the Eye and showed me my granddaughter."

"I knew you were looking for Gerolyn. It seemed the best way."

"Where is Desirol now?"

Stebben answered. "He is with Nomed's nephew, Esán, and his friends. Corvus informed me that WoNa sent them to Nesune Ruins. That's as much as I know."

"And where is Nissasa?"

A brief glance at Wolloh brought a nod. "My informants tell me he and his men have joined forces with the Sebborr, and that they were stuck in a desert storm. It is now waning.

Lorsedi placed his hands on the table, pushed himself to standing, and walked to the end of the room, where double doors opened onto a small garden. He cracked open the louvered blinds. A linear pattern scattered across the floor. Silence cloaked him. The closing blinds erased the light.

With a soft inhale, he pivoted to face the table. "I owe you a debt of gratitude, High DiMensioner od DerTah."

"You owe me nothing, Lorsedi. I would, however, appreciate your thoughts on what to do next."

A knock at the door forestalled his response. Wolloh's nod sent Stebben to open it. The Major Domo's back tensed. He stepped aside. A kcalo-draped figure strode into the room. He threw back his hood, exposing a rugged face filled with despair.

Wolloh grabbed his cane and rose from his chair. "Narrtep, what is it?"

"The Sebborr have taken the Atrilaasu Oracle. WoNadahem Mardree is their prisoner. She told me if anything happened to her, I was to come to you."

A chilled silence settled over the room.

Brie felt only a deep sense of calm as Desirol's grip tightened around her throat. A momentary loosening of his arm sent air into her lungs in a rush of fluid coolness. The ruins faded. Bone and flesh melted into the shimmering liquidity of water. She flowed from his grasp over the floor and into a pool before the Statues of Sinnttee.

Water filled her senses. Heady with delight, she relished its cool silkiness. Deep in her last speck of Human awareness, she knew that water was all she ever wanted to be.

Even as a droplet from the statue of Ceeconni's bowl splashed from the basin into her pooled essence, sealing her to humanness, Brie felt her water self swirl into the resulting eddy and spiral upward.

Esán could not take his eyes off the rising form. Composed solely of water, it assumed a feminine shape. The ConDria's glistening eyes opened in Brie's fluid countenance. Her smile flowed into being. Curls the color of liquid glass fell in a waterfall down her back. She held up her right hand and touched the center of her palm with her left forefinger. It rippled and calmed. Laughter surged from her throat and became a song so full of beauty it made his heart ache. When she turned away, Esán knew he would die of loneliness.

With mercurial grace, and as crystalline and shimmering as Evolsefil, she flowed to Desirol and touched the knife in his hand. Efillaeh slipped into hers. Offering it hilt first, she sang out, "If you take a life with the sacred knife, it will end your own. If you save a life, it will fill your heart forever."

He backed away, bumped into a bench, and sat down with a jarring thud. Sobs shook him as he buried his face in his hands.

Brie's watery form trembled. Her silver-blue eyes glinted brighter. A single tear slid down her cheek. She caught it and watched it merge into her fingertip. A distant voice called her name. WoNa's eyes gazed up at her from her shimming palm.

"Shift, Brielle."

The transition from water to matter left her shaken. Her eyes found Esán. She opened her mouth, but WoNa's voice, not hers, filled the temple.

"You must all go to Shu Chenaro. Wolloh knows—" The Oracle's alto tones ended mid-sentence. Brie crumpled to the floor, a spasm of despair tearing through her.

Corvus hastened to her side. A quick touch on her moist brow cleared her confusion. She grasped his arm. "WoNa is in trouble."

"I know. And so are we. She left a message in your subconscious, Brielle. Will you allow me to help you uncover it?"

"How?"

"Close your eyes and let yourself relax."

Again, he touched her forehead. Her eyes grew heavy. A red curtain filled her vision. Sand whirled around her, whipping and slapping her kcalo and bringing tears to her eyes. She rotated, straining to see. Gradually, the wind ceased its bansheed-wailing. The sand pelting to the desert floor settled. On the horizon, dark specks climbed upward and grew bigger. *Horses. So many horses. Nissasa travels this way.* The scene changed. She crouched on the top of the outcropping at Eissua. Below her, men in dark kcalos crept through the palm trees. One lifted his face. Dahe's eyes trapped hers. Wind tossed sand between them. When it settled, her frantic gaze searched for her friends. Only the desert stretched for miles in all directions —blood-red sand and the dark, menacing shapes moving toward her from the horizon.

The sound of WoNa's voice called from the distance, "Brielle? Brielle. Beware..."

A cool touch sent the remnants of the storm flying into nothing. The horses and men scattered over the sand. A face came into focus. "You did well." Corvus said. "Nissasa is closing the gap. He will be here soon. We have to leave Nesune."

Ira, Torgin, and Yaro were standing behind him, their faces filled with questions.

She scrunched her forehead, straining to remember. "Ohhhh..." "Dahe is..." The image eluded memory. She shook her hair back from her face. "The storm is almost over. Where's the Mindeco?"

Esán knelt beside her. "It hasn't discovered the passage to the temple, but it won't be long. What about Dahe?"

Frowning, she shook her head. "I can't remember. I..." She scanned the faces of her friends. "Where's Desirol?"

Esán's eyes glazed over and refocused. He groaned. "He's heading for the Mindeco. I'll go."

Corvus stopped him. "I'll go after him. You teleport everyone to Shu Chenaro. Do you know the raptor center?"

"I know it, but what about the energy trail?"

"Wolloh will deal with it. When you get there, stay hidden. Someone will meet you, probably Stebben. Don't let anyone else know you're there. Do you understand?"

"I understand." Esán gathered his belongings. "Hurry. Grab your packs and hang onto me."

Brie slipped her hand into his. Ira put his arm around her and a hand on Esán's shoulder. Torgin grabbed his kcalo and backpack and joined them with Yaro in spider form, clinging to the inside of his flute case.

The last thing Brie saw before she blinked to adjust to the dark interior of the raptor center were the flashing eyes of the Statues of Sinnttee.

Corvus allowed his internal radar to guide him through the passages leading to the temple's lower level. Not far ahead, he could hear the soft tread of Desirol's footsteps. A low growl rolled through the darkness. A gasp smothered into silence. Corvus cloaked his movements and tiptoed forward. The stench of fear and the sound of rapid breathing alerted him to the boy's presence a short distance ahead.

Beyond Desirol's immobile form, Corvus picked out the crouched shape of the Mindeco. It raised its ugly head; its single eye bored a hole in the dark; its wide-nostriled nose sniffed the air. A rumble of satisfaction ricocheted off the walls, crumpling the boy to his knees. With the speed of a cheetah, Corvus shot forward, grabbed Desirol by the back of his kcalo, and teleported.

Their sudden appearance in front of the Statues of Sinnttee in the upper temple left them both staggering. Desirol rounded on Corvus, his face pale and his dark eyes flooded with horror. "Why did you save me? I betrayed you."

Corvus propelled him along the marble path. "We'll talk later. I must get you to safety without leaving a trail for the Mindeco.

A loud snarl made them both glance back. The hideous creature lumbered into the main temple and straightened to his full height. A booming roar heralded its triumph. Corvus' eyes locked onto Desirol's. Sheer terror screamed back at him. Grabbing the boy's hand, he charged down the path, veered right, and leapt, pulling Desirol after him into the Abyss of the Dead.

45
Myrrh

Almiralyn loved the Dojanack Caverns. The sense of antiquity engendered by stone always calmed her nerves and put her in a contemplative state. History lived in these caverns, the history of Old Earth...its shattering...its return to life with the birth of Myrrh.

She skimmed her fingers along the rough wall as she walked, touching the treasures of another age. The muffled sound of her footsteps sang a song of centuries past. Secrets in the lightless depths of the caverns called to her, enticed her to leave the worries of The Unfolding behind and discover the hidden mysteries of forgotten times.

The Cavern of Tennisca, the place where Wodash od DerTah had snatched her from the air, beckoned. She had not revisited it since her capture and ultimate return through the heart of Evolsefil.

On the landing at the top of the Stairway of Retu Erath, she arranged her memories into their proper perspective. Today, her journey was a different one. Today, she planned to bring Elcaro's Eye back into being.

The stone stairs tingled, sending a pulsing message up her legs and along her spine. Continuing her descent, she tuned her vibration to that of Tennisca. Ancient whispers caressed her cheeks and filled her mind. Initiation...resolution...release and acceptance, all were necessary for a traveler on the Stairway of Retu Erath. She opened her heart to the ancient power until she stood at last before the entrance to the Cave of Canedari, the home of the Evolsefil Crystal.

The double doors swung inward, admitting her into the silent emptiness. She crossed the stone floor to a second set of doors and stepped beyond them. The Hall of Priestesses stretched empty and quiet to the end of the corridor. A lengthened stride carried her to the Reading Room, across its carpeted floor, and through a door on the far side.

Warm colors summoned her to a stained-glass window that spanned the breadth of the massive stone wall and angled away from the room's center. Raising her arms, she whispered a soft command. Colored shapes in rose, green, and royal blue flew from the window and scattered across the purple velvet drapes covering three sides of the room, leaving the star-spangled heavens framed in delicate panes of glass.

Veersuni, the room established for quiet contemplation and meditation, thrummed with soft, musical harmonies. The Guardian Priestesses of Canedari would protect Elcaro's Eye.

Almiralyn bowed her head and allowed the music and the beauty to fill her. When she felt ready, she removed the miniature fountain from her pouch and placed it on the floor at the center of the sanctuary. With the window imbuing her vision with stars and moons and spiraling galaxies, she chanted,

> *"Elcaro, the All-Seeing-Eye,*
> *Return to size that I may spy*
> *Within your depths, the heart of things,*
> *And all that The Unfolding brings.*

*Allow your magic heart to be
The center of the Veer-su-ni.
I clap my hands to call you forth.
Spring to size from your true North."*

Three sharp claps melted into velvet and glass as the fountain grew to its normal size. Almiralyn's gaze traced the silhouetted form of the carved woman on the fountain's rim. Bending forward, she touched the tip of the Vesen Crystal where it protruded from the top of the alabaster pedestal into the curved bottom of the fountain. Three more claps brought water streaming into the bowl. It stilled. The window's reflection settled on the surface. It dissolved and reformed to show Almiralyn's face. She stepped back, observing the beauty of Elcaro's Eye juxtaposed against the night sky. Gurgling water called her back to the rim. A new image sent a thrill of fear up her spine.

Allynae paced his quarters. The thought of using DiMensionery chilled him, but his daughters and their friends were in grave danger. He paused, his gaze fixed on a gleam of crystal light on the opposite wall. An image of the twins flashed. *Ari, Brie, I've only just met you, but you have stolen my heart.* After a long, slow inhale, resolve squared his shoulders. "The time has come to embrace the Arts of DiMensionery and my training." He sank down on his bed and allowed the lessons of his youth to rise to the surface.

One Man had suggested they shape shift to the DerTahan hawk. Both had seen one, knew its habits, and felt comfortable with it. Unwilling to embarrass himself at the portal, he had slipped away to his quarters where he could practice shaping the hawk and returning to his Human form. A rush of uncertainty almost overwhelmed him. *I've ignored my training for a long time. What if I can't shift?*

The memory of saying goodbye to Sparrow distracted him and left him drenched in more emotion. *The Unfolding is in full swing. Everything is in flux. There's no guarantee I'll see her again.*

With his jaw set, he came to his feet. *Stop it, Alli. Concentrate.* His eyelids lowered and the image of the hawk filled his mind. The sudden shift sent him, in hawk form, gliding around the small cave. As his talons touched the ground, he returned to his Human form and laughed. *I had forgotten the thrill of flying.*

He turned to the mirror on the dark stone wall of his quarters. "Remember who you are, Allynae Nadrugia. Remember the reason you're doing this. Get the job done so you can return to your quiet life." A long exhale hissed between bared teeth. "A quiet life may be a long time in coming." He stared again at his reflection—water-blue eyes, a nose almost too big for his face, dark brown hair shot through with silver. "You'd best be going. One Man is waiting."

Without a backward glance, he made his way to the Nervac Portal.

One Man bid his farewells and promised Merrilea he would be careful. Now, he waited for Allynae and Almiralyn at Nervac. The cavern portal's destination point would deposit them too near Nissasa's camp. One Man felt no fear, only the need to move. Esán needed him. Urgency nagged at him to be on his way.

Allynae rounded the corner. "Sorry to keep you waiting. I needed to practice."

"And..."

He laughed. "I remembered how to shift, fortunately in both directions. Where's Almiralyn?"

One Man shook his long, wheat-colored hair back from his face and twisted it into a knot at the nape of his neck. "Still in the Hall of Priestesses."

"I can tell you're impatient to be off. Do we wait or go?"

"Something has happened on DerTah. The balance of power is shifting...and not in our favor. We need to go."

Allynae's expression changed from curiosity to concern and back again. "And you know this because..."

One Man tapped his chest. "The Seed of Carsilem is like radar. When there's trouble, it lets me know."

"Then we'd better leave." His eyes searched the passageway. "Sure wish we'd seen Almiralyn one last time."

One Man followed his gaze. "She has her own problems, my friend. Come. On the count of three, shift. One. Two. Three."

They shot into the portal, their hawk wings mere stabilizers in the silent flash of time.

Soldiers from both Idronatti and RewFaar had searched *Antiques by Q,* Dom's shoppe in the Borderlands, a dozen times. Not one soldier had acknowledged his presence with a look or a word. When darkness sent the brigands back to their respective camps, Dom gave a sigh of relief, snuggled down in his favorite chair, and fell asleep.

Pounding on the front door woke him with a jolt and sent him shuffling down the hall, his slippers flip-flapping against his heels. His interrupted snooze left him groggy. Another volley of fists on the door made him cranky. *One invasion after the other.* He yanked it open and glared over the top of his spectacles. What he saw made him shove them higher on his nose.

Fadin glared back at him. "Ya gonna let us in, Dom, or leave us on the doorstep?"

He moved aside. Fadin ushered a tall, well-built black man into the shoppe, closed the door, and bolted it. "Can we chat in your office?"

"O' course." Dom preceded the men into the office and cleared papers and books from two chairs. He poured a mug of coffee and handed it to Fadin. "How 'bout you? Coffee?" He noted the PPP uniform and bit back his dislike.

"Please."

The strain in that one word made Dom look at him more closely. "Ya need sugar or milk?"

"No, thanks." The response was subdued.

Dom settled in his chair. "How can I help?"

Fadin glanced at his companion. "This be Wilith Whalend. Remember them three kids that came through close to a moon cycle ago?"

Dom nodded. "The red-haired gals and their friend Torgin."

Whalend swallowed a swig of the fragrant, dark liquid. "Torgin's my son. I need to find him."

"And you came to The Borderlands...how?" Dom kept his tone even despite his natural inclination to distrust any member of the PPP.

The man opposite him wrapped tapered, black fingers around his mug and stared into its contents. When he looked up, his broad-featured face gleamed ebony. Dark irises, made even darker by the whites of his eyes, held a touch of panic. He inhaled, took another swallow of coffee, and set the mug on the paper-cluttered desk next to him.

"A PPP officer brought me as far as the SunSpire. I traveled the rest of the way alone. My son is in danger. The Guardian of Myrrh helped me to locate him."

Dom folded his arms and narrowed his eyes. "You had your brain rearranged as a kid. How'd you remember Myrrh?"

Impatience edged the deep voice. "When Myrrh appeared above Thera a few turnings ago, the people of Idronatti received a shock. The mind-altering of their childhoods had removed Myrrh from their memories. Its appearance rekindled them." Fear flecked his dark eyes. "My son has been missing for three Theran sun turnings. I can't locate his best friends, which means they must have persuaded him to visit Myrrh." He swallowed. "Something happened—" He pressed shaking hands together. "It is vital that I find him."

Dom shook his head. "Your kid's been missin' for three Theran turnings, more than a moon cycle on Myrrh, and you're just lookin' for him?"

Fatigue and worry fought for supremacy. "When Torgin didn't come home, Renn, Torgin's mother, and I decided not to alert the PPP. He has never broken rules of *The Plan*...his record is clean. Hoping to keep it that way, we filed a stay-at-home request because of illness. I received a summons from the Five Fathers." He rubbed a hand across his brow. "RewFaaran soldiers, but not Largeen Joram's, entered the city. Torgin has something they want. They're holding the Five Fathers hostage. If they don't get whatever it is Torgin has, they will kill the Fathers one by one. And..." His shoulders sagged and he dropped his head into his hands.

Fadin gave him an awkward pat on the back. "Well, Dom, will ya take 'im to Almiralyn?"

"How do I know he isn't a spy for the PPP? Is his story true?"

Wilith Whalend lifted his head. "You do not know." He met Dom's gaze. "I swear on my life what I say is true. Torgin *and* his friends are in danger. Please help me."

Dom picked up his crystal paperweight and tossed it from hand to hand. *"Wish the fountain was workin'."* He placed the paperweight on top of his favorite book and studied the dignified man across from him. The tailored blue uniform suggested Whalend was an elite PPP official. *Dare I show him the way into Myrrh? He isn't sharing something. Something too difficult to face, I'm guessin'.* Dom removed his specs, cleaned them on his vest, and glanced Fadin's direction. His old friend nodded. Fadin, who saw stuff most folks missed, trusted the man.

He peered through his clean lenses. "I'll take ya, but you'll have to wear a blindfold, and you'll need to do exactly what I tell ya. Agreed?"

Wilith Whalend straightened, his handsome features filled with relief. "I remember the way to Myrrh through the mirror. I even recall some of my visits. Torgin's mother and I met there." His voice tightened, and the panic reignited in his eyes. "I'll do whatever. Please—"

Dom handed the man his mug. "Finish your coffee and let's make a plan. RewFaaran soldiers are all over Myrrh."

Fadin smiled. "You're a good man, Dom. Take care of yourself. These soldiers are playin' for keeps." He chugged the rest of his coffee and stood up. "I'll let myself out." He looked at the man beside him. "Good luck finding your son." His back merged with the shadows in the dark hallway as he disappeared.

Dom swallowed a load of questions and looked at Torgin's father. "You gotta name you prefer?"

"Wilith would be fine. How soon can we leave?"

"Here's the challenge. Soldiers have set up camp on Almiralyn's land. Tropal Gateway from The Borderlands sets us down right at the edge of her front garden." He removed his spectacles, muttered under his breath, and replaced them on the bridge of his nose. "I'm imagining that we need to sneak you past the soldiers..." He stuffed the handkerchief in his pocket. "Sure wish I knew..."

A clipped meow interrupted him and brought a grin to his face. "Well, I'll be. Just the cat I was wishing for. Wilith, this is..."

The man's expression stopped him. Surprised bewilderment dance across his features. Recognition lit his eyes and curved his generous mouth into a smile. He held out a hand. "You're Majeska. I remember you."

She crouched and jumped to his lap, her purr rumbling and her amethyst eyes fixed on his face.

"Well, just ignore me, Jeska," Dom picked her up and held her next to his chest while he rubbed her belly. "What's the news from Myrrh?"

With a meow and a wiggle, she squirmed free, landed on all fours, and leapt to the top of the desk. She looked at him, and swished her tail back and forth, then lowered her nose and nudged his crystal paperweight into sight.

He scuffled to the desk and picked it up. "Well, I'll be darn. Elcaro's back in business." He peered into the crystal and frowned. "Looks like I'd better find my boots, Wilith. We have a journey to make."

Tinpaca Mondago stood over the traitor tied to a chair in his tent. A trusted soldier had escorted Cantruto and his other cohort to different tents at the camp's border. Guards were in position and ordered to allow no one to see the prisoners. If the traitors escaped, the guards would pay the price. Now, he would question the least experienced of the trio. His nostrils flared in disgust.

"What is your name, soldier?"

"Dupits, sir."

Mondago held out a hand. A large dragonfly landed on his palm. "You plotted with Cantruto to kill me, Dupits. You have broken your pledge to the Largeen Joram. Why? Answer me!"

The soldier remained silent. Mondago circled the chair. Dupits' muscles tensed. Mondago glared down at the stubborn face. "Tell me what I want to know. You will fare much better at my hand than at Nissasa's."

Dupits' eyes flew to his face.

"I will make sure Nissasa hears you are *my* informant. He is a cruel man. And he is merciless where traitors are concerned."

The man's Adam's apple rose and fell. His face remained blank. His eyes reflected the beginnings of fear. Mondago brought his face level with his. "You will provide a list of Nissasa's traitors—those here, at Shu Chenaro, and in RewFaar. I want to know everything you know about his plans, Dupits. Now!"

Eyes straight ahead, the soldier pressed his mouth closed.

"Perhaps I can entice you to respond to my request." The shimmering silver-blue dragonfly on his hand fluttered its wings. "This insect is as deadly as it is beautiful. Were I its enemy, I would tremble at the sight of it."

Dupits gave a nervous laugh. "You threaten me with a dragonfly, and you expect me to shake with fear?" Arrogance leaked into his voice. "A dragonfly will not make me talk, *sir*."

Mondago backed away from the chair. "Then perhaps this will."

The dragonfly disappeared, and a panther materialized in the middle of the tent. Dupits' face lost its color. His eyes bulged. The panther sniffed at his face, threw its head back, and snarled. A rough pink tongue appeared between its huge teeth and licked Dupits' cheek.

"Second thoughts?" Mondago remained at a distance.

Dupits jerked his head away. The panther's paw shot out. Blood warmed his cheek. It opened its mouth. Large incisors flashed in the light. The huge predator stretched its mouth around his neck.

"Death or talk. Your choice, Dupits. The panther will do as I say."

"I have nothing..."

The mouth began to close; the teeth clamped down on his throat. He shuddered. "I'll talk. Just get it away from me."

Mondago ran a hand along the feline's sleek side. "If you fail to answer even one of my questions, I will not hesitate to let my friend end your miserable life, Dupits."

The panther tightened its grip.

"I'll tell you everything, upon my honor."

Tinpaca Mondago glared down at him. "You have no honor, Dupits. Swear on your life."

"I swear on my life, sir, to answer all questions to the best of my knowledge, sir."

"Back, my friend."

The panther released its hold, licked its lips, and sat back on its haunches.

For the next chron-circle, Mondago grilled Cantruto's man. The panther listened. Dupits spilled his guts, his eyes darting from one to the other. Satisfied at last, Mondago ordered him taken away, and addressed the panther. "Did you get all that?"

Voer materialized. "Every word. I must travel to DerTah via the Dojanack Mountains."

"How soon can you reach Lorsedi?"

"Almiralyn will provide me with an introduction. I will leave as soon as we have spoken." He gave a low whistle. A miniature man darted into the tent and landed on his hand. "This is Kieel, the Matrés of the Terces Wood Nyti. He and Stee will continue to keep watch. They will warn you of any other traitors or strange activity here or at Demrach Gateway."

Mondago acknowledged Kieel with a smile. "Thank you for your help."

Kieel tapped his walking stick on Voer's palm. "My pleasure. If you need me, whistle and I'll come." He levitated and zipped out the entrance.

"I'll report back as soon as I can." Voer bowed his head and shifted. His dragonfly form buzzed after Kieel.

After the Pentharian departed, Tinpaca Mondago stood at the tent's center, wrapped in thoughtful silence. Things had certainly become interesting. He opened a box on his table, picked up a cigar, and rolled it between his fingers. Deep in thought, he clamped it between his teeth, touched the tip with a match, and drew in a deep breath. The exhaled smoke formed a cloud of whitish-gray. He squinted through the haze, thinking how fitting it was. An impatient shake of the head cleared his thoughts. He had things to do. Nissasa Rattori's infiltration of his platoon must end—now.

46

Der Tah

Nomed cursed under his breath. WoNa's capture meant a shift in the balance of power. He saw Wolloh's face, ashen at the best of times, turn even paler. Narrtep's stricken expression confirmed the seriousness of the situation.

Stebben pulled another chair to the table and offered the Dansmen a tumbler of water. When he had quenched his thirst and tossed his kcalo aside, Narrtep slid onto the proffered seat and looked to the High DiMensioner for guidance.

Wolloh raised his good hand and nodded to those gathered at the table. "Allow me to provide you with the names of my colleagues: TheLise, the Dreelas od Trinuge; Gerolyn AsTar, the Guardian of Myrrh's emissary and grandmother of the twins; Lorsedi Telisnoe, the Largeen Joram of RewFaar and grandfather of the twins, Seyes Nomed, the DiMensioner and uncle of Esán; and of course, you know my Major Domo, Stebben."

Narrtep acknowledged the introductions with an interested nod and returned his attention to the High DiMensioner.

"I believe it is best if you share your story. Then we can decide how to proceed."

Narrtep composed himself. "WoNa called up a storm to hide the departure of the children from Eissua. It raged across the entire desert and succeeded in confusing Nissasa's troops. However, when the wind began to howl and the sand blinded man and beast, Dahe Terah, the head of the Sebborr, called his tribesmen to a halt; gathered them into a tight formation; and led them forward. With unerring accuracy, he maintained the correct course, and while the RewFaaran soldiers hunkered down to wait out the storm, Dahe and his men crept closer to their target."

Lorsedi leaned back and steepled his fingers. "You seem to have a clear picture of what *you* did not see."

Narrtep gave Lorsedi a tight-lipped smile. "The Oracle Stone informed us of the storm's progress. It also showed us Nissasa, the Sebborr, and the children. What the Stone could not show were Dahe and six tribesmen circumventing the oasis, camouflaged by curtains of swirling sand. When three fellow Atrilaasu and I left WoNa to make our rounds of the oasis, the intruders jumped us and knocked us unconscious. Even though my attacker made a poor job if it, I did not reach WoNa before they took her prisoner and disappeared into the dissipating storm. I rode post haste to Shu Chenaro."

Wolloh placed a clawed hand on the man's arm. "You are lucky to be alive, my friend."

Narrtep touched his heart. "There is a saying in the desert: 'Kill the Oracle's Dansmen and burn to death in SeDah.' There are few who would ignore it. Dahe knows the touch of WoNa's fire. He will do his best to disarm her, to make her harmless—helpless." His voice broke, but his face remained stoic.

Wolloh's expression hardened. "This is a serious blow to our defenses. Lorsedi—" Wolloh's grip on his cane tightened. He hoisted himself to standing. Stebben arrived at his side in an instant. The High DiMensioner steadied himself. A slight smile touched his lips—a malicious spark ignited in his good eye. "We have good news and bad. I have just received a telepathic message from Corvus: Four children to raptor center. Stebben, meet them. Desirol tracked by Mindeco. Off to rescue."

The Largeen Joram pushed back his chair and surged to his feet. "If the Mindeco captures Desirol—" His expression hardened. "Corvus had better be as good as you say, Wolloh Espyro."

"He is, however—"

Lorsedi's leadership persona slammed into place. "I can only trust that he will do his job. I must meet with my staff and secure the borders of Shu Chenaro. When Nissasa discovers the children are beyond his reach, he will turn his focus here. We will be ready." He marched from the chamber.

Wolloh gripped the crystal knob of his cane and surveyed the room. A glint in his good eye informed Nomed he had arrived at a plan.

"Stebben, obscure the children's energy trail. Beware the Mindeco. It will not worry about the flames of SeDah. Be quick. I need you back here."

With a slight bow, Stebben vanished from sight.

"You didn't tell us he could teleport." TheLise's expression showed her surprise.

Wolloh twirled his cane between clawed fingers. "I told you I trained him..." He left the sentence hanging. "Gerolyn, meet the children and bring them to my hidden study. Do you teleport?"

"I'm rusty, but I can make it happen."

"Good. I'll put an image of the study in your mind. If you need help, Esán can provide it. You'll know him by his energy and his almost-bald head. Now go. And don't let anyone see you or them."

"I'll be quick. See you in the study." She stood and was gone.

Wolloh smiled at the Dreelas. "I have a task I know you will thoroughly enjoy. Find Tissent and ask her to help you distract Roween Rattori. Keep the woman occupied. We'll see you at dinner."

TheLise's face reminded Nomed of a cat after prey. She planted a quick kiss on Wolloh's withered cheek and slipped from the room. Nomed observed his mentor with interest. "And you need me to do what?"

Wolloh looked down, his thoughts cloaked by the scarred profile. When he finally raised his head, his face registered a touch of surprise. "Almiralyn has reinstated Elcaro's Eye."

Nomed's eyebrow shot up. "How do you know that?"

Wolloh tapped the round crystal in his cane and limped to the middle of the room. "Crystals from Evolsefil share a connection. Come. We have children to see, and then..." His good eye twinkled.

Nomed bit. "And then...what?"

Wolloh rested a hand on his arm. "You are going to pay a visit to the Guardian of Myrrh."

Brie's retina retained the flash of light from the Statues of Sinnttee for several long moments after she and her friends arrived in the raptor center. When it faded and she could finally see, her heart jumped to her throat. She could not tear her gaze from the woman who smiled down at her.

She was tall with chestnut curls piled on top of her head and eyes the color of sun-drenched emeralds. The lovely face reminded Brie of someone. Her brain scrambled to find the answer. It settled into a vague image that refused to come into focus.

The woman drew them into a close huddle. "I'm Gerolyn AsTar. Wolloh sent me."

Gerolyn...the name reverberated in Brie's head. "You're my grandmother!"

The woman nodded but pressed a finger to her lips. That and the ominous sound of soldiers marching through the barn attached to the raptor center kept Brie's many questions at bay.

Her grandmother spoke to Esán. "You can teleport?"

"Yes."

"Good." She clasped his hands. "I'll put a picture of our destination in your head." She motioned everyone closer. "Ready?"

Esán nodded again. The raptor center vanished. They arrived in a small, comfortable room. Gerolyn looked relieved. She smiled at Esán. "Thanks for the help. I'm a bit rusty." Her gaze traveled to Ira. Curiosity sparked as she offered a hand. "You are..."

"I'm Ira Raast. You're Sparrow's mother, aren't you?"

"That I am. It is nice to meet you, Ira. Very nice indeed."

Ira's tanned face reddened as he nudged Torgin forward. "This is my friend, Torgin Whalend."

Gerolyn smiled. "You're the musician. I can't wait to hear you play."

For Brie, it felt like several sun cycles passed before her grandmother's smile enveloped her. When Gerolyn put arms around her, she relaxed against her and sighed. "I've wanted to meet you for—"

Two men materialized at the room's center. Seyes Nomed looked from one of the room's occupants to the next and raised an eyebrow at Esán. "Hello, nephew."

"Hello, sir."

Nomed's companion rested his hands on the crystal knob of a cane; an unreadable expression masked his thoughts.

Brie stared at the face with its two very different aspects. *The High DiMensioner, Wolloh od DerTah...Nomed's mentor—*

"Hello, Brielle."

The words in her head startled her. She closed her mind with a slap.

Wolloh's smooth profile angled her direction. The intelligent hazel eye gleamed, and the mouth curved upward. "Good girl." He adjusted his body to bring his eye in line with Ira. For a long moment, he said nothing. "Brielle, please introduce your friends."

Swallowing her desire to know more about him, she smiled. "May I present Ira Raast and Torgin Wilith Whalend, who are both from Idronatti."

He inclined his head. "Welcome to Shu Chenaro, Ira and Torgin. And Esán...we are glad to have you back." With calculated slowness, he lowered his body into an overstuffed chair. "Take off your packs and kcalos and get comfortable. Boys, please arrange the chairs in a circle. We have many things to discuss."

Brie moved to her grandmother's side. "Mother looks like you."

Gerolyn smiled down at her. "And you bear a resemblance to her. I understand you have only recently met your father."

The sudden appearance of a tall man produced a hushed silence in the room.

"Well?" Wolloh's impatience flickered in his good eye.

"It is done, sir. I also erased the trail from the raptor center to here."

"Good work, Stebben. Any sign of Corvus and Desirol or the Mindeco?"

"None. The ruins were empty."

Wolloh's good eye sought Torgin. "I believe you have someone to introduce."

Torgin gave Nomed a challenging look before he placed his flute case on the floor. A small brown spider scuttled onto the polished tile. Yaro materialized beside him. "My heart brother, Yaro, Pentharian from ReTaw au Qa."

Nomed's eyes narrowed. Gerolyn smiled an interested smile. Stebben put a protective hand on the back of his master's chair. Wolloh eased to standing. With his clawed left hand on his heart, he extended his right hand palm up. "Oid eo daize rao, Yaro."

The golden Pentharian placed one hand on his chest and the other palm to palm with Wolloh. "Oid eo daize rao, High DiMensioner. I honor you heart to heart."

"And I you. Join us in our council. Your thoughts are most welcome."

Yaro hesitated with his focus on Nomed.

The DiMensioner frowned. "So we meet again, Yaro. As I recall, you switched loyalties on a whim."

Ira and Esán exchanged glances.

Yaro's alien features did not change. "I know not this whim. I supported my heart brother."

Brie caught the edge of a thought. Wolloh's sightless eye rested on her face. The disfigured cheek transitioned to smooth as he turned his head and locked his good eye on Nomed. The DiMensioner relaxed, stood, and extended his hand. Yaro bowed his head and touched the offered palm with his. The tension in the room dissolved.

Wolloh sank back into his chair. "Tell us what happened in Nesune. Esán, please begin."

Brie listened with only half her mind. The other half speculated about Wolloh, The High DiMensioner od DerTah, the man she had seen on the Throne of ReNin RepPosu when the future rolled out before her like a saga on a V-Screen.

The rising sun had not yet begun to erase the shadows from the desert landscape when two DerTahan hawks shot from the portal into the pale orange dome of the DerTah sky. One Man noted a dozing guard with a sense of relief. To his left, Allynae pressed hawk wings against the chill of dawn's first light. The shift had gone against the grain for the twins' father. One Man respected his willingness to put his personal preferences aside.

Banking to the northeast, he set a course for Eissua Oasis. He considered landing and teleporting but thought better of it. The Mindeco could follow the energy trail left by teleportation, and there might be others who could, as well. Glad for whatever remained of the tepid temperatures of early morning, he forced his mind into stillness and pressed ahead.

Allynae relished the feel of his wings against the air, of the wind skimming his feathered body, and of the beat of the hawk's heart. Conscious of the need to keep his humanness ever present, he trained hawk eyes on One Man and his mind on the reason he had chosen never to practice the Art of DiMensionery. Too many initiates succumbed to the dark side of the art and used it for their own gain. Not even Almiralyn's strict adherence to the rules of service and good works had changed his mind. Need had caused him to forsake his self-imposed abstinence. His daughters' well-being meant more to him than life itself.

He banked and soared after One Man. Some distance ahead, silhouetted palm fronds rose above the horizon. Each wing stroke brought them closer to Eissua Oasis and the Atrilaasu Oracle. Almiralyn revered WoNadahem Mardree. Allynae looked forward to meeting her.

One Man picked up speed. Allynae followed suit.

One Man's hawk eyes searched the desert below. Something had activated the Seed of Carsilem, something dangerous and unseen. Caution made him swoop behind a towering, wind-blown dune and land in Human form. When Allynae materialized beside him, he sent a telepathic message. *"Can you hear me?"*

Allynae's eyes narrowed. *"It's been a while."*

"Danger at the oasis. Fly in low. Not too close. Right?"

"Got it."

They shifted. Soaring just above the dunes, they streaked toward a group of palm trees on the outskirts of the oasis. From the top of the tallest tree, they studied the terrain.

Grateful for the hawk's excellent eyesight, One Man scanned the length and breadth of the lush basin—the lake, the outcropping, the waterfall. Echoes of activity, like fleeting memories, mingled with sunlight and shadow and the rhythmic sounds of water. Not one footstep of man or beast marred the rippled sand. As though someone had waved a magic wand, life at Eissua Oasis had ceased to exist, leaving behind empty tents, outbuildings, and animal pens.

Still worried but unable to pinpoint a threat, One Man swooped down and landed in Human form within a cluster of palms near the water. His narrowed eyes confirmed his hawk's sight. The deserted oasis felt as eerie as a town filled with ghosts.

Allynae shifted beside him. *"Telepathy or voice?"*

"Telepathy. I can't shake the feeling that danger lurks behind every tree. Let's separate and do some reconnoitering. I'll meet you on top of the outcropping."

With the stealth of a cat, Allynae skirted the north side of the oasis. The heat sent sweat trickling down his neck and face. He scrubbed the dampness away with a handkerchief and shoved the wet cloth back in his pocket. *Where are all the Dansmen? And WoNa? She knows we're headed her way.*

Alerted by sand sliding down the sloped side of the basin, he dropped behind a scraggly bush. Above him on the pitch of the dune, a pock-like indent was filling with sand. He crouched lower. Every instinct screamed danger, yet he saw nothing.

A slight sound shouted a warning. Halfway to standing, the weight of a heavy man hit him and sent him sprawling on his belly. Sand in his nose and mouth threatened to smother him. His assailant straddled his back, grabbed a handful of hair, and yanked his head back. A knife gleamed by his cheek. A scarf-covered face appeared next to his. "One sound and you die." The dark eye peering at him was hard as flint.

47

Myrrh

At *Antiques by Q* in the Borderlands, Dom tied his bootlaces, secured his paperweight in its special hiding place, and trundled down the hall to where Wilith Whalend waited, head in hands. The man sure was closed-mouthed about his real purpose for seeking the Guardian of Myrrh. "Ah, well." Dom grabbed a lightweight jacket from the coat tree in the corner and shrugged it on. Slapping his favorite hat on his head, he scuttled down the hall to lock the front door. "Won't keep 'em out but might slow 'em down.". The click of the ancient brass key in the lock reverberated in the empty hallway.

Majeska appeared in the shaft of light from the office entrance and meowed.

"Don't just sit there yowling. Get our guest and let's go."

She flicked her tail. Torgin's father appeared in the light behind her.

"You ready, Wilith? Jeska's impatient to be off."

The man scratched the smoky gray cat under the chin and straightened. "I'm ready."

Following Majeska down the dusty corridor, Dom pondered the best way to the Dojanacks without raising an alarm at the RewFaaran camp. He'd received word that Lorsedi and Almiralyn were joining forces. He'd also heard about traitors amongst the soldiers on Myrrh. Best to avoid any problems and just slip on by.

He pulled open the door to the basement. Wilith followed him down the rickety stairs. Majeska nosed a tapestry aside to reveal the mirror. Dom placed a hand on the cloudy glass. As soon as the keyhole appeared, the cat leapt through. Dom made no move to follow.

Wilith fidgeted beside him. "Are we going or not?"

"We wait for Jeska unless you wanna get caught."

The gray cat landed at Wilith's feet and meowed. He shot Dom an inquiring look. "Can we go?"

"Yep. Follow Majeska."

The cat obliged by leaping once more through the keyhole. Dom followed, with Wilith at his heels. Intense quiet and blurred streaks of color suspended them in time. A flare of light sent them rocketing through the portal exit into the field of sunflowers bordering Almiralyn's front garden. A breath-catching moment later, they snuck through the rows of green stems and bobbing yellow blossoms. The sound of footfalls a short distance ahead brought them to a halt.

Like a shadow, Majeska crouched and crept through the foliage on her belly. When she trotted back through the green growth, a Nyti rode on her back. A wide grin stretched his mouth almost bigger than his face. He zipped around Dom and Wilith and finally landed on a large leaf. "I'm Ashor. It's not safe to be running around out here. Those soldiers have weapons."

Wilith's expression of disbelief melted once again into impatience. "I must speak with the Guardian of Myrrh. I can't afford to wait."

Dom patted his shoulder. "Easy, Wilith. We'll get ya where you need to go."

Ashor ignored Wilith and landed on Dom's upturned hand. "Whatcha need?"

Dom explained. The Nyti listened attentively and looked Wilith up and down. "I'll find Kieel. You'd better follow me. You're pretty close to a lookout station." He flitted through the sunflowers and hovered by a grove of ancient hemlocks. "Stay here. I'll hurry."

Wilith sank to the ground and rested his back against a tree. "Do you think we'll have to wait long?" Strain and frustration made his face grim.

Dom eased his fanny down on a stump. "The Nyti are quick little creatures. Shouldn't take him long." He pulled off his hat, reshaped the crown, and jammed it back on his head. From under the droopy brim, he observed the strength in the man's face and the panic. *You are in for a ride, Wilith Whalend, one you can't even begin to imagine.*

Voer had followed Kieel to a small clearing some distance from the camp. He shifted and breathed in the smells of pine and spruce, of dark, damp earth, and of lichen and moss. The Terces Wood titillated his senses, reminding him of the forests of his home planet. His fondness for Myrrh deepened every turning, but ReTaw au Qa would always come first in his heart.

Kieel landed on a branch at Voer's eye level. "You will travel the Intersect?"

"It is the fastest way. How far is Nemttachenn from here?"

"As the raven flies...a short distance."

Ashor zipped into the clearing and hovered near Kieel. "Dom is near Tropal Gateway with a man from Idronatti. The man needs to find Almiralyn."

"Did Dom say why?" Kieel's lips puckered.

"The man is looking for his son, and it's important."

The Nyti Matrés landed on Voer's upturned palm. "Are you interested in learning about this? Or do you wish to go ahead?"

Voer's negative remembrance of Dom was colored by his loyalty shift from Almiralyn to Seyes Nomed, but then the Pentharian had also changed allegiance—Nomed to the Guardian. He let his bias go. It would be imprudent to ignore what might be important.

"Take us to them, Ashor." Once again, a dragonfly, Voer followed the two Nyti.

When Dom and his companion were still a short distance ahead, Voer shifted to his natural form and observed the men from the cover of the trees. Dom twirled a sprig of hemlock between his fingers, his face hidden beneath the battered brim of an old hat. An impressive-looking black man in a PPP uniform sat on the ground with his head in his hands.

Voer left his hiding place. The soft snap of a twig made the man tense. His dark eyes widened as they took in the Pentharian's alien presence. In one fluid movement, he came to standing, prepared to fight.

Dom rubbed his knee and pushed himself to standing. "Relax, Wilith. This be Voer. He's a friend. Voer, this is Torgin's pa. He needs to find Almiralyn."

Voer kept his voice low, and his stance relaxed. "I am a Pentharian, a friend of the Guardian, and of your son. What brings you here from Idronatti?"

In a hesitant voice, the man provided a brief explanation. Behind the obvious agitation caused by the threat to the Five Fathers and the demand to bring Torgin back to Idronatti, Voer sensed deeper emotions tearing the man apart. Yet, nothing in his demeanor suggested lies or a threat to Almiralyn.

"You must come with me, Wilith, father of Torgin. Your son is the heart brother of my comrade, Yaro. Because of this, I, too, honor him as brother. I will take you to Almiralyn."

Wilith tried to make sense of Voer and the Nyti and Torgin as a heart brother to a Pentharian mercenary. He rubbed his throbbing temples. *How can my son be a brother to such an alien creature?* Forcing his confusion aside, he squared his shoulders. "I would be grateful for your help. How soon can we leave?"

Voer conferred with Dom and the Nyti about the RewFaaran camp and ended his conversation with a query. "Do you have any news for Almiralyn?"

"Tell her to take care. I'll head back to my shoppe. Now that Elcaro's Eye's workin' again, I can keep her posted on The Borderlands." He extended a hand. "I wish ya the best, Wilith. Hope ya find your boy."

Wilith marveled at being treated with respect by these people—creatures. He clasped Dom's hand and shook it heartily. "Thank you, Dom. I hope we meet again."

Kieel and Ashor hovered near the Pentharian. "We're off to keep an eye on the camp. If you need us, let Paisley know. Good luck to you both."

Wilith shook his head as they whizzed away through the trees.

Voer smiled down at him. The gold of his Reptilian eyes glowed in the dim light. "You aren't in Idronatti anymore, my friend. And you have only just begun your journey. I am a shape shifter. To attain the best possible speed, I will shift to a panther so you can ride on my back. Can you manage that?"

Wilith opened his mouth, but words would not form. He clamped it shut and nodded. The Pentharian disappeared, leaving an enormous panther in his place. Wilith stifled the temptation to run back to the portal and return to Idronatti. Still unable to move, he stared as the black head swung toward him. Golden eyes questioned. Disoriented and more than a bit taken aback, he gathered his courage, mounted the broad back, and gripped the black fur. As panther muscles rippled into action beneath him, he shook his head. *The sheltered environment provided by The Plan did not prepare me to face such unknown creatures and events. How am I ever going to manage?*

Paisley sat across from CheeTrann in the Tower of Nemttachenn, studying the chessboard and mulling over his options. He bit his bottom lip, moved his rook, and captured a pawn. CheeTrann rested his forearms on the table and considered his next move. Medium length gray hair falling over his face hid it from sight. Paisley relaxed back in his chair. He couldn't believe he'd found a friend in the apparition on the other side of the chessboard.

A low laugh alerted him to CheeTrann's arrival at a decision. The big man straightened. A hand hovered over the chess pieces. The opaque fingers gripped a knight. With a satisfied chortle, he moved it two to the right and one down, picked up Paisley's bishop, and grinned. "Your move."

Paisley hunkered down to examine his damaged defense. Footsteps entering the tower broke his concentration. Voer peered down at him. Behind him, a uniformed member of the PPP stared in astonishment as CheeTrann faded into a blue haze.

"Howdy, Voer. Who's your friend?" A tingle of recognition made him stare harder at the man's dark features.

The Pentharian drew the man forward. "This is Wilith, the father of Torgin."

"Ahh." Paisley hoisted his towering bulk to standing and offered a hand. "Paisley Tobinette. You have one terrific son."

"It's a pleasure to meet you." The man released his hand. "You know Torgin?"

"I've much respect for your son. He's done some pretty tough growing up in the past weeks. You'll be proud of the man he's becoming."

Voer explained the situation. "Wilith wishes to meet with Almiralyn. We'll travel through the Intersect. I have much news for her." He provided a brief description of his time with Mondago and the young traitor.

As he finished, CheeTrann appeared from the haze. His voice boomed in the confined space of the tower. "It is good you have shared this with us. We will be vigilant. We will keep Evolsefil safe. Go quickly and share your news with the Guardian."

Paisley smiled at the astonished expression on Wilith's face. It reminded him of Torgin and his introduction to Myrrh and The Unfolding. He touched the man's shoulder. "You, like your son, will learn much in Myrrh. May your journey be a good one."

He accompanied them to the Intersect entrance, tempted to go along for the ride just to see Wilith's face while he experienced the vastness of Intersect space. But the chessboard called. He couldn't let CheeTrann win by default.

Wilith Whalend stared, spellbound, at the expansive skyscape, stretching into the foreverness of the universe. Stars, like a multitude of miniature gemstones, winked and blinked below him. The full moon, a hovering goddess dressed in shimmering white satin, cast her gracious light around her in a haloed corona of pastel colors. The tangled roots of the Terces Wood, swirls of turquoise—all of it took his breath away.

He turned to Voer, hoping for an understandable explanation of the extraordinary vista. The Pentharian merely smiled and put a hand on his arm. Together, they repeated the sacred words Voer had taught him prior to descending the steep staircase. A flash of light, air brushing his cheek, the sweet odors of early spring, and they arrived on another platform where slender tendrils trembled above them. A third platform gave him a glimpse of geometric patterns composed of amethyst, citron, ruby, and minerals of every sort. At last, they arrived at the bottom of a stone staircase.

The awesome wonder of the Intersect eased the burning fear that gripped him...only to have it return with a vengeance when they arrived at the Meosian central square. He focused on Voer's scale-sprinkled spine to keep from gaping at the white fur-covered creatures who stared at them from luminous, pale blue eyes in an obsidian black face. His growing sense of panic almost overwhelmed him. *How many more surprises will challenge everything I know? And how will I find my son?"*

Almiralyn left the Hall of Priestesses, traversed the Cave of Canedari, and flew through the Cavern of Tennisca. It was a short flight, but one that she savored. From the top of the Stairway of Retu Erath, she teleported to the tunnel leading into Meos and arrived at the Central Square to find Zugo waiting.

"Father asked me to meet you and bring you to him. Voer is here...and Torgin's father."

"Torgin's father?" She increased her pace. Zugo knocked at the double wooden doors to Yookotay's chambers. A young female with one green eye and one blue answered.

Almiralyn smiled. "It is good to see you, Elae. The last time we met, you were still recuperating from your unexpected trip to Nevah Efas. You look well."

"I'm fully recovered, my lady, and ready to help in any way I can. The ReDael awaits you in the room next to the council chamber. Zugo and I will wait here in case you need us."

Zugo lifted his chin in a gesture of defiance. "I'm going with Almiralyn."

Yookotay opened the carved wooden door of his office and stuck his head out. "You will remain on guard with Elae until we call you. Don't go wandering off."

Almiralyn addressed the ReDael. "If it meets with your approval, Yookotay, I have a job for them."

The ReDael joined them. "How can they help?"

"I have returned Elcaro's Eye to its full size in Veersuni and require trustworthy guards to watch over it." Her solemn gaze rested on Zugo and Elae. "I am asking you to do this important job because I know you will guard the fountain and its secrets as I would. If it shares information, one of you must come to tell us. Please keep a journal. When I visit the fountain, you can bring me up to date. This is a very important job. I can't be everywhere at once."

Yookotay nodded his approval.

Elae linked arms with Zugo. "We'll go now."

"We won't disappoint you, Almiralyn." Zugo waved and escorted Elae from the chamber.

Almiralyn smiled. "Zugo is having a difficult time not bolting for DerTah. Hopefully, Elcaro's Eye will keep him occupied. He mentioned that Torgin's father is here?"

"And Voer with news from the RewFaaran Tinpaca. Torgin's father will speak only to you. Voer will join us when you're ready. Things move quickly, my lady." He ushered her into the cave and withdrew.

A tall man in the elegantly tailored uniform of a PPP official waited with his back to the room. His close-cropped black hair accentuated the shape of his head and the powerful muscles of his neck. When he turned, expectation lit his dark eyes. At the sight of her, it dulled. She shifted to the form of Mira, the older, more comfortable woman who welcomed the children of Idronatti to Myrrh.

"Hello, Wilith. It has been a long time since we last met."

The strong, ebony features showed a broad sweep of emotions—astonishment when she shifted, relief, the happy memories of a small boy, sadness, and fear—fear that ran so deep it left him drained of speech.

She sank onto a chair and tucked a lock of gray hair into her bun. "Please sit. Tell me what has brought you to Myrrh."

"Mira, I thought you weren't real, even though I continued to dream of you after they expunged my memories. Then, when Myrrh appeared over Idronatti and memories of you surfaced, I—" He sat down and massaged his furrowed forehead. "I never expected to be sitting opposite you."

After an emotion-filled silence, he breathed in a sustaining breath. When he looked up, he had regained his equilibrium. "I came to deliver a message to Almiralyn, The Guardian of Myrrh." He spoke with professional formality.

She shifted form and let his mind readjust to her slender, blonde beauty. When he nodded, she answered with formality to match. "I am pleased to receive you, Wilith Whalend, official of the Peoples Plan Protectors. What is the message?"

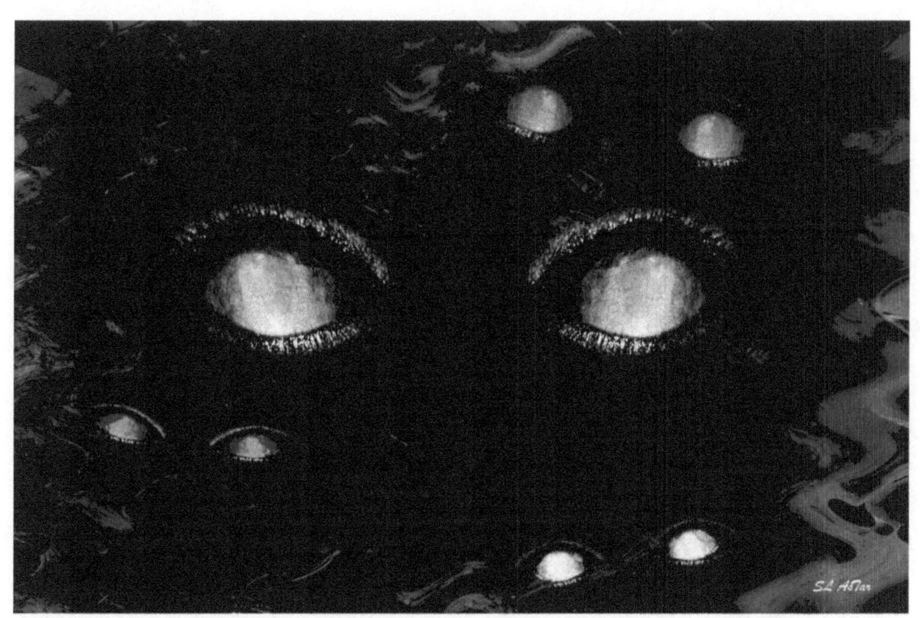

48
Der Tah

At the Nesune Ruins, Corvus and Desirol plunged feet first through a darkness sticky and thick as molasses. The Abyss of the Dead embraced them, caressed their skin, and burned tears from their eyes. Invisible fingers stroked their hair and tugged at their clothing. Like a siren's song, their names rang out in a repeated chorus.

Corvus tightened his grip on Desirol's hand. *The deeper we go, the better our chances of teleporting without leaving a trail. Deeper also means greater danger.* A shield of protection shot up around them. Before he could seal it, Desirol's panicked struggle destroyed his concentration. The shield shimmered into nothing.

He pulled Desirol around to face him. "We can survive the abyss." His stern whisper continued. "Navigating its dangers is the key. I can get us out of here, but I need your help."

"W-w-hat?" Desirol hissed through chattering teeth. Terror quacking through his body sent a circle of tiny wavelets into the syrupy darkness.

"Listen to me. Look nothing in the eye. The dead can't harm you if you don't see them." Sour darkness lathered his tongue. He sucked saliva into his mouth and spit. "Don't swallow the darkness. Hold on to the belt of my kcalo and do not let go." Again, he spit. White and spider-like, the foulness floated beside them.

Desirol gripped his belt. "H-h-hurry, C-cor—" He choked and tightened his hold.

Freed to direct their course, Corvus pressed his hands against the blackness as though sculling a small boat through the water. Gradually, he gained control of their downward drift. Syrupy nothingness undulated around them. Distorted faces flashed into view. Corvus dropped his eyes and prayed that Desirol remembered his instructions.

A distant sploosh sent a tremor quaking through the abyss. Creatures, dulled and without the luster of life, began to gather in the rush of current preceding the Mindeco's descent. Vacant eyes drifted around them. Their chanted names grew louder and louder.

The sudden pressure of Desirol's arms around his neck strangled the air from Corvus' lungs. Grabbing the boy's wrists to ease the pressure on his larynx, he forced himself to breathe through his nose, one small breath at a time. A choked sob, a smothered moan... Sagging weight tore at his arms. Adrenaline pumped through him. He hauled Desirol's limp body forward until his armpits rested on his shoulders. Caught in the sloshing aftermath of the struggle to regain control, he floundered with the unconscious boy in the thick intensity of the abyss.

Above them, the Mindeco's torpedoed-weight hurtled rapidly downward. The darkness responded to its progress like water to a plunging stone. Around them, the dead gathered. Their chanting quieted to a whispered whoosh. Their collective presence chilled the darkness. Gooseflesh rushed over Corvus' body. Frost began to form on his exposed skin. Time was running out. The only way to save Desirol and himself—teleport.

The sipping of water and the chewing of food were the only sounds in Wolloh's hidden room. After the adults had departed, Stebben returned with a hot meal, their first since the celebration at Eissua Oasis. Ira stuffed his fourth piece of roasted zeegall in his mouth. Stebben told them a zeegall was a type of deer. Ira didn't care what it was. It was food, and it tasted great.

Distracted and quiet since the adults departed, Brie sat across from him, nibbling at her meal. He was glad they were gone. Nomed inspired a deep anger in him that exhibited itself in snide comments and bitter asides. His friends had banished him to a corner. He bit an odd-looking vegetable and chewed it with relish. *Wolloh. Now there's one strange guy. Sure hope I don't have to deal with him much.* Another mouthful of zeegall sent juice dribbling from the side of his mouth. He mopped it up with a napkin and stuffed in another piece.

For some unknown reason, Gerolyn fascinated him. He envied Brie's immediate closeness to her. *Wish she were my grandmother.* Brie caught his eye and smiled. *Is she reading my mind?* He gave her a belligerent stare. She looked down at her plate and shoved her food into small piles.

We will meet the Largeen Joram later. That'll be interesting. Brie's grandfather sounded pretty dreadful back on Myrrh. But then things have changed...changed a lot since then.

Esán shot a smile in his direction. "You over your grump, Ira? Come join us."

"I like my corner. No one's picking on me here."

"Suit yourself."

Stebben appeared, carrying a plate piled high with sweet-smelling pastries. "Our cook made these especially for you. They're a rare treat... taccus berry and steerro fruit sweetened with DerTahan honey. The berries and fruit only ripen together once each sun cycle. I think you'll find them not only delectable, but energizing. When you're done, pull the bell cord, and I'll return to clear the table."

"When do we meet Lorsedi?" Ira shaped the question around a mouthful of meat.

"That is up to the High DiMensioner."

Brie stirred her food with her fork. "Any word on Corvus and Desirol?"

"Not that I'm aware of." He looked from her plate to her face. "Perhaps, Brielle, eating your meal would make you feel better."

"Who said you could call her Brielle?" Ira snapped, rubbing the tip of his forefinger against his pant leg.

Wolloh flashed into the room, his distorted profile to him, his smooth side to his Major Domo. "I will manage things here, Stebben. Please alert Lorsedi that we will need him soon."

Stebben bowed and vanished.

Ira squirmed under the High DiMensioner's penetrating gaze and wondered how a sightless eye could make him so uncomfortable. "What're you looking at?"

Wolloh's good hand rested on his shoulder. Before Ira could brush it aside, he stood facing the High DiMensioner in a cozy room with comfortable looking chairs on either side of a rustic stone fireplace.

Easing his crippled body into the chair, Wolloh relaxed back and observed him with a slight smile. "I thought you could use some time without your friends. Please have a seat."

"Who asked you for..." Ira bit his tongue, sat down, and massaged his fingertip.

Wolloh lifted a hand. A tingling sensation ran through Ira's body.

The High DiMensioner smiled. "Welcome to Shu Chenaro."

"Oh my!" Ari wrinkled her brow. "Do I know you?" She frowned. "Of course, I do. You're Nomed's mentor. He slapped me, you know."

"I think you will find him changed, Arienh. How do you feel?"

"Confused." She traced a figure eight on the arm of the chair with a very feminine finger. "How did you know?"

With the two aspects of his face turned purposely toward her, he touched the disfigured cheek and rubbed the arch of his feather-like brow. "I understand the intricacies of shifting better than most. WoNa did you a major favor. Are you calmer?"

"I am. But I have to maintain my disguise, don't I?"

"You do, I'm afraid."

Sighing, she nestled back in the softness of her chair. "I really want to know my grandmother."

"Even as Ira, she knows you."

Ari adjusted her angle to peer more closely at him. "She does?"

He nodded.

"Will my grandfather know?"

"He would not have known—but because Nomed told him about his twin granddaughters, I have explained the reason for your disguise and why you must continue to maintain it. I believe you will like him, Ari. And as Ira, he will find you most interesting."

She pursed her lips and clasped her hands together in her lap. The bagginess of her boy's clothing made her want to giggle. Sobering, she sought his good eye. "It's time, isn't it?"

Wolloh stroked the crystal knob of his cane.

Ira opened his eyes and glanced at the man across from him. Placing the palms of his hands together, he rested his chin on the tips of his fingers. An exhaled breath restored his sense of place.

"Thank you for bringing me here, sir. I am much better. I don't know why I get so grumpy."

"Sometimes a few moments alone make all the difference. Are you ready to return to your friends?"

Ira stood up. "I am. Sure hope they didn't eat all the pastries."

Wolloh angled his uninjured side to Ira. "I'm sure they saved you a couple." He tapped his cane on the tile. The click, click faded.

Ira laughed at the expressions on his friends' faces. "Wow! Got here by myself." He eyed the dessert plate where three pastries waited, picked one up, and took a huge bite. "Darn good." Savoring the tangy sweetness of fruit and honey, he grinned.

Alone for the moment, Wolloh focused his attention on the predicament of the Atrilaasu Oracle. His ally and friend since he arrived in DerTah, WoNa had been his mentor and he hers. Of all the women he had met in his travels across the Inner Universe, WoNadahem Mardree was the one who held claim to his total allegiance and respect.

He closed his eyes and slowed his breathing. In a meditative state, he made a systematic search of Fera Finnero. Nissasa had divided his troops. A small group gathered at Nesune; a larger group waited near the borders of Shu Chenaro. Dahe and his men wavered into focus. Wolloh gripped the arms of the chair. He focused his power to hold the vision steady. Someone fought to tear it from his grasp. Nissasa's sneering face shimmered like a mirage and melted away, but not before Wolloh glimpsed WoNa lying on the ground behind him, the Oracle Stone missing from her forehead.

Wolloh roused himself from thoughts of WoNa as Lorsedi strode into the study, energy bristling around him. "My men are in place, and I have sent scouts out to gather information. I expect word at anytime as to the whereabouts of Nissasa's troops." He pulled off his riding gloves and tucked them over his belt. "There are times, Wolloh, when I wish I had your gift for shape shifting. It would be much more efficient to fly over the enemy than to creep around on horseback."

Wolloh relaxed his grip on the chair. "Nissasa has divided his troops, Lorsedi. Some are at Nesune Ruins, some at the border between Fera Finnero and my land. Nissasa himself is with the Sebborr."

Lorsedi shook his head and sank into the opposite chair. "Why I didn't think to ask you..." His voice trailed off. He sat upright. "Desirol?"

"I wasn't looking for your son. WoNa is my priority."

"And Desirol is mine. Can you do whatever it is you do and find him?"

Tempted to deny the request, Wolloh studied the RewFaaran leader. *I require his cooperation.* With an affirming nod, he closed his eyes. The instant he slipped into a trance state, a shadowy form reached for his throat. He dodged and sent a shield slamming into place around him. The menacing figure formed a zigzag of light and hurled it in his direction, the wind in its wake and rain pelting after it. Wolloh sent out a call for help. A hand gripped his arm. Energy infused his body. With a wave of his hand, he doubled the power of the attack and deflected it back to its sender. It hit the shadowed form, shattering it and tossing its pieces on the wind.

When he opened his eyes, Nomed bent over him.

"Thank you, Seyes. I was unprepared for the strength behind the attack."

Lorsedi moved into view, his freckles three dimensional on a face filled with concern. "Who attacked?"

"Nissasa. But with far more power than he possessed when he arrived at Shu Chenaro." Wolloh held his gaze. "Did you know, Lorsedi, that he is a trained DiMensioner?"

"A DiMensioner?" He sank into a chair. "I did not. Who trained him?" His tone verged on accusatory.

"The Mocendi League, my friend. Roween made the contact and the arrangements."

"I should have guessed. She is a viper, Wolloh, one that I intend to eliminate. What has increased Nissasa's power?"

Wolloh reached for his cane. With it stabilized between his feet, he waved a hand above it. White light flew from the crystal knob, scattering pastel rainbows over the walls, ceiling, and floor. The light softened. An image of a teardrop shaped crystal on a beaded headband came into focus. A hand snatched it from view, leaving Wolloh's crystal empty of light.

Nomed paled. "Nissasa has stolen the Oracle Stone. That means he can access Elcaro's Eye. We have to warn Almiralyn."

Wolloh squeezed the bridge of his nose. "And we can't use my crystal." He leveraged his tired body from the chair. "Which means you and Gerolyn must go to Myrrh and warn her. Nissasa will also know where the Compass of Ostradio is, as well as Efillaeh. The children are not safe here."

Lorsedi cleared his throat. "I certainly hope Corvus has spirited Desirol out of his reach, or my oldest son will hold all the best cards in the deck."

Allynae awakened in the dark with a resounding headache. His forehead rested on his bent knees. He realized with a sinking feeling in the pit of his stomach that some kind of bag covered his head. And his shoes were gone. When he tried to move his arms, he discovered his hands and ankles tied together like a turkey ready for the oven.

Since seeing was impossible, he strained to pick up any sound, which might give him a clue to his whereabouts. The external hush, heavy as stone, told him nothing. All could hear was his breathing and his heart striking his ribs. Lifting his head, he sniffed the air. The musty smell of dust and goat filled his nostrils. His sneeze hit an absorbent surface and muted into silence.

He wondered if One Man had met with the same fate. He thought about Sparrow and the twins. *Will I ever see them again? Who are the men who attacked me?* He'd heard stories about the Sebborr—stories that made his hair stand on end. *Maybe Nissasa's men have me. I'd be a great bargaining chip.* Panic started to push its way up from his stomach. *Calm down, boy. What would Almiralyn do?*

The quiet tread of footsteps approached and stopped. Soft breathing told him whoever it was knelt beside him. A knife cut the rope between his wrists and ankles. Rough hands straightened his legs and released them from their bonds. More muffled steps...another pair of hands helped to hoist him to standing.

No one spoke as they led him, with the bag still over his head and his hands tied in front of him, along what seemed to be a trail. His bare feet felt the cutting bite of stone. Heat hit him, dragging sweat from his body and leaving his throat and tongue so dry he couldn't swallow. Still, no one spoke. Only soft breathing assured him he wasn't alone.

49
Der Tah

In the depths of the Abyss of the Dead, Corvus clung to Desirol's limp body. Only a little more and he could teleport them to safety without leaving an energy trail for the Mindeco to follow. Above them, the enemy plummeted; around them, the ghosts of the abyss pressed closer. Molasses-black darkness wavered and rolled. The screams of the dead shrilled higher.

A single, unblinking eye locked onto his. Long, gangly arms reached out to snatch his burden away. Corvus frog-kicked backwards, broadening the distance between them, focused his intention, and teleported. The Mindeco's howl followed for only an instant before Corvus breathed in the odor of rough wood and desert air. He staggered under Desirol's weight, dropped to one knee, and lowered him onto a pile of straw.

After assuring himself that the boy's vitals were strong, he rubbed his tired shoulders, shook out his arms, and took a moment to regain his composure. His first concern—return Desirol to his father and Wolloh; his second—find and rescue WoNa. He gave him a gentle shake. "Des, we're safe. Wake up."

A shudder ran through the boy's body. He opened his eyes and jerked into a sitting position. His frightened gaze darted around the center. "Where's the Mindeco?"

"It's still in the Abyss. You're safe."

"Where are we?"

"Wolloh's Raptor Center."

A DerTahan hawk swiveled its head and blinked a feral eye. A squawked warning brought them both to their feet in one scrambled motion.

Corvus relaxed and grinned. "Hello, Stebben. Good to see you."

Wolloh's Major Domo returned the smile. "And you, Corvus."

Desirol looked wary. "Where's my father? I want to see him. I want to see him right now." Each word grew louder and more agitated.

"Better keep your voice down, Master Desirol. There are soldiers around here who aren't too friendly." Stebben put a hand on his shoulder. "I'll take you to the Largeen Joram." He glanced at Corvus. "You know about WoNa?"

"I'm headed to Eissua now."

"Take care."

Corvus released a relieved breath as Stebben and Desirol flashed from sight. *One less thing to worry about.* A shadow fell across the doorway. A kcalo-clad man slipped into the center. Corvus narrowed his eyes, poised for battle if need be.

"Easy, my friend." The man threw back his hood. "I'd like to go with you."

"Narrtep. It's good to see you." Corvus offered his hand. The Dansmen gripped it, his expression tense.

A shout in the barn and the thunder of soldiers' running sounded a warning. Corvus grabbed Narrtep's arm and teleported.

Brie waited in Wolloh's personal study for her grandfather. The High DiMensioner had decided they should meet for the first time in private. Her encounter with the Largeen Joram via Elcaro's Eye had left a foul taste in her mouth. That Wolloh trusted him made this meeting only slightly less nerve-wracking. To help neutralize her mixed feelings, she pulled a book of poetry from Wolloh's bookshelf and thumbed through it.

The soft sound of the door opening loosed butterflies in her stomach. Swallowing her nervousness, she set the book on the shelf. The Star of Truth gave a faint tingle. The door clicked shut. She grasped the blue velvet pouch at her throat and turned.

Her grandfather stood motionless in the center of the room. He was taller than she had imagined, with hair as red as hers and the dark eyes she remembered from the fountain. The expression on the strong-featured face made a tear slip down her cheek. She had not expected to see love, nor the almost overwhelming rush of it through her heart.

"I am Lorsedi Telisnoe, your grandfather." His voice was deep and controlled. The gentle words soothed her fears and overrode the terror of their first meeting at the fountain.

More tears welled up and spilled one after the other down her cheeks. He touched one with the tip of his finger and touched it to his heart. "I have wanted to meet you for so long."

The paralysis keeping her still released. "I am Brielle AsTar. I am so happy to meet you, sir."

And then they were both laughing. He pulled her down beside him on the love seat by the window. "I want to know all about you. What your life has been like, your mother, your..." He laughed again, then sobered. "But things are moving fast, Brielle, and I think I should meet your friends before Wolloh joins us."

"May I ask a question first?"

"Of course, my dear. What is it?"

She felt a little breathless. "What do I call you? I mean, how do I introduce you?"

He put an arm around her shoulder and smiled down at her. "Call me Grandfather. Will that do?"

A wide smile spread across her face. "It will do very well. Wait here, and I'll bring my friends. I think you'll like them, Grandfather."

She crossed the room and twisted a sconce by the fireplace. The wall slid away. Esán entered the sitting room, followed by Torgin, Ira, and Yaro.

Lorsedi stood as she brought them forward. "It's good to see you again, Esán." He flashed him a quizzical smile. "As I recall, you prefer not to have your mind probed."

Esán grinned. "That is true, sir. I am happy to answer your questions."

"I'll bear that in mind." He turned to Torgin. "I understand you are from Idronatti."

"Yes, sir. I'm Torgin Whalend."

"I also hear you are a fine musician and an excellent mathematician."

Torgin blushed. "I am good at math, but it is music I love."

Another charming smile lit Lorsedi's face. "I look forward to hearing you play." His gaze shifted to Yaro. "You must be Torgin's heart brother."

"I am Yaro." Gold-brown braids tumbled over his shoulder as he bowed and touched his heart.

"I have had dealings with Pentharian in the past and found them most interesting. It is good to meet you, Yaro." He, too, bowed his head and touched his heart before offering Ira his hand. "And you are Ira." Curiosity flickered in his dark eyes.

Brie watched her friend straighten as he took her grandfather's hand. A memory struggled to surface. *What am I forgetting?* She looked again at Ira and then at her grandfather. They had fallen into a discussion about RewFaar.

"I'd love to visit it sometime." Ira's eagerness made Brie smile.

Lorsedi assumed the demeanor of the Largeen Joram. "After we have resolved the issues at hand, we will discuss a visit."

A tap on the door announced Stebben's entrance into the room. "I am sorry to interrupt, sir, but someone across the hall requires your presence."

Lorsedi's persona changed. "Of course. I'll go immediately." With a gracious smile that encompassed them all, he left the room.

Stebben shut the door and smiled.

Brie clapped her hands. "It's Desi, isn't it?"

"Corvus brought him. He's had a bit of a scare. I gather they visited the Abyss of the Dead on the way here."

"He's alright?" Esán glanced past him at the door.

"A bit shaken, but fine."

Brie smiled to herself. She had seen the sudden light in her grandfather's eye as he hurried from the room.

From taccus tree to taccus tree, Gerolyn and Nomed made their way to the raptor center. Teleporting would have been quicker, but Nomed was being watched. Omudi, the Dreela of Geran, and Thaer of the Plains of DoOlb remained in residence. Their alliance with Gidtuss made it imperative that they take extraordinary care not to be detected.

They paused behind a screen of desert bushes to watch a group of soldiers exit the barn and scatter in various directions. Nomed squeezed her arm and jerked a thumb at two more who remained at the barn doors.

She edged closer to him. "Dare we teleport?"

"No. I suggest we wait a few moments. If things don't quiet down, we'll shift and leave from here."

Although waiting for nightfall would have been preferable, time and a crisis dictated they leave immediately. She wished they'd been able to wait, especially with soldiers swarming the ranch. They were Lorsedi's, but traitors remained within their ranks.

The soldiers regrouped near the barn and moved toward the house. As soon as they rounded the corner, Nomed took her arm. They dashed to an outbuilding opposite the raptor center.

He whispered, "Stay here. I'll check things out."

Staying low, he ran to a single-wide door, opened it a crack, and sidled inside. When he reappeared, he held it wide. She dashed across the open space, glad she'd taken time to change to slacks and boots. Inside, Nomed hurried her into the raptor center and closed the door.

Leaving from the center had been Wolloh's idea. Since he had both owls and ravens in his collection of birds, it would arouse less suspicion. She focused on the enigma that was Seyes Nomed. After a lifetime of hating Myrrh's Guardian, how would he manage his meeting with her? He appeared both solemn and nervous—the latter quite contrary to his public façade.

"What made the Guardian ban you from Myrrh, Seyes? I've known her for a long time. She is a reasonable woman."

His expression went blank, and she thought he would ignore the question. Then the scar at the corner of his mouth pulled downward. "The most honest answer—I was a bully. I hurt small children and animals. My only excuse—my father beat me and one turning I went too far."

"Too far?"

Deep green eyes searching his face brought a flush to his cheeks. Ignoring the impulse to rub it away, he met her gaze. "I threw a kitten. It hit the wall and its neck broke." His face reflected a child's confusion. "I wanted to take it back, but it was too late. Almiralyn caught me and forbade my return."

Gerolyn kept her response easy. "I'd say confronting her is past due."

He rubbed the scar with a forefinger. "You didn't cringe or look shocked or horrified."

"You were a child, Seyes. I'm surprised a woman of Almiralyn's training and sensitivity missed the signs of abuse. Meet her with an open mind. A friendship and an alliance with the Guardian of Myrrh will benefit all of us." She prepared to leave. "Shall we go?"

He seemed to shrug away the past and smiled. "After you."

Blue-black feathers encased her. Powerful raven wings carried her high above Shu Chenaro. The DiMensioner's great horned owl soared beside her. Soon they would be at the portal. With luck, they would make it into the vortex without incident.

One Man skirted the south side of the lake at Eissua Oasis, his senses stretched to the limit. As empty as the oasis appeared, life vibrated close at hand. He crouched behind a tent. His attention focused, he sent out a sounding and waited for the sonar-like waves to bounce back, telling him what existed nearby. It was a technique he had perfected prior to leaving his cabin at Timreh Pass in the Dojanack Mountains.

He rocked back on his heels. Sequestered deep underground, he discovered several Humans still occupied the oasis. Allynae was not among them. He closed his eyes and tried another sounding. *Nothing.* His concern escalated. *Where are you, my friend?*

The Seed of Carsilem stabbed a warning. Danger moved closer to his position. Shifting, he lifted into flight in his hawk eyes trained on the land below. Where Allynae had been scouting, sand obscured the signs of a conflict. No footsteps led to or from the spot.

He landed at the top of a desert pine. *Who has captured you? Sebborr? RewFaarans?* Swooping down to a cluster of palm trees, he touched down in Human form and allowed the Seed take the lead. At the sound of a softly expelled breath, he swung around. His gaze darted over the oasis; his senses searched the surrounding area.

A flash of desert orange caught his eye. "You can come out. I mean no harm."

A Dansgirl peeked around a tall palm. "You father of Esán." She stepped from behind it. "WoNa say you come."

He kept his voice low. "My name is One Man. Esán is my son. I seek to find him."

"I Nichook. You call me Nichi." She dropped into a crouch and motioned him to the ground. "Wicked men come. Follow Nichi." Staying low, she headed for the outcropping at the far end of the oasis. Midway, she ducked into a tent. When he entered, she pressed a finger to her lips and pulled the tent flap closed. After a brief wait, she moved away from the entrance. "Wicked men take WoNa. My people search. Do not find. She told me two men come...Father of Esán and father of twins. Where twins' father?"

"I was hoping you might know."

She pursed her lips and fingered her beaded headband. "We wait till sun spirit sleeps. Then seek your friend. You rest. I wake you soon."

One Man shoved his impatience aside. *In my heart I know Allynae lives. The girl seems honest and unafraid. Right now, she's my best hope for finding him.* He sank onto a cot in the dark tent and allowed himself to take a much-needed nap.

A noise outside startled him awake. Nichi was not in the tent. Alert and ready to fight or shift as necessary, he crept closer to the door and crouched in the shadows. A man's hand pushed the tent flap aside. A kcalo-draped figure slipped into the tent and pushed his hood back from his face. Another man followed.

One Man relaxed and straightened. "Good to see you, Corvus. Who's your friend?"

"This is Narrtep, WoNa's guardian. Nichi informed us you were here. Any idea who has Allynae?"

"None. Where's Nichi?"

Narrtep closed the tent flap. "I sent her to do some spying. She'll be back soon."

"I suggest we exchange information while we wait." One Man grabbed a cushion and sat down. The others followed suit. Soon, they were deep in conversation. Corvus shared what he knew of Nesune and the events at Shu Chenaro.

"I'm glad the children are at the ranch." One Man nodded his relief. "That gives us some time to find Allynae and rescue WoNa. Any idea where she is?"

Narrtep raised a hand and pointed at the tent flap. Nichi slipped inside and fell to her knees, sobbing. She held out her hands. On her palms lay a small, red-orange snake. "I think it dead."

The men gathered around her. Narrtep ran a finger down the snake's slender length. "WoNa's." Horror filled his eyes. "Without the snake and the Oracle Stone, she will slip into deep stasis. Whoever awakens her will have the power to control her."

Nichi's sobs grew louder. Narrtep put his arms around her. "Shh. You will bring the enemy to our door."

She hiccuped and placed the small, limp body in One Man's outstretched hand. He sat back on his heels, held it to his heart, and closed his eyes. *Ah, wee one, you live.* Holding it level with his mouth, he blew one soft breath, then another, and touched the small head. The tiny eyes glittered. Its tongue licked the air. It hissed a series of sounds.

One Man returned the serpent to Nichi. "The snake tells me WoNa slipped into stasis a short time ago."

Narrtep's face paled. "My worst fear."

"That means Nissasa can gain control of her." Corvus paced to the tent's entrance. "We need to get moving."

One Man joined him, stared up at the caravan of moons overhead, and contemplated WoNa's vulnerable state. "I hope we rescue her before Nissasa discovers what her total blindness means."

50
Myrrh

In the private cave adjacent to Yookotay's council chamber, Almiralyn flicked a quilled pen over paper. She added her signature and reread her reply. It was brief and to the point—she did not support the traitor's behavior—but would do her best to get their message to Torgin Whalend.

Folding the paper, she slipped it into an envelope. Nissasa's representative instructed Wilith to return with her answer. *A bad idea since the Five Fathers have recently appointed him the next Premier of Idronatti.* She affixed her seal to the envelope, picked it up, and stared at it, contemplating her next move. *If I send Wilith back to Idronatti, the rebels will have one more bargaining chip.* She set her reply aside. *I'll get the message there by other means.*

In her meeting with Voer, he had shared the information he and

Mondago had gleaned from the young traitor. She must get it to Shu Chenaro.

Wilith's true motive for coming to Myrrh had been the most vexing revelation of all. *Nissasa makes Seyes Nomed look like a saint. I will not underestimate his hunger for power or the means by which he intends to achieve his goals.*

Zugo loved Veersuni. The window, with its expansive view of this sector of the Inner Universe, always filled him with awe. His thoughts, as he watched a shooting star streak across the sky, however, were mixed. *Esán, Torgin, and the twins are in danger in another dimension—on another planet. I want to help my friends. Instead, I am trapped, incarcerated in Veersuni.*

Elae joined him, her different-colored eyes glowing in the faint light. "DerTah's heat would destroy you in less than a chron-circle, Zugo. You can help the most by staying alive and healthy. There are things we can do here."

"I know. It's just..." He gritted his teeth. "I feel helpless, useless."

"We aren't useless or helpless. Almiralyn trusts us to monitor Elcaro's Eye and report to her. We can even ask questions and see if it will give us some answers."

Water bubbling made them hurry to the fountain's side. A haze floated above its turbulent surface. As it cleared and an image floated upward from the bottom of the bowl, Elae pulled Zugo back into the muted light in front of the velvet curtains. The evil face—the dark hair and square-cut beard, the eyes filled with a lust for power, and the cruel sneer that twisted the mouth—made him cringe. Beside him, Elae whispered a series of words and clapped three times. The image dissolved. Water dripped from the carved statue's upturned palms, its sound in counterpoint to his throbbing fear.

Elae's serious expression made the hair on his neck rise. "Go! Warn, Almiralyn. She will know who it is and what to do."

Zugo needed no urging. He sprinted from Veersuni to the Cave of Canedari, gulped a revitalizing breath, and started the long trek up the Stairway of Retu Erath. *Sure wish I could shape shift like Esán.* When he reached the landing, he glanced back and shuddered. The cruelty and malice of the image haunted him. *I sure wish I were with my friends.*

The great horned owl swooped from the Nervac Portal and landed in Human form in the Dojanack Caverns. Nomed swung around, his attention riveted to the whirling vortex. *Where's Gerolyn? She should have been right behind me.*

A DeoNyte male stepped from the shadows. "You are Seyes Nomed?"

"I am. And you are?"

"I am Sitrio. I understood the Guardian's emissary was coming with you."

Nomed paced back to the vortex. "She was right behind me. If she doesn't—"

A raven shot over his head and landed. Gerolyn appeared, her green eyes flashing. "The soldiers at the portal are Nissasa's. A short distance from their camp, they had staked four of Lorsedi's men out in the sun to die. I couldn't leave them there."

Nomed's eyebrow shot up. "How do you know they were the Largeen Joram's?"

Her chin lifted. "Lorsedi would leave no one to die in that fashion."

"Tell us what happened."

"I created a small sand storm and released Lorsedi's men. Nissasa's soldiers were running around like scared rabbits. You'd think they'd never been in a sandstorm before." She gave a disdainful laugh and grew serious. "I left Lorsedi's men hidden near the portal and came here. They're outnumbered, so I doubt they can take over the gateway, but they might make it back to Shu Chenaro."

Nomed shook his head. "You are quite a woman, Gerolyn." He gave her a mock bow. "We'd better find Almiralyn and make our report."

"Allow me to escort you to Yookotay and the Guardian." Sitrio prepared to take the lead.

"What about the portal?" She peered at the faint spin of the vortex. "It shouldn't be left unattended."

Two DeoNytes stepped from the darkness.

"My men stand guard at all times." Sitrio led them to the Central Square and into the anteroom of the council chamber. "Wait here. I'll inform Yookotay and Almiralyn of your arrival." He disappeared beyond the door.

Nomed looked at Gerolyn. "You are a woman of many surprises. I was preparing to return for you."

"I know. The time differential between DerTah and Myrrh is a good thing. Otherwise, we might have collided in the vortex. I couldn't leave them, Seyes. I didn't mean to worry you."

He was about to answer when Sitrio appeared with Yookotay. The ReDael acknowledged Gerolyn with a smile before his penetrating gaze came to rest on Nomed. "When last we met, Seyes Nomed, we were fighting as enemies. I am honored now to fight at your side. Welcome to Meos." He offered his right hand palm up, his left on his heart.

A rush of feelings left Nomed speechless. With his palm on Yookotay's, he touched his heart and bowed his head. When he raised it, he saw only respect and welcome in the ReDael's light blue eyes.

Yookotay indicated the door. "I'll stay here with Gerolyn. Almiralyn awaits you in the room off the council chamber."

Nomed stepped into the chamber, crossed to the round table at the center, and rested his hands on the smooth wood. A sapphire that matched the one Yookotay wore on a gold chain around his neck gleamed between his hands. Guilt warmed his face. During the battle to destroy Myrrh and Almiralyn, he had stolen Zugo's Pendant of Ascendance, the sapphire that matched his father's. In his pocket, its weight pressed against his leg. *I will find an opportunity to return it.*

A door opened. The Guardian of Myrrh, backed by the light in the cave beyond, observed him from eyes hidden in shadow. His hands fisted and then flattened against the table. A knot in his throat forced him to swallow. The heartbeat pounding in his ears made him exhale the breath he had drawn when she appeared in the entryway.

She crossed to the table and stopped opposite him. "I cannot undo the damage my unjust banishment caused you, Davin. I can only express my gratitude that you are here today."

The quiet of the chamber following her statement filled him with a sense of peace. He had no words to express what her apology meant to him... to Davin, the small, abused boy who had begged so long for relief from pain.

His rage cooled. It would take time to extinguish it completely, but today the flames died to embers, leaving him lighter and freer than he could ever remember.

He walked around the table. She placed her palm on his and touched her heart, and then his. "I pledge to fight by your side, Seyes Nomed, and to honor you as my ally and friend."

The word friend rolled around his mind and settled into the void in his heart. Warmth radiated throughout his body. He took a breath and touched his scarred cheek. "I pledge to fight at your side, Almiralyn, Guardian of Myrrh. I honor you as my ally and..." He smiled. "...my friend."

She blinked away tears. "Thank you, Seyes. I suggest we take a moment before we call the others." With a smile of gratitude, she slipped into the antechamber, leaving him time to collect his thoughts.

It crossed his mind that confronting her sooner would have made his life simpler. It would also have made it different...him different. He caressed the scar and remembered when he had cut his cheek with a shard from the portal mirror. He had done it out of anger and hurt. That turning he had gone numb. Today, the feelings Esán's appearance inspired surfaced and settled. Again, he touched his cheek. *Henceforth, this scar will remind me to embrace my life and my emotions...to be true to myself.*

He gave Almiralyn a slight nod as she reappeared with Yookotay and Gerolyn. Behind them trouped Sparrow; the Theran major, Jordett; Pentharian Yuin and Voer; Esán's Aunt Merrilea; and Sitrio. A dark-skinned stranger was the last to enter. He had expected Somay and Allynae, but there was no sign of them.

Almiralyn smiled at the stranger. "I'd like to introduce a recent member of our company. This is Wilith Whalend, Torgin's father. He has information for us. Yookotay has offered his council table. I suggest we sit and share our knowledge."

Nomed joined the others. Opposite him, Torgin's father cast an anxious look around the table. Nomed felt a flash of sympathy. *He's definitely out of his element. Bet he hasn't left Idronatti since he visited Myrrh as a child.* Nomed fingered the ruby marking his place. *Well, Wilith Whalend, you're not alone. The Unfolding is shaking the foundation of all our lives.* He noted with a bemused smile that a short time ago, those gathered at the table had been his enemies.

Jeet's carnelian scales glowed in the late afternoon sun, a beacon for the Nyti Matrés. Kieel carried a message from Tinpaca Mondago. One guard at the portal was a traitor.

Skirting the Demrach Gateway, he landed on a branch by Jeet's head. The Pentharian's eyes narrowed. "Trouble?"

The man to the right is a traitor. Stay alert."

Mumshu and Ashor zipped into view. Kieel waved them forward and introduced them. "If you need help, send one of them to the Tinpaca with a message. I'm off. Take care." He darted away through the trees.

The tension hanging over the woods rubbed his nerves raw. The trees were too quiet, and the birds had stopped their constant chirping. Something was amiss. Tinpaca Mondago had already imprisoned Cantruto and his two cohorts. Five rebels were missing. They would apprehend the one at the gateway when his watch ended. Kieel's instincts told him that would be too late.

Skimming just above the level of a tall Human, he searched the forest near the gateway. His sharp eyes caught a subtle movement in a gully between two hills. Zipping to a maple branch, he hid under a large leaf. Five men in full battle gear huddled below. At their leader's signal, they spread out, flanking the gateway on both sides.

Kieel shot through the trees, warned Jeet, and headed for the RewFaaran camp. With one traitor at the portal already, Lorsedi's solitary soldier didn't have a chance. He flew into the tent, where Mondago and Stee were discussing battle tactics, and hovered, his eyes darting from one to the other.

The Tinpaca held out his hand. "You look harried. What's happening?"

Kieel landed. "Your five missing men are on the move. They're headed for the portal. Jeet is staying close to your loyal soldier, but he can't hope to handle six men—the five and the guard duty." He fluttered to the tabletop.

Mondago strode to the entrance, whispered to a young soldier posted there, and returned to the table. Grantese Tesilend strode into the tent and saluted. His gaze flicked to Stee and back to the Tinpaca.

"You need me, sir."

"Take some men and secure the gateway." He provided him with the details. "Do what you have to do, Tesilend. We can't afford to let *any* of Nissasa's rebels use that portal."

"Yes, sir." He did an about face and departed.

Stee flipped his braids over his shoulder and stood up. "I think Jeet might need some help." He shifted to a dragonfly and shot out of the entryway.

Mondago shook his head. "What a strange time."

Kieel lifted into the air. "I'll go as well. I'll send one of the Nyti to you if anything goes awry." He streaked toward the trees, hoping it would not be too late for Lorsedi's soldier.

From the branch of a tall oak tree, he watched Mondago's men closing in on Demrach Gateway much faster than he expected. Relieved, he zipped ahead.

Jeet remained hidden in trees at the gateway. Kieel shot down and informed him of the Tinpaca's plan. A dragonfly hovered and shifted.

Stee knelt beside his comrade. "I'll keep to this side of the gateway. You take the other one. Use serum to numb the traitors. I'm sure Mondago will want to question them."

"And if I have to use venom?"

"Protect the portal at all costs, Jeet. Good hunting."

"Good hunting, my comrade."

Jeet shifted and shot away on iridescent wings.

Kieel followed Stee's panther form. Like a forest shadow, the big cat slipped from tree to tree. A muffled cough brought it to a halt. Crouching low, it waited, its ears swiveling, its nostrils wide.

A man broke cover, zigzagged his way to a large stump, and squatted behind it. The panther vanished. A small brown bat shot after him. Tiny teeth sunk into the tender flesh at the base of the man's neck. He sank to the ground in a silent heap.

Stee shifted to his natural form, hefted the man over his shoulder, and carried him deeper into the trees. After concealing his weapons, he left him hidden in tall ferns and underbrush.

Again, the bat appeared and flew soundlessly through the woods. A second soldier dropped to one knee and drew his weapon. He gave a soft whistle. An answering whistle made him adjust his course. Creeping forward, he crouched low and strained to see through the dense forest growth. He flinched, grabbed his neck, and folded to the ground. Stee materialized and stuffed the weapon in a hollow beneath a log before he gripped the man by the armpits and dragged him deeper into the woods.

With a hummingbird's speed, Kieel dodged between trees, searching to see how many of Nissasa's traitors remained. He spotted three clustered together, camouflaged by a group of short needled pines. He flew closer.

"I'm telling you, something in these woods is hunting us." The speaker scowled.

"Don't be ridiculous." Their leader shot him a hard look.

The first man scanned the trees. "Where are the others? We made it on time. Why didn't they?"

"Shut up, Stich, they gotta be close by. Let's move."

The three separated. Stich skulked between the trees on one side of the vortex. The other two hid opposite. They were closing in fast.

Mondago's men hid on the camp side of the gateway. Their orders were explicit. Nissasa's men must not use the portal. If it meant killing them, so be it.

Kieel shuddered at the thought. *Life in the Terces Wood has become far too dangerous.*

51

Der Tah

At Eissua Oasis, dusk leached the landscape of color as One Man and Corvus followed Narrtep along a trail that crawled up the side of the outcropping. They had left Nichi behind with WoNa's recuperating snake. Danger stalked them, and they stalked it. She was safer hidden in her tent.

Narrtep hunkered down behind a ridge of sand and rock. Corvus crouched next to him. One Man held back, his senses searching like a bloodhound after a scent. He discovered men up ahead. Frenzied-anger buzzing around them warned him, emotions blurred their judgment. He knelt beside his companions. "Trouble up the trail."

Corvus nodded. "Sebborr or RewFaaran?"

"Can't tell."

Narrtep motioned for silence, then stole up the trail, ducked beneath an overhang, and peered around a large rock. His quick retreat and silent descent back in their direction held a warning. Apprehension formed a lump in One Man's throat. The expression on Corvus' face told him he shared his heightened concern.

Narrtep knelt and whispered. "On the opposite side of the ridge is a sacred site, one used for celebrating the desert spirits. Your friend is there. The men holding him are from the LaTiru, a nomadic tribe who believe in blood sacrifice. They worship WoNa and the Oracle Stone and will do anything to find them. She is one of their deities."

The lump plummeted to One Man's stomach. "You think they plan to sacrifice Allynae?"

He nodded.

One Man looked at Corvus. "Options?"

"Shift and see what we can learn."

One Man motioned up the trail. "I'll go. If I call, come running." He crept to the overhang, shifted to a desert lizard, and scurried from one clump of dried desert vegetation to the next until he reached the outer edge of a circled-throng of unkempt and ragged men and women. The scene turned the lump in his gut to ice. His telepathic message to Corvus held a warning and a summons.

Allynae, tied to a pole in the scorching desert sun, felt himself fading. A feeble tug at his bonds left him frustrated and disheartened. *I need water. And I need to see.* He struggled to lift his head. The effort left him panting.

As the coolness of dusk dried the sweat on his body and the night's creeping cold began a slow crawl over his exposed skin, a pebble struck the ground nearby. Rough hands untied him from the pole and held him upright. A second pair tested the ropes lashing his wrists together in front of him and then grabbed his arm. In total silence, his captors dragged him up a steep trail.

Blinded by the bag covering his head, he stumbled over the rock-strewn terrain. Sharp stone cut the soles of his bare feet. He clenched his teeth around the pain and sagged against his captors.

The rancid odor of Human sweat and a low murmured-mix of voices brought him to a standstill. He strained to hear or smell anything that would give him a clue to his surroundings. The hands gripping his arms tightened. A menacing quiet settled around him. The warmth of a fire behind him soaked up the cold of the encroaching desert night, but did nothing to assuage his growing apprehension.

The bag, yanked from his head without warning, left him blinking back tears and confusion. He squinted, straining to clear his vision. A narrow, dark face, made more threatening by the flicker of flames, loomed in front of his. Wild black hair, a long, filthy beard, and eyes filled with a fanatical gleam sent goose bumps flying over his skin.

Rapid blinking brought the face into clearer focus. Tattooed on the man's forehead was the Oracle Stone. Hope evaporated. *I'm as good as gone. These aren't RewFaaran or Sebborr. They aren't even Atrilaasu.* He stared at the tattoo. The LaTiru of the Oracle Stone were a small, uncivilized tribe of scavengers who roamed the desert, making blood sacrifices to their deities.

The man held up a long knife. His followers cheered. At his signal, they grew still. Anticipation and excitement bristled in their midst.

The leader sheathed his weapon and jerked the gag from Allynae's mouth. "Speak, thief. Tell us where you've hidden WoNadahem Mardree. Tell us or roast in SeDah."

Allynae tried to moisten his lips with a dried and swollen tongue. His throat, raw from heat and lack of water, made it difficult to form words. "Water," he choked. "Can't speak." He coughed and savored the one-drop of spittle it produced.

"Water!" The leader's shout brought a rumble response from his followers.

A tribesman detached himself from the crowd and tossed a water bag. The leader caught it by the neck, held it above his head, and rotated slowly. With a vicious laugh, he took a drink, smacked his lips, and let the water drip down his beard and onto his ragged kcalo. "Ahh..."

The crowd chanted and pushed closer. "Water, water, water."

Again, he tipped the bag up. A stream of water shot into his mouth. He swished it around, held it in puffed cheeks, and spewed the contents in Allynae's face.

Laughter rustled through the crowd. He corked the bag and lobbed it at the man who had produced it. Grinning, he wiped his mouth with the back of his hand. "Answer or die, thief."

Allynae's tongue sought the splatter of liquid and drew what it could capture into his mouth. "I am Allynae, brother of Almiralyn, Guardian of Myrrh." He licked his lips in search of more moisture.

The tribesmen muttered nervously. A minute change of expression on the leader's face encouraged Allynae to continue. "Let me go. My friends and I will find and rescue the Atrilaasu Oracle."

A soft rush of cool air produced a look of alarm on the LaTiru leader's face. The men on either side of Allynae stiffened. He glanced over his shoulder. His knees went weak with relief.

One Man shifted to human form beside the LaTiru's fire. Tribesmen and women scrambled backwards. Allynae's guards whipped their heads around. Their leader reached for his knife.

One Man stayed his hand with a look. A spark of fear flitted across the man's face. The tribal members retreated further from the fire.

"I am One Man, the Guardian of Myrrh's ambassador. What Allynae says is true. Do you wish to anger the Guardian, who is his sister and WoNa's good friend?" He let the words sink in.

A large raven landed on his shoulder. Marcasite-hard eyes glinted in the firelight. "I am Karrew, the protector of Almiralyn, the Guardian of Myrrh and friend of WoNa. This is my lady's message. 'Release my brother and remain at peace with me. Sacrifice him, and I will judge you as I will judge those who kidnapped WoNadahem Mardree.'"

Hatred filled the leader's grimy face. His lip curled, displaying decayed teeth. A long hiss whistled them as he slid his knife beneath the ropes binding Allynae's wrists. One quick cut scattered them on the ground. "Tell the Guardian her brother is free." He spat out the words. A wad of sputum followed, splattering over the ground. "Tell her if he does not rescue the Atrilaasu Oracle, another will die in his place."

The circle parted. A tribesman dumped a kcalo-covered body on the ground. Nichi raised terrified eyes to One Man's face.

"You would harm one of the Oracle's chosen children?" Karrew's caw rang like a warning bell.

"If you do not rescue the Oracle, this girl dies."

One Man stroked the raven's breast. "Deliver the message, Karrew. Tell Almiralyn we will seek those who kidnapped WoNa."

The raven cawed and lifted into flight, his dark feathers blending with the night.

Narrtep walked into the ring of firelight and hurried to Allynae's side. He offered a water bag. "Drink slowly, friend."

Corvus walked from the shadows and placing himself between Allynae and the LaTiru leader.

One Man knelt and wrapped his arms around Nichi. "We will not fail."

She hugged him. "Save WoNa." The small snake slithered from her sleeve down the neck of his kcalo. "WoNa need snake."

He helped her up and looked at the leader. "Where will we find you?"

The man grasped Nichi's arm and passed her to a woman in the circle. "When the Oracle is safe, we find you." With a wave of his hand, the LaTiru tribe disappeared into the darkness, leaving only the fire as a reminder that they had been there.

Lorsedi hesitated outside the door to the room where Desirol waited. Many moon cycles had passed and much had occurred since he had last seen his youngest and favorite son. Allowing himself a moment to prepare for the reunion, he reviewed the circumstances that had brought him to this juncture.

He had chosen Desirol to rule instead of Nissasa because of his more developed sense of right and his potential to become a fine strategist. When he disappeared, he left no hint of where he had gone or why. Although suspecting Nissasa, Lorsedi could find nothing to prove his involvement. After a long and disheartening search, he had called a halt.

Explaining his disappearance to his mother was tough; explaining why he called off the hunt was even harder. He had chosen Chyneria, the only woman with whom he had shared time after his Joining to Gerolyn, because she was so different from the woman to whom he had given his heart.

Chyneria was petite; Gerolyn was tall. Her hair was dusty brown with no hint of the rich chestnut luster of Gerolyn's, and her eyes were the soft, tawny brown of a RewFaaran zeegall. Except for the intelligence they shared, Chyneria was everything Gerolyn was not—and vice versa.

When it became obvious that Nissasa could not rule and he must sire another son, he chose her. Unwilling to dissemble, he had told her of his love for Gerolyn. She had never questioned it or doubted the depth of his feelings for her. After Desirol's birth, they continued to spend time together, sharing their delight in the son they had created. With luck, he would take Desirol home to RewFaar and the mother who cherished him beyond measure.

Setting the past aside, he turned the doorknob and stepped into the present. Dark eyes, huge in a fair-skinned face, widened. Auburn hair, much longer than Lorsedi remembered, brushed the broad shoulders of a boy well on his way to manhood. The youngster of his memory was not the youth standing in front of him. The scars of tragedy and loss replaced the innocence once so prevalent in Desirol's face and eyes. *My dearest son, what have they done to you?*

Desirol stared at his father, afraid if he moved, the man in front of him would disappear like the demise of a dream. *How could I not remember the handsome ruggedness of his face, the blaze of red hair, the kindness in his eyes?* He cleared his throat and tried to speak.

Two long strides brought his father to his side. The arms embracing him were strong, the chest well-muscled and broad, and the hand stroking his hair filled Desirol with the knowing that his father's love had never floundered. Lorsedi held him at arm's length and studied his face. "I have missed you, my son, more than you can imagine."

Desirol soaked up the words and reveled in the deep timbre of the sound. He wanted to remain cool and mature, but emotions stripped him of breath and voice. *How could I have forgotten the loving man who raised me?* A flash flood of memories left him trembling. Teardrops heralded a choked sob. "I'm sorry, Father, I..."

Strong hands caught him as his knees gave way and guided him to a chair. Lorsedi sat opposite him, enclosing his trembling hands in his steady ones. "Tears are not signs of weakness, my son. They are salve in the wounds of the heart. I was told what happened to you. When you are ready, I would hear your story from you."

Desirol composed himself and accepted the handcloth his father offered. He dried his tears and refolded it in a neat square. "Things are moving quickly, Father. I think I should tell you now. We may not have an opportunity again soon."

Lorsedi nodded and gave him an encouraging smile.

Desirol shared what he could remember of his story. Some parts were sketchy, but the part Nissasa had played was clear. He left nothing out—not even his own erratic behavior at the ruins. When he finished, he sat back in his chair and let out an expansive sigh. A weight had lifted from his shoulders. From the expression on his father's face, he knew Lorsedi had taken on the burden of retribution. Nissasa would soon feel the full power of his father's wrath.

Wolloh soared above the ranch, his osprey body shrouded in the night's darkness. Below him, Nissasa's troops patrolled the desert border of Shu Chenaro. To the east, DerTah's buttery moon, Fasfro, crested the horizon, heralding the imminent arrival of her two sister moons. The beauty of the celestial trio had been one of the deciding factors in his decision to reside in DerTah. Tonight, however, he would have foregone their beauty for a cover of clouds.

He crossed into Fera Finnero and increased his speed. An urgent need to reach his destination and return to the ranch before dawn kept his focus sharp. Close to the border, Nissasa's traitors gathered. The quiet of their camp told him an assault on Shu Chenaro would not begin until morning.

Swooping in a wide arc, he scanned the desert for signs of life...the Sebborr...the LaTiru. He let his senses roam the sands. *When I find Nissasa, WoNa will be close by.* The glow of a fire and the shadowed shapes of tents nestled at the base of a desert plateau lured him to a lower altitude. He landed a safe distance from the camp, shifted, dropped to his knee behind a stocky taccus tree, and sent out a subtle probe. *Nissasa has done his work well. Gidtuss' Fire ConDra guard all sides of the camp, and the protective wards at the entrance to WoNa's prison quiver with power.*

A quick thought, and he assumed his osprey form and headed for Eissua Oasis. *One Man and Corvus will benefit from the information I've gathered. It will increase their chances of a successful rescue and decrease the time needed to accomplish it.* Impatience tempted him to land and teleport. Nissasa's heightened power kept him in the air. Osprey wings carried him with good speed. He would reach the oasis long before daybreak.

When it finally came into view, he coasted to a landing near Narrtep's tent and shifted. A probe informed him three men rested inside. The tent flap flipped open. A man appeared, his eyes scanning the oasis. Narrtep appeared behind him. Wolloh stepped from a group of palms into the golden light of Fasfro and that of her sister's cool blue. Narrtep whispered and withdrew.

The man crossed the sand, his silver blond hair glistening and his blue eyes filled with moonlight. "I'm One Man, Esán's father. Please come in and join us, High DiMensioner od DerTah."

Wolloh preceded him to the tent. Narrtep closed the flap behind them. The third occupant sat in the circle of dim light cast by a small oil lamp. Wolloh noted the blistered lips and feet wrapped in torn strips of cloth. Choosing not to play games, he turned his full face to the man.

Narrtep introduced him. "This is Wolloh, High DiMensioner od DerTah."

Allynae studied him with interest. He had heard so much about Nomed's mentor, he found it difficult to ignore his preconceived bias. One Man pulled up a cushion and Narrtep provided Wolloh with a chair before he spoke. "I apologize for not getting up. I'm Allynae, but you know that already, don't you?"

The man smiled and settled his crippled body on the chair. "I am glad to see you safe, Allynae. And Corvus?"

Allynae noted the turn of his head as his good eye searched the tent. "Patrolling the area. But you know that, as well."

The smooth side of the High DiMensioner's face caught the light. "I am here as a friend, yours and your sister's. Nissasa and the Sebborr are east of here. They have imprisoned WoNa in a cave under the plateau. Fire ConDra guard the camp. Nissasa has put up wards at the entrance to her prison. Any tampering with the shields will alert Nissasa to an intruder's presence. I offer you a way into the cave without disturbing his wards—and also a gift for WoNa when you find her."

Allynae let his chagrin show on his face. "I apologize. My negative bias toward Nomed has colored my view of you. I...we thank you for risking a trip through the desert to warn us."

The cool intelligence in the dark eye held a glint of light. "The Unfolding is at work, brother of Almiralyn. You will feel the force of it before its cycle is complete. I believe we had better hurry if you are to rescue WoNa."

One Man adjusted his cushion to face Wolloh. "Tell us about the Fire ConDra."

"The ConDra are sluggish at night. Their fire's heat is tied to the heat of the sun. Although they can rise if threatened, their fire, like the desert night, will remain cool until the sun crests the horizon. To minimize the risk of detection *and* death by the ConDra's fire, you must perform your rescue before the sun rises."

The High DiMensioner withdrew his hand, which he had pocketed upon sitting, and held it out. A crystal rested on his palm. "This is from the Evolsefil Caverns on Tao Spirian. It carries the signature of the Prima Crystal's power and connects to Elcaro's Eye and any other crystal mined from there. Since Nissasa has stolen the Oracle Stone, also from the caverns, it will not trigger an alarm. One of you must enter the perimeter of the wards with the crystal. As soon as you are through, place it on WoNa's forehead. It will free her from the total blindness, which is keeping her in a state of stasis. With your help, she can use it to get you away. You must hurry. If Nissasa is the first to awaken her, she will be under his control."

Allynae took the crystal and cradled it in his hands. Its power prickled up his arms. He handed it to One Man. "You are a better guardian for this."

One Man held it to the light, smiled, and slipped it into a pouch at his waist. "As soon as Corvus finishes his patrol, we'll head out. Thank you again for the warning and the information."

Allynae leaned forward. "Before you go, Wolloh, please tell us about our children."

Wolloh's face softened. "All the children are at Shu Chenaro. For how long, I don't know. They are not safe as long as Nissasa is free. Your son, as you know, One Man, carries dual seeds of Carsilem. He is learning about his gifts, but he needs coaching if he is to attain his true potential." His gaze rested on Allynae. "As for the twins, they are well. Brie's talents are many. She, too, requires coaching. Ari remains in her Ira form. Her talents differ from her sister's, but are just as strong. It will be interesting to see how she proceeds. Their friend, Torgin, continues to surprise himself and everyone else. I like him."

Allynae's parched lips spread into a smile. The first, he realized, since his capture. "Thank you, Wolloh, for protecting them."

Wolloh eased his body from the chair. "I must return to the ranch. At dawn, Nissasa's troops will begin their attack. If they get too close, I will remove the children from harm's way. When WoNa is safe, join me there. A feathered eyebrow above an opaque eye pulled down, furrowing his forehead.

Moving more quickly than Allynae thought possible with his maimed leg, Wolloh crossed the tent, threw open the flap, and stepped out under the three moons of DerTah. Before anyone could say goodbye, he shifted and lifted into the air. His osprey body, graceful and unhindered by his Human disfigurement, soared upward, following the ascending path of the moons toward Shu Chenaro.

52

Myrrh

Karrew winged his way through the desert night to the Nervac Portal. He had been away too long. The length of the separation from Almiralyn was taking its toll. He understood her need to have him in DerTah, but his heartache grew more intense with each sun turning.

Skirting the RewFaaran camp, he swooped into the gateway. The power of the spinning vortex sped him through the dimensional tunnel and deposited him at its anchor point in the Dojanack Caverns. Two DeoNyte guards barred his way. He landed and croaked... "Karrew. I have a message for the Guardian."

A guard knelt and offered an arm. Karrew hopped on and tilted his head to show the single white feather at the base of his neck.

The DeoNyte stood up. "She's in her quarters."

Karrew flew along the tunnel that would take him to the woman he had protected since her infancy. At his approach, the curtain at the entrance to her quarters whipped aside. His heartbeat quickened. Almiralyn appeared. He landed on her arm, reveling in the beauty of her smile and the intense wonder of her presence.

"I have missed you." She stroked his breast feathers. "Did you find Allynae? Is he unharmed? How are the children?"

He flew to the back of a chair and flapped his wings. "So many questions!" He cawed and ruffled his neck feathers. "I just want to look at you."

She laughed. "I know, my dearest friend. I'm also longing for time together, but things move quickly.

He bobbed his head in agreement. "Allynae is safe." After a quick account of his rescue and Nichi's subsequent capture, he made his report on the whereabouts of the children and gave her a message from Wolloh. "Nissasa has stolen the Oracle Stone. Use Elcaro's Eye with great care."

"Gerolyn and Nomed arrived earlier and shared that piece of information. It explains the increase in Nissasa's power. Does WoNa still have her snake?"

"No. The kidnappers left it for dead. Nichi found it. One Man revived it."

"Then she is truly blind and more vulnerable than even Nissasa knows. If he gains control of her, it could have a catastrophic impact on The Unfolding. You must return to DerTah. Too much is at stake. You cannot remain here."

She ran her hand down his back and planted a kiss on his head. He cawed and ruffled his feathers. "Who supports you with One Man and Allynae in DerTah?"

"Nomed is here."

"The DiMensioner...here?"

"He is a man of great power, Karrew, and he pledged to protect Myrrh."

"You trust him?"

"Until he proves unworthy...which I doubt will occur. The Unfolding has worked its magic on him. I think you will like the changes. Now go." She pulled the curtain open.

Karrew fluffed his neck feathers. "Take care. I will return when I can."

Enlivened by his visit, he soared down the tunnel, shot past the two guards, and entered the portal. Dimensional time tugged at his feathers. He shot from the vortex into the light of the three moons of DerTah.

Far from the Dojanack Caverns near the Demrach Gateway in the Terces Wood, Stee, the emerald Pentharian, crept through the forest in panther form. Kieel had reported that a traitor called Stich headed his way. Jeet also sent word. He had downed one rebel. Two remained at large, and a man guarded the portal.

Mondago's soldiers crept closer, but time was running out. If one traitor made it into the vortex, Nissasa would know Mondago still lived and had gained access to his plans.

Quiet breathing and the odor of sweat warned Stee of a Human nearby. His nostrils flared as he swung his head toward the scent. Directly in front of him, the man called Stich crouched behind large-leafed ferns. Lorsedi's loyal soldier stood guard a few paces away. Stich ducked beneath a low branch and skulked closer to his prey.

Stee shifted to bat and darted after him. A tiny claw snagged on a thread of the man's uniform jacket, left it struggling to get free. Stich shook like a dog, dropped to the ground, and rolled on his back. Stee's panther form heaved him into the air with powerful paws. Shifting to a dragonfly, he shot upwards. Stich slammed into a stump and clambered upright, searching the woods for his adversary. He gave a growl, loped towards the gateway, and slouched down nearer to Lorsedi's man. With a quick look over his shoulder, he dodged around a tree and lunged. Lorsedi's soldier went down. With the help of the second traitor, he pinned the man to the ground. Well-placed kicks rendered the loyal man unconscious.

Stich yanked his comrade off the ground and pushed him toward the vortex. The man stumbled, slapped at something on his neck, and slumped to the ground. Stich took one frantic look around the clearing, raced for the portal, and jumped.

Stee shifted again to a panther and leapt after him into the vortex. Color streaked past. The destination point blazed brighter. Stich flailed in front of it. Stee tensed for the exit and landed just short of the scrambling traitor. Crouched for the kill, the panther attacked. The man beneath him gave a terrified cry. Stee silenced him with a paw to the head and teeth filled with venom, sinking into his neck.

A shout warned of company. In his natural form, he slung Stich over his shoulder and leapt into the portal. With luck, the sand covering his emerald-scaled lower body had provided enough camouflage to confuse whoever followed.

When he hit the ground in the clearing in the Terces Wood, armed soldiers circled the portal. Their expressions and their weapons aimed at his chest told him they did not know that the Pentharian mercenaries helped in the battle to protect Myrrh.

Grantese Tesilend pushed his way through the ranks. "You were with Mondago."

"I am called Stee. My allegiance is to the Guardian of Myrrh. This man fought for Nissasa Rattori."

The soldier Stich had tackled rested with his back against a tree. He cleared his throat. "I saw him follow Stich into the portal."

Behind Stee, the vortex began to spin. Two soldiers pulled him into the trees. He laid Stich on the ground and crouched between them. Their comrades melted into hiding, leaving the clearing empty and silent. The spin in the vortex sped up. Four soldiers leapt free of the portal and assumed a defensive stance.

Lorsedi's men stepped from the trees, weapons aimed and ready. Soldier faced soldier, neither group willing to take the first step in a battle that could kill a comrade. The tension eased as the highest ranking of the new arrivals placed his weapon on the ground and straightened. His companions followed his lead.

The ranking officer stepped forward. "We are here to see Tinpaca Mondago. If you are his enemies, kill us now. If you are loyal to Lorsedi, take us to the Tinpaca."

Tesilend addressed the leader. "I am Grantese Tesilend. Come with us peacefully and meet with Mondago."

The four nodded their agreement. Mondago's men gathered up their firearms and prepared to escort them to camp.

Stee moved into the clearing. "Grantese Tesilend, may I speak?"

The Grantese waved him forward.

"Besides the man in custody, four unconscious traitors lie in the woods.

The man who escaped through the portal is dead. I am sorry. I could not leave him alive to tell Nissasa that Mondago lives."

Tesilend dispatched two men to bring the traitors to camp. Two more stood guard at the portal. He returned his attention to Stee. "You'd better come with us, but not in your natural form." He turned to his men. "Until Mondago gives the word, no one here has ever seen a Pentharian. Am I clear?"

A chorused "yes, sir" confirmed his order, and then they were on the move. Stee shifted to a dragonfly and landed on Tesilend's shoulder. *Life is a gift.*

Almiralyn splashed water on her face and ran a brush through her hair. With deft fingers, she wove its length into a single, thick braid. Small, uncomplicated actions always refreshed her, and right now she needed to revitalize her energy and her brain. A bowl of fruit by her bed caught her eye. She picked up a piece, settled in a chair, and savored the sweet, tangy taste as she reviewed both the discussion in Yookotay's council chamber and Karrew's news.

Spending time with her personal guardian had given her a moment's respite from her worries. She sighed and relished another sweet bite. *I wish you could have stayed with me, Karrew, but you're needed in DerTah more than I need you here.*

WoNa's capture worried her more than she cared to admit. Nissasa's theft of the Oracle Stone compounded the seriousness of the situation in Myrrh and DerTah. *The sooner the Atrilaasu Oracle is rescued, the better. Regaining control of the Stone will be more difficult. Nissasa will not let it out of his sight.*

Gratitude for Allynae's rescue had left her light-headed with relief. Nichi's capture by the LaTiru anchored her thoughts in the present. *We cannot trust the LaTiru to keep their word. For them, sacrifice is an addiction. If their lust for blood takes over...* She refused to think about that possibility. It made her wonder at the workings of the Human mind and whether The Unfolding could shift humanity's killing mania.

The exchange of information at the round table had been fruitful.

Tinpaca Mondago requested via Voer that Jordett take his adjutant's place. The Major and Yuin departed immediately after the meeting. Yuin planned to join Jeet at the Demrach Portal; Stee would act as personal guard and advisor to Mondago and Jordett. After the meeting, Voer and Gerolyn left via the Nervac Portal to report to Lorsedi in DerTah.

She chewed another bite of her pommaletta. *Today's biggest surprise... Nomed wishes to remain with me to help defend Myrrh. The Unfolding works in mysterious ways. Now...how to deal with Wilith Whalend?* She swallowed and stared beyond the half-eaten pommaletta. *His inability to shift makes him a liability. As much as he wants to deliver Nissasa's message to Torgin, getting him there creates problems for which I have no solutions. Until Lorsedi captures and holds the desert portal, I can't send Wilith to DerTah.*

In the middle of the meeting, Zugo hurried into the chamber. Nissasa had found Elcaro's Eye. Since shutting it down would leave her blind again, she and Nomed planned to go to Veersuni. Between them, she felt certain, they could set up an energy field that would obscure the Eye from outsiders.

After the last delicious mouthful of fruit, she drank cool mountain water from her obsidian chalice and teleported to the Council Chamber. Nomed, there and ready to leave for Veersuni, met her with a smile. They spoke with Yookotay and left. The hidden door ushered them onto the stairway of Retu Erath.

Almiralyn gazed into the dark cavern. "I suggest we fly."

Nomed looked down at her. "I have not yet passed the test of Tennisca. Will the ancients allow me to fly?"

"I believe you should make the journey on foot, Seyes. I will be at the bottom to welcome you to Canedari."

"What if..."

She smiled. "You won't fail. I'll see you at the bottom." Stepping onto the stairs, she shifted, her heart filled with the delight of flying.

Surprised by how easily they had developed a cordial relationship, Nomed watched her white form fade into the darkness. The small boy in him wanted to please her; the man that he had become wanted her to respect him. He shoved the thoughts away and began his descent down the stairway of ReTu Erath.

The quiet of the cavern, which stifled the sounds of his breathing and heartbeat, magnified the slap of his footsteps on stone. A gentle breeze cooled his cheeks. He was eleven again, standing in front of the mirror into Myrrh. When he cut his cheek, his world had become a muted and colorless place.

Whispering voices called him from that other time and sang him a song of beauty and wonder. His mother's voice joined the ancients. She sang to him of love and gentleness. She apologized for her inability to protect him from his father's rage. 'I love you, Davin.' Her last words echoed in his heart long after the sound faded into the depths of the Cavern of Tennisca.

The whispered voices stilled. The air grew rich with the scents of life, the feel of his breath, and the profound resonance of the galaxies. Last, as though a theater curtain opened, vibrant color flooded his senses. Astonishment and wonder propelled him down the stairs. The double doors stood open. Almiralyn waited by the entrance to the Hall of Priestesses.

She held out her hands. "I see your triumph in your face."

He squeezed them and smiled. "How could I have forgotten about color and smell and the feel of life's pulsing energy?"

"It is enough, Seyes, that you have remembered *now*. Come. I will show you something of great beauty."

He followed her through the door at the end of the hall. The elegance of the Reading Room left him breathless. "I only remember this in muted shades of gray."

She led him to a second door and ushered him through. "This is Veersuni."

He scanned the space—absorbed the splendor of the stained-glass window that covered the entire breadth of one wall, the exquisite color of the velvet curtains surrounding three sides of the room, and the two young DeoNytes who stood guard by an alabaster fountain. Their smiles for Almiralyn transformed into wariness with his entrance. Elae, the DeoNyte priestess, observed him with thoughtful interest. Yookotay's young son, Zugo, glowered.

Nomed withdrew a gold and sapphire pendant from his pocket. "I believe this belongs to you, Zugo. I don't expect forgiveness, but I apologize for my previous behavior."

Zugo's expression remained neutral as he accepted the pendant and cupped his hands around it. "Thank you, sir."

A radiant smile brightened Elae's serious face. "We are glad to have you on our side, Seyes Nomed."

Almiralyn gestured toward the door. Elae and Zugo slipped away, leaving him to watch as she waved a hand in front of the spectacular window. The patterned colors fled the glass to hover behind them in front of the curtains. In their framed spaces, the night sky stretched into the expansive magnificence of the Inner Universe. The clarity of his recovered sight filled him with astonishment as he stared, spellbound at its beauty.

He turned to Elcaro's Eye. The simple elegance of the fountain reached out to him. Slow, measured steps carried him around it. His newly awakened senses assimilated the alabaster detail of the carved statue kneeling on its rim, the smoothness of the satiny bowl, and the ivy weaving its way up the pedestal. Drops from the statue's hands created a calming sound that sang in his heart.

Almiralyn drew him back to observe the effect of the fountain's white alabaster against the vastness of space. Finally, she spoke. "We have work to do."

He closed his eyes and inhaled a deep breath. When he opened them, he smiled his crooked smile. "Thank you, Almiralyn, for your willingness to give me a chance. Where do we begin?"

A clap of her hands sent the hovering color flowing back to the window. A new picture emerged...Old Earth hung in the sky, soaking up the light of its solitary moon. She smiled. "We begin at the beginning of things."

With one hand in Almiralyn's and one hand on the alabaster rim, he bowed his head. *I, Seyes Nomed, DiMensioner od DerTah, share in the creation of shields to protect the fountain Elcaro's Eye and the last remnant of Earth.* He peeked at Almiralyn's profile and smiled to himself. *I have come full circle.*

53
DerTah

One Man lay on a cot in Narrtep's tent. Allynae had curled up on the floor and fallen asleep soon after Wolloh's departure. The rest would do him good. His experience with the LaTiru had drained him. As events sped toward a conclusion, he needed all his faculties and energy.

Narrtep had gone to confer with the Atrilaasu in their hiding place beneath the outcropping. He had decided WoNa would want him to remain with their people. One Man agreed.

The tent flap rustled aside. A splash of moonlight illuminated Corvus; the closing flap erased it and left him in shadow. One Man gave him a moment to adjust to the dark interior before he patted a cushion next to his cot.

"What did you discover on your patrol?"

Corvus shoved his hood back and settled on the cushion. "The LaTiru's camp is south of here. Nissasa and the Sebborr are east. Giduss' Fire ConDra guard their camp. Wards surround WoNa under the plateau. We have a choice to make. The third moon has reached the western horizon. Soon the sun's light will brighten the land. We must strike now or wait for nightfall."

Allynae's voice penetrated the dim interior of the tent. "Wolloh paid us a visit." Shuffling sounds announced he was up and fully awake. A cushion landed on the ground by the cot and whooshed under his weight. "Based on his information and your patrol, I suggest we go now. We don't want to give Nissasa the opportunity to wake her."

One Man withdrew the crystal Wolloh had given them and handed it to Corvus. While he studied it, Allynae briefed him on the Fire ConDra.

Corvus held the crystal to his forehead. "Like all Evolsefil crystals, it is powerful." It hovered above his hand, floated to One Man, and landed on his palm.

Allynae shook his head. "Telekinesis...not in my skill set, I'm afraid. As much as Almiralyn would like me to believe that I am her equal..." He shrugged.

Corvus gave him a sidelong glance. "Your gifts are equal, Alli, simply different."

One Man curled his fingers around the crystal. "Did you locate the entrance to the caves under the plateau?"

"I did. There are no wards. Two soldiers guard it."

Allynae frowned. "How do we deal with guards without raising an alarm?"

Corvus loosened the top two ties on his kcalo. "I subdued a guard at the outskirts of the camp and 'borrowed' his uniform. Once we're past the Fire ConDra, I'll change my appearance to resemble his. With luck, I can deal with the other guards without causing a commotion."

"And if they catch on?" Allynae unwrapped the rags from his injured feet.

One Man tossed him a pair of soft leather boots. "One step at a time. We'd better go."

He pulled them on, stood up, and walked gingerly around the tent. "Narrtep was right. The boots help. The pain is manageable. He told me they're tough. Drango, I think he said." He gave a brisk salute. "Thank you,

Narrtep." He faced Corvus. "I'm ready to go. What happens once we find WoNa?"

Corvus pushed the tent flap aside and made a cautious inspection of the oasis. "We'll know when the time comes. All clear." He shifted to raven and shot upward, banking to the East. Allynae made the shift to hawk and followed.

One Man examined the crystal one last time and stowed it in his pouch. Shifting, he soared into the late-night sky. Their challenge was formidable. He prayed the desert spirits would protect them.

Wolloh swooped into his inner garden and shifted from osprey to Human. Urgency tempted him to push his crippled leg faster; prudence kept his pace unhurried. Stebben met him in his sitting room. "You have visitors, sir."

"I know. Gerolyn has returned with a Pentharian."

"The Pentharian's name is Voer. They have information for the Largeen Joram."

"Bring them to me and fetch Lorsedi. Nissasa's men are stirring. No teleporting and no telepathy. Omudi and Thaer are most likely monitoring our every move."

Stebben withdrew. A short time later, the panel by the fireplace slid open. He ushered Gerolyn and Voer into the room and left. The panel clicked shut.

Wolloh remained sitting. "I would rise to greet you, but I must conserve my strength. Good to see you, Gerolyn. Welcome to DerTah, Voer. I am most glad to have a second Pentharian in our ranks. Battle is imminent."

Voer made the ritual bow of his people. "I am honored to meet the High DiMensioner od DerTah."

As he straightened, the panel by the fireplace reopened. TheLise preceded Stebben into the room, followed by Lorsedi and Tinpaca Granier. Lorsedi's face softened at the sight of Gerolyn and then shaped the masked efficiency of his military training. "This is Tinpaca Granier. I have asked him to join us. I hear trouble heads this way and that you have important information for me."

Wolloh spoke from his chair. "Gerolyn, please make introductions, and then I want everyone to join me."

"TheLise, Dreelas of Trinuge, may I present Voer, the leader of Almiralyn's Pentharian?"

TheLise held out a hand, palm up, upon which Voer placed his. "Welcome to DerTah, Voer."

The sapphire Pentharian removed his hand and bowed. "Thank you. I have always wanted to visit your home."

With a graceful motion of her hand, Gerolyn shifted focus to the Largeen Joram. "Lorsedi...Voer. He has a message to you from Tinpaca Mondago."

Lorsedi eyed the Pentharian with interest. "I am eager to hear your report."

When everyone had taken their place in the chairs Stebben had arranged, Wolloh shared a truncated version of his meeting with Allynae and One Man. "They are, as we speak, preparing to rescue WoNa."

"Are they capable of succeeding?" Lorsedi's tone was mild.

Wolloh angled his uninjured profile toward him. "There are none better. Corvus will join them. One Man is a man of many talents and Allynae is Almiralyn's brother."

"I understand he chooses not to embrace his training in DiMensionery."

Gerolyn's expression held the hint of a smile. "He has set aside his bias to help protect his daughters and to support our cause."

Wolloh added a PostScript to her statement. "Although his power differs from Almiralyn's, it is something to be reckoned with. He will serve us well. I have one more thing to add before Voer makes his report. Nissasa's troops are preparing to advance in this direction. They are one, perhaps two chronometer circles away. Stebben's contacts will let us know when they are on the move."

Lorsedi's face grew hard. "My men are in position and ready."

Wolloh picked up his cane and placed the tip firmly on the floor. "Voer, please make your report."

Voer allowed himself a moment to examine the members of the small group. "I would like to suggest that we include Yaro in this meeting. If he is to help, he needs to be part of the discussion."

"Are there any objections?" Wolloh's hazel eye glinted as he scanned the group.

When none were forthcoming, he dispatched Stebben to bring Yaro to the sitting room. Refreshments laid out on a table by the window prior to the meeting provided a welcome respite from talk of war. Gerolyn and Lorsedi moved apart. Granier sipped a cup of tea and perused the bookshelves. Wolloh leaned back and closed his eyes.

Voer noted the signs of fatigue in the tremor in the High DiMensioner's clawed hand and the crescents of smudged color under his eyes. He poured a cup of tea, put a few tasty tidbits on a plate, and set them down on the table next to his chair. "I've brought you a snack, Wolloh."

"Thank you, Voer. I am conserving my energy for what's coming." He picked up his cup and sipped. "It is good that Yaro joins us. I believe you have news—"

The panel opening interrupted. Voer greeted Yaro with a nod and a hand to his heart.

Wolloh set down his cup. "Thank you for joining us, Yaro. Please help yourself to refreshments, and then we need to continue our meeting."

When everyone had returned to his seat, Voer introduced his fellow Pentharian to Gerolyn and Granier. At a nod from Wolloh, he described the assassins' attempt on Mondago's life and what followed.

"Cantruto has created difficulties in the past." Lorsedi's brows bridged. "He is a stubborn man. How did you entice him to provide information?"

"Once we broke one of his younger men and threatened to send Cantruto to you for questioning, he talked." Voer paused and looked at Lorsedi. "Nissasa's goals are to take over DerTah, Thera and Myrrh, and RewFaar. With the Prima Crystal and the fountain in his possession and Wolloh, Almiralyn, and, you, Lorsedi, neutralized, he's certain he can do this and then gain control of the entire solar system. I have a list of traitors from Mondago. It includes soldiers in his platoon, the men in your regiment here, and those on RewFaar. We are certain there are others." He handed over a courier's folder with the list and other documents Mondago had felt were important.

Lorsedi withdrew the papers and selected the list. No emotion showed as he read. When he was done, he turned to Granier. "I appreciate your loyalty. Nissasa must have been hard to withstand."

"He did not approach me, sir. My allegiance to you is common knowledge."

"And did you know of his treachery?"

"There were vague rumors when you and Nissasa arrived at the ranch, but nothing I could substantiate. The talk stopped almost as fast as it began. I would have alerted you without delay, sir, if I had possessed any proof."

"Are you aware of who is loyal to me?"

"I know who supports you, but not who remains neutral or sides with Nissasa, sir."

"One more thing. I understand you were an ungracious guest when you first arrived at Shu Chenaro."

Granier colored. "I was, sir." He turned to Wolloh. "There is no excuse for my lack of courtesy, High DiMensioner. You intimidated me, and I responded by behaving like a boy. If there is a way, I can make amends..."

"I accept your apology. Remain steadfast in your loyalty, Granier. We need good men. Lorsedi, what is your first move?"

The Largeen Joram outlined a plan for gathering up Nissasa's supporters, one that would allow no one to slip away to sound a warning. When his instructions were complete, Stebben and Granier left via the hidden passage to carry out his orders.

Voer waited until the panel slid shut and then continued his report. "You need to be aware of one more problem. Nissasa has taken over the Five Towers in Idronatti and put the Five Fathers under lock and key. He will kill them one at a time unless Torgin Whalend returns to Thera with the Compass of Ostradio. And if that isn't enough to bring Torgin running back, they have kidnapped Coala Renn Whalend, his mother. She is being held somewhere on DerTah."

Voer observed Yaro's face change from interest to controlled anger. As Torgin's heart brother, he must explain to Torgin that even though his mother was at risk, he could not trade the compass for her life.

Ira squirmed in his chair. Ever since his arrival at Shu Chenaro, he and his friends had remained hidden in Wolloh's secret study or rooms near to it off the underground passage. *I hate not knowing what's happening. And I really hate feeling like a prisoner.* He changed position again and grimaced. Although no one said anything, he knew his friends felt the same. Esán paced one direction, rubbed the recent growth of hair on his head, and tromped back across the room. Brie flipped through a book without stopping to read. Desirol had joined them and apologized for his behavior at the ruins. Now he sat tapping his fingers on the arm of his chair. The only one unaffected was Torgin, who played a passage on his flute and then scribbled on paper Stebben had provided. Engrossed in his music, he seemed unaware of anything else. Ira watched him with growing envy. *Wish I had something like music to keep my mind busy.*

He propped his legs on a footstool and put his hands behind his head. *I would love to spend more time with Brie's grandfather. What an interesting man.* During their conversation, the strategies of warfare had intrigued him, and he wanted to learn more. He glanced across the room where Desirol rested—his face in repose so like his father's. *I wonder what it would be like to have Lorsedi as a father or a grandfather?*

When he thought about his own family, his father, he couldn't quite pin down his memories. He knew he had parents and a sister, but... *There it is... that feeling I've forgotten something important. What on Thera is it?*

Brie flipped through the pages of a book, her thoughts in turmoil. *I can't sense WoNa anywhere in the Desert of Fera Finnero. I feel like a part of me is missing.* She set the book aside and closed her eyes. The details of the DerTahan map etched in her memory from her Aunt Mira's book did not distract her from her distress. *I realize Wolloh banned telepathy, but...* With great care, she had made a subtle mental search. *WoNa, where on DerTah are you? Are you hurt? Please help me find you.*

Although she found no trace of the Oracle, she discovered her father and One Man on DerTah. *What are they doing here?* She opened her eyes and tracked Esán's restless pacing. *I think I'll wait to tell you until we're alone.*

Torgin's music penetrated her thoughts. The melody's dreamy quality made her smile. He glanced up, gave her a distracted nod, and submerged himself in the transcribing of notes to paper. Another musical passage, more dissonant this time, made him smile to himself. Finally, he put the stylus down, looking satisfied, and a bit bemused.

"Play for us, Torg." Esán plopped down on a chair. "We could use a few moments of beauty."

When he hesitated, Desirol added his plea. "I've never heard you play, Torgin. Please."

Torgin straightened his notes. "I'll play what I just composed. It's rough, but I believe it is a good beginning." Lifting the flute to his lips, he closed his eyes.

Like the blowing desert sand, notes flitted around the study. Allegro and light, with a quick repeated passage, it infused with sunshine and heat into the melody. Lower notes pushed the lightness away and burdened the air with a tremor of fear that ended in a series of high-pitched phrases. A transition to a fluid, rippling adagio, reminiscent of water and flight, filled the room with its beautiful refrain, trembled, and then skittered into a short repeat of the opening allegro before it finished, one note sliding into the other until the room was silent.

Brie's eyes glistened. "It's about the Water ConDria, isn't it?"

Puzzled, Torgin studied the flute in his hand. "I..." He gripped it tighter. "That wasn't what I wrote. I thought of you, and the piece took on a life of its own. While I played, I saw the Fire ConDra and you rising to meet it."

She crossed the room and hugged him. "It was so beautiful. Thank you."

"You're great, Torgin." Desirol grinned. "The melody you just played is unlike anything I've ever heard."

The panel slid aside, and Wolloh stepped into the room. Yaro ushered Gerolyn ahead of him.

The High DiMensioner's face was grim. "Brielle, you must come with me. Stebben will disperse our energy trail."

An image flashing through her mind made her hurry to his side. She linked her arm through his. "I'm ready."

Room and friends flashed from sight, replaced by red dunes caught in the diminishing dimness of the night's last moments.

54
DerTah

In bird form, Corvus, Allynae, and One Man soared in opposite directions above Nissasa's camp, searching the landscape for any signs of Fire ConDra. Although Corvus had dealt with the great flaming beasts in the daylight, he'd never encountered one at night. Swooping lower, he caught an updraft slightly warmer than the chilly night air and continued his search. Three more places at the perimeter of Nissasa's camp where a tepid temperature warmed the air suggested a ConDra kept watch.

A wide arc carried him to the rendezvous point he and his comrades had agreed upon earlier. Allynae squatted at the northwestern side of the plateau. Only the most discerning eye would pick out the tented-darkness of his kcalo. Corvus materialized beside him. "Found four possible ConDra. You?"

Allynae reached out of shadow and sketched the plateau in a patch of moonlit sand. He pointed at three spots. Corvus nodded, showed the fourth, and drew a circle to represent the cave entrance.

The softest whoosh announced One Man's return. He crouched by the sketch and added one more X to the map. "This ConDra roves the entire area. It sticks to the same pattern. He pointed to a place at the western edge of the plateau. Once it passes here, we can slip through. There are soldiers and Sebborr patrolling the inner perimeter, so we'll need to stay alert." He shed his kcalo and straightened his RewFaaran uniform.

One Man handed him the crystal. "This will help you find WoNa's prison. She knows you, so you take the lead. Allynae and I will be close by."

Concern registered on Allynae's face. "I'm not sure I can shape anything but the hawk. It's been a long time..."

Corvus shoved the crystal deep in his pocket. "You will do what must be done, Alli." He pointed at the white moon hanging overhead, halfway to full. It had begun its descent toward the western horizon. "Time is running out." He shifted, flew a low trajectory around the end of the plateau, and landed by a clump of desert brush in bird form. Two hawks landed nearby. A ConDra's night-cooled heat passed overhead. When Corvus was sure it was gone, he shifted to Human form and made a cautious approach to the encampment.

His circuitous route to the cave entrance beneath the plateau gave him an opportunity to learn the layout of the camp and find Nissasa's headquarters. No sign of Dahe alerted his senses. Careful to keep his mind focused on the innocuous thoughts of a soldier taking an evening walk, he ambled by the camp's headquarters and paused behind a tent pitched a short distance away.

He could feel Nissasa and realized with a jolt the breadth of his power. What surprised him the most, however, was the subtle tremor within it. Something made it unstable. He filed the information away for later. Moving at a leisurely pace, he circled the next several tents and stopped to observe the cave entrance.

The tingling touch of a mind probe held him motionless. Only the moon and the heavens and the sudden feeling of discomfort as a Fire ConDra flew overhead infused his mind with images. When the tingling ceased, he dulled his thoughts and strolled back the way he had come. Once beyond Nissasa's tent, he veered toward the plateau's vertical rise and obscured his thoughts with a sense of deep slumber.

A Sebborr sauntered in his direction. Corvus adjusted the angle of his hat, nodded as the man passed by, and moseyed past the next tent. Surveying the area around the entrance to the caves, he noted two hawks perched on a parched, barren bush near the edge at the top of the plateau. Tents, pitched to create a wide semi-circled barrier, left an open space between them and the rise of the plateau. They would see anyone trying to approach.

He was straight across from the cave entrance when a young soldier marched up to the guards. A short, agitated conversation ensued. One guard motioned him forward. He tilted his brim down and joined them.

"Need you to stand guard until I get back. Won't be long." The guard and the other soldier hurried back through the camp.

Corvus exchanged a curious glance with the remaining guard. "What's all the fuss about?"

"Something about an intruder." The guard shrugged. "Rattori is pretty paranoid."

"I've noticed." Corvus jerked his thumb toward the caves. "Anyone looked in there lately?"

"She hasn't moved a muscle since they brought her here. Go check on her."

"Think I will. Wouldn't want anything to happen to her on my watch." Corvus ambled into a roughed-out tunnel, ending with piles of rubble on either side of a man-made cave. Nissasa's wards shimmered in front of the opening. Beyond them, an oil lamp glowed beside a mat on the ground. WoNa lay unmoving, her arms crossed over her chest like a body prepared for burial.

Using Wolloh's crystal to create an opening in the wards, he stepped through, and sealed them behind him. He knelt beside the Oracle and placed the crystal on her forehead. She did not respond. Stasis continued to hold her in its grip.

The sound of scuffling and the thump of fists against flesh shouted a warning. Nissasa's wards began to sing. With the crystal above his head, he placed a hand on WoNa's arm and teleported to the northwestern side of the plateau.

One Man stepped from the shadows. "Nissasa is right behind us.

Another mass teleport will bring him down our necks faster than a bee to nectar."

Corvus noted a tear in his kcalo. "A fight?"

"A diversion." He knelt and placed WoNa's snake on her chest. It thrust its head forward and flipped its tail to form a circle around her heart.

Corvus placed the crystal on her forehead. A breath inflated her chest. The saffron and glacier eyes flew open. The snake hissed. Removing the crystal from her head, he laid it within the snake's circled length.

A hawk landed and shifted. Allynae joined them, rubbing his cheek where a bruise had already begun to show. "Sorry for the commotion, but at least we kept them busy for a time. The Fire ConDra are massing, and the sun is close to the horizon. We have to move."

The snake slithered into the neck of WoNa's kcalo. She wrapped her fingers around the crystal.

"WoNa, it's me...Corvus." He put an arm around her and helped her to sitting. "Can you shift?"

She shook her head, tucked the crystal in a small drango skin medicine pouch on a thong around her neck, and grasped his hand. "Help me stand."

Corvus and One Man helped her as a chorus of fluttering flames warned of the Fire ConDra's rising. A shrieked call announced preparation for flight.

Allynae sensed the chaotic bustle of men on the opposite side of the plateau. He searched the sky, hoping the Fire ConDra hadn't discovered their position. A glow of wavering light coloring the southeastern side of the plateau spurred him into action.

"Gotta hurry." He reported his findings. "If WoNa can't shift, what do we do?"

WoNa held out a hand. "Come to me, brother of Almiralyn. Your daughters and I are blood-bonded. Their blood pulsing in my veins ties me to you. Corvus and One Man will distract the soldiers. And you, my friend, will carry me home." She lifted her arms to the sky, where a swath of stars sprinkled the heavens with specks of diamond light.

Allynae gasped as stars flew earthward, swirled around him, and engulfed him in a current of cool, pristine air. His body trembled and shifted. He shook a midnight mane from moonlit eyes and flicked his haunches with a midnight tail. Star-spangled hooves pawed the ground as One Man lifted WoNa onto his back. She grasped his mane and whispered his name. "Starfire!"

A stallion's power sent him racing across the sand. A canyon yawned wide a short distance ahead. The Human part of his mind balked, almost panicked. WoNa urged him faster. He hit the lip and leapt forward. Night dark wings unfurled. Tremendous power carried him into the star-studded sky. WoNa's voice in his head sent him soaring over the desert after the white moon, where it slid below the horizon.

A rush of air and the flickering of pale flames surrounded them. Three Fire ConDra, one on each side and one overhead, tried to force horse and rider to land. Allynae pressed his powerful wings against the air, striving to put distance between WoNa and the ConDra's fire. The faint beginnings of heat enveloped them in a blur of colors—golds and oranges, blues and greens. WoNa's knees squeezed his sides. His wings pressed harder, sending them through the haze of flames into the first faint light of morning.

"Starfire, faster." Like a blast of fuel, her command sent him soaring higher, his mighty wings pushing the air, his legs pumping a galloped path. A wafting inferno of flames licked his flanks and tangled in the midnight strands of his tail. He raced the sun across the sky, the heat of the ConDra's fire increasing as the moon slipped lower and the sun's rays flared golden along the eastern horizon.

On his back, WoNa's voice filled the pale morning sky. "Water ConDria, rise!"

Silver glistened against the shadowed land below. Liquid wings fanned the sand into a small tornado as the ConDria lifted skyward. It arced above them, a sparkling gem in the first bright rays of morning. A song burst from its throat. A Fire ConDra roared a response and swooped to meet it. Shimmering water wings opened to receive the blazing beast. The air filled with the crackle and hiss of water against flame. Blackened bones rained from the sky.

Allynae registered the sound and the sight. His shifted form raced onward, the blaze of a Fire ConDra's heat searing his sides as the sun topped the horizon line. Its flaming partner banked away, streaking ahead of him toward its target.

Again, the ConDria soared to meet its fiery adversary. The song from its throat made the air tremble. The glistening body absorbed the Fire ConDra's blazing red hue. Like partners, they danced a duet, circling and swooping around him and his rider. The ConDra's lava tongue splattered the air with specks of blistering heat that hit the ConDria and sizzled into nothing as it closed the gap with a sudden thrust of liquid wings. Howling its rage, the second Fire ConDra fled.

The third lashed its tongue along his horse's flank before it arced away into the rising sun. Starfire's body spasmed in response to the searing heat, then calmed as the ConDria's wing tip swept the pain away.

Ahead of them, the lake at Eissua gleamed. Relief flooded Allynae's Human mind. His massive wings carried him to the shore of the lake near the outcropping. He landed, tossed his star-speckled head, and snorted the heat from his nostrils. WoNa slid to the ground and felt her way along his side until she faced him. "Thank you, Starfire." She blew a soft breath that tickled his nose and flitted over the surface of his horse's body.

Conscious of his human feet planted firmly on the desert sand, Allynae tried to blink the stars from his eyes. He heard a woman's voice. "Allynae, you're back." He strained to gather the pieces of himself into an order he recognized. The hiss of a snake and the flick of its tongue on his forehead cleared his vision. He searched the dome of soft morning light. "I saw a ConDra made of water. It saved us." His voice sounded strange to his Human ears.

An osprey soared over the oasis and landed atop a tall palm. A melody of fluid notes filled Allynae's heart. The ConDria crested the top of the dunes. Its glistening wings rained sparkling drops of water over the oasis. For a brief instant, it hovered above Eissua, and then joined the departing osprey and disappeared behind the sand dunes of DerTah.

Allynae's heart, emptied of song, ached.

WoNa moved beside him. "You will be with your daughter soon."

He sucked in a breath. "That was *Brielle*?"

A hawk swooped over the palms and landed next to WoNa. One Man appeared and touched her arm. "You must hide WoNadahem Mardree. Sebborr ride this way."

"And what about us?" Allynae couldn't contain a shiver.

Corvus appeared from a stand of palm trees. "You and One Man must go to Shu Chenaro. I will take WoNa to safety and bring Nichi back to her people. I'll join you when I can."

Allynae gathered the Oracle's hands in his. "Thank you, WoNa, for a ride I will never forget."

"Starfire is a part of you, brother of Almiralyn, or I could not have called him forth."

"Do you mean I can shape him again?"

She smiled. "Time is the revealer of all things. You must go."

Awash with the wonder of a creature created from moonlight and stars, Allynae watched Corvus guide her through an opening in the outcropping. With a horse-like shake of his head, he shaped a hawk and soared after One Man.

The dramatic departure of Brie and Wolloh left Torgin pondering his recent adventures. Those on Myrrh seemed like nothing compared to those on DerTah. He sorted his latest compositions into piles, and, grinning, put them in a folder, and slid the flute into its case. Composing always made him happy.

He glanced up to find Yaro looking down at him, his face grim. "We need to talk, Torgin. I have disturbing news. I can tell you alone, and then we can share it with your friends. Or they can join us, and you can hear it with their support."

"Why do I need their support?"

"Because what I have to say won't be easy to hear."

The good mood fled. A tinge of his old trepidation flared. "I'd rather you told me first."

At a signal from Yaro, Gerolyn herded Ira, Esán, and Desirol beyond the panel. Yaro shoved his braids away from his face and sat down. "Voer is here in DerTah. He brought a message to you from your father."

"M-m-y father. How did he speak to my father?"

"He came to Myrrh to ask Almiralyn to help find you."

"*Father?* In Myrrh?" Confusion fogged his brain. He shook his head.

"My father doesn't even believe in Myrrh. What made him remember it? How did he get there?"

"Your father remembers, and he is there now." Yaro's expression hardened. "Nissasa's men have taken over the Five Towers and have imprisoned the Five Fathers. They sent him to find you. Unless you return to The City and give them the Compass of Ostradio, they will kill the Fathers one-by-one."

Torgin heard without hearing. *The predicament of the Fathers is important, but there's something Yaro's not telling me.* "That's not all, is it?"

"No, Torgin. To make sure they get what they want, they have kidnapped your mother."

Air blasting from his lungs almost doubled him over. "M-m-mother! Nissasa has my mother?" The voice was his. The words were his. He wanted to yell, but they came out in a choked whisper. "I have to find her, Yaro. I have to go back to Idronatti."

"She's here in DerTah. Going back won't help her."

Torgin pulled the compass from beneath his shirt and removed the thong from around his neck. He forced himself to think, to be logical. *Fear will cloud my judgment. Mother's life is at stake. I have to use everything I've learned during the past few cycles.* The weight of the compass in his hand reminded him of the first time he held it—*when Almiralyn entrusted it to me.* He swallowed. The stringent taste of bile left its bitterness on his tongue. He hated what he saw in Yaro's face.

"You are going to tell me I cannot trade the compass for my mother."

Yaro's expression provided the answer.

"They won't let her go, even if I do. My father is in line to be the next Premier of Idronatti. They will keep her and me, if I go back, and use us to control him. Help me, Yaro. I do not know what to do." He dropped his head in his hands, hoping that when he looked up, the nightmare would be over.

55

Myrrh

Almiralyn stretched out on her bed, resting from the strain of shielding the fountain from enemy eyes. She and Nomed had encoded a list of specific individuals who could access Elcaro's Eye from DerTah through the shields: One Man, Allynae, Karrew, Wolloh, and Gerolyn. They would add WoNa after her rescue. An attempt by anyone else would shut the fountain down.

Nomed's power added to hers had surprised them both. Already, the personal changes he was making enhanced his skills. He had left Veersuni in an introspective mood. The Stairway of Retu Erath and his work with her had given him food for thought.

She stared at the glitter of quartz in the curve of the stone ceiling. *What to do next? I wish I were closer to the action.* Her concern forced her from the bed into a restless circuit of her quarters. *I could restore the cottage and stay there; then I'd be nearer the fight.* She pivoted and paced back the way she had come. *I'd also be vulnerable. I can't afford to put myself in harm's way. That would play right into Nissasa Rattori's hands. At least in the Dojanacks, I'm safe, and so are Sparrow and Merrilea.*

Her pacing ended with the rustling of her entryway curtain. The subjects of her final reverie greeted her with tentative smiles. "I was just thinking about the two of you." She motioned them inside. "I imagine you are as restless as I am."

"We are." Sparrow smiled, picked up a forest green pillow, and plopped down on the bench. "We realize we're safest here." She hugged the pillow to her chest. "But we're feeling out of touch. How are the children, Mira? What about Allynae and Jordett? Can you tell us anything?"

"Or show us in the fountain?" Eagerness filled Merrilea's expression.

"Neither of you has visited the Cavern of Tennisca. The ancient ones initiate all who enter. Are you willing to face your personal fears?"

"Isn't that what The Unfolding is about?" Sparrow smoothed her hair. "Coming to grips with who you are?"

"For those of us directly involved, that is part of it."

Merrilea looked thoughtful. "Life is unfolding in every moment, right? If walking the Stairway of Retu Erath helps, I'm all for it."

"So am I." Sparrow jumped up and tossed the pillow on the bench. "What do we have to do?"

Almiralyn laughed. "For everyone, it is different, Sparrow. I'll take you to Tennisca. I require a moment alone. I'll meet you at the Central Square."

After the women departed, she pondered the workings of The Unfolding...change and upheaval on all fronts. Settling into her chair, she allowed herself a few moments of quiet contemplation. *Taking Sparrow and Merrilea to see the fountain will be interesting. With luck, it will confirm WoNa's rescue and whether Nissasa's troops have attacked Shu Chenaro.* She narrowed her eyes. *I hope Elcaro's Eye will recognize our need to know and answer our questions. It is impossible to know what it will share.*

J ordett and Yuin arrived at Nemttachenn Tower via the Intersect. After conferring with Paisley and CheeTrann, Yuin shaped a vulture and carried the major to a clearing near the RewFaaran camp on Almiralyn's land. The ruby Pentharian then flew on to join Jeet at Demrach Gateway.

Jordett peered after him. *Wonder what kind of reception I'll get when I walk into camp?* He straightened his crumpled uniform jacket, adjusted his tie, and strode from the woods.

A RewFaaran soldier stepped into view. "Who goes there? Stop where you are."

Jordett complied. "Major Jordett of the Peoples Plan Protectors. The Guardian of Myrrh sent me. I'm here to see Tinpaca Mondago."

The soldier saluted. "This way, sir. We've been expecting you." He hurried between tents. "A Nyti girl and her dragonfly let us know you were on the way. The Tinpaca asked me to bring you straight to him." He stopped by a large tent. "Please remain here."

While he waited, Jordett examined his surroundings. He liked what he saw—soldiers at their posts, soldiers on patrol, and soldiers talking to each other with the quiet dignity of well-trained troops.

The tent flap flipped open. "Tinpaca Mondago will see you now." The soldier stepped aside and motioned Jordett to enter.

A stocky man with dark graying hair met him with an offered hand and a harried smile. "Good to meet you, Jordett. I have my hands full. The soldier who brought you here will escort you to your tent so you can settle in." He handed him a packet of papers. "Take a quick look through these. They'll help you familiarize yourself with RewFaaran protocol. When you're ready, come back here. Hopefully, things will have calmed down."

Jordett accepted the packet. "Thank you, sir. I'll let you get back to business." He exited the tent and fell in step with the soldier who had waited for him outside. "What's your name, soldier?"

"Tunet, sir." They stopped by a tent pitched a short distance from the Tinpaca's. "This is your quarters, sir. We were told you arrived with no belongings. You'll find a clean uniform and a kit on your cot. Can you relocate headquarters on your own?"

"I can. And thanks, Tunet."

"You're welcome, sir. We're glad to have you join us." He saluted and walked back the way he had come.

Jordett ducked into the tent. A cot, a collapsible washstand, and a camp chair were the only furnishings. A clean uniform lay on the cot with a fresh cigar and matches next to it. He picked up the cigar, sniffed, and smiled. *I've heard of these but never expected to hold one.* After washing away the dust and dirt, he changed clothes and perused the papers from the Tinpaca. They summarized the camp's resources: the number of men, available weapons, technology, etc., as well as an organizational chart and list of ranks for the RewFaaran military. Aware of how important his first impression on Mondago's men was, he committed the information to memory and headed back to headquarters.

His arrival at the tent coincided with the return of soldiers from Demrach Gateway. From the sidelines, he watched Mondago dispatch Nissasa's men to be placed under guard and interrogated and the one dead soldier to be prepared for burial. Last, he placed a guard on the four soldiers who had used the portal from DerTah. Finally, he invited Jordett and the Grantese who had been in charge of the returning soldiers to join him.

Once they were inside the tent, he made introductions. "Major Jordett... Grantese Tesilend. Jordett will act as my adjutant and Theran advisor."

Jordett offered his hand. "It's good to see you, Grantese."

Tesilend shook it. "I look forward to working with you, sir."

A dragonfly buzzed to a clear spot, and an emerald Pentharian materialized.

Mondago gave him a nod of recognition. "Tesilend, I see you've met Stee. He will also act as an advisor. I imagine the men are aware of Pentharian in Myrrh.

"I swore them to secrecy, sir." He shrugged. "You know how word travels here."

"I do. We'll deal with that soon. Jordett, what do you consider yourself?"

"A civilian consultant, unless you prefer otherwise. My allegiance is to The Guardian of Myrrh and to your service, Tinpaca."

Mondago picked up a stylus and tapped it on the tabletop. "I would like you to keep your rank and title. Your military status will be important to the troops. After Tesilend's report, I will introduce you to the platoon. Please, take a seat, gentlemen."

Chairs shuffled into place, and everyone settled but Stee, who remained standing beside the Tinpaca. Tesilend's report was succinct and clear. When it was complete, he ushered the top-ranking man of the four soldiers from DerTah into the tent.

"Your name, soldier?" Mondago watched him through narrowed eyes.

"Tranwar Dresutt, sir."

"You realize you put yourself and your comrades at risk by coming through that portal unless, of course, you are Nissasa's men and expected to capture it?"

"Sir, we are loyal to the Largeen Joram. Nissasa's men captured us and staked us out in the desert to die."

"And yet you are here?"

"You won't believe this, sir. I hardly believe it myself. A raven landed beside us and then this beautiful woman stood there. She waved her hands in the air and the wind began to howl. Sand started flying around the camp. While Nissasa's men were tying things down, she released us and hid us behind a dune near the portal. Then she disappeared."

"That's quite a story, soldier."

Jordett smiled. "If I may, sir?"

Mondago nodded.

"The woman was Gerolyn AsTar, the Guardian's emissary to DerTah. She told Almiralyn that she had rescued four soldiers at the portal destination point."

"Thank you, Major. Tranwar, what made you decide to use the portal?"

"We had heard there were Pentharian in the Guardian's service. When one came through the portal after a soldier we knew to be a traitor, we decided our best bet was to follow him when he entered the gateway with the body. Nissasa's men outnumbered us, sir. At least here, we can fight for the Largeen Joram."

"Thank you, Tranwar Dresutt. Wait outside." Mondago paused, watched him leave, and turned to Tesilend. "One of his men is in terrible shape. Take him to the infirmary. After you arrange for the others to relax and eat, post two men to monitor them. Let the rest take a break. I want a full platoon meeting at half the chron-circle."

When Tesilend had departed, Mondago picked up a cigar, rolled it between his thumb and finger, and inhaled the smell of tangy tobacco. "Nothing like a good cigar to stimulate one's thought process." He returned it to the box on the table. "Nissasa has control of the portal's destination point in DerTah. Jordett, I suggest we develop a plan of action. "Stee, please take a seat and tell us your version of the confrontation at the portal."

Jordett paid close attention to Stee and the Tinpaca. Mondago's intelligent questions gave him insight into the training he had received on RewFaar. Working with him would be an excellent learning experience.

When Stee had completed his report, Mondago sat back. "I believe these four men are loyal to the Largeen Joram. Thoughts?"

"I agree." Jordett glanced at the tent entrance. "I also think they may provide valuable information regarding the camp at the destination point. It seems important that we gain and maintain control at both ends of the portal."

The emerald Pentharian scooted his chair nearer to the table. "I agree on both counts. I also suggest we consider the situation in Idronatti."

Mondago looked at Jordett. "You're the expert on The City and Thera."

Jordett nodded. "The issues as I see them are as follows. Wilith Whalend is in line to be the next Premier of Idronatti. His term of office begins in two moon cycles. If his wife is a prisoner on DerTah and if Torgin returns to The City…" He paused. "I think the problem is self-explanatory. Almiralyn does not intend to send Wilith back to Idronatti. She has also sent word to Wolloh and Lorsedi that Torgin is to remain with them. That leaves the problem of the Five Fathers and regaining control of The City. We are the most logical ones to deal with that situation."

Tinpaca Mondago sighed. "I feared it would come to this. You realize we have only twenty men, including the four who just arrived. We also have traitors to guard." He tapped his box of cigars. "Wish we could get some reinforcements."

Jordett pushed his chair back and walked to the entrance. Anticipation hung in the tent. He knew the Tinpaca waited for him to speak. After taking the time to develop a concrete plan, he retraced his steps and rested his hands on the table. "I believe I may have a solution, sir."

After an insightful journey down the stairway of Retu Erath, Sparrow arrived in the Cave of Canedari first. She paused inside the double doors, her emotions a vibrant parade across her face.

Almiralyn watched her changing expressions and smiled to herself.

Finally, Sparrow sighed. "I faced Standin's death, my fear for the twins and Allynae, and the changes in my mother. The ancient ones whispered my name, Almiralyn. They told me to open my heart to the potential of serving. Do you know what they meant?"

Before she could answer, Merrilea strode into Canedari. Her gray-blue eyes overflowed with tears. She gave them a tremulous smile. "I didn't know what to expect. Voices whispered my name and Esán's. They shared that his destiny is greatness and that my job of caring for him is done. They even spoke of Jordett. I need to digest it all.

Almiralyn hugged each woman and smiled. "You have both passed the initiation of Retu Erath. Now, I have something to show you."

She led them down the Hall of Priestesses. Zugo met them at the Reading Room door and hurried them into Veersuni.

When they arrived beside Elcaro's Eye, the image on its surface held them mesmerized. Three Fire ConDra surrounded a winged horse and a rider with hair the color of fire. Eyes flaming and tongues licking the air, the ConDra chased them across the sky. A shimmering, silver ConDra-like creature composed of water rose from the desert floor. The watchers gasped and then cheered as the two remaining Fire ConDra fled. Finally, the stallion landed beside a sparkling lake. Folding its star-speckled wings, it raised moonlit eyes to the sky. The rider whispered a series of words and blew in its nostrils. Stars and sky fled back to the heavens, leaving Allynae standing lakeside at Eissua Oasis.

Sparrow gasped. "That's Alli! I didn't know. How did he…" She laughed and shook her head.

Almiralyn's eyes twinkled. "You realize, Sparrow, that Brielle is the Water ConDria of the Atrilaasu?"

"Oh my…" Sparrow shot her an incredulous look and gripped the rim of the fountain.

Merrilea put an arm around her shoulders. "Brielle is a ConDria and Allynae, who hates to shape shift, formed a horse from the night sky. You have quite a family."

Sparrow hugged her. "You do, too. It's hard to believe Alli did that."

Almiralyn smiled. "I believe my brother will return to Myrrh a changed man."

"Can we see if the fountain will show us Esán?" Merrilea looked hopeful.

"And Ira and Torgin?" Sparrow pleaded.

Almiralyn waved a hand above the water. A scene rose from its depths and settled. Esán waited for his friend to speak. Compassion filled his eyes. Across from him, Ira and a boy they did not know wore shocked expressions.

"Nissasa has your mother? How?" Ira demanded.

"His men kidnapped her." Torgin's voice was steady but bleak. A gold Pentharian rested a hand on his shoulder.

"At least Yaro is with him." Merrilea moved closer to Sparrow.

The scene blurred, and a new one formed. Soldiers crept across the sands of DerTah. Within their ranks, the Mindeco prowled. Wherever he went, soldiers cringed and moved away. The fountain zoomed in on the ugly, bear-like skull. The single eye filled the bowl. Reflected in its black depth was the glowing silhouette of a boy.

56
Der Tah

Brie and Wolloh landed on the outskirts of Shu Chenaro and teleported to the Raptor Center.

Stebben stepped from the shadows, his demeanor alert. "Nissasa's men approach the boundary between the desert and the ranch. They will be here sooner than expected."

A flurry of wings cut Wolloh's reply short. Two desert hawks swooped to a landing. Allynae and One Man materialized as their hawk talons touch the ground.

Brie threw her arms around her father. "You were so amazing, Father. I didn't know you could shape a winged horse."

A laugh shook his chest where her head rested. "I didn't know you could become a ConDria. Thank you for saving me."

She hugged him harder and turned in his arms so she could see One Man. "Thank you both for rescuing WoNa."

Wolloh cleared his throat. "If you have finished admiring one another, we have another crisis brewing." He told them about Voer's news.

"Nissasa has Torgin's mother?" Brie wished she had heard it wrong.

"He does. We have to decide what to do. Stebben, please make sure all is clear. Gentlemen and Brie, shield your minds. No telepathy."

Stebben slipped from the center and returned within a short time. He led them through the barn and between several outbuildings. The arena loomed ahead of them, opposite the ranch house. He sprinted ahead, crouched behind a group of taccus trees, and waved them forward. Before they could move, a group of RewFaaran soldiers marched around the corner of the arena and headed toward the barn. Pressing into what shade they could find, they remained rooted to the spot.

When the soldiers were beyond hearing, Wolloh took Brie by the hand. "You and I will stroll to the house. One Man and Allynae, please go with Stebben. We're too big a group to remain undetected. I don't want your presence discovered."

As the others slipped away, Wolloh looked down at her. "I believe an illusion is in order." He touched her forehead.

A soft breeze whispered around her. "What did you do?"

"Anyone who sees you will see someone who resembles your great-aunt." He drew her arm through his. "Shall we?" They walked into the brightness of morning. "Thank you for humoring an old man, my dear. A walk before the sun rises too high in the sky always invigorates me."

She smiled up at the disfigured face. "I love walking in the morning. And you are not old, Wolloh."

He opened a door to the inner garden and gave her an elegant bow. "Beauty before age, my dear."

Laughing, she stepped into the cool interior and followed him through the quiet halls to his study, where her father and One Man had just arrived.

Wolloh picked up his cane and stroked the crystal. The illusion faded and left Brie smiling at her father.

Allynae returned her smile. "Nice trick, Wolloh."

"Where's Esán?" One Man looked hopeful.

Wolloh leaned on his cane. "We must reunite you before we tackle the problems at hand. Allynae, I believe you should see Ira as well. Lorsedi's men have been alerted regarding Nissasa's troops, so we have some time. Of course, we don't want to keep Torgin waiting too long. He's struggling."

Brie hugged herself. *I can't imagine how I would feel if Nissasa kidnapped my mother.*

Esán waited for his father in the small room next to the library. "I can't believe my father is here on DerTah. I haven't seen him since Nomed kidnapped me on Myrrh." A series of quick mental vignettes filled him with emotion—learning that One Man was his father, the discovery that his father and Seyes Nomed were half-brothers, the vortex that carried him away from the father he had only just met...

A panel in the wall opened, framing the man of his memories. Two long strides closed the gap between them. "I knew you would come for me, Father. Welcome to DerTah."

One Man hugged him and then held him at arm's length. "You look good. Your hair is growing back, you have some color in your cheeks, and I even believe you're taller. The desert must agree with you."

"WoNa told me it is Thera that makes me ill. You rescued her?"

"She hides in a place the Sebborr do not know exists." He pulled up a chair.

Esán drew up a second one and sat down opposite him. "I can't believe you're here."

One Man studied him for a long moment. "I was afraid for a while that I might have lost you." A comfortable silence settled between them as they basked in the pleasure of being together. Finally, he sighed. "We had better make this time count, my son. The Unfolding has set a rapid pace for all of us, so we may not be together long."

Esán leaned forward and rested his forearms on his knees. "Tell me everything, Father. How did you rescue WoNa? How is Almiralyn? Have you seen Zugo? Is Evolsefil still safe in Nemttachenn Tower?"

Allynae and Brie talked non-stop until Wolloh appeared with Ira in tow. Before the High DiMensioner departed, he tapped the crystal knob on his cane. In the center of the room, Ira's male form faded and identical red-haired twins stared at one another.

"Oh!" Brie laughed softly. "That's what..."

"We forgot," Ari finished and threw her arms around her sister. "I have missed you so much!"

Brie's eyes filled with tears. "I can't tell you how lonely I've been."

Ari squeezed her hand and pulled her down on a small sofa. "You don't need to. I know."

Allynae watched the panel close behind Wolloh and sat down to enjoy his daughters' reunion. Their animated faces made him smile. His heart filled with longing. Because of their adventures, subtle changes defined them. Ari's deep voice held a note of maturity he did not remember. Brie's sounded melodic, no matter what she said. It was the depth in her words that impressed him. *My little girls are growing up. How I wish...*

He realized they were looking at him. With one simultaneous movement, they threw their arms around him. His joy skyrocketed. His laughter joined with theirs. "How I wish I had been with you all your lives!"

A twin raised her head from his shoulder. "What's important is that you're here now." Brie's melodious words teased a tear from his eye. She planted a kiss on his wet cheek.

Ari squirmed and pulled them to a group of chairs. "Tell us everything. What's happening on Myrrh?"

"How're Aunt Mira and Mother?" Brie sat down beside him.

He filled them in, and a thoughtful silence settled over the study. He looked at his girls' serious faces. *They have so much to bear for ones so young.*

Brie tugged at a stray curl. "Isn't The Unfolding amazing? I mean...look at Seyes Nomed. He wanted to destroy Myrrh and Aunt Mira. Now he's helping to protect it and her. And then there's Torgin...he's changed so much."

Ari gave her an impatient look. "Hey, I want to know about WoNa's rescue."

The contrast between his daughters made Allynae chuckle. He began the story, and Brie completed it.

"I wish you had seen him, Ari! The winged horse was the most beautiful thing I've ever seen...all stars and midnight sky and huge wings and—"

"Change now, Father. I want to see." Ari pulled him from his chair.

He put his arms around her and rested his cheek on her soft curls. "I'm not sure I can shape it again." A sigh rustled her hair. "Now is not the time, anyway."

Sad eyes look up at him. "I guess I need to become Ira, don't I? Torgin needs our help."

Brie joined them. "Wolloh believes Ari and I are safer when she's a boy."

He held them close, savoring every moment.

A final hug and Ari walked to the center of the room. She closed her eyes, then opened them. Ira frowned at Allynae. "I know you, right?"

Allynae grinned. "I know your mother. She sends her love."

"Oh, well, ah...thanks. Torgin's this way."

Allynae followed his daughters through the panel. A wave of pride washed over him. *The Unfolding will achieve its fullness and restore to the Inner Universe—with their help.*

Wolloh left Allynae and the twins to catch up and made his way to Roween Rattori's suite. Clearing his thoughts, he rapped on the door.

An older woman answered and curtsied. "LaChett Rattori will receive you in her sitting room. This way, please." She led him through a set of double doors. "The High DiMensioner od DerTah, Ma'am." Bowing her way past him, she scurried away.

Nissasa's mother stood at the center of the room. Her angular face held neither warmth nor welcome. "You realize, Wolloh, that I am departing under duress. If you had not ordered it, I would not be leaving Lorsedi's side."

Wolloh bowed. "I understand your desire to remain, but as I have already explained...your safety is my priority. The Sebborr gather along the border. They are vicious fighters, Roween. In Trinuge, you will be out of harm's way, and Lorsedi can concentrate on the coming battle.

She pursed her lips in a pronounced pout. "I don't know why Lorsedi wastes his time with a DerTahan quarrel. And what of Nissasa?"

"Lorsedi is an honorable friend. I appreciate his willingness to help. As for Nissasa, I understand he is dealing with personal affairs and will return when he can."

A mind touch tingled and withdrew. She smiled and moved toward him. "I imagine TheLise is ready to go. Will you escort me to her rooms?"

"Better than that, I will escort you to her coach. I believe your servants await you there."

She took his arm and glanced at his face. "You were a handsome man before..." Acerbic sympathy dripped from her words.

He limped beside her down the hallway. "I have learned to live with my differences, Roween." He guided her out the front door and handed her into the coach, where Tissent waited with a patient smile and an aura of tranquility. "I will check on the Dreelas. Take care of yourselves and stay safe." A quick bow and he withdrew into the house.

The door to TheLise's rooms stood ajar. He stuck his head inside. "TheLise?"

She appeared at her bedroom door, sent her serving woman out to the coach, and smiled a sardonic smile. "*That* RewFaaran woman is going to drive me insane. She is the most spiteful, self-serving—"

"And you, my dearest TheLise, are the most wonderful woman on DerTah." Wolloh took her hand and pressed it to his lips.

"Oh, Wolloh, you are..." She shook her head. "There are no words to describe you. Is the 'hornet' in the coach?"

"She is. Pay attention. I will set wards as soon as you cross the border into Trinuge. Keep Roween focused on anything but Shu Chenaro. Tissent will help. Take care of yourself, TheLise. Roween Rattori is, as you so aptly noted, a hornet. She will do her best to destroy you if she catches even a hint of your true intent."

"I'll be careful. I will not underestimate her as I did her son. Be in touch when you can. Tell Seyes he'd better come and rescue me. See me to the coach?"

He took her arm and drew it through the crook of his elbow. "I am in your debt, TheLise. I realize you would prefer to stay here."

They reached the front door. "You take care of yourself, Wolloh." She swept out into the courtyard, checked her luggage, and allowed her footman to hand her into the coach. After seating herself across from Roween, she leaned out the window and waved.

Wolloh watched the coach pull away, his heavy sigh of relief obscured behind a wall of mental shields.

Torgin wanted to curl up in a corner and cry. His mother's kidnapping left him feeling empty, alone, and more frightened than he could ever remember. Yaro's wonderful support helped. His friends had listened to the news with shocked expressions and sworn to help. He glanced around. The hidden study seemed to overflow with people. Wolloh explained it was the most secure place in Shu Chenaro, and its permanent shields insured privacy.

Torgin counted thirteen people, including himself. The only one missing was Corvus. One Man had told them he was on the way to rescue Nichi. When he had accomplished the task, he would return to Shu Chenaro. Torgin thought about his arrival in the Nesune Ruins and how he had helped to save Yaro. *If I needed rescuing and Yaro couldn't get to me, Corvus would be my choice.*

A dull headache made him massage his temples. He sighed, dropped his hands to his lap, and looked at Esán, talking quietly with his father. Ira and Brie sat on either side of Allynae, their faces animated and happy. Allynae said something. Brie laughed and leaned her head on his shoulder. *What would it be like to have my father with me?* He couldn't imagine Wilith Whalend in this room. But then he couldn't imagine him in Myrrh either. *I'm so glad I have Yaro.*

Wolloh tapped his cane on the floor. Conversation stopped. All eyes turned toward the High DiMensioner. "Gathered here are some of the best minds in this solar system." His good eye traveled the room. "I have some decisions to share, and we have decisions to make."

Torgin's hyperactive mind wandered. *How am I going to rescue my mother? We don't know where she is.*

Ira elbowed him in the ribs. "Listen up, Torg."

Shooting him a dirty look, he returned his attention to Wolloh.

"One Man and Allynae have offered to find the Oracle Stone and return it to WoNa." He nodded their direction and continued. "Lorsedi has already dispatched troops to secure the desert portal, a step vital to our success. Voer brought word that Jordett and Mondago would deal with the situation at the Five Towers in Myrrh, which takes that situation off our already full plates."

A murmur of relief filled the room. Somehow, nothing so far made Torgin feel better.

The crystal knob on Wolloh's cane glowed. The High DiMensioner glanced down. When he looked up, his expression was grim. "Coala Renn Whalend is being kept on an island off the shore of Geran. It is only accessible by water. The Geranian Guard has a small contingent stationed there. She will be safe as long as Nissasa believes we are unaware of her presence in DerTah. The moment we turn our interest in that direction or Lorsedi dispatches troops to Geran, he will do one of two things..."

Torgin swallowed.

"Move her...or kill her. We have to act with extreme caution. Coupled with that, we have the Compass of Ostradio, the knife Efillaeh, Brielle, Esán, and Desirol. He wants them all."

The panel in the wall slid open. Tinpaca Granier stepped through and hurried to Lorsedi's side. The Largeen Joram's face hardened. A commander's authority filled his voice. "Nissasa's soldiers are closing in on the border. I suggest we conclude our meeting and prepare to defend ourselves." He put a hand on Desirol's shoulder. "I need you to do whatever Wolloh believes is best. Don't fail me, son."

Desirol's posture took on a military stance as his father followed the Tinpaca into the passage behind the wall.

Corvus hid at the outskirts of the LaTiru encampment. A mental search pinpointed the Dansgirl, Nichi, imprisoned in a tent near to its center. He touched the orange stone in his pocket. WoNa sent it as a sign of her successful rescue. Unsure of his welcome, he made a final mental scan, pushed his hood back, and walked into the camp. LaTiru tribesmen appearing from all sides enclosed him within their ranks. A messenger darted ahead to warn the LaTiru leader.

The man who had spit in Allynae's face waited for him in front of a shabby tent, his arms folded across his chest, his knife sheathed at his waist. "Release him."

The tribesmen moved back as he turned fanatic eyes to Karrew. "You bring news of WoNadahem Mardree?"

"I bring you a sign and a message. She is safe with her people." He held up the orange stone. "She sends this as proof of her freedom, and she asks that you release Nichook into my care."

The leader cradled the stone in his hands. His tongue poked in and out through the gap created by two missing teeth. He sucked in a breath and placed the stone on his heart. Eyes closed, he began to hum. Tribesmen joined him, crowding closer. The humming intensified and grew louder. The hooded eyes snapped open. Silence weighted with anticipation filled the camp. He slipped the stone into a pocket beneath his filthy kcalo and withdrew the knife from its sheath. With the tip against Corvus' chest, he bared blackened teeth. "You are a man of much courage." He raised the knife above his head. "The man speaks the truth. Bring the girl to me."

Corvus kept his face blank. A threat in the man's stance shouted a warning. The knife, still unsheathed, caught the sunlight and gleamed. The crowd parted. A man pushed Nichi ahead of him. Keeping his distance from Corvus, he passed her to the leader.

"The LaTiru make sacrifice to the Oracle Stone in gratitude for WoNadahem Mardree's rescue."

"Sacrifice, sacrifice, sacrifice!" The chorused shout rang through the crowd.

Fear flooded Nichi's eyes. Corvus moved an unobtrusive step in her direction. The crowd shouted louder. The leader slashed the air with his knife. "Who will pay the debt?"

"Sacrifice, sacrifice!" A frenzied edge crept into the chanting voices. "Sac-ri-fice."

The leader grabbed Nichi by the arm and pulled her to him. "Sacrifice to the Oracle Stone!" He raised the knife higher.

Nichi yanked away from her captor and threw herself at Corvus. The crowd howled as he caught her and flashed from sight.

At the top of the outcropping at Eissua Oasis, Nichi buried her face in his kcalo and sobbed. When she raised her head, he motioned for silence. A scan of the Oasis showed a small group of Sebborr hid near WoNa's cave.

He leaned close to her ear. "Is there another way into the caverns?"

She dried her tears and smothered a hiccuped sob. "I show." Creeping around the overhang, she sprinted past the sacred site where the LaTiru had held Allynae and dropped to her knee behind a stocky taccus tree. Corvus knelt beside her. She pointed to a group of tall, angular oragasu cactus some distance away. "We go there. Stay low. Move fast."

She darted away, dodged around rough patches in the terrain, and vanished into the small, prickly forest. Corvus arrived to find Narrtep and no Nichook. "Thank you for bringing Nichi home. I have sent her to her family. WoNa says you are needed elsewhere. Come to her when time allows."

Corvus shook the man's hand. "Sebborr tribesmen hide near WoNa's cave. Stay safe." He shifted and flew east, hoping to make the ranch before dusk.

With Lorsedi's departure to oversee his troops, everyone's attention returned to the High DiMensioner. Wolloh could see the questions in their faces and hear them pounding in his brain. He ran the palm of his uninjured hand over the head of his cane and viewed the room from beneath lowered lids. *We must prevent Nissasa's soldiers from overrunning Shu Chenaro, and we must remove the young people from harm's way. Nissasa knows exactly where they are.* His fingers caressed the crystal's smooth roundness. *Our next move must push the enemy back and obscure the departure of the children from the ranch.*

He leveraged his fatigued body to standing. The anticipation in the study deepened. "I've developed a plan. Everyone will need to help, including Corvus. It is vital that we put up wards around the ranch. By combining our power, Nissasa will find it difficult to break through. Once the wards are in place around the arena, we will widen their breadth to include the entirety of Shu Chenaro's acreage. I know we can't sustain them for long, but they will buy us some time." He paused a moment to allow the import of his words to sink in. "Removing the young people to safety is tantamount. This will occur after the wards have reached their expanded level. The children will teleport, their energy trail erased by the breadth of the wards. I will also shield Efillaeh and the Compass of Ostradio, making it next to impossible to track them."

A wave of fatigue made him clasp his cane with unsteady hands. "It is time for a break. Omudi and Thaer have put their tails between their legs and stolen away with their retinues, and TheLise has departed with Tissent and Roween." He smiled at his Major Domo. "Stebben has arranged for a meal to be served in the conference chamber and will escort you there. Esán, please remain with me."

When the room had emptied, he eased his aching bones onto a chair and leaned his forehead on the knob of his cane. He straightened and flexed his clawed hand. "Pull up a seat, boy. We have much to discuss."

Esán rubbed the recent growth of fuzzy hair on his head. Somber blue eyes narrowed. "Are you alright, sir?"

Wolloh forced a smile. "Just feeling my age."

Esán positioned a chair opposite him. "It is my responsibility to teleport The Prima Crystal Evolsefil back to the Cave of Canedari on Myrrh. How can I do that and help Torgin find his mother here on DerTah?"

"Almiralyn sent word that, for the time being, Evolsefil is safe. CheeTrann and Paisley will take care of it. Rescuing Coala Renn Whalend is vital. You will find her. Then you will take her to Myrrh."

Esán sat back and stared straight ahead. Again, his eyes narrowed. "So much to accomplish, and time pushes hard at our heals."

With a touch of nostalgia, Wolloh observed Nomed's nephew. He remembered Seyes when he first arrived at Shu Chenaro...his talent, his anger, and his desire to achieve. *Esán resembles him. Fortunately, he does not possess the anger. And he carries dual Seeds of Carsilem. He is young but has the talent to do what is required. If he fails...* Wolloh clutched the crystal knob. *Failure was not an option.* He locked his good eye on the boy's face. "I have a vital job for you, Esán. Listen closely."

57

Der Tah

Brie glanced up as Esán preceded Stebben into the Conference Chamber. Stebben paused by the door, his eyes on her. The Star of Truth tingled. Finishing her last bite, she excused herself from the table and followed him down the hall.

Stebben opened a door and ushered her through with a slight bow. Two leather chairs sat side by side in front of a fireplace. Wolloh's dark head leaned against the back of one.

"Join me, Brielle."

She hurried to the chair next to him and studied his smooth profile. Happy to be seated on his 'good' side, she noted the intensity of his gaze and sensed the seriousness of his expression even before he faced her.

"You, my dear, are about to embark on another journey in pursuit of your destiny. Your skills will be honed and your abilities challenged. It is time to awaken your gifts. I don't have time to explain them all. You will discover them as you need them. However, two things you must remember. A DiMensioner's power increases with practice and use. Never forget the desire to serve magnifies that power."

Her heart beat hard in her chest. "Are you suggesting I'm a DiMensioner?"

"I am saying you have the gifts. When The Unfolding's cycle is complete, you will become my apprentice along with Esán."

The throne of ReNin RepPosu flashed into her memory. *Wolloh's face...*

He nodded. "You remember. Good. Kneel in front of me, and we will awaken your power. Almiralyn gave you the Stone of Remembering. I will need it."

Brie touched the Star of Truth. It responded with a warm flow of energy down her spine. Kneeling in front of the High DiMensioner, she removed the blue stone from its velvet pouch and placed it in his uninjured hand.

"You must trust me without question, Brielle. Close your eyes and clear your thoughts."

For a moment, she kept her eyes on his face. Her lids lowered. His fingertips rested on her temples. The coolness of Almiralyn's gift touched her forehead. Awareness of each tiny particle composing her body, each synapse in her brain, and each molecule of air as it traveled into her lungs flooded through her. WoNa's face appeared and faded. Her mother and father...Ari...Almiralyn...Gerolyn...Lorsedi...her heritage surged through her veins until she thought she would drown.

Soft words called to her. "Brielle, open your eyes."

Heavy lids lifted. Her eyes rebelled against the light. A touch on her forehead awakened her fully to Wolloh's serious face.

"Please stand."

Using the chair arms to steady her trembling, she pushed herself to her feet.

"How do you feel?"

She swallowed. "Shaky."

"Sit down and rest."

She eased herself to sitting and gulped a breath. Her gaze sought his face.

He nodded, returned the Stone of Remembering, and handed her a goblet of water. "Sip it, and pay close attention while I explain what happens next."

When Brielle returned to the conference room, Ira noted a flush in her cheeks and a brightness in her eyes he hadn't seen earlier. She went straight to Gerolyn, and the two of them left together. He wished they'd invited him. Instead, he sat tracing infinity signs on the conference table. A tap on the shoulder interrupted him.

Stebben stood by his chair. "Wolloh would like to see you. If you'll come with me."

He swallowed a desire to lash out and followed the Major Domo into the hall. "At least someone wants me around." He muttered his frustration under his breath.

"I beg your pardon, Ira?"

"Ah...nothing, Stebben. Just talking to myself."

"I see." He opened a door. "Wolloh awaits you here."

Ira entered and glanced around the room. Its comfort welcomed him.

A voice from a chair by the fire invited him to have a seat. He rounded the chair and stared at the distorted side of Wolloh's face.

"Please sit, Ira. We have little time."

Curiosity won over his inclination to disobey. He plopped down in the chair and studied the High DiMensioner.

Wolloh's opaque eye seemed to drill a hole in him before his good eye caught the gleam of the dying fire. He lifted his cane and tapped the crystal.

Ira yawned and leaned back in his chair. When he opened his eyes, fragments of strange dreams clung to his memory. "What did you do?" He scowled.

"I put a shield around Efillaeh and placed important information in your subconscious."

"What kind of information?"

"You will know when you need it."

Ira considered pushing for an answer, but the look on Wolloh's face canceled the inclination.

"Go join your friends and be ready to help Esán later today."

"Yes, sir." He rose from his chair.

"Take care of yourself, Ira." Wolloh's serious expression made him pause.

"And you, sir." Troubled thoughts tumbled through his mind as he left the room.

Torgin poked at the food on his plate. His appetite had vanished with the news of his mother's abduction. The assurance that others would rescue the Five Fathers kept him from fretting about them, as well. *The people involved are smart and capable. They'll get the job done.* His forehead wrinkled. *My parents...my poor father must be so worried about Mother.* A shudder of dismay squeezed his throat tight. *How am I going to rescue her?*

Stebben beckoned him from the doorway. Shoving his plate away, he stood up and followed him from the room. He had seen Brie and Ira leave with Stebben and couldn't imagine what Wolloh would want with him.

The rhythm of their shoes on the tile floor almost dispersed his nervousness, but not quite. When the Major Domo held a door open, he steadied his breathing, squared his shoulders, and walked into the sitting room.

Wolloh leaned against the mantle of a stone fireplace, gazing into remnants of the morning's fire. As he turned, the different aspects of his face emerged in the light. "Thank you for coming, Torgin." He tapped a chair with his cane. "Please join me."

Torgin sat on the edge of the proffered chair and folded his hands in his lap. The High DiMensioner, who would have scared him to death a few moon cycles ago, inspired respect and curiosity. Unsure what to expect, he waited. So did Wolloh.

When at last he broke the silence, Wolloh spoke with quiet gentleness. "I am very sorry about your mother, Torgin. How do you feel about helping to rescue her?"

"I want to, sir." He fidgeted with his tunic. "I don't know what to do."

"First, I need to see your compass."

Torgin knew his face went blank. *Everyone wants the compass. Can I trust this man?*

"I promise to return it. I want to shield it so Nissasa cannot track it, and I would like to add to its information base."

"What do you want to add?"

"I'd rather not say. You will discover it when you need it."

Torgin studied his hands. His brain ran a quick inventory of potential reasons for secrecy. He looked up. "You don't want anyone to read my mind, right?"

The odd mouth shaped a smile. "You are a bright young man, Torgin." He held out his hand.

Torgin placed the compass on the High DiMensioner's palm and watched with interest as he held it face down over the crystal knob on his cane. Chron-clicks flashed by. Finally, he flipped it, tapped the face, and handed it back.

"That should do it. You are the perfect person to carry this. Guard it with your life." He sat back in his chair and studied Torgin's face. "Since Lorsedi requested Yaro join him at the front, I am sending Corvus to help you find your mother." His good eye seemed to sparkle. "If that's alright with you, of course."

The burden of his mother's kidnapping felt suddenly less overwhelming. "Oh, sir, thank you. I trust him almost as much as my heart brother. But can you spare him?"

"I can for a time. Please ask Stebben to bring Desirol to me."

"I will, sir. Thank you for your trust. *And* for helping me to find my mother."

When he returned to the conference chamber, Ira, Brie, and Esán sat together at the end of the table. Withdrawing to watch them unobserved, he noted how much they had changed and realized how much he, too, had changed since the start of their adventures several moon cycles ago. He wondered what was next and then decided it didn't matter. As long as they were all together, they would manage.

Desirol did not trust the High DiMensioner, and he couldn't understand why his father did. The last thing he wanted was to meet with him alone. He glared at Stebben's broad back. When the Major Domo opened the door to the study, the temptation to walk away held him rigid.

"Desirol, please come in." Wolloh's voice held an edge of authority that he dared not ignore.

Standing by the chair next to his, Desirol tried to hide his dislike and his discomfort. The odd face made him nervous.

"Sit down, boy. I don't bite."

"I'd rather stand."

"Sit down, Desirol. I will not get a crick in my neck because you dislike me."

Desirol rubbed his flushed cheek, sat ramrod straight in the chair, and tried to ignore the face.

"You will accompany your friends later today. Before you leave, I would like to share some information.

"I am staying here with my father. You can't make me leave."

Wolloh placed his cane between them. "As I recall, your father told you to do as I asked. You are not safe here. The Mindeco is at the border, sniffing to find you. Since you refused to wear your drango tunic, he left his mark on you at Nesune Ruins. His goal, Desirol Telisnoe, is to take over your body. Do you know what that means?"

He gulped. "Yes. But my father won't let him get me."

"Your father's responsibilities prevent his protecting you. He needs you to go."

"Well, I won't."

Wolloh tapped the crystal knob with his forefinger.

A light shot from its center. Desirol's forehead began to burn. The room blurred, then refocused. "What did you do?"

"Helped you relax."

"Go? Oh. With Esán." He rubbed his forehead and wondered if he had forgotten something. Unable to track down what it was, he shrugged and prepared to listen to the High DiMensioner od DerTah.

When Desirol left, Wolloh sat back in his chair and closed his eyes. The desire to give in to his fatigue almost overpowered him. He massaged his feathered brow. *Wards around the ranch are vital in order to remove the children from harm's way.* With a frustrated sigh, he lowered his hand. He wanted nothing more than time free from The Unfolding. *I need*

quiet, my house emptied of people, and time to regain my strength. This is not to be, however...

A soft knock made him grasp his cane. "Come in, Stebben." He watched the man he had rescued so many sun cycles ago enter and close the door. "What have you discovered?"

"I can find no trace of Corvus. You may need to send the children on their way without him."

Wolloh cupped the knob on his cane in unsteady hands and peered into its depths. "Nissasa has interfered with my crystal. He is closing in, and the Mindeco is pacing the borders. I can sense Lorsedi and his men, but I cannot find Corvus anywhere."

"Could he be in the oasis caverns? They would obscure his whereabouts." Stebben sat down in the leather chair vacated by Desirol.

A tremor ran the length of Wolloh's left side. He flinched and massaged a muscle cramp in his shoulder.

Stebben leaned toward him. "You are too tired to construct wards. You need to rest. We can hide the children longer."

Wolloh straightened and fixed his good eye on his Major Domo. "I don't have the luxury of resting just because I'm tired. We have too much to accomplish."

"At least take a quick nap, Wolloh. I'll wake you in one chronometer circle."

"Half a circle...and I'll nap."

Stebben nodded his agreement and prepared to leave. He paused and shot Wolloh a stern look. "I'll keep everyone at bay. Rest." He exited and shut the door without a sound.

Setting his cane aside, Wolloh leaned into the comfort of his chair and closed his eyes. *Too many tangles to untangle...too many...* He yawned, blanked his mind, and slept.

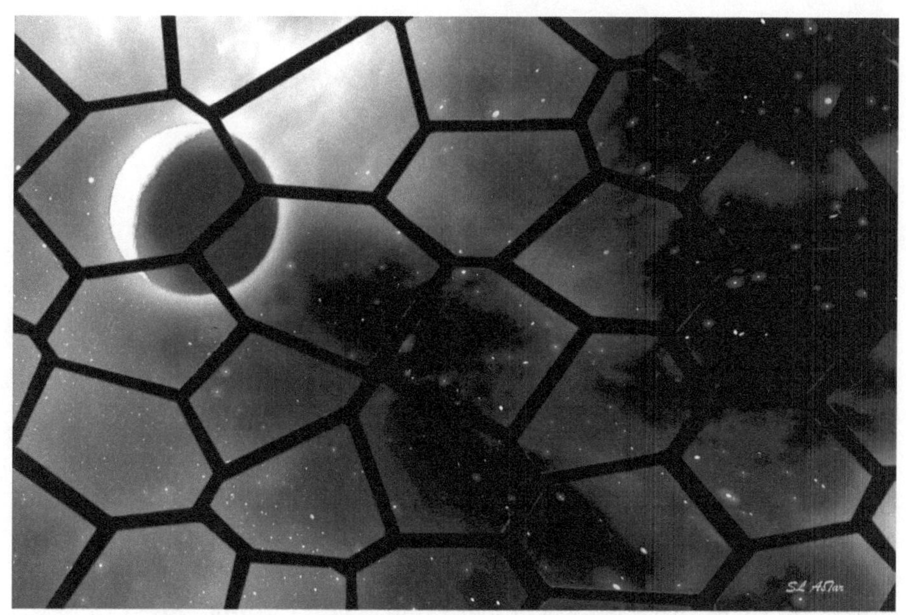

58
Myrrh & Der Tah

Almiralyn stood in the serene quiet of Veersuni. The colored pieces of light from the window still floated in front of the velvet curtains. Beyond the emptied panes of glass, stars scattered across the panoramic expanse glittered. A crescent moon gleamed in the vast heavens.

The image of the Mindeco in Elcaro's Eye had sent both Merrilea and Sparrow into a panic. Almiralyn did her best to calm their fears. None of them knew whose reflection shone in its eye. She tried to assure them it wasn't necessarily one of the boys. The women remained unconvinced, and the Guardian did, too. When the fountain refused to show anything more, Elae and Zugo escorted them back to Meos.

Dread she could not explain, and had not mentioned, kept her from returning with them. *Why am I so uneasy? WoNa is safe. Allynae is safe. He and One Man are at Shu Chenaro. The children are with them.*

She turned her back on the window and stared at the fountain. *What I need to know requires looking into the enemy's camp. Dare I try it without Nomed's support?*

The door from the Reading Room opened. A man's silhouette paused, then moved into the light. Almiralyn smiled. "Seyes, I am glad you're here."

He crossed to the fountain and met her gaze. "When Merrilea and Sparrow came back without you, I felt you might need my help."

She joined him beside the fountain. "I believe there's trouble in DerTah. I was just about to use Elcaro's Eye. You must have felt my need. I didn't want to use it again without your help. You can monitor the wards while I see what the Eye will share."

Nomed gave her a worried half-smile and placed his hands on the bowl's rounded rim. "I'm concerned about Esán. Perhaps it will show us where the children are." He closed his eyes. His breathing deepened, then he looked up and nodded grimly. "The wards are solid, Almiralyn, but something strange vibrates at their outer edges. Do you think Nissasa is attempting to break through?"

"I believe he is trying. Let's hope he's too distracted by events in DerTah to pursue it. Please let me know if you need help to maintain them."

She waved a hand over the fountain. "Show us the events unfolding in DerTah."

The water swirled and grew calm. On the surface, an image took shape.

Corvus and a young Dansgirl knelt at the top of the outcropping at Eissua Oasis. Below them, at the water's edge, three Sebborran warriors hid near WoNa's cave entrance.

"That must be Nichi." Almiralyn smiled. "Karrew told me Corvus was on the way to rescue her."

The girl darted across the top of the sandy ridge and disappeared into a group of oragasu trees. Corvus followed.

Rippling water erased the image and stilled to a mirror-like finish. Wolloh's face, infused with fatigue, focused and faded into a closeup of the children clustered at the center of a large, round arena. The scene blurred.

Worry filled Nomed's voice. "Wolloh looks ill. He should be resting." He summoned a small smile. "I'm glad to know Esán is with his friends." An emerging image claimed his attention.

One Man, Allynae, Gerolyn, and Stebben gathered in a group near the children. The picture reeled out, showing Wolloh conversing with Torgin.

"We can't wait any longer, Torgin. Nissasa is on the move. He is much stronger than we expected. The wards have to go up."

"But, Wolloh, you promised. How can we find my mother by ourselves?"

Brie put an arm around him. "Ira has Efillaeh, and you have the compass. We'll be fine."

Wolloh raised his cane to stop further discussion. "It is time. Please take your positions."

The crystal knob flared golden. Like shafts in a wheel, light shot from its center to form five pools on the ground in a tight circle around Esán and his companions. The High DiMensioner stepped into a pool of light. The remaining adults followed suit, their backs to the arena's center. With arms raised, they began a whispered chant.

Almiralyn watched a shimmering curtain of light rise from the ground, enclosing the arena and its occupants in a humming, luminous circle. Wolloh traced a sign in the air. The curtain shot upwards to form a dome high overhead. Moving within their pools, the adults began a measured pacing toward the outer walls of the arena. Their chanting grew more insistent. The space within the wards expanded. Almost invisible, it moved beyond the arena walls.

The image scattered, reformed, and sharpened.

For the second time, the Mindeco's hideous face filled the bowl. The image pulled out. Behind it, the wards glowed in the intense light of the DerTahan sun. Nostrils flaring, it rose from all fours to its full height and howled. Nissasa's soldiers fought to steady their frightened mounts. On the ranch side of the shield, Lorsedi's men moved without a sound into a long, narrow gully that ran parallel to the border of Fera Finnero. Voer and Yaro stood on either side of the Largeen Joram.

Almiralyn glanced at Nomed. "I'm glad the Pentharian have joined forces with Lorsedi. He will need their help."

Nomed leaned closer, peering into the water as a kestrel swooped into view, hovered above the wards, and streaked away. "That's Esán. He's scouting for Wolloh."

Elcaro's Eye followed the course of the kestrel. A wide arc carried it east, where the wards stopped at the Sea of Fire. On it flew until the Plains of DoOlb came into view beyond the shimmering curtain. In the distance, a coach led a caravan through the deep green of the rain forests of Trinuge. The kestrel made a last pass along the desert boundary, soared above the dome, and dropped through the central opening. Esán appeared with the other youngsters and signaled Wolloh. "It is done."

A series of different scenes flitted across the water's surface. Warriors lined both sides of the border, preparing for battle; a red sun beat down on the translucent light dividing them; and the Mindeco prowled the perimeter of the wards, its single eye focused intently on the almost invisible curtain. It lifted its head and sniffed the air. A frustrated howl churned the water in the fountain. White waves crashed against its alabaster sides. Frothy spray misted the air with fine droplets of water. The creature crouched. With a powerful leap, it landed partway up the wards. Clinging with its massive claws, it began a labored climb.

With the back of his hand, Nomed wiped the water from his scarred cheek. "Why didn't the wards repel him?"

Almiralyn leaned over the fountain and studied the beast. A glint of light caught her eye. "Look, it has a crystal around its neck. Not just any crystal. That's the one WoNa carried in her medicine bag. It's from the Evolsefil Caverns. Thank Emit, it's not strong enough to damage the wards."

The water swirled and stilled. Wolloh's arena snapped into view. The High DiMensioner's voice rose loud and clear. "Seal and secure. Protect all who reside within. Allow no one to enter whose intent is to harm."

He made a sign in the air. The chanting ceased. Golden pools coalesced, enclosing the children in glowing light. The adults turned to face them.

"Shoulder your packs, everyone, and hold on to me." Esán closed his eyes.

Elcaro's Eye rocked on its pedestal. The water roiled and quaked. Nomed gasped. "Help me, Almiralyn!"

Joining forces with the DiMensioner, she fought to reconstruct the protective wards. When they were in place, she backed away from the fountain, drawing him with her.

For an instant, his hazel eyes gleamed with the wildness of the Great Horned Owl. He blinked. "What happened?"

She fingered the weave of her braid. "Nissasa, or someone as strong, tried to break through. I redesigned the wards. Hopefully, that will slow them down. Let's see what else we can learn." Winding her braid into a tight bun, she returned to her place by the fountain, snapped her fingers, and whispered a single word.

Quiet filled Veersuni. Elcaro's Eye remained calm and empty. Almiralyn clapped her hands. Small white caps appeared, turned into a seething whirlpool, and steadied. An image formed at the bottom of the bowl and spiraled upward.

Nissasa Rattori's face slammed into focus. Anger flushed his complexion. Cold blue eyes focused on a cowering Fire ConDra. Soldiers scattered. Sebborr huddled to one side, their dark eyes following Nissasa's every move. The ConDra cringed away from his fury.

"How could you let WoNadahem Mardree and her rescuers escape?" A flip of his wrist froze the flaming bird in mid-flight. He removed the Oracle Stone from the black pouch at his throat and chanted,

> *"Oracle Stone, torch your bier*
> *And be filled with ConDra's Fire.*
> *Burn into my heart sublime,*
> *Burn there 'til the end of time."*

"Brosba!" He lifted the crystal above his head. "Brosba Nerofin!"

The ConDra roared in terror as flames fled its body. Sucked into a twister, its fire spiraled downward, infusing the Oracle Stone with the deep red-orange of an inferno. Blackened bones fell, shattered into brittle shards, and scattered over the plateau like pieces of glistening obsidian.

Nissasa held the stone high. His voice rang out, loud and clear and filled with power. "I claim thee for my own and christen thee, Souvitrico, the Stone of Fire." He returned it to its black pouch.

Almiralyn tensed, her eyes glued to the water. Beside her, Nomed murmured under his breath. "The man grows stronger with each chron-click."

Nissasa threw his arms wide and shifted form. A DerTahan bearded buzzard lifted into flight on blazing wings and swept over the desert. At the border between Fera Finnero and Shu Chenaro, where the wards held his army at bay, he landed and resumed his Human form. Throwing his head back, he laughed. His men exchanged questioning glances and backed away from the venomous sound.

He turned. His shout pierced the air. "Guardian of Myrrh… I know you watch! High DiMensioner od DerTah, you know not with whom you are dealing. I, Nissasa Rattori, have stolen the ConDra's fire. Fear me! I shall burn your heart and all you love in the furnace of my desire." He strode forward, raised the crystal, and rent a gaping hole in the wards. The Mindeco's howl echoed through time and space as it flashed from sight.

Shu Chenaro's arena burst into view. Wolloh flung his arms wide. A cry of despair broke from his lips as the children vanished. Body rigid and face convulsed in a spasm of pain, he crumpled to the ground. Around him, the adults struggled to maintain the wards.

Almiralyn glanced at Nomed's ashen face and back at the fountain. "Show me the children."

The water rolled and splashed. Light exploding on the surface brought a dark, dank forest into focus. The children knelt in ferns that towered high above their heads. An animal's predatory roar shook the ground. Torgin crouched lower. "What was that?"

Desirol's grim expression matched his tone. "Where did that horrid man send us?"

Torgin gave Desirol a hard stare. "Wolloh isn't a horrid man. He sent us away to keep us safe. And he sent us where we can get the help we need to save my mother."

"Well, Nissasa can track us because of Ira's knife and Torgin's compass."

Esán interrupted. "Wolloh shielded both of them before we left the ranch, so your brother can't use them to find us." His eyes caught Brie's and then darted around the terrain. "We have a problem."

Torgin clutched the compass. "This isn't where we were supposed to teleport, is it?"

Esán gazed at his friends, one by one. "This looks nothing like the picture Wolloh put in my head. We were supposed to end up in a seaside village called Atkis, not in a rain forest."

Brie touched Torgin's arm. "I think we'd better have a peek at your compass."

He withdrew it from beneath his tunic and held it out. "Where are we?"

The needle spun. A map appeared on the face, levitated above it, and enlarged to readable proportions.

"It's never done that before." Ira angled to see it better.

"Look." Brie pointed at a glowing green spot. "We're in the Tinga Forest in Trinuge."

"Great. So now what?" Desirol folded his arms across his chest and glared.

The picture faded.

Nomed's eyebrow arched. "The Tinga Forest is one of the most dangerous places on DerTah. With Wolloh weakened and the Mindeco on the loose, the children are in peril. I think—"

A maniacal laugh erupted from the depth of the fountain. Bloodied water splashed over the rim of the bowl. A picture danced erratically and settled. Almiralyn's heart jumped into her throat. Her hands gripped the rim.

Cage bars, encased within shimmering wards, jumped into focus. A raven's tortured eye fastened on hers. Scorched feathers covered a wing that hung at an odd angle. A jagged gash at the base of its throat soaked a single white feather with oozing drops of blood.

Almiralyn sucked in a shocked breath. Tears flooded her eyes. "Karrew. What have they done to you?"

Another crazed laugh bounced off the walls, surrounding them with an echoed taunt that went on and on.

The image faded from the fountain's surface, leaving the water in Elcaro's Eye tinted crimson. Beyond the emptied panes of Veersuni's window, DerTah spun into view and blinked from sight.

Water slipping from the carved woman's palms overflowed Elcaro's rim, staining the white alabaster red.

> *The children of many continue their course*
> *To defy and destroy a sinister force;*
> *The Unfolding pulls them along in its wake*
> *Toward worlds to protect and the wicked to break.*

And the Unfolding continued.

GLOSSARY LINK

A searchable glossary for the
VarTerels' Universe™ is available online at:

www.skrandolph.com/glossary

ACKNOWLEDGMENTS

A book needs many pairs of eyes upon it before it is ready for print.

The ConDra's Fire has had the benefit of astute professionals and critical readers. To everyone who has offered their support and their help, I express my heart-felt thanks.

To Tom Krantz, my partner, publisher, book formatter, and marketing manager, I thank you for listening, for hearing, for reading, and for critiquing. Your support helps me to stay on track, to keep writing, and to truly love what I do. I cannot imagine doing this without you.

To my editor Linda Lane, without whose patience and commitment this book would still be in draft form, I can only affirm my delight at our working relationship and my pleasure at our developing friendship. You are important to every aspect of the VarTerels' Universe™ and to the development of my talent as a writer. Words cannot express the depth of my gratitude.

To Ms. Lane's assistant, David A. Lane, I express my thanks for a sharp eye and a willingness to say it like it is.

To Ann McEntire, for her willingness to read, reread, and critique each volume of the VarTerels' Universe™.

To Linda White, clay artist, I express my thanks for not only your creative input after reading and rereading but also for applying your talent as a clay artist to the characters. Your imagination and astounding eye for detail deepens my visual understanding of the characters and brings them to life as Chapter headings in ConDra's Fire.

To Leslie Randolph for her willingness to critique and correct each volume. Your insightful observations always take my work to a new level.

To Sean and Courtney Krantz, you are the reason I smile and laugh and embrace life. The lessons we have learned together inform everything I do.

To my mother Emma Randolph for her painting of the Terces Wood and for her ongoing encouragement.

To Sally Yorke, for always supporting my efforts and cheering me on.

To Maureen Miller for her gorgeous pictures of sunflowers.

To FreeNaturePictures.com and Public-domain-image.com, thank you for desert pictures to supplement my photography. And to Pixaby.com and all the wonderful photographers whose photos enhance mine.

And...to all the Alaskan Ravens depicted throughout this book for their raucous, funny, and winsome personalities.

ABOUT THE AUTHOR

FROM DANCE STAGE TO WRITTEN PAGE

STORYTELLER

Dance, humanity's most ancient narrative art, captivated S.K. Randolph as a child living and dancing in the British Crown Colony of Bermuda. After graduating from the University of Utah with a BFA in Ballet, her dance career spanned four decades of performing, mentoring, teaching, choreographing, and directing. Over sixty of her original choreographic works were brought to life for theatre audiences around the globe, establishing her deep foundation in pacing, movement, and narrative structure. She was the Ballet Mistress of the Colorado Ballet and the Alberta Ballet as well as cofounder of the Bermuda Dance Theatre. For the last two decades of her dance career, she educated the next generation of creatives, as Director of Dance at Interlochen Center for the Arts, named the "#1 Best High School for the Arts in America", and at St. Paul's School.

S.K. at the helm of her forty-foot boat leaving Seattle, Washington on a transformative seventy-five day voyage up the Inside Passage to Sitka, Alaska. Then a decade writing while living afloat swinging on the anchor rode in one remote Alaskan cove or another. 2010

DIGITAL ARTIST

S.K., a pioneer in the digital art sphere, has been creating original digital art since 1997. Utilizing a unique, self-taught technique, she transforms photographs into vibrant, otherworldly masterpieces using Adobe Photoshop. Today, her VarTerels' Universe™ series features nearly 500 of these hand-crafted digital illustrations.

VOYAGE TO WRITING

In 2010, S.K. retired from the dance world to live with her partner on their boat in the world's largest temperate rainforest along the remote and rugged coast of Alaska. Isolated in nature, she spent a "gap decade" afloat honing her writing, refining her digital art style, and mastering shipboard skills (including catching dinner). It was during this creative voyage that she transitioned her storytelling from the dance stage to the written and illustrated page, self-publishing her first novel, *DiMensioner's Revenge*, in 2011.

TODAY

Now, in 2026, S.K. is currently writing the twenty-first installment of her saga. She and her partner reside in the lower-48 states, living on the side of the largest flat-top mountain in the world. From her mountain studio, she continues to cultivate her "Illustrated by the Author" Science Fantasy series, VarTerels' Universe™, dedicating her life to the timeless journey of a true storyteller.

S.K.'s website
www.skrandolph.com

Facebook
facebook.com/skrandolph11

Substack
skrandolph.substack.com

Encounters

VarTerels' Universe™ Book 6
Part I - UnFolding
Novella
29 pages

When a vengeful DiMensioner forms an unholy alliance with a death shadow to steal a legendary crystal and destroy the Guardian who banished him, he discovers that the children he saves along the way may hold the key to his own redemption—or his ultimate damnation.

Available in the paperback *Agothany 1* and as an individual eBook.

An epic science fantasy saga told through art and words
in companion shorts and illustrated novels,
available as paperbacks and eBooks.

Illustrated by the author, color in eBooks
and black and white in paperbacks.

Presented in suggested reading order.

DiMensioner's Revenge

Illustrated by the Author
VarTerels' Universe™ Book 1
Part I - UnFolding
Novel
642 pages, 73 illustrations

Four young people from a regimented city discover their destiny when they journey to Myrrh—the hidden remnant of Old Earth—only to find themselves hunted by a vengeful DiMensioner, his death shadow, and alien mercenaries determined to destroy everything they've come to cherish.

Available as a paperback with black & white illustrations and eBook with color illustrations.

Gifts

VarTerels' Universe™ Book 2
Part I - UnFolding
Novella
34 pages

A pregnant art student must deceive a ruthless surveillance state about her twin daughters' true father, the brother of a powerful Guardian, or become the perfect hostage in a deadly political game.

Available in the paperback *Agothany 1* and as an individual eBook.

Discovery

VarTerels' Universe™ Book 3
Part I - UnFolding
Novelette
32 pages

Fourteen-year-old Torgin must choose between protecting his passion for music and spying on the only friends who understand him in a dystopian city where the government controls every aspect of life.

Available in the paperback *Agothany 1* and as an individual eBook.

Rescue

VarTerels' Universe™ Book 4
Part I - UnFolding
Novella
31 pages

In a dystopian city where surveillance is constant and conformity is mandatory, twin sisters Ari and Brie must navigate secret portals and evade ruthless patrollers to rescue a lost boy and return him home before their forbidden act lands them all in the dreaded Five Towers.

Available in the paperback *Agothany 1* and as an individual eBook.

ConDra's Fire

Illustrated by the Author
VarTerels' Universe™ Book 5
Part I - UnFolding
Novel
504 pages, 59 illustrations

Kidnapped to a hostile desert planet, Esán must survive while his friends race to rescue him, unaware that their rescue mission will unleash ancient powers and reveal family secrets that could destroy three worlds.

Available as a paperback with black & white illustrations and eBook with color illustrations.

Encounters

VarTerels' Universe™ Book 6
Part I - UnFolding
Novella
29 pages

When a vengeful DiMensioner forms an unholy alliance with a death shadow to steal a legendary crystal and destroy the Guardian who banished him, he discovers that the children he saves along the way may hold the key to his own redemption—or his ultimate damnation.

Available in the paperback *Agothany 1* and as an individual eBook.

Metamorphosis

VarTerels' Universe™ Book 7
Part I - UnFolding
Novella
31 pages

Wrongfully banished from his home planet and left disfigured by a catastrophic magical accident, Laurent must shed his arrogance and accept his broken reflection before he can master the ancient art of dimensional magic and discover his true purpose.

Available in the paperback *Agothany 1* and as an individual eBook.

MasTer's Reach

Illustrated by the Author
VarTerels' Universe™ Book 8
Part I - UnFolding
Novel
686 pages, 60 illustrations

As the UnFolding reaches its climax, teenagers wielding legendary artifacts must evade deadly hunters across multiple worlds while uncovering shocking truths about The MasTer's identity and a centuries-old conflict that threatens to destroy the Eleo Preda people forever.

Available as a paperback with black & white illustrations and eBook with color illustrations.

Wanted

VarTerels' Universe™ Book 9
Part I - UnFolding
Novella
33 pages

A fugitive with a dark past escapes prison only to discover he's being hunted by a powerful mystical league that wants to control his untapped ability to bend reality itself.

Available in the paperback *Agothany 1* and as an individual eBook.

Jaradee's Legacy

Illustrated by the Author
VarTerels' Universe™ Book 10
Part I - UnFolding
Novel
336 pages, 51 illustrations

Separated as children during a brutal genocide, birth-mate twins Rayn and Rethdun must survive across galaxies while carrying the genetic legacy that could save their dying civilization or destroy them both.

Available as a paperback with black & white illustrations and eBook with color illustrations.

Agothany 1

An anthology of
the Companion Shorts
*Gifts, Discovery, Rescue Encounters,
Metamorphosis,* and *Collision*
in VarTerels' Universe™
Part I - UnFolding
256 pages

Available as a paperback.
Each Companion Short also
available as an individual eBook.

Incirrata Secret

Illustrated by the Author
VarTerels' Universe™ Book 11
Part II- CoaleScence
Novel
428 pages, 45 illustrations

Racing against ruthless enemies across mystical dimensions, the Universe's youngest VarTerel and a prophesied leader with legendary eyes must rescue kidnapped mentors from a cloud-shrouded island where a phantom octopus guards secrets that could reshape their world—or destroy it.

Available as a paperback with black & white illustrations and eBook with color illustrations.

Lessons

VarTerels' Universe™ Book 12
Part II- CoaleScence
Novella
26 pages

On the desert planet of DerTah, blind oracle WoNadahem Mardree must overcome devastating loss and her deepest fears when a mysterious shape-shifting DiMensioner arrives seeking knowledge, challenging everything she believes about fate, power, and love.

Available in the paperback *Agothany 2* and as an individual eBook.

Corps Stones

Illustrated by the Author
VarTerels' Universe™ Book 13
Part II- CoaleScence
Novel
438 pages, 52 illustrations

A young VarTerel and her friends journey to 1969 New York City to recover three stolen Corps Stones before their entire solar system collapses into chaos.

Available as a paperback with black & white illustrations and eBook with color illustrations.

Fishing

VarTerels' Universe™ Book 14
Part II- CoaleScence
Novella
30 pages

A twelve-year-old boy with extraordinary powers must survive slavery, betrayal, and the relentless pursuit of a deadly league that murdered his parents and will stop at nothing to control him.

Available in the paperback *Agothany 2* and as an individual eBook.

Duplicity

VarTerels' Universe™ Book 15
Part II- CoaleScence
Novella
30 pages

A sworn protector with shapeshifting abilities and a future Guardian destined to unite worlds must outwit a ruthless League of sorcerers determined to claim her before she can fulfill her destiny.

Available in the paperback *Agothany 2* and as an individual eBook.

Mocendi's Gambit

Illustrated by the Author
VarTerels' Universe™ Book 16
Part II- CoaleScence
Novel
328 page, 35 illustrations

Stripped of her protective Star of Truth and held captive aboard an enemy ship young VarTerel Brielle AsTar must trust an unlikely ally—a former enemy seeking redemption—and escape through folded time before The MasTer's followers destroy everything she loves.

Available as a paperback with black & white illustrations and eBook with color illustrations.

Destiny

VarTerels' Universe™ Book 17
Part II- CoaleScence
Novella
32 pages

Brielle AsTar, the youngest VarTerel in the Inner Universe, must hide her genetically engineered babies and their surrogate mother from ruthless spies while battling a dangerous gene threatening to resurrect an ancient evil.

Available in the paperback *Agothany 2* and as an individual eBook.

Cimondeli

VarTerels' Universe™ Book 18
Part II- CoaleScence
Short Story
12 pages

Sixteen-year-old Desty has never seen the sky, but when she ventures beyond her underground refuge for the first time, she discovers her telepathic gifts, befriends a majestic flying lizard, and learns that healing a poisoned world may begin with bridging the divide between enemy tribes.

Available in the paperback *Agothany 2* and as an individual eBook.

Queen's Quest

Illustrated by the Author
VarTerels' Universe™ Book 19
Part II- CoaleScence
Novel
420 pages, 44 illustrations

A young VarTerel, a bearer of cosmic seeds, a musical genius, and a street-smart boy with magical spectacles must unite their extraordinary powers to shatter an impenetrable dome, defeat a rogue demi-god, and complete a universal cycle before time runs out.

Available as a paperback with black & white illustrations and eBook with color illustrations.

Collision

Prequel to VarTerels' Universe™
VarTerels' Universe™ Book 20
Part II- CoaleScence
Novella
64 pages, 14 illustrations

A genius physicist barely out of university must lead a team of Galactic Guardians wielding ancient instruments of power to rescue Earth from total annihilation, even as enemies from his past conspire to ensure the planet's destruction.

Available in the paperback *Agothany 2* with black & white illustrations and as an individual eBook with color illustrations.

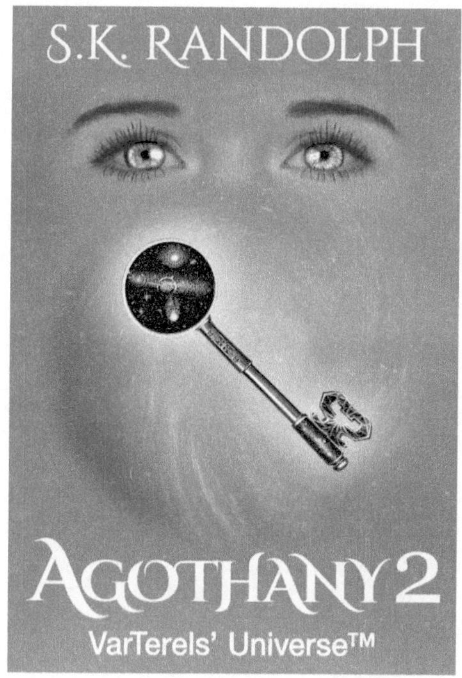

Agothany 2

An anthology of
the Companion Shorts
*Lessons, Fishing, Duplicity
Destiny, Cimondeli,* and *Collision*
in VarTerels' Universe™
Part II - CoaleScence
284 pages

Available as a paperback.
Each Companion Short also
available as an individual eBook.

Divided Destinies

Illustrated by the Author
VarTerels' Universe™ Book 21
Part III- QuicKening
Novel
a Work In Progress

Divided Destinies is a work in progress with a targeted release date of late 2026. An illustrated novel, it starts QuicKening, Part III of the VarTerels' Universe™.

See www.SKRandolph.com for current status and subscribe to S.K.'s newsletter to receive progress updates.